WHITE HORSE BLACK NIGHTS

THE GODKISSED BRIDE
BOOK ONE

EVIE MARCEAU

Content Note:

The Godkissed Bride series is a fantasy romance with sexually explicit scenes, violence, trauma, and adult language.

What do you do with sleeping gods?

Pray they don't awaken.

THE ANCIENT IMMORTAL COURT

Vale the Warrior, *King of Fae*
Iyre the Maiden, *Goddess of Virtue*
Artain the Archer, *God of the Hunt*
Solene the Wilderwoman, *Goddess of Nature*
Popelin the Trickster, *God of Pleasure*
Meric the Punisher, *God of Order*
Thracia the Stargazer, *Goddess of Night*
Alyssantha the Lover, *Goddess of Sex*
Woudix the Ender, *God of Death*
Samaur the Sunbringer, *God of Day*

CHAPTER I
SABINE

Shivering in my father's courtyard in the cool morning air, I feel naked beneath my robe, yet I'll lose even that scrap of silk any minute now.

I shift from bare foot to bare foot in the spring mud as I fix a hard stare at the gate, waiting. A maid sweeps the front stairs behind me, acting like today is like any other day, and for her, maybe it is.

But for me?

Today, everything changes. Today, I'm a sold bride.

The church steeple chimes from three blocks over. Each clang shoots straight into my chest as though the iron clapper slaps directly against my heart. *Bong. Bong. Bong. Bong.* A tremor reverberates through my bones until I squeeze the cockleshell hanging on a cord around my neck like a protective talisman.

Bong. Bong. Bong. Bong.

Eight chimes for eight o'clock in the morning. This is the hour the ride is supposed to begin—so where is he?

Soft, feminine footsteps pad through the mud behind me, and in the next moment, Suri rests a gentle hand on my shoulder, making me flinch.

"He's late," I rasp, my voice hoarse.

She doesn't answer right away, and instead smooths her umber brown hand along the thick rope of a braid that circles the crown of my head, then runs down the length of my back all the way to kiss the ground. She spent an hour last night braiding it into the intricate style called an "immortal crown," named in honor of the sleeping gods. All the different regions of Astagnon call the deities by different names: *Immortals* in the capital city of Old Coros. *Fae* in the northeast. *Gods* in the south. Whatever name they go by, legend tells us they went to sleep one thousand years ago in underground realms and will wake again to rule the human world. Until then, we keep their memory alive by mimicking their fashion with elaborate braids, swipes of colored kohl to wing the corners of our eyes, and golden caps on our ears to make the tops look pointed.

Today, though, I'm just me, unadorned. That will have to be enough.

"Are you so anxious for the ride to begin?" she asks.

I fold the robe tighter across my chest and hug my arms over top. "It's cruel, on top of everything, to make me wait."

Then again, what isn't cruel about this day? This ride and its obscene rules are the definitions of cruelty. I know my future husband's reputation, and "cruel" is a common word used to describe him, followed by "arrogant," "rich as sin," and "just like the rest of the Valvere devils."

You have to wonder about the type of man who would buy a bride only to require her to ride naked across half of Astagnon to his castle.

If you ask me? *Not* the best way to begin a marriage.

"Maybe he just got held up?"

I snort. "At the bottom of an ale tankard, maybe."

"Lord Rian holds a powerful position in the Valvere family," Suri chirps in a tone that rings with false optimism. "They're second in wealth only to the king. The ride may be challenging, but you'll never know hardship once you arrive in Duren. Your husband will drown you in gifts."

Petite, pretty Suri with her round cheeks and warm walnut-brown eyes takes her role as my stepmother with a comical amount of gravity, considering the fact she's only two years older than me. When she married my father over the winter, I wasn't allowed to leave the convent to attend the wedding. I had no idea what kind of woman my father's new bride was, nor could I find the energy to care; I figured I'd be carted off from the convent walls to my new husband's walls with barely a chance to give my new "mother" my regards, anyway.

The last thing I'd expected was to adore her. Kind-hearted Suri. Quick-to-smile Suri. I've only known her three days, and she's managed to bring me to tears twice in that time out of kindness. The first was at dinner on my initial night home from the convent, when she leaned over to whisper that I had a speck of spinach lodged in my teeth. The second time was when she snorted when I called my father a *duette di marcer* to his face, knowing he didn't understand a word of the Immortal Tongue.

In the twelve years that I spent as a ward—or rather, prisoner—of the Convent of the Immortal Iyre, no one ever checked my teeth for spinach. Hell, I'd have killed for a *taste* of spinach instead of week-old gruel. And kindness? Laughter? Those were as absent as the sleeping gods themselves.

Now, Suri clucks over me like a mother hen. "You're shivering," she chides.

I deadpan, "And to think, I'm not even naked yet."

The manor's front door swings open, and my father stumbles down the freshly swept stairs. He checks his pocket watch, then squints at the courtyard gate with a frown before trotting over to Suri and me.

"Lord Rian's guard will be here soon," he informs us. "I have no doubt."

"Maybe he died on the way," I mutter under my breath. "One can only hope."

My father's cheeks redden in irritation.

"You're twenty-two, Sabine," he says forcefully. "You've been granted more freedom than most girls your age. I could have secured a marriage contract ten years ago, and the courts would have allowed it."

I know better than to visibly balk in my father's presence at the word "freedom," so instead, I press my lips together to seal my anger. I don't know any girls who would call spending the last ten years imprisoned in a convent, beaten and starved by Sisters with hearts as sour as withered lemons, any type of freedom.

"Twenty-one days." My father rubs his hands together in a farce of joviality. "The ride is only twenty-one days. Soldiers march for months at a time."

"Yes, but *clothed*," I point out wryly. As soon as I say it, his lips work like he has choice words to throw back at me, but Suri rests her tender hand on his arm before he can.

"Charlin," she entreats sweetly, "let's keep the peace on Sabine's last day here." She bats her long lashes at him. Their marriage is still so new, and he is still so besotted with his pretty young second wife, that he forgets the bulk of his ire.

"Lord Rian set the rules of the ride," he mutters to absolve himself of some guilt. "Not me."

And yet you didn't object, either.

When my father sold me as a bride to Lord Rian Valvere in exchange for settling our family debts, I was the last person consulted. After all, why would anyone have bothered to include me in the talks? Since I was born, all I've been is a bargaining chip to be dangled before powerful men. But out of all the wealthy lords my ass of a father could have chosen, did it have to be *him*?

Lord Rian might be sinfully rich, but he's also simply *sinful*. On my first day out of the convent, Suri whispered to me that he earned the moniker "The Lord of Liars" when he took over his family's empire of lawful vices in Duren. The Valveres own every vice establishment in West Astagnon, from gambling dens to brothels to racing grounds—and if the rumors are true, they dabble in their share of *un*lawful vices, too. I suppose this ride is all just another game for Lord Rian.

Every game has rules. According to our engagement contract, these are mine:

No dress.

No chemise.

No slippers.

To honor the gods, Lady Sabine Darrow will recreate Immortal Solene's legendary ride by traveling on horseback from Bremcote to Duren for twenty-one days with only her hair to cover her.

I'm all too familiar with the story this ride supposedly pays homage to. We had an ancient, well-thumbed-through copy of the Book of the Immortals in the convent. I'd spend hours pouring over the sacred text, memorizing the fabled accounts of each god and blushing at the scandalous accompanying illustrations. There was Immortal Vale, the King of Fae, who ruled over the godly court with an iron fist and tanned abs. Immortal Popelin, God of Pleasure, depicted with scantily clad women feeding him grapes. Immortal Alyssantha, Goddess of Sex . . . her illustration, complete with tangled limbs of multiple sexual partners in impossible positions, piqued my curiosity the most.

But one of the book's most famous tales is when Immortal Solene, Goddess of Nature, celebrates her upcoming marriage by traveling naked on horseback to her husband's home as a demonstration of her bared soul. The illustration shows her immortal fey lines—the glowing, faintly blue marks that run up the gods' limbs and necks—on full display across her entire body. *"I come to you not as a god, but merely as a woman,"* she says. *"I come as nature forged me."*

And the man my father chose for me? Apparently, he loves that story, too. Or at least the idea of a naked girl groveling to him.

6

And yet, even though I'm about to be paraded nude across half of Astagnon, a part of me is still hopeful. It's probably false hope, and I'm probably setting myself up for an even more shattered spirit, but at least—finally—I'm out of the convent walls.

That small chance for something greater keeps my head high.

I rub the cockleshell necklace between thumb and forefinger, trusting in its secret promise. Overhead, the sun breaks free of clouds, gracing us with a bath of light that makes my skin sing.

In the next instant, however, a man saunters through the gates, and my fragile ray of hope dissolves like morning mist.

He stalks in like a storm cloud made flesh, all midnight hair, hooded eyes, and a scowl that says he'd rather be anywhere than here. There's no question who he is: there's a bow on his back, and he bears the Valvere crest on a leather chest plate harnessed around his shoulders.

This was the final rule in my future husband's game: *My most trusted guard will escort Lady Sabine for her safety.*

Lucky me.

Lord Rian's guard drops his rucksack and bow on the ground and then stands tall enough to eclipse my father, who isn't a small man. The guard's shoulders strain his shirt so the fabric is taut over his biceps, which are as thick around as my thigh. His brows are low over dark eyes that glint even from across the courtyard. His jaw is square and symmetrical, but his nose is slightly dented in several places, as though it's been broken more than once.

His shoulder-length hair is the rich color and texture of a raven's wing. He wears it loose, not at all in keeping with fae-inspired fashion.

He's striking. He's savage. He's undeniably gorgeous.

And yet all I can think is: *They sent a beast for me.*

Lord Rian called this man my escort in the marriage contract, but one glance at his thuggish frame and it's clear: he is my jailor. His job isn't to keep me safe on the ride—it's to prevent me from running away.

The blood in my veins ices over as he looks our way and barks, "Lord Charlin Darrow?"

My father jumps at the call and shuffles forward like a schoolboy instead of the privileged lord protector of Bremcote. They exchange words I can't hear, but my ears are buzzing with so many internal questions that I feel besieged by a cloud of gnats.

Beside me, Suri's hand trails to her collar as she appreciatively remarks, "He's certainly *large*, isn't he?"

I snort. A married woman can't say aloud that anyone but her husband is a dark god of a man.

"I wouldn't know," I say flatly. "There weren't exactly a lot of men traipsing through the convent."

I see movement in the manor's front windows—a gaggle of maids is also ogling Rian's guard from inside the house.

"His name is Wolf Bowborn," Suri whispers conspiratorially. "One of our family's messengers knew of him when we lived in Buckwen. He's served the Valvere family since he was an orphaned boy. Even as a child, he made his way with his fists in the combat games. The Valvere family heard about his godkiss, brought him on as a hunter, and renamed him a Bowborn."

A child in the combat games? I'm certain that isn't legal, but I'd be naive to think such things don't happen.

The wind changes, causing my robe to flutter around my thighs. My skin erupts in gooseflesh as I wrangle the silk back into place.

Wolf Bowborn's head suddenly jerks toward me as whatever words he was about to say to my father are lost. He sniffs the air, sharp and sampling, and then his gaze targets me.

It's the first time he's looked directly at me, and with my legs bare up to my thighs, I expect him to leer. But that isn't the look he gives me. His eyes run down my length like I'm a filly at auction, and he wants to gauge how much trouble I'll be.

I think I'd prefer a leer, all things considered.

"He's godkissed?" I ask, surprised.

Suri nods. "Heightened senses, people say. That's how he made his name in the fights, and now, as a hunter." Her gaze lowers to my own godkissed birthmark on my breastbone, half hidden by the robe's folds. "The Valveres like to surround themselves with godkissed people."

Feeling self-conscious, I close the robe tighter so it hides my mark completely. The fae gods may be sleeping, but threads of their magic remain in a few of us, who are called the godkissed. We are gifted with talents beyond the bounds of human ability. No one knows who the gods will bless from within their slumbering dreams, though magic does have a slight tendency to run in a family. Not in mine, however—neither of my parents were godkissed.

9

It is only once a baby is born, with the birthmark or not, that the gods' favor is revealed. And only many years later that the magical nature of their ability manifests.

Suri goes back to eyeing Wolf like a decadent dessert, and I half expect her to lick her lips. With the face of an angel on a beast's body, it feels like a crime for the gods to have given someone so brutish such beauty.

Despite my wariness, my curiosity gets the best of me. My hand goes to a loose lock of hair that's slipped out of my braid, twisting it around my little finger. For the last ten years, I've barely seen a man. The convent was run by elderly women who swore a vow of chastity, so they rarely even spoke of men.

Are all males this . . . impressive?

My throat bobs with a hard swallow.

Wolf's head turns sharply toward me again, and I gape.

Did he *hear* me gulp?

He says a few final words to my father and then strides across the courtyard in my direction. I feel myself shrinking despite my resolve to stand tall. He moves with a sort of heavy grace, though he holds one shoulder stiffly, as though an old injury still gives him trouble. His boots come to a squelching stop in the mud a pace away from me.

"Lady Sabine." His voice rumbles like rough stones. "Lord Rian sent me to escort you to Duren. It's an easy road, but given the nature of the ride, I anticipate we might have trouble. Obey my commands, and I will ensure your safety."

Nature of the ride. He means the fact that I'll be

paraded around bare as a babe in the name of some sleeping god who couldn't care less.

His eyes bore into me, and my jaw clamps in a feckless attempt to tame my anger. Obey him? He's a stranger, and yet he thinks I'm his to command?

Overhead, the clouds shift, and a dark shadow swallows us.

This isn't the first time I've been told to obey. I was taught obedience at the end of a heavy rod in the convent. *Eyes down. Lips silent. Thoughts on the Immortal Iyre.* Matron White's sadistic voice still rings in my head like those damnable church bells.

Distracted, I slide my middle finger along the base of my ribs. They're still tender, not yet fully healed.

A songbird swoops down from the rooftop to alight on my shoulder. It's a nuthatch. As tiny as a plum with soft gray wings and a black cap of feathers.

Heart, it whispers to me. ***Take heart.***

At its gentle reassurance, I remember to breathe.

Thank you, little one, I speak back in my thoughts, knowing it can hear them as clearly as I could ascertain its message in my own mind.

The bird's presence reminds me that I'm not locked away anymore with a cadre of cruel-hearted women. And that I'll have a friend on the ride, too.

Myst will be with me.

At the end of the courtyard, one of the stable boys brings her out. She's been groomed to perfection for the occasion. Her white coat gleams the color of freshly fallen snow, her mane and tail as soft as a swan's down.

The church bells chime again. *Bong.*

It's time.

As the stable boy brings around Myst, I uncinch my robe's belt and, forcing a steady breath, slide the fabric off my shoulders. My arms tremble, and not just from the chill. Suri takes the robe from me, draping it over her forearm, keeping her eyes averted out of respect.

After all her work to create the immortal crown braid last night, she unties it now and begins combing out the locks. She separates, shakes, and flounces each long curl like she's unraveling the strands of a woven rug. Then she takes great care spreading out each curl in an attempt to cover my bare breasts and the hollow between my legs in a way that will uphold my modesty.

"See? I told you the braid would make nice thick waves. It's practically like you're still dressed!" she says with forced optimism.

Right. Nice try.

Lifting my chin, I fix a sharp look on Wolf Bowborn, the man who expects me to obey him for the next twenty-one days. "Don't you dare look."

Wolf is so busy gawping at the nuthatch perched on my shoulder that I'm not sure he hears me. But then the nuthatch flits away, and his eyes drag to meet mine, straight on and piercing.

He clears his throat in a gruff assent. "I won't look, Lady Sabine."

CHAPTER 2
WOLF

I look.

Of course I look. Even a blind man would take a good long eyeful at Sabine Darrow, though I permit myself only a single sidelong glimpse. And it's entirely for her benefit, not mine. If I'm to keep her safe, I need to know this girl down to her bones—what she's capable of, if she has injuries I need to make accommodations for, how men along the road might react to her naked body before my fist pounds the ogling out of them.

All it takes is one peek, anyway, to know that the legendary rumors of her beauty are true. If anything, she exceeds what's whispered about her at Duren. She's small and round, her skin like fresh morning milk. Her hair is the color of honey, flowing all the way to her toes in thick waves that, despite her stepmother's best attempts, cover her nakedness about as well as a sieve holds water.

I snap for the stable boy to bring her horse closer. It's a striking mare, with pure white coloring, a proud bearing, and flawless conformation. The horse is much too fine for the likes of this utter ass, Lord Charlin Darrow. I know a little about horses from the Valveres' racing stables, and this pristine white mare must be worth a fortune.

So how did a daughter of a minor lord, who's drowning in debt, come by such a horse?

The stable boy halts the horse beside Sabine and removes its lead rope. This is another one of Lord Rian's conditions: Sabine must ride bareback, just girl and horse, the same as Immortal Solene. The requirement is a thorn in my side, making my job more difficult. If the horse bolts or Sabine decides to make a break for it, I have nothing to grab onto except the girl's bare calf.

Still, I'm confident that the girl will be easy to manage. She can't weigh more than a doe, and it isn't like she has a lot of places to hide a blade on her.

As Lady Sabine swivels to face the horse, I spot something gleaming at the base of her neck and grab toward her throat. She sucks in a sharp breath as my fingers make contact. Ignoring her fear, my fingers curl around a cockleshell dangling from a cord.

"No dress," I remind her. "No chemise. No slippers. Lord Rian was very clear in his instructions—you aren't to wear anything, my lady."

"It's a necklace." She speaks through clenched teeth as her flinty eyes glare. "Not clothes."

"Just the same." With a flick of my hand, I snap the cord and shove the seashell into Sabine's open palm. "Get rid of it."

The sound of her blood rushing in her veins jumps

across the small distance between us, but she reins in her temper and faces the mare again, sliding a hand over the animal's back.

I wrap my hands around her waist to help her up, fingers digging into her hipbones, but she starts writhing in my hands even before I lift her negligible weight.

"Put me down!" She squirms until I lower her, and then she spins on me in a way that makes her carefully positioned locks threaten to give everyone in the court-yard an eyeful. "Don't touch me!"

I hear the fear in her voice. I smell it, sweet and pungent in her sweat. She's scared of me—but not as much as she should be, or else she wouldn't dare to give commands to Lord Rian's guard.

I could bend her to my will, but the best way to handle a skittish girl is like a skittish horse—give it space to make it think it has power.

So I hold up my hands and take a step backward.

"There's no mounting block," I explain in painstaking slowness that strains my patience. "A little thing like you can't climb on a horse that tall."

"I don't need your help."

Pinning me with a distrusting look, she turns back around to the horse. Her soft hand goes to its neck, stroking the flawless white hair. Her lips move silently. She says nothing aloud, and yet I sense some form of understanding pass between girl and horse.

The mare lowers itself to one knee, then the other. It folds its hind legs in until it crouches on the flagstones.

Swinging a graceful leg over its back, Sabine easily

mounts. She whispers, "Up, Myst," and the horse lumbers back to its hooves.

I'm riveted, as is the stable boy and the gaggle of maids peeking through the manor's windows. I've seen horses trained to bow at a whip's crack, but this is something different. This is no trick.

Sabine smooths her hand gratefully over the horse's flank like it's a friend, not a beast of burden, and gives me a triumphant look.

"Didn't your master tell you I'm godkissed?" Sabine asks with her chin high, like she enjoys looking down at me.

For a second, something ugly twists in my gut. I don't know why, but it spikes me with a jealous vein to see such tender harmony between girl and beast. I'm not used to seeing any kindness at all. Certainly not in the Valveres' household.

I regain my composure. "He said you could talk to animals. Not control them."

"I *can't* control them. With kind words, no one needs to."

Can this girl be serious?

The breeze shifts, and her scent wafts to my nose again, snaring my attention for the second time.

Violets. That's what she smells like. *Goddamn violets.*

The wind keeps shifting, splashing her scent around the courtyard—and it's distracting. I need to stay sharp, aware of the scents that matter. Scents that could portend danger: smoke, steel, sickness.

But now that her aroma is in my nose, I can't stop

thinking about violets. On the list of things that interest me, flowers have to be at the bottom, right down there with royal gossip and the latest favored eyeliner shade. But there was one time that wasn't the case. I killed a prized wild boar for Sorsha Hall's midwinter feast that no other hunters had managed to bag. As a reward, Lord Rian gave me a seat at the high lord's table. I, a bastard son from the streets, dined among lords and ladies. The feast was decadent. Cheeses from the Clarana hills. Spiced mead by the barrel. The boar itself, roasted and served with braised root vegetables and buttery sage sauce. But the finest of all was dessert: delicate honey cakes dripping with iced sugar and dotted with violets. Those little candied buds were the most sinful thing I ever put in my mouth.

Earthy, sweet, delicate.

I'd do anything to get the taste of violets in my mouth again.

"Wolf Bowborn. Wait." Lord Charlin waves me over, his beady, bloodshot eyes blinking fast.

I adjust my bow slung over my shoulder and make my way to join him.

He props his hands on his hips like he's about to give me a lecture. *What a fucking oaf.*

"This marriage means I'm to be Lord Rian's father-in-law. You tell the high lord and his family that I have certain expectations. When I next come to Duren, I want gratis coins to spend at the gambling houses. As well as choice seating at the arena."

This buffoon has reeked of whiskey since he first stepped out of his house. Not the expensive kind the

Valveres drink, either—something cheap, probably cut with turpentine. Fuck, it's not even mid-morning.

"Let me make one thing clear," I say slowly, so that his pickled brain can process my words. "Lord Rian bought himself a wife, not a father-in-law. If you set foot in Sorsha Hall without an invitation, I will personally see to dragging you back to Bremcote myself."

Lord Charlin's eyes bug out in indignation. He takes a few rageful breaths before sputtering, "She's *my* daughter."

"Not anymore, she isn't. You sold her to save your own skin. The only man with a claim on her now is my master."

I can see that this painful truth eats him alive, but there's nothing he can do about it. He might have the finest manor house in Bremcote, but that makes him a king among ants. The Valveres are interested in him only as far as his humiliation is entertaining to them.

Still, a slow, sly smile crosses Lord Charlin's face. He stuffs a hand into his breast pocket and comes back with a letter, sealed with wax and stamped with his crest.

"Give this to your high lord," he sneers, smashing the letter into my palm. "Tell him that if he wants what I've written about in there, he'll have to be more welcoming to his father-in-law."

As much as I'd like to shove the letter back in his face, I begrudgingly accept it. Who knows what scheme or secret is scrawled inside—it's up to Lord Rian to determine its value, not me.

When I return to Sabine, anxious to get on the road,

my keen eyesight sharpens in on something in the horse's mane that wasn't there a moment ago.

The seashell now hangs from a strand of its mane.

Now this is interesting, I think.

The girl tried to hide the shell there while my back was turned. Lord Rian didn't permit her any clothes, bags, or belongings, so she had no place to hide the bauble on her own body.

What does such a paltry shell mean to her? Why cherish it so?

I file this curiosity away as I look toward the rising sun. We need to be moving.

"Say your farewells," I order her.

Lord Charlin's dark-skinned wife, who can't be much older than Sabine herself, approaches the horse and clasps hands with Sabine. In a sweet chirp, she says, "We've put out the order that no one in Bremcote shall look upon you. All doors will be closed, all windows shuttered. Beyond that . . . " The young woman's voice breaks. "We've sent requests to the towns beyond also to close their shutters, but we have no official influence over them."

"Thank you, Suri," Sabine says solemnly. "You've been so kind. I won't forget it. I wish we'd had more than a few days together."

Bored with their womanly talk, I scrape my eyes over the sky, looking for any sign of rain. The last thing I want is for this damnable ride to be delayed for the weather. Twenty-one days are twenty-one days more than I should be away from Duren.

I *should* be in the Blackened Forest north of the city,

tracking that troublesome bear that's been wreaking so much damage in the villages up near the border wall with the neighboring kingdom of Volkany—the cursed kingdom. My mind can't let go of it. It dragged off a fifteen-year-old girl, and no one has seen her since. Her parents wailed my ears off. She was their pride and joy, godkissed with the ability to find misplaced objects. But it's strange: When I tried to track the bear, the claw marks it left behind seemed too large—unless it's the largest fucking bear anyone's ever seen. I found a clump of its fur that shimmered like fine strands of precious metal.

Lord Charlin climbs the manor's front steps precariously as he raises his voice to the small crowd of servants.

He slurs drunkenly, "We of House Darrow bid farewell to my daughter on this, um . . . on this joyous occasion of her ride to meet her husband . . . uh . . . " He trails off stupidly, smacking his lips.

Like a ripple of smoke, Sabine's scent changes. Her tang of fear is gone, the violets are gone, replaced by the smell of two iron blades striking.

The scent of anger.

Can I blame her? I prefer having no father, if my option is this one.

Suri Darrow saves her husband's lackluster speech by piping up, "May the wind be at your back, the sun on your face, and the gods' blessing on your journey, Sabine."

It's childish, these theatrics. They aren't sending her off to her doom. Lord Rian will shower a girl like her with jewels. She's about to know finery as she's never fathomed. All she need do is acquiesce to my master's occasional whim—and granted, his whims can be impulsive—and he'll lay down the earth at her feet.

Lord Rian's words slingshot back into my memory.

"*I want her, Wolf,*" Rian said. "*Sabine Darrow will be my wife, come hell or hounds.*"

I remember it like it happened yesterday, not a year ago. My master came to Bremcote for business to evaluate some young brute for the combat games. The fighter's father wanted to charm Lord Rian, so he took him to a Preview where young maidens eligible to be wed in the next few years were put out on display.

Up to that point, he'd sworn never to marry—until he saw Sabine Darrow.

"*Her father's a drunken lout,*" he told me after. "*But he knows he has a prize in that girl. Honeyed hair down to the floor. A face that rivals the statues of Clarana. And she's godkissed. She's young—not ready for another year. And her father won't give her up for less than a fortune, but I'm not going to pay a penny for her. Watch and see, Wolf.*"

Lord Rian could easily afford to buy a bride at any price, but it's never about money with the Valveres.

It's the win.

It's the game.

And in the end, he *hadn't* paid a penny for her, just as he'd vowed.

"Open the gate!" Lord Charlin calls.

Servants roll back the wooden gate, and Sabine's pulse jumps in her veins. She's not the only one less than thrilled about this ride. I have more pressing work. I can't stop chewing over that strange bear activity up near the border with Volkany and the missing godkissed girl. But Lord Rian said it had to be me.

I trust you to bring her to me, Wolf, he said. *You and you alone.*

"Listen, little violet," I say to her now as I sling my rucksack over my shoulder. "You are the property of Lord Rian Valvere of Duren, who has entrusted me to bring you to him safely and without incident. You will obey my commands on the ride, do you understand?"

She looks down at me through her long lashes, and I have to pretend that I don't notice the obvious bare curves of her body.

"Oh, I have plenty of experience with people who expect me to obey," she says evenly.

There's a challenge in her tone, yet I can't quite suss out its exact nature. This pampered princess? She's known no hardship, of that I feel certain.

I tighten my jaw. *The little flower might yet have thorns.*

"Good," I snap, and the two of us—me on foot, her on horseback—begin the ride.

CHAPTER 3
SABINE

Bremcote is a provincial town with middling importance in East Astagnon, best known for its wool market. A network of dirt roads connect wooden houses, a few garden plots, the mill, and of course, my father's manor house.

The furthest I've ever been from Bremcote is nineteen miles away, at the Convent of the Immortal Iyre. After my mother died, my father didn't know what to do with me. I was ten years old, no longer an easily-ignored child, and not yet breedable collateral to be married off. So he made a deal with the Matron to take me in as a ward. Of the ten Immortals, only Iyre, Goddess of Virtue, has any reputation for chastity. The nine others are a debauched collection of licentious pleasure-seekers. Iyre served the other gods with sweetness and light, maintaining her purity even with Immortal Popelin always trying to look up her skirt. As far as gods go, I always found her boring and meek; the spirit of the convent reflected those traits. My one saving grace during my miserable years there was that I was allowed to bring Myst, though it pained me every day that they drove her hard pulling work carts. A horse like her should never be yoked.

Now, my curiosity flits around the rusty hand pump in the village green, a goat-head door knocker, bottles of milk left at someone's doorway. After ten isolated years in that place, everything is new, thrilling, strange. Even *milk bottles!*

I left the convent only once in those twelve years, and on that particular occasion, I sooner would have remained imprisoned. They called it the "Preview." The memory alone steeps me in nausea.

A Preview is to a high-born maiden as an auction is to a broodmare: a chance to show off merchandise to potential bidders. Ten girls stand on ten chairs in the church nave, of all places. The men come to find a young, ripe wife they can eventually sire children on with their grunting old bodies, and they pay handsomely just for the chance to attend.

Bachelors from all corners of East Astagnon spoke about us girls like we couldn't hear them, comparing our beauty, our ripeness for childbirth, our family names. There was one other godkissed girl there, a pretty brown girl from Covery who could change an apple's color from red to green. A useless power, if you ask me, but a power all the same, and the status of having a godkissed bride—regardless of what they can actually do—is all some men care about.

Balancing on that damned chair, unsuccessfully begging a thrush in the rafters to come peck out the eyes of every man there, was the first and only time I saw the man I'm now to marry.

Lord Rian's presence was magnetic from the moment he stepped into the church, but the others' responses to his appearance truly made me take note. Every bachelor stiffened in jealousy. Every girl jutted out her chest and ass, hoping to catch the attention of the handsome young lord.

He never spoke to me. He never asked my family name or about my godkiss. To my recollection, he looked at me only once—just a flitting pass—before continuing on to the other girls.

So why, in the name of the Immortals, did he pick me now?

Wolf and I pass a shuttered apothecary shop. True to Suri's word, we haven't seen a single soul in a dozen blocks. At this time of day, the streets should be bustling with wagons and market-bound vendors, yet it's utterly empty. Every shutter is closed, even on The Wilderwoman Tavern, with its carved sign of peach-skinned Immortal Solene with ivy woven in her braid and glowing fey lines along her hairline. I glower. She isn't exactly my current favorite of the gods, given this damn ride is supposedly in her honor. The quietness is eerie: not even the convent was this still. There should be the crack of a blacksmith's hammer, feet squelching through the mud, the shrieks of playful children.

Wolf rubs his shoulder that looks like it might have sustained an old injury. He seems as unnerved by the quiet as I do. "I guess the townsfolk respect your father's orders, after all," he says, his surprised tone making it clear how low he thinks of my father.

At least we agree on one thing.

"Not him," I clarify. "His new wife, Suri. They like her. Everyone likes her. If she asked them to throw themselves into the Tellyne River, I think they would."

Wolf snorts.

I shift my position on Myst's back. From this angle, I can almost see down the front of Wolf's shirt. The leather breastplate hugs his torso, but his shirt is loose at the collar, unlaced. On a hard swell of muscle, I glimpse the edge of his godkiss birthmark.

Gripping Myst's sides more squarely with my calves, I lean over to try to see more . . .

Wolf snaps his gaze to mine. Amused, his eyes taunt me. "See something you like, my lady?"

My legs clamp harder around Myst and, sensing my embarrassment, she warns me, *He smells like a predator.*

For good reason, I communicate back bitterly.

"We'll follow this road as far as Polybridge," Wolf says with matter-of-factness, like he's giving orders to a soldier. "From there, it's north through Middleford, and then across the Innis River. It would be safer to traverse backroads, but my master desires that we pass through towns and villages so the whole kingdom knows of his impending marriage. If the weather holds and we move swiftly, we can make the journey in as few as nineteen days. Rain could delay us, or trouble on the road."

"You fear bandits?"

He flicks a hand like the suggestion is nothing but a

gnat in his ear. "Bandits know better than to attack a guard wearing the Valvere crest."

Right, I think wryly, *because the Valvere family pays the bandits' salaries.*

He continues, "We'll make camp each dusk in a forest or field, and rejoin the road at dawn. It's too much of a risk to spend nights at inns. Word of the unusual nature of this ride is spreading fast. There are those who might wish to harm Lord Rian and his family by attacking his future bride. Safer to be out in the open."

"Camp?" I ask hesitantly.

He tosses back his wild mane of hair, pinning me with a derisive look. "I realize you've never slept a night beneath the plain sky, my lady. Don't worry, you won't wither without a feather mattress and bed warmer."

I almost laugh. So this is what he thinks of me: that I'm a pampered aristocrat. While it's true that I've never slept without a roof overhead, for the last twelve years, that roof has been leaky and bee-infested.

As for a feather mattress? More like a flour sack stuffed with moldering straw. But there's no point in disabusing him of his beliefs about me; he can think whatever he likes.

They can have my body, I repeat in my head. *My mind is my own.*

That incantation has been my guiding principle to get me through my imprisonment in the convent. How fortuitous that it fits with my current reality, too. Previously, it was malicious Sisters beating me daily; now, riding naked is just another form of controlling my body.

At least this way doesn't leave bruises. Should I thank my future husband?

"There is a chance the bridge will be closed at Middleford," Wolf continues as we turn the corner at a bakery. Stacked crates block its window, though I glimpse the bakers inside moving around through the cracks. "If that happens, we'll go west instead, toward Marblenz."

A black cat noses its way past one of the crates and blinks at me lazily. I tell it about the milk bottles I spotted earlier, encouraging it to knock one over for a drink.

"I'll purchase food and supplies in the towns we pass through," Wolf states evenly, "If you must stop to rest, tell me at once. Lord Rian won't wish you to arrive fatigued."

"How very considerate," I mutter.

A door slams from somewhere nearby, making me jump. Myst draws to a stop, and Wolf halts, too, resting a hand on her mane.

She flinches, not liking his touch.

A man steps out of the Lucky Love Tavern and stands by the side of the road. He faces us square on, chin raised defiantly, a mean gleam in his eyes. He pointedly takes his time cocking his head this way and that, getting as much of an eyeful of my naked body as possible.

Annoyance snaps in my chest as I comb my hair into place, trying to hide what he wants to see.

"That's Thom Wallsor," I mumble under my breath to Wolf. "The second largest landowner in Bremcote after my father."

Wolf's presence changes immediately, crackling with coiled aggression. His hands curl into fists at his side, but he does nothing to stop the man from looking.

"Aren't you going to protect my modesty?" I prompt cynically.

"No."

His direct answer still surprises me. "*No?*"

"I'm tasked with getting you safely into Lord Rian's hands. He said nothing about your modesty and, in fact, if he worried after it, I doubt he'd command you to ride naked. Every man from here to Duren can fuck you with his eyes for as much as I care."

I didn't think much could shock me after what I've endured at the convent, but my face goes slack at his crudeness.

Hurt him? Myst asks hopefully.

It's a nice mental picture to imagine Wolf trampled under her hooves, but I swallow my ire and think, **Not yet.**

A middle-aged woman sticks her head out of the tavern's upstairs window, calling down, "Thom Wallsor, turn 'round your meaty arse and get back inside! We aren't to look at Lady Sabine. Don't you go bein' the one rotten peach in the whole town!"

Thom Wallsor folds his arms petulantly.

"Lord Rian stole that girl from me," he shouts loud enough for the whole street to hear. "Lord Charlin promised to give her to me as a bride. The least I am owed is a long look at what should have been mine to take on my wedding night!"

Wolf jerks around to face me. "Is there truth to his claim?"

"No." I sear Thom with a scorching look. I knew him vaguely as a child—he was a miserable teenage lout then, and I've heard nothing but ill about him since. "My father

29

might have strung him along to wring coin or favor from him, but he would never have married me to a commoner. His aspirations were always as big as his thirst."

It's all Wolf needs to hear. He drops his rucksack on the ground and then eats up the distance between Thom and us. The sneer instantly melts off Thom's face to see a beast of a man closing in on him.

Wolf's fist smashes into Thom's face before his sneer fully fades.

Blood spurts from the wound like a mouse crushed beneath a wagon wheel. Thom screams. I don't think the possibility of violence entered his head when he devised this little stunt. But he didn't know about Wolf Bowborn.

Thom cups his shattered nose as he doubles over, but Wolf takes no pity on him. He pulls back for another swing. His fist slams into the side of Thom's head, knocking him to the ground. Thom curls in a ball. Plaintive little squeals come from his throat. Wolf drops to a knee in the dirt, bringing his fist down on Thom's shoulder.

He hits him again, again, again, until my stomach feels hollowed out.

Beneath me, Myst prances, wanting to bolt. There isn't much that spooks my brave mare, but something about Wolf has her as on edge as if we were facing down his namesake.

The woman in the tavern's upstairs window blanches and runs inside for help. Mud streaks both men now, but Wolf doesn't seem to care as he beats the man bloody.

I have no love for Thom, but I still look away.

Even with my eyes closed, the sound of Thom's whines sting like wasps.

They can have my body, I recite. *But my mind is my own. They can have my body . . .*

At the convent, the beatings stopped one month before I returned to Bremcote. Sister Gray received my father's letter about the engagement contract and delivered it to Matron White. The next morning, I was dragged from my cell into the main living quarters and locked in a room to give my wounds time to heal. Sister Gray and Sister Red force-fed me rich butter and fatty veal to plump me up in order to hide the evidence that they'd starved me. After a few days in that room, I started to go stir-crazy and walked in circles on the floor and did exercises.

They didn't like that, so they tied me to the bed, so that I'd stay soft and slight. Silk ties so as not to leave bruises on my wrists and ankles, of course.

For the next thirty days, I stared at the ceiling, listening to Myst whinny for me from the stables, hating every one of those blackhearted women, hating my father for trading me to a stranger, hating him for stupidly gambling away our fortune in the first place, and most of all, hating Lord Rian for shaming *him* by making *me* endure this twisted game.

Wolf finally stands, tossing back his loose hair. Blood coats his bare knuckles. He wipes them on Thom's shirt back as the man moans pitifully, the only sign he's still alive.

Wolf strides back toward me as though nothing happened.

"Let's continue," he says, checking the sun's position.

There's no point in thanking him for defending my honor. He didn't do it for me. He did it because another man dared to claim the property of his precious master.

As Myst walks on, I run the pads of my fingers over the cockleshell braided into her mane.

If I had any doubts that I had to escape this ride, they're gone now.

Wolf Bowborn is a devil.

And something tells me his master is the same, only dressed in a finer suit and with a lot more coin in his pockets.

CHAPTER 4
WOLF

True to their word, no one besides that one peeping bastard watches Sabine ride naked down the streets of Bremcote, but that goodwill doesn't last in the next town. Or the next.

Once we're outside the boundary of Lady Suri's influence, people flock to the streets, anxious to see if the rumor about Lord Rian's shocking command for his new bride is true. They hang out windows, calling down slurs to Sabine. Pubescent boys snicker from the alleyways. Men hoot and holler, trying to get her to flinch so that her carefully arranged hair will give them a glimpse of curves they can beat off to later.

Through it all, Sabine remains a mask of indifference, almost as if she's used to taking abuse and giving nothing back.

I'll admit that I'm surprised, maybe even a little affected.

The little violet is made of tougher stuff than I

thought. And frankly, that could be a problem. Pummeling that asshole at the start of the ride wasn't just for Lord Rian's sake—I wanted to impress upon Sabine the utter futility of trying to escape. Because I know how to sniff out a scheme, and she reeks of one.

First clue: All day, she hasn't once asked me about Lord Rian or Duren and what her life will be like there.

Second: There's that cockleshell she thinks she hid so well.

Third, the cincher: The taste of hope on her breath.

Put together, it tells me that Sabine Darrow has no intention of ever reaching Duren. If I had to guess, I'd wager some erstwhile lover gave her that cockleshell, and she plans to run away to be with him. Inwardly, I scoff at the idea that anyone would be so foolishly lovesick. Lord Rian will give her the world on a silver platter. She'll never know a day of hunger, or cold, or pain.

But there could be pain, couldn't there?

I shut up that internal voice as soon as it whispers in the back of my head. It's true that Lord Rian can be unpredictable. It isn't his temper that worries me—I've never seen a man more in control of his temper—but he tends to take out his frustrations in more calculated ways. He'll drive a racehorse to run until it's lame. He'll pit brothers against each other in the arena.

And the things he does with the whores . . .

But Sabine is different, I assure myself, and scold my inner voice for doubting Lord Rian, who has given me everything. Sabine will be his bride. She'll be his cherished prize to show off at Sorsha Hall's parties as she converses with fucking squirrels to the amazement of his guests. He'll want her pristine, protected at all times.

He won't hurt her, I tell myself. *Not like the others.*

By the time we leave the next village, I can see the torment is wearing on Sabine. Though her back remains ramrod straight, dark smudges now ring her eyes, and the blood in her veins flows sluggishly.

"We'll stop for the night soon," I say, signaling to the forest ahead. "We'll find shelter among the trees and a stream for the horse."

She nods wearily, finally too tired to argue.

Some of her curls are still damp with spilled ale from a drunken group of men who tried to grope her in the last town, before I knocked the biggest one on his ass. The smell of it—sour brew mixed with the men's pungent sweat—turns my stomach as much as the thought that their grasping hands were almost on her. Not that I'm looking—*you know you are, Wolf*—but Sabine's skin is flawless, and something inside me will do anything to keep it unspoiled. Only my master's hands belong on her.

In another half hour, we reach the outskirts of Mag Na Tir Forest, where the road winds among beech and oak trees. I lead us along a side path to a gently sloping clearing.

"Here?" Sabine looks around in bewilderment. "There's no stream."

I point deeper into the forest. "It's fifty paces that way."

At first, confusion pinches her pretty face, but then her eyebrows slowly rise. "Ah. You can hear it, can't you?"

My gaze drops from her face to her upper chest, where her godkiss birthmark rides above her breastbone.

Do I tell her I can hear the blood in her veins?

That I can hear her little sighs, her exhales?

That the small slip of her fingers caressing that cockleshell is as loud as the crash of ocean waves to my ears?

"Yeah. I can hear it." I toss down my rucksack and start clearing fallen limbs.

She gracefully dismounts and leads Myst in the direction of the stream, but I shake my head and point to the base of an elm tree. "No. I'll water the horse. You stay there and don't move."

"I can—"

"Sit and stay there. I told you to obey."

Her little hands fist, but she's too tired to put up a fight. Letting out a huff, she drops to her pretty ass at the tree's base. *Good girl.*

The routine of making camp is second nature to me. Clearing a space, collecting wood for a fire, checking the perimeter for any signs of wild animals nearby or, more dangerously, other people. Since Lord Rian pulled me out of the combat ring when we were both still boys, and years later put a bow in my hand, my life has been the hunt, the woods, the crackle and sighs of nature.

But this time, making camp is different. *She* makes it different. I find myself second guessing where to build the fire so the smoke won't drift in her face, how to make a berth soft enough for a noblewoman. I spend so much time thinking about Sabine's comfort that the moon is already up by the time I have the fire going and have led her horse to water.

Her stomach rumbles.

I stand up from stoking the fire, dusting off my hands. "I'll hunt us something to eat. Stay here."

She touches a hand to her stomach, eyes widening as it dawns on her that I heard her body's hunger signals. She glances toward the darkness beyond the campfire's glow, biting her bottom lip.

"I won't be gone long enough for any danger to reach you."

She swallows. "Okay."

She hugs her knees. She's shivering—fuck. Balled up like that, with her honeyed hair loose over her bare skin, she looks about as helpless as a fawn left alone by its mother.

Immortals help me.

I unbuckle my breastplate, tug my shirt free from my trousers, then drag it up over my head.

I toss her the shirt in a messy ball. "Put it on."

Her hands knead the fabric as she looks at me with utter bewilderment. For a second, neither of us speaks. Finally, she says, "No dress. No chemise. No—"

"I know the fucking rules, Lady Sabine."

She still looks baffled as her attention darts between me and the shirt. "But . . . "

"Who is going to tell Lord Rian? The trees? Look, little violet, if you want to spend all night shivering without a stitch on you, be my guest. But it's only you and me here. I don't give a shit about honoring Immortal Solene's ride —the gods have earned none of my favor. Tomorrow, you'll continue the ride unclothed, as my master has declared. Tonight, in the privacy of our camp, if it brings you peace to cover yourself, then do so. It's all the same to me."

In the firelight, her round eyes look especially large. My heightened vision lets me see all the flecks of gold in her blue-green irises, like the sparks rising into the night have found a home in her eyes.

"You don't honor any of the gods?"

I snort. "People are idiots to hope for their awakening. Yeah, I know the legends are thrilling to read, but in reality, the gods would be the same as any rulers with unchecked power—fucking tyrants. In a year after their return, it would be war and enslavement. We're fortunate they went to sleep. I hope they never fucking wake."

Her eyes stretch even wider.

"Why, does that offend you, little violet?" I snap.

She gives a laugh, surprising me. "Not in the slightest."

Without another word, she shimmies into my oversized shirt, so big it hangs past her hips. Her heartbeat slowly calms as her hands smooth over the rough fabric. Undyed linen stinking of a man's long day is no prize for a girl surely used to taffeta and silk, but she acts like it's damask from the far isles.

"Why do you call me that?" she asks.

"Call you what?"

Her eyes skip to the godkiss visible on my bare chest. "Little violet."

I grunt, not about to tell her a story of how a ruthless hunter once swooned over candied violets on a cake.

Because you smell like them.

"You're soft," I snap. "Fragile, like a violet. Now stay there."

I snatch up my bow and tromp into the woods. It's a relief to be here, where the space between trees feels like a homecoming. The smell of wild tartberries, the tiny snores of a chipmunk.

Immediately, I spot prints in the dirt and ready my bow.

As I stalk the rabbit's trail, my mind drifts to my current charge. It's easy to see why Lord Rian wants her. She's a beauty by any man's standards, and her hair might as well be a godkiss in itself. It's no surprise Rian wanted a bride favored by the Immortals. His family might possess wealth and influence, but not a single one of them is godkissed. It's the one thing they don't have, so they're drawn to it.

Will he be pleased with her? *By the Immortals, he's going to be fucking obsessed.* I've collected him from enough brothels on the morning after a rager to know the kind of woman he likes, and Sabine will not disappoint. A body built for carnal pleasure with the grace of a lady.

For a moment, my mind drifts to the possibility of taking a bride for myself one day. It isn't a thought I've ever entertained, if I'm being honest. I swore my life to serving the Valveres. My work takes me into the forest for weeks at a time, and there's always the chance I'll be finished off by a wild animal, like the stag that speared my shoulder with its antler the summer before last.

Let's be real—I'm hardly husband material.

Besides, look at the way she flinches around me, like she can see all the blood on my hands. Even her horse shies away from me. The whore who birthed me couldn't be bothered to keep me, nor whatever bastard got her pregnant by coin or by force, so why would anyone else? There's something inside me that's twisted like tree roots, broken like a faulty arrow. The fae gods made a mistake when they blessed me with my abilities. Only Rian saw the damage but dragged me out of the gutter anyway.

I'm anxious to see this ride through and return to more important ways of serving him. I can't stop thinking about that bear that dragged off the godkissed girl. It was strange; I should have easily scented her corpse but never found it. Never even scented a drop of blood. Likewise, if she survived and was still alive, I'd have smelled her, too.

I should be there, staking out the bear, I think with a growl of frustration. *Not babysitting some scrap of a girl.*

When I told Lord Rian about the bear's unusual fur and size, he only laughed. *"What are you suggesting, Wolf? That the goldenclaws are back? There hasn't been one in a thousand years. They went to sleep along with the gods."*

Ahead, in a grassy thicket, a rabbit blinks its black eye, and I draw my bow.

A few minutes later, I drop a brace of rabbits by the campfire. Sabine has rolled up my borrowed shirt sleeves to fit her shorter arms. She braided her hair, too. Not in the fancy fae style, but a simple rope.

At the sight of the dead rabbits, Sabine's jaw tightens, the scrape of her teeth striking my ear.

"What, friends of yours?" I ask.

She levels an unamused glare at me that, for some reason, makes me smile. Now that she's clothed, she's regained some of the bullheaded attitude she started the ride with.

As I clean the rabbits and roast them on a spit over the fire, I feel the heat of her gaze. It's like candlelight on my skin, flickering over my scars. Has a lord's daughter seen a bare-chested man before?

I glance up to catch her interest, and she quickly looks away.

After a moment, she says, "I don't know any other godkissed." She points the tip of her finger toward my birthmark. "I was the only one in Bremcote."

There aren't many of us godkissed, it's true. One out of every thousand babies is born with the small, sunburst-like birthmark that designates us as blessed by the ancient ones. What particular gift we're given is impossible to predict—I've seen godkissed with the strength of an ox, godkissed who can sculpt a woman's beauty like clay, godkissed who can call the rain.

"Well, you'll meet more," I say, plucking off a hunk of meat to test it. "There are many in Duren."

The juices drip down my chin as I relish the rabbit haunch. I tear off another piece.

Sabine shifts on the ground, wiggling closer to the roasting meat as her stomach rumbles. "Is it true the Valvere family collects godkissed?"

"Collects?" I snort. "Hell, we aren't horses. But, yes, they employ many like us. It makes sense given their businesses."

"Extraordinarily strong fighters bring a larger audience to the arena?"

I concede with a nod. The legal vices comprise all

manner of games of chance and spectator competitions—and brothels, of course. I no longer involve myself in those aspects of Lord Rian's work. Ever since he named me Duren's official huntsman, it's my job to keep meat on the table and wild animals from killing villagers. How he runs his vice houses is of no consequence to me anymore.

Sabine's fingernails suddenly become very interesting, and she clears her throat. I think she's about to ask for food, but she says, "I can pay you. To let me go, I mean."

Her heart claps like thunder in her chest—she's intensely nervous. As well she should be. It's no small crime to offer a bribe to a Valvere guard. I could punish her for this, and Lord Rian would back me. I could tie her up. Choke her with a fist around her throat until she recants. Until those big eyes look up at me beseechingly, those rosebud lips beg for forgiveness.

Instead, I only let my gaze hang on her small frame, drowning in my borrowed shirt. "Where exactly are you hiding a pouch of gold coins, my lady?"

Her heartbeat changes, thumps lighter with hope.

"I have a friend who can get you money if you take me to a rendezvous location twenty miles inland from Salensa."

Inwardly, I groan deep in my bones. As I suspected, this girl has some lovesick scheme with a boy she met somewhere. That damn seashell. The way she caresses it.

Turning the spit buys me time as I consider how to handle this foolish girl's artless plan. I suspect the boy is the supposed brains behind it, not her. Sabine may be clever, but like any pampered lord's daughter, she is uneducated on such things as geography and roadways. This is trouble. Not because she'll escape—she won't under my watch—but because I don't know how much this boy might have already spoiled Sabine.

She's still a virgin—of that, I'm certain. It's crass, but I can smell it if a girl is untouched. Lord Rian used to use that particular skill of mine when evaluating new whores for the brothels. Since virgins are worth far more, every girl claims to be one, and he needed my nose to suss out the liars.

Unlike most, Sabine has the scent of innocence all over her.

But this lover of hers could have had his mouth on her, his hands in places reserved for her future husband. And that would be unacceptable.

Standing, I take my time removing one of the rabbits from the spit, picking off the ash and charred bits, then stalk around slowly and hold the roasted meat above Sabine's head.

Her stomach growls. Saliva floods her mouth. Her big eyes look up at me with so much goddamn hope it takes my breath away.

In a hard voice, I say, "Never attempt to bribe me again, Lady Sabine. It won't go as well for you the second time."

I pop a chunk of the meat in my own mouth.

Her face falls. I'm never keen to see a girl's hopes dashed like a rotten pumpkin, but she doesn't realize what a favor I just did her. What a favor I'm about to do for her now, though she'll hate me for it.

Setting the stick back on the spit while her stomach

rumbles louder, I rummage through my rucksack until I find a length of rope.

"Hold out your hands," I command, and measure enough to bind her wrists.

Her eyes fill with fear.

Violets, I think as her scent mixes with the savory juices in my mouth. *Goddamn violets.*

CHAPTER 5
SABINE

My wrists are bound.

My ankles are tied.

My stomach growls like a newborn pup.

And all I can think is: *I hate Wolf Bowborn with all the marrow in my bones.*

My captor sits on a log by the fire, confident I can't escape, taking his time picking the meat off a rabbit haunch like he enjoys watching me try to squirm out of my binds.

After he torments me long enough, he comes around the fire in unhurried steps, then lowers the roasting stick with the second rabbit toward my mouth.

"Eat," he commands.

Seething, I glare up at him, but I'm too hungry to refuse. It's pathetic how a single day without food sends all my resolve flying out the window. As I think of all the ways I'd like to stab him with that pointy stick, I part my jaw. He holds out the meat, and I take a bite, ripping its flesh with my teeth. Grease drips down my chin.

A dark smile plays on his lips—he's enjoying this far too much.

"You're a beast," I mutter around the bite in my mouth.

The insult doesn't phase him. "A beast? Sure. A beast who will get you to Duren even if I have to bind and gag you every night. So any ideas you have about escape, you give up now, do you understand? Because I'm happy to repeat this act every night. I assure you, I don't mind."

"I wasn't planning to escape!"

He reaches into his pocket and takes out a small object, dropping it in the grass beside my bound feet.

It's Adan's cockleshell.

Oh, shit.

At my silence, he wipes the rabbit grease from my chin with his thumb, then slowly pops his thumb in his mouth to lick off the juices.

I gape at him—there's something deeply carnal about that action, something that stirs a buzz in me I can't place a name to.

"What is his name?" Wolf asks, licking his lips.

I'm not sure which emotion is greater—fury that he seems to somehow know about Adan or baldfaced awe that he figured it out so easily. Does his godkiss let him read minds, too?

"Answer me, Lady Sabine." Wolf grips my jaw, forcing my head upward.

"You wouldn't hurt me," I mutter between squished lips.

"Oh, I've hurt plenty of women."

My eyes narrow with seething anger as I explain, "I don't doubt it, but I mean that Lord Rian wouldn't like his bride bruised."

He snorts to concede that I'm right. "Perhaps. But I don't have to be kind."

"Ha! What kindness have you done?"

"I could take back my shirt and have you stand before me bare, little violet."

My heart thundering, I twist my head out of his grip, keeping my eyes on the cockleshell in the grass.

Adan's sunlit voice reaches out from my memory:

"I'll show you the sea, Sabine. You and me, we'll cross the waves together and leave this place once and for all."

Wolf snorts. "As you wish. When you feel like telling me the details of your plan to run away with your lover, I might feel like loosening your binds. Until then, finish eating this before it attracts every predator in the valley."

He thrusts the stick at me. I manage to take it awkwardly in my bound hands, then tear into the rabbit.

Wolf settles back on the far side of the clearing, extending his legs and using a log for a pillow. I have nothing—no blanket, no bedroll, only the borrowed shirt steeped in his masculine scent.

His eyes close.

At least now I can scowl at him openly without fear of punishment. He's even more of a devil than I first suspected. That untamed long hair that flaunts every social norm. Those honed muscles that've doubtlessly bloodied countless men like Thom Wallsor. The scars on his torso from a lifetime of fights.

I take my time searing Wolf with a long, assessing look. Do all men look like that bare-chested? So raw? Battle worn? So dominant, like a ram?

They can have my body . . .

My head feels cloudy. I'm too frustrated to get through my recitation. But I grit my teeth and force it.

. . . my mind is my own.

And my heart? Well, my heart belonged to Adan the first moment he ambled through the convent gate.

Because of the strict chastity vows, no males were allowed to set foot in the Convent of the Immortal Iyre, and frankly, the Sisters didn't need them. For as mean-hearted as those old crones were, I have to give them credit for their mettle. They hauled stones for the new chapel. They bricked and mortared the buildings themselves. They repaired the wagon when the axle broke.

And yet there was one thing they needed men for:

The goats.

Immortal Iyre's teachings forbid Sisters from touching any male anatomy, even that of a goat. So once a year, a farmer was admitted into our sacred feminine space to castrate the newborn male kids. During my first eleven years at the convent, it was blind old Mr. Porter with his steady hands and oak-handled knife. But the fae gods called Mr. Porter to join them in eternal rest, and the following year, Adan came in his place. Beautiful, golden-haired Adan, who the animals called "The Boy Who Shines Like Sunlight."

Now, my stomach clenches with longing, but it's all I can do to fish the cockleshell he gave me out of the grass with my bound hands and hug it to my chest.

I'll show you the sea, Sabine.

Another voice squeaks its way into my head, this one in the here and now. A tiny nut-brown mouse noses out of the grass by my feet.

Food?

Its curious little face breaks through my frustration. I can't help but smile.

For you? I tell it. **I'll gladly share.**

Shifting my feet under me, I manage to lower to the ground and pluck off a piece of the rabbit meat to hold out, though Wolf's rope certainly doesn't make it easy. The mouse's nose works double-time as it scampers closer.

"What are you doing?" Wolf's bark from across the fire makes me jump—I'd thought he was asleep.

"There's a mouse," I answer coldly.

"I know there's a fucking mouse. I heard it rustling the grass ten minutes ago. What are you *doing*?"

One of his eyes is open, glaring at me suspiciously like feeding a mouse is somehow part of a grand escape plan.

Scoffing, I don't give Wolf another second of my time and turn back to the mouse with a smile reserved only for it. In a softer voice, I murmur, "It's hungry."

The mouse creeps up to my hand, whiskers exploring as it happily accepts the scrap of meat, making a dining table out of my palm.

Wolf is silent for a long time, but I feel his eyes studying me. His energy chews up the air around us as surely as the fire devours the wood.

"Never seen a mouse before that you didn't want to stomp?" I mutter in a hard tone. "I'm not surprised you've never had a pet. Or anything else to love, I'd wager."

He adjusts his position, arms clenching tighter. "I'm trying to figure out what you hope to gain by feeding a fucking mouse."

A sigh slips out of my lips. I'm prepared to have choice words for Wolf, but when I turn to him, I'm surprised to see that his suspicion has vanished. Instead, he looks positively fascinated, even gobsmacked, by what I'm doing.

Something about that look softens my anger.

Taking a deep breath, I explain, "It isn't always about personal gain. All creatures, even a mouse, deserve to be understood."

Judging by his pinched brows, this concept is completely foreign to him. There's a challenge in his voice when he says, "Even the wildcat that will eat that mouse later tonight?"

"Yes, even the wildcat."

His jaw works for a moment, and then he says in a guarded tone I haven't heard before, "And me? Can you understand what's in my head?"

An owl hoots from the dark canopy, unseen high in the trees.

I roll my eyes. "My gift only works on animals. You're a person."

His eyes devour me as he says in a dangerously low voice, like a warning, "No, little violet. I'm a Wolf."

A shiver runs through me, spooking the mouse enough for it to scamper away. The darkness of the night feels palpable, heavy. The fire burns low, sending sparks skating toward the stars overhead. Suddenly I can't look at Wolf without feeling like he can sense every fear in my body.

I roll away from him, curling up in the grass, using my bound hands as a pillow. My heartbeat wallops.

Does he sleep?

Does he stay awake all night, guarding me? Watching me? Jailing me?

The owl hoots again like it's sending out a warning to all the forest. The clouds are loud overhead as the wind drags them across the stars.

When I dream, I dream of wolves.

In the morning, Wolf's shadow blocks the dewy morning sun.

My heart kicks into a gallop, and I keep my eyes mostly closed, afraid to alert him to the fact that I'm awake.

He's standing over me. Why is he standing over me?

A breeze ruffles my borrowed shirt hem, and it dawns on me that while tossing and turning in the night, his shirt has ridden up over my hips. My bare legs and the curve of my ass are on full display. With my wrists and ankles bound, I must look like a trussed pig for him, ready for the feast.

He hasn't hurt me yet. Maybe he never will. Maybe his blind loyalty to my future husband will keep him from sampling the goods.

At least, that's what I've told myself until now.

Steeling my nerves to mask my fear, I snap open my eyes and glower, "You promised you wouldn't look."

His eyebrows raise as his gaze drags from my legs to my face. A hint of amusement wrinkles the skin around his eyes. "I wasn't looking at your ass, Lady Sabine. There's a deathrattle snake curled up at your back."

Oh.

My face flushes as I sit up. Twisting around, I spot the snake's black-and-red pattern coiled against my flesh.

"Don't move," he orders, drawing his knife. "I'll kill it."

"Don't you dare!" I gently nudge the snake awake with my bound hands. It raises its head, flicks its tongue at me in silent thanks for the good rest, and then slithers off toward the woods. "It was only seeking some warmth."

As the venomous snake disappears into the under-brush, Wolf stares at me with that same gobsmacked look as when I fed the hungry mouse. Finally, he pinches the bridge of his nose, mutters something under his breath, and then starts kicking dirt onto the fire.

"Get up. It's dawn. Time to move."

I hold out my bound hands pointedly, and he uses his knife to slice through the ropes on my wrists and ankles.

Rubbing my wrists, I make my way to where Wolf tied Myst to a tree. She tosses her head insistently.

Worried for you, she says.

"I know, my brave girl," I whisper, running a calming hand down her velvety muzzle. "We'll both be okay."

Leave now? Run?

I sigh, glancing over my shoulder at Wolf packing his rucksack. "It still isn't time." She knows about my plan to run away with Adan to the extent that a horse is able to comprehend complex ideas. She wasn't fond of Adan any more than she is of Wolf, but that's only because she's overprotective of me and generally distrustful of men.

I wonder who she learned that from, I think wryly, remembering all the times I complained to her about my father.

"Soon," I whisper.

Escaping will be trickier than I thought, now that Wolf has determined my aims. Of course, Lord Rian's stipulation that I ride with no lead or bridle is actually a godsend; Myst and I can bolt whenever we like. But we have to be smart about it. I didn't anticipate my future husband would send a godkissed huntsman to escort me.

Myst and I can run, but Wolf can track us anywhere. A few hours' lead on him doesn't mean much when we'll have to stop eventually for rest and directions. I have to figure out a way to run so that he can't follow us.

After combing my fingers through the knots in Myst's mane and tail, I feel Wolf move up behind me.

He says almost apologetically, "My shirt, Lady Sabine."

My hand falls on the rough linen collar that smells like him. Of course, word cannot get to Lord Rian that I broke a single one of his rules. No one can know that I was clothed for even a second of this ride.

Keeping my back to him, I start to tug his shirt over my head, but before it's over my shoulders, he takes ahold of my braid like seizing a stallion's reins. He coils it around his fist and then yanks my head back.

Gasping, I cry, "Don't touch me!"

"Quiet," he orders, low and hard. He moves his hand to feel along my back ribs, prodding and testing the skin gingerly, with a heightened sense of touch that seems to tell him cryptic details about my body.

He grunts low in his throat. "You have a cracked rib."

I try to look at him over my shoulder, but he still has my braid in a fist. I hiss, "It's fine."

His grasp tightens on my braid. "It's an old wound. Five weeks and a day. There's still some bruising."

He finally loosens his hold, and I twist away, tugging the borrowed shirt back down so I can face him clothed. Tipping my chin up, I snap, "I said it's fine! It's almost healed, anyway."

His brows are set low, dangerous, like a predator. "Who did this to you?"

"Couldn't it have been an accident?"

He doesn't bother to respond to the suggestion. "Answer me, my lady."

He isn't going to let me get away with silence. My heart clenches like a fist, wanting to protect me from my memories. Lowering my eyes, I admit reluctantly, "I was a ward of the Convent of the Immortal Iyre. The Sisters struck me until a month ago, when my father informed them he'd sold me to a wealthy husband. Then they locked me in a room, tied to a bed, to fatten me up and let the wounds heal. I guess it wasn't quite long enough. No one else has noticed the bruises, but no one else has your eyesight."

Wolf's gaze burns into me with the intensity of an August sun. "How long?"

He means the beatings.

"Years."

He briefly closes his eyes. "How many years?"

"Twelve."

His face reddens as he drags in a breath that trembles with rage. He holds it, then lets it ebb away slowly, and only then can he speak. "You'll be safe at Sorsha Hall, my lady. I swear it."

I snort a mirthless laugh as I tug the cord off the base of my braid, freeing the strands and combing them loose with my fingers.

He frowns. "You doubt my word?"

My eyes are sharp and rebuking as I work through my hair. "I think you're so besotted with your master that you're blind, despite your godkissed vision."

His jaw tightens. I've angered him. I said the wrong thing. But I don't get the impression he's angry that I insulted *him*, but rather that I implied a flaw about his master.

Fighting to maintain composure, he vows again, "No harm will come to you in Duren, Sabine."

"What do you call *this*?" I explode with more verve than I knew I had in me, as I toss a hand toward my naked legs. "You think I'll be safe with a husband whose first action toward his new bride is to make her a spectacle?"

Wolf's neck burns with threads of red. "This ride is meant to honor the gods."

"Oh, come on, you know that's bullshit!"

He hesitates but doesn't deny it. "Alright, then, but it

isn't meant to shame you. If anyone, it's meant to shame your father."

My response is to tug his shirt off despite the fact it leaves me naked. I ball up his shirt and shove it against his chest, breathing hard. "And yet I'm the one punished, aren't I, Wolf?"

CHAPTER 6
WOLF

The next few days pass with the same leers and catcalls, until every town blends together. I knew men could be vile, but the wicked delight that shines in their eyes as they line the road makes my stomach sour. My knuckles are raw from all the smart mouths I've punched, but it's worth it.

To shut them up.

To relieve the needling frustration coursing in my veins.

And, dammit, to see her smile.

Sabine was uneasy at first, but gradually, she started to smile when I pummeled a mouthy asshole. Maybe after so many years on the receiving end of a stick, she relishes being on the team doling out the beatings. If I had to sucker-punch Immortal Vale himself, the King of Fae, to earn more of her smiles, I'd do it.

As we near Polybridge, the forest grows marshier. It isn't long before we catch glimpses of the serpentine

Tellyne River in the distance. Once we cross the river, we'll head north, and that's already got me prickling with dread. North means bigger towns, bigger crowds.

I'll just say it—north means trouble.

For now, though, the road is quiet, save Myst's hoofbeats and a jay's chittering as it perches on Sabine's shoulder. It makes a particularly loud squawk, and Sabine gives a gentle laugh that tinkles like bells.

What the hell do the two of them have to laugh about, worms?

My thoughts keep chewing over the abuse those Sisters doled out on her. For fucking *years*. It shouldn't have taken me as long as it did to spot the bruises. That's what I get for trying to be a gentleman and not gawk at her naked body. I should have demanded to inspect every inch of her before we left Bremcote. Fuck, how I'd like to get my hands around those old Sisters' necks. Such hypocrites, claiming to be acolytes of Immortal Iyre. Me? I've never wanted anything to do with the Red Church. In name, the church upholds the worship of the old gods, spreading hope that they'll reawaken. In reality, the church's Grand Cleric is just the same scheming asshole as every other power-hungry ruler. King Joruun, in his palace in Old Coros, may be the official sovereign of Astagnon, but he's getting old. And you can bet the Red Church is crouched like a fox, ready to pounce as soon as he dies and a power vacuum opens.

After the river crossing at Polybridge, I feel at ease enough to allow a stop at an inn for a midday meal. I've been running Sabine ragged, anxious to get her to Duren, and she deserves to rest her ass on a chair for once.

The Stargazer Inn, named for Immortal Thracia, Goddess of Night, is barely more than a few boards slapped together, but there's a spacious common room with a large fire in the hearth warming a soup kettle. One side of the common room holds shelves with staples for purchase—rope, tin pots, flour sacks. Wooden tables span the other side, occupied by a few patrons: two single men, a young couple with a baby.

"Can I help . . . *oh!*"

A white-haired innkeeper stops short in her boots at the sight of Sabine dressed only in her flowing hair.

"A meal, madam," I order sharply, gesturing toward the kettle. "We'll have a bowl of that soup for Lord Rian Valvere's new bride."

I allow the two men to take a brief look at Sabine—it's only human nature—before extending a warning growl that has them both immediately fascinated by the bottoms of their tankards.

Satisfied no one is going to bother us, I drag out a chair and jerk my head toward it. "Sit."

Sabine collects her curtain of hair in front of her as she slips into the seat. The innkeeper brings two bowls of soup, half a warm loaf of bread, and ale.

"Her horse is hitched outside," I say. "Make sure it's fed and watered."

"Yes, sir." The elderly woman scurries to the kitchen, where I hear her giving orders to someone.

As a chicken wanders in through the open back door, pecking at crumbs under our table, I relax as much as I dare. Being indoors makes me nervous, but something about this humble place, with its sturdy earthenware pitchers and cozy tallow lamps, calms Sabine's pulse.

And that, in turn, relaxes me.

As I tear into the bread, I watch her spoon a hunk of potato toward her mouth, only to pause, looked fixedly at the chicken, and then offer it the morsel instead.

My toe taps anxiously under the table. Four days on the road now, and she still hasn't asked about Lord Rian or Sorsha Hall. That means that even after my theatrics with the rope, she still plans on never reaching Duren.

I sigh. *Foolish girl.*

Trying to sway her is useless, if she has her heart set on escape. I suspect she will have to learn her lesson the hard way, but I find myself piping up to try to steer her away from disaster.

"You'll be a good match," I say gruffly. "You and Lord Rian."

She gives a scoffing laugh as though she doubts my words but is willing to humor me. "What makes you say that?"

I shrug. "You're clever. You're observant. Lord Rian will like you."

"I can match his wit at his mind games, you mean?"

I hesitate. *Oh, little violet. No one matches Lord Rian at his games.* But that's a lesson for her to learn another day.

At my pause, mischief sparkles in her eyes. "Wolf, you came dangerously close to complimenting me just now, did you know that?"

A silence moves in between us. For four days, we've passed long hours at each other's sides, and grown familiar with each other's habits, but we've spoken only when necessary, and about practical matters. This hint of banter throws me. For my whole life, I've been in the company of other men. First in the fighting rings, then in the army barracks, and now in the hunting regiment. I'm used to gruff ribbing, but this is different.

Sabine and I aren't friends. We never will be. Every part of her belongs to someone else—even her quips.

My attention drops to my tankard as I try to steer the conversation back to Rian. "You'll find things to like about Lord Rian, too. He's twenty-eight years old. Your father could have sold you to a man twice his age. He's known for his physical prowess and his shrewd dealings. Every woman in Duren would kill to wear his ring, probably even in all of Astagnon. But he chose you."

Sabine takes her time swallowing a few bites of soup. "So because he's young and attractive, I should be pleased that I was bought without being consulted on the matter?" Her amicable tone has soured.

I drink deeply from my tankard, the sour ale splashing down my throat to settle uneasily in my belly. I wipe my mouth with the back of one hand. "He's richer than sin, too. Don't tell me that doesn't matter."

She scoffs, shaking her head like I can't possibly understand, and returns to the chicken, presumably for better conversation.

The innkeeper hesitantly interrupts. "Can I get you anything else, sir? My lady?"

I push to my feet, the chair groaning as it scrapes on the stone floor. I jerk my head toward the mercantile corner. "We need supplies."

While Sabine converses with the chicken, and a cat

that's sauntered in to take my place at the table, I browse through the wares for sale.

"A length of rope," I tell the innkeeper. Tying Sabine's ankles and wrists every night has left me short on supplies. "And three apples. Oh—and that blanket."

As I make room for the goods in my rucksack, I spot Lord Charlin's sealed letter. It's none of my business, but I am curious about what secret it contains that he believes is so powerful that Rian will acquiesce to his demands.

Does Sabine know what's in it?

I'll have to let my curiosity go hungry, because of that damn seal. The sealing wax Lord Charlin used turns black if reheated, so there's no way to open it stealthily.

The innkeeper keeps flinging anxious glances out the window like she's skipping rocks. When I pay her, she distractedly drops the coins in her apron pocket.

"Eh? Oh, yes. Thank you, sir."

I frown. There's something wrong if *I'm* not the primary source of her worries. Whenever I'm in the room, people usually keep their eyes on me, my bow, or the nearest exit.

"Something the matter?" I ask slowly.

Her fingers move to clutch her dress's uppermost button. "I was just keeping a close eye on your lady's mare outside. That's a fine horse, and, well, we've seen a bit of trouble these past few days."

A warning instinct prickles along my spine. "What manner of trouble?"

Her eyes skate nervously around the common room, as she lowers her voice so as not to alarm her patrons. "A boy from a village about three miles from here went missing. Not but six years old, the poor thing."

"He could have run off. Boys do at that age."

Chewing her lip, she confides, "A shepherd claims he saw Volkish riders take him north."

Volkish riders? Impossible. The border between Astagnon and Volkany closed five hundred years ago, after a war that nearly decimated both kingdoms. Our two lands' struggles began when the Immortal Court, who'd woven themselves deeply into the threads of both kingdoms, simply went to sleep one day without warning. In other words, they fucking abandoned us. Overnight, crops that had thrived under Immortal Solene's earthy magic withered. Entire towns built with Immortal Vale's framework magic crumbled.

Astagnon fared better. We had arable land, and we'd never been as dependent on the gods. But Volkany, with its large godkissed population, had thrown all their cards in with the Immortal Court. Every aspect of their kingdom ran on godly favor—a necessity in a wild land filled with rugged mountains and impenetrable forests. Volkish rule fractured into lawless regions run by banditlords, who soon set their sights on our rich soil. After a century and a half of attacks on our lands, the Volkish rulers came together to create a godkissed army, and the great war began. When we defeated them, the Astagnonian army built a towering wall along the entire northern border to seal off Volkany, reinforced by godkissed spell craft that was supposed to be permanently impregnable.

For centuries, that's been it. Ancient history. No one

has seen or heard anything from the Kingdom of Volkany besides a few tidbits that sailors traveling from our coast to theirs gleaned. Apparently, a new king named Rachillon managed to reunify the fractured regions and now rules under one Volkish crown, but little is known about him.

Everything else is just rumors:

Rachillon is mad with power.

A deadly monoceros woke from its thousand-year slumber and slaughtered a village.

A woodcutter found Immortal Vale's resting place in the Volkish side of the Blackened Forest.

To the innkeeper, I say with an edge in my voice, "The shepherd must be mistaken."

The old woman presses a hand to her throat. "Perhaps, sir. But also—also, the boy was godkissed."

A stitch pulls in my side. The great war was fought in part because Volkany tried to bring all godkissed into their borders. But that was five hundred years ago. "What was his power?"

"He could rot tree roots. It was useful for falling trees. He could clear an entire forest in a day if he wanted to. His father planned to take him to a logging camp in Mag Na Tir, where his services would be highly compensated. He isn't the first godkissed to go missing around here, either. There was a godkissed soldier stationed in Marblenz who vanished two weeks ago. He could scry."

I let this information find fallow ground in my mind. It could be more baseless gossip, but if it's true, what would Volkany want with a godkissed boy who can fall trees and a scrying soldier? And how the fuck did their soldiers get over the wall?

"I'm just saying, take care on the road, sir." The innkeeper entreats me as her eyes slide behind me to where Sabine is holding court with the chicken and cat. "That's her, isn't it? The noblewoman everyone's been talking about, who was sold to one of the Valvere sons?" She pauses before saying meaningfully, "She's godkissed, too, isn't she?"

I tighten my jaw. I don't like what the innkeeper is implying about Sabine being a target for raiders. "Thank you for your warning. We'll be fine."

Mulling over our options, I pull Sabine to her feet by her upper arm, interrupting whatever silent conversation she was having with livestock. This news has me on edge. We're headed north, in the same direction as these supposed Volkish riders.

"Wolf?" She skitters as I drag her backward toward the door. "What's wrong? What happened?"

"Nothing."

"*Something* happened."

"Nope."

I shoulder open the door, thrusting us into bright sunlight. My eyes case the road in both directions. I can see about three times farther than the average person and in much greater detail. There's no sign of any other travelers.

I pitch my head up to judge the position of the sun. "I've decided that we'll bypass Middleford and take the road west through Mag Na Tir Forest instead."

She frowns. "Lord Rian ordered us to pass through Middleford."

By the gods, does she *want* to be kidnapped by Volkish raiders? I remind myself that she knows nothing about them or the missing godkissed people, and I intend for it to stay that way.

"You'd prefer to pass through cities? More jeering men? More women spiteful that you've stolen their husbands' attention?"

Sabine holds both hands up. "You know what? You're right. The forest road sounds lovely."

The rest of the afternoon, we get no more trouble other than some farmhands who sprint to the edge of a wheat field to watch us pass, and a crow who perches on Sabine's shoulder and refuses to leave until I throw a rock at it.

That earns me one of her scowls.

As the afternoon drags on, my thoughts cycle back to the innkeeper's warning about the missing godkissed. It isn't unusual for godkissed to go missing more often than regular people. By our nature, we're coveted. Men want godkissed wives as a sign of status, and they aren't above stealing them.

But a young boy? The Marblenz soldier? And what about the godkissed girl the bear supposedly dragged off in the northern border villages? Something still feels particularly off about that last one.

The mental map of Astagnon's northern border forms in my head. I'm intimately familiar with the border's contours, since it cuts through the Blackened Forest, where I do much of my hunting. The wall, built thirty feet high, divides not only the forest but also the two king-doms. There have never been stairs or openings in the wall. I've only seen it once with my own eyes, and even then, it was from a distance. To reach the border means traversing through a nearly impenetrable section of the Blackened Forest.

Suddenly, my feet go still.

If my mental map is correct, the area where I tracked that odd bear was less than a mile from the border wall. It's been five hundred years, for fuck's sake. What if the wall's protective wards broke?

A dark certainty fills me, though I know nothing for sure. If raiders did come from Volkany, they would have had to tear down part of the supposedly-impenetrable wall. A bear—a goldenclaw, who hasn't been seen in our lands for nearly a thousand years, but might have awoken *north* of the border—could have entered after they opened it.

Rian dismissed my previous warning about the gold-enclaw, but with this new information, he'll have no choice but to take the possibility more seriously. It's strange to think the Valveres, with their network of spies, haven't heard of any strange border activity.

Ahead, Sabine draws Myst to a stop and peers at me inquisitively over her shoulder "Wolf? Why did you stop?"

My muscles prickle, wanting to return to the Black-ened Forest and inspect every inch of that wall. Timing is critical if enemy raiders are entering our land to abduct godkissed. I can only imagine what King Rachillon of Volkany—mad or not—intends to do with them.

And yet, as Sabine looks back at me with those doe-like round eyes, I'm beyond torn. *This* is where I should be. Protecting her. There's no chance in hell I'd let any other person alive do the job. She's far too valuable. If anything were to happen to her . . .

"Wolf?" she prompts again. "Hel-*lo*?"

"Keep moving," I bark, snapping out of my thoughts as I stalk forward. "I didn't tell you you could stop."

She rolls her eyes at my gruffness, but dutifully urges Myst forward.

Good girl, little violet.

As we enter the Mag Na Tir Forest, fears about what is really happening in Astagnon claw my insides to shreds.

CHAPTER 7
SABINE

"Is this *really* necessary?"

As Wolf coils rope around my wrists, I glare up at him through my lashes, trying to impress upon him the full extent of my indignation. His shirt, which is normally tight on him, hangs on me like a chemise. The collar is so loose that my godkiss mark shows on my breastbone, but I can't tug it higher with him tying my wrists.

"That's up to you," he says. "Are you ready to tell me the boy's name?"

My face settles into a scowl.

My look makes him smirk. He gives the rope an extra tug to check its tightness and then moves on to my ankles.

"I told you, little violet. Tell me your lover's plan to steal you from Lord Rian, and I'll trust you enough not to tie you up. I won't even kill the lad, how about that? I'll just remind him there's a price to pay for coveting another man's property."

Resting my back against the tree, I heave a sigh that travels all the way to my navel. I suppose there's no point in denying anymore what Wolf already knows.

I mutter evenly, "He didn't sully me, if that's what you're so concerned with."

Wolf loops the rope around my bare ankles, trussing me up with the same well-practiced knots he probably uses on his quarry. "I know he didn't."

I snort. "How could you possibly know that? I could have slept with half the boys in Bremcote, and you'd be none the wiser."

His hands go still for a brief moment, and then he finishes the knot. Tossing his hair back, he stands. "I just know."

"You're a liar, Wolf Bowborn. Come on. That can't even be your real name."

He runs a hand over his chin like he knows better than to let me goad him, but then levels me with a dark look that says he's run out of patience for my prodding. In a steady voice, he explains, "Whenever Lord Rian gets a new whore for the brothels, he brings her to me first. Many claim they're virgins—few actually are. I can . . . tell. And I can tell with you, too."

He sniffs the wind once, like an animal.

I gape, mildly disgusted. "You can *smell* that? No. Impossible."

His eyes gleam like hot coals. "If you don't like it, take it up with the Immortals."

I fold my bound arms into my chest, feeling pink-cheeked and mortified. All the while Wolf goes about setting up camp, I pity myself for having to be stuck with this beast of a man. He was right when he warned me he was an animal—but not a sweet one like my mice and birds.

He seemed nervous at the inn. Something happened while he was buying supplies. Whatever the innkeeper told him was significant enough to spook him away from the road to Middleford to take the forest road instead.

This detour complicates my plan significantly. Adan anticipated what route the ride would take through the major towns, and our rendezvous hinges on that path. Now that Wolf and I veered off course, Adan will have no way of finding me.

I still have his seashell, tucked into the cradle of my ear. It's the only place I could hide it on my body. As badly as I want to clutch it now for reassurance, I don't dare risk Wolf seeing. The man has the eyes of a hawk.

Well, Wolf Bowborn can't see or smell or taste *inside* my head. My mind is my own. And that's where I keep Adan, tucked away among my few good memories. Myst. Suri. Adan. The only souls in this world who ever gave a damn about me.

Supper passes with few words exchanged between us. Wolf leaves to take a piss. Myst seems spooked, uneasy, as she stamps her feet next to the tree where she's tethered.

What is it? I ask.

A predator nearby, she answers. *Wildcat.*

I scan the dark woods, but if the wildcat is close, it isn't inclined to speak its thoughts to me. I wonder if Wolf is already aware of it. If Myst can pick up on its scent, surely he can, too.

It won't come near the fire, I reassure her. *Besides, Wolf will protect us.*

She snorts, hardly comforted that our safety is secure in Wolf Bowborn's hands.

When he returns, he says nothing about sensing a wildcat. He digs around in his rucksack and pulls out three apples—real, fresh apples that make my mouth water.

He tosses one to me. "Here. A fine dessert for a lady."

I catch it with my bound hands. His tone was heavy with irony, but an apple *is* a decadent treat to me. I smooth my thumb over its glistening peel like it's a precious jewel.

To my surprise, he offers the other apple to Myst in his open palm.

She snorts. *Poison apple?*

Oh, stop being so suspicious, I say to her. *There would be easier ways to kill you.*

She snorts again, doubtful.

I take a theatrical bite to demonstrate to her it isn't poison. Still dubious, she accepts the apple from him but bares her teeth as she does.

He snorts right back at her.

For a few minutes, the three of us enjoy the apples. The Sisters grew apple trees in the convent orchard, but I was rarely permitted a taste. Instead, they made me mash the fruits for long hours into fermented cider that they'd guzzle by the gallon, despite their abstinence vows. At night, the scent of the juice on my skin drew the bees that lived in my thatched roof. I let them crawl over me as I lay in bed, whispering to them that they were lucky to be able to fly away. They were always careful not to sting me—but one night, I rolled over on one accidentally. The prick of pain soon faded, but my face began to swell. My neck and chest itched so badly that I wanted to scratch my skin off. I'd heard of bee venom sickening certain people, but never knew I was susceptible. My throat closed up; I couldn't breathe. In the morning, the Sisters found me unconscious, bees crawling over every inch of my skin to keep me warm. If not for them, I might have died. The Sisters drenched me with a bucket of cold water to shock me alert. Then, they made me return to work.

As the delicate juice now flows down my throat, my mood also sweetens.

The convent is behind me.

"So. Your name," I say between bites. "Did your parents really name you Wolf?"

He shakes his head, keeping his eyes on the fire. "Didn't know my parents."

"*Someone* named you."

He rolls his half-eaten apple from one hand to the other as distant thoughts scroll through his eyes. I don't actually expect him to open his mind's vault to me, so it's a shock when he says, haltingly, "There was a—a thief. Jocki. He kept an eye on me as a boy. He used to set up street fights. Children aren't allowed to fight for pay in Duren, but it happens."

I raise my eyebrows. This situation feels delicate, like any sudden move will freeze Wolf up like a skittish rabbit. "I'm sorry to hear it."

He looks at me oddly, like he's never heard sympathy before. Then, he clears his throat. "Lord Rian saw me in one of Jocki's fights. He decided a godkissed fighter around his age would make a good sparring partner, so his father, Lord Berolt, allowed me to train in the academy for the Golden Sentinels. That's the Valveres' private army. They gave me Bladeborn as a surname, then later, when they decided my skills were better suited as a hunter, changed it to Bowborn."

"And your first name?"

"Rian started calling me that for my ability to track— like a wolf."

I nibble the last scraps of apple flesh from its core. Softly, I ask, "What's your real name?"

His head jerks to the side, an instant head shake. He doesn't want to say.

"Tell me?" I swallow the last bite of my apple. "Please?"

His body flinches at that word as viscerally as if I had slapped him. I can tell now that kind words make him uncomfortable. They raise his defenses as much as if I'd drawn a knife. He throws his apple core deep into the woods, and I'm sure he isn't going to tell me a thing for the rest of the night other than to bark commands.

But he quietly mutters, "Basten."

The way he says it is rusty, like his tongue hasn't made the sound in years. He immediately stands, as though ashamed, and finds something urgent to dig through his rucksack for. The patter of falling acorns, loosened by the wind, tap around us.

Basten, I repeat in my head. Something about it unlocks a door I didn't see in him before. A godkissed boy on the streets, living on his own, blessed and cursed at the same time. Hell, it isn't that different from how I grew up, only instead of the combat arena, I was caged by convent walls.

"It suits you," I say encouragingly.

He snorts. "Basten the Bastard—you're right."

"That isn't what I meant."

Silence falls between us as the sun sinks further. The stars begin to make their debut overhead, one at a time like they don't want to rush each other. We finish eating, and I take my apple core to Myst so she can savor the last bite.

He told me his real name, I tell her.

Doesn't matter. Still don't trust him. She sniggers derisively in Wolf's direction before munching on the apple core. *But the apple helps.*

Wolf pulls a folded blanket out of his rucksack. Stalking over with that stiff way he holds his shoulder after a long day, he drops it in my lap with as little care as if it was a dirty sack. But it's actually luxurious, soft wool that doesn't appear to have ever been used, as fine as the coverings in my father's manor house.

Night after night, I've slept on hard ground. *Now* he gives me a blanket?

I look up, baffled. "What's this for?"

"I got tired of hearing you shivering all night. It keeps me up." When I still stare at him in bewilderment, he grumbles, "Take it. That's an order."

Unfolding the blanket with bound wrists is not the easiest task, and after a few pathetic attempts to stretch it out over my legs, he sighs impatiently and crouches down.

"Let me."

His hands make quick work of smoothing the blanket over my body. He wraps it around my back and brings it around in the front to tuck under my bound hands. Like he's bundling up a child, he rubs my shoulders.

"There, little violet. Maybe this way I'll get some goddamned sleep for once."

For all his grumbling, he doesn't pull away. He stays close enough that I can see the stubble on his jaw, a small scar above his left eye I hadn't noticed before. He really is as gorgeous as the gods themselves, illustrated so exquisitely in the Book of the Immortals. All he lacks are pointed ears and glowing fey lines. How many times did I flip through that book, sighing over the scantily clad portraits of Vale and Woudix and Artain?

My heart starts clanging in my chest, and I curse my traitorous body, knowing Wolf can hear every thrust of my heart. What else can he sense about me with his godkiss? Does my sweat smell different when I'm thinking about him? Can he feel my sped-up breath clouding against his skin?

His rough palm cups my jaw, gently tilting my head toward his. The move is so bold that I'm left speechless. He's never touched me before, unless it's to bend me to his will. His eyes drop to my lips. There's a look in them I haven't seen before.

Dark, glistening, hungry.

My own gaze lowers to his bare chest like it's pulled there by invisible ropes. When he gave me his shirt to wear that first night, I didn't think about how it would leave *him* shirtless. It's not my fault his scarred body

76

fascinates me. It's the damn convent's fault. My damn father's fault. Keeping a libidinous teenage girl locked up with no one to look at for over a decade but wrinkled old women and some faded illustrations, and it's no wonder I'm aching with curiosity about the first man I see.

Damn Immortals.

His thumb drags down my cheek to my jugular, and my eyes sink closed. My lips part. He has to hear how my heart is racing. He has to know what that means.

"Sabine."

His voice is hoarse. His hand falls to his borrowed shirt on my shoulder, fingers twisting in the fabric. His touch sets my skin on fire, and all I can think is:

I shouldn't want more. I want more . . .

His mouth is only a breath's distance from my own, and I wait, and wait, but nothing happens. I open my eyes, overwhelmed and unsure, not knowing if I should kiss him, slap him, or shove him away. His brown irises are filled with such powerful want that they're as velvety dark as Myst's.

Our eyes lock, and a spark shoots straight from my head down to my toes.

A muscle jumps in his jaw.

Then, an owl hoots from the canopy. It breaks the moment, and he looks away. He drops his hand.

For a long time, neither one of us speaks.

Eventually, he finishes tucking the blanket edges roughly around me, then stands.

"Good night, Lady Sabine."

His voice is hard as iron.

I'm voiceless. My lips are still parted. The shock of

what I just felt begins to dawn on me, and it's leaving me quaking, despite the blanket's warmth.

What was I thinking?

As soon as Wolf's back is turned, I fish Adan's shell out of the cradle of my ear. I squeeze it, trying to shock some sense back into me. Would I have let Wolf *kiss* me? Have I gone mad? I would have betrayed Adan—for what? A grumpy, godkissed hunter who hates me?

My toes curl as I try to make sense of the altercation. For as much as I tell myself it was simply a fleeting attraction fueled by curiosity, I'm not sure I believe it. Seeing that Wolf thought to get an extra apple for Myst, and the fact that he shared his real name with me, let alone that he's had every opportunity to hurt me but hasn't, has made a small but irrevocable shift in the way I feel about him.

I can't sleep, and it seems to take forever before I hear Wolf's snores from across the clearing. Once I'm certain he is deeply asleep, I call to the tiny forest mouse who's been riding in Wolf's rucksack since the first night, when I shared my rabbit meat with it.

Little friend, will you help now?

Ready! it answers as it pops its head out.

I hold my wrists out to the mouse, who gnaws at the rope with stalwart determination. In ten minutes, it chews through all my binds.

Onto my shoulder, I tell it. *Hurry.*

The mouse scampers up my sleeve and settles in beneath the shirt's collar. I move as silently as I can toward Myst, fully aware that with Wolf's keen hearing, even a rustle of leaves could wake him.

But it has to be tonight. I hadn't intended to run until we passed Middleford, but since Wolf changed our route, he's forced my hand. I can't afford to head in the opposite direction from where Adan waits.

I climb onto a fallen log and slip onto Myst's back. I allow myself one final look at Wolf, asleep by the fire. He looks troubled in his sleep, twitchy like he's dreaming of a fight.

Absently, I run my hand over the sleeve of his shirt hugging my shoulder, dragging my fingers to end at my breastbone, the hollow where my godkissed birthmark rests.

I saw a different side to him tonight—but that's just one more reason why I have to run. The last thing I need is to start caring about a beast.

Go, Myst.

It won't be easy to evade a godkissed hunter, but I'm confident that as skilled as Wolf is, I'm cleverer. I've had time to study his power and think through how to evade him.

With careful, silent steps, Myst leaves the clearing behind. It isn't until we're half a mile away that I finally dig my heels into her sides.

Beneath my collar, the mouse clings on tight.

Now, run as fast as you can, I tell Myst.

CHAPTER 8
WOLF

When I wake, the coals are cold. The moon cuts a jagged sliver in the black night. Judging by her lingering scent, Sabine has been gone for about two hours.

I crouch next to her blanket, examining her binds' frayed ends, which could only be made by a set of small rodent teeth.

The hunt is on, I think.

I've known this was coming since the first day of the ride. It was only a matter of time before Sabine and Myst bolted to meet up with that moronic lover of hers. And I can't deny that a dark part of me has been looking forward to this moment. The anticipation of Sabine's escape has been like an itch prickling at my skin, hooking my interest, needling my heightened senses.

Damn, I love the chase.

My veins are already blowing up with adrenaline that throbs incessantly, demanding I chase after her *now*. But I tuck that urgency away. I can't let the thrill of the chase dull my reason. This is no simple fox hunt, and my quarry is much more precious than any deer or grouse. It complicates things that Sabine is godkissed, too. For all I know, she could send a swarm of locusts to devour the flesh from my bones.

The thought, though dark, does nothing to lessen my arousal. Hunting someone with a power rivaling my own is nothing short of intoxicating. Yet as I make quick work of selecting arrows for my bow—not to harm her, only to threaten her—momentary darkness sobers my excitement.

She left you, Wolf, a voice spits. *Just like everyone leaves you.*

My own parents couldn't be bothered to claim me. Jocki only wanted me for my godkissed skills in the ring. The other street boys avoided making friends, knowing we'd eventually have to fight each other.

Can I blame Sabine for running? I'd run, too, if I were stuck with me.

A twig snaps nearby, and I banish my self-pity. Judging by the scent, it's a doe about a hundred paces away. Ignoring it, I scan the dirt around the tree where I tied Myst.

Between the rotting leaf cover from last fall and new ferns sprouting underfoot, tracks would be impossible for most hunters to spot. But with my eyesight, Myst and Sabine might as well have painted red blazes on every tree they passed.

Adrenaline courses through my veins as I stalk their

path. Sabine's lingering, sweet floral smell laces the air like perfume. I'm not concerned about their two hours head start. Myst is in good shape, but she can't gallop all night. Neither can Sabine ride that hard on no sleep, without a saddle or even a skirt. Her bare thighs are going to be rubbed even rawer than they already are. Sooner or later, they'll have to rest. It isn't about speed, it's about stamina.

Myst's hoof prints lead me on a series of switchbacks to the main road, where her pace changes to a gallop. I follow for a few hundred paces, sensing from the slightly hesitant prints that this is a deception. And sure enough, the trail soon veers off the road back into the forest.

Clever devils.

They wanted me to think they hit the road and kept going to Middleford.

The creaks and scuffs of the forest snap in my ears, awakening my already-heightened sense until the influx of stimulus is almost painful. I appreciate that Sabine has some subterfuge in her. It will serve her well at Sorsha Hall, where cunning is necessary for survival.

I eventually track their path to a stream, where Myst's hoof prints disappear. There's no way to follow her tracks in water visually, but Sabine's scent still hangs in the air. My boots splash over river rocks as I follow the barely-there aroma of violets.

I'm impressed Sabine knows to double back and ride in a stream. But it doesn't matter. Her evasions would stop a hunting dog, but not me. The truth is, such tactics would be rudimentary, even laughable among hunters, and yet I'm not laughing. Sabine has never trained as a hunter. She's spent most of her life within a single convent's stone walls. So how the hell did she figure this out?

She's even cleverer than I suspected, and so damn determined. But that doesn't mean I'm going to take any pity on her when she's mine again.

I *will* get her to Sorsha Hall.

Though, as I track her and Myst over the next few hours, I start to worry about what comes next once we reach Lord Rian's home. Sorsha Hall can be a lawless place. No clear-headed individual would dare touch Lord Rian's bride, but Valvere revelries make wise men foolish. Drunk, dazed, and stupid, some few foolhardy men might set their eyes on Sabine.

Rian will need a bodyguard for Sabine, and it's imperative that it's someone he trusts. He decided I was the only one loyal enough to bring her to Duren safely, so why not continue the service? He can find another lead huntsman to replace me. Hunters are as common as whores—maybe not as skilled as me, but perfectly capable of bagging dinner for the Valveres. I'll need to take some time to investigate the border wall, but that won't take me away from Sabine for long.

Sabine will never agree. She hates you. She's going to hate you even more when you catch her.

This thought sobers my mood as I pick up Myst's tracks again where she exited the stream, and follow her still-damp hoof prints east. Well, Sabine won't have any say in the matter of her bodyguard. She might loathe me, but she'll have to suck it up and get used to me.

Her disdainful voice rings in my ears: *I'm not surprised*

you've never had a pet. Or anything else to love.

But she's wrong. I have loved. I have cared for another creature. And it royally fucked me up.

Jocki had no affection for any of the boys he managed. He acted like a half-decent surrogate father whenever the Valveres' agents were around, but the moment we were alone in the dilapidated old stables he'd converted into our barracks, he reveled in punishing us. Starving us, taunting us, pitting us against one another. It wasn't in his interest for any of us boys to be friends, so he made sure we weren't. He wanted us to loathe one another so that the aggression would spill out in the fight ring to make for more realistic entertainment. Besides, we weren't idiots. We knew there was no point in getting to know a boy you might break, even kill, the next week.

But Jocki kept fighting dogs in the old stables, too. Most of them were vicious curs off the street, just like us. Onno was different. He was so massive in size that he didn't need to snarl to earn the other dogs' respect. He fought in the dog fights just as we did in ours, but as a means of survival, not pleasure.

I liked Onno, and he liked me. I'd share whatever scraps of supper I had with him, and he would curl up against his cage's bars at night, with me on the opposite side, to keep each other warm.

I should have known that was a big fucking mistake.

Jocki thought it would make his boys weak to have a pet. So that fucked-up brain of his devised a new kind of fight. Boy against dog. Once we were forced into the ring together, Onno wouldn't even try to fight me. He just looked at me with his big brown eyes, knowing only one of us would be allowed to make it out alive. Letting that one be me.

I snap out of the dark past as Myst's tracks reach a fork in the road. The forest path veers left, with the main road to Middleford continuing straight ahead. Sabine is riding a few feet to the side of the road to try to hide their tracks, but it's easy to see they went straight.

What's in Middleford? Her lover?

On the horizon, the first haze of morning crests. Fuck. How have I not found them yet? I can't risk anyone seeing her during the daylight hours, when word could get back to Rian that his bride is running wild through the Astagnonian countryside. Or worse, someone could find her before me and decide she's a tempting little morsel.

Moving faster now, I give myself over to the hunt. No more messing around. She's had her fun. A part of me has always got a charge out of the chase. When Rian agreed to make me a huntsman, I took to it like a fish in water. It's a pleasure to unleash my heightened senses to see what exactly I'm capable of.

My pulse raps in my veins, urging me on. I'm getting close. I block out all other stimuli and hone my senses on tracking the girl and horse.

The aroma of violets swells until I'm practically choking on it. Myst's scent is there, too: wet horsehair.

I stop and close my eyes to listen.

It takes me a while, but I hone in on an animal's labored breath. They've stopped to rest, but Myst is still breathing hard from the exertion. Focusing my attention more, I eventually pick up on Sabine's breathing, too.

Slow and steady. *She's asleep.*

A hard smile curls my mouth as I silently draw my bow and move through the forest. Myst will smell me coming, but by then it will be too late. Sabine will hear her warning snicker, wake up, and find an arrow aimed at her dear mare's chest.

To save her horse, she'll do anything. She'll beg me for mercy with those perfect rosebud lips.

I spot Myst ahead, partially sheltered behind a rocky outcropping, eating grass with her head turned away from me. She's slathered in dark mud to mask her white color, which would make her stand out starkly in the dark forest. Once more, I'm struck with Sabine's resource-fulness—

But then I see Sabine, and my thoughts go blank.

She's asleep, curled against a dip in the rocky outcrop-ping that partially hides her. There's mud all over her hands and bare feet, and she looks utterly exhausted, like a rabbit that's run and run until its muscles gave out. My shirt is up around her hips, giving me an obscene look at her naked ass, rubbed red from riding all night.

My breath stalls in my throat.

By the fucking Immortals, I'm bursting with need. My body was already flushed with adrenaline from the hunt, and now it wants its prize. And gods be damned if I don't want to claim Sabine as my reward. For days now, I've fallen asleep to her heartbeat. I've drowned in her violet scent. I've stroked my own hand after touching her silky skin. Now, more than anything, I want to taste her.

And I know it's fucked up. She belongs to Lord Rian, not me. There's no way I would ever touch her, and I'm plagued with guilt for even thinking of it. But Rian would forgive my desire, wouldn't he? He's trained with soldiers. He understands that men get aroused in battle as a purely physical response. Hunting is no different.

It doesn't—*doesn't*—have anything to do with the fact that she's the most beautiful fucking woman I've ever laid eyes on.

Hanging back beyond the line where Myst could pick up my scent, I take a moment to get my head on straight. My body is still shaking from the rush of pursuing Sabine, the charge taking too long to drain from my limbs. I wipe my hand over my face to get the blood back up where it needs to be, away from my groin.

I drag as much air as I can into my lungs. The sun is rising. Sabine's jaunt has taken us far off course. We need to end this charade and get back on the road to Duren.

Bow raised, I step around the rocky outcropping into the clearing.

Myst tosses her head up, her eyes flashing wide. The instant she scents me, she lets out a whinny.

Sabine stirs immediately, jumping out of sleep with a small cry.

Her eyes latch to mine and immediately fill with fear.

"I don't want to hurt Myst," I say in a steady voice. "It's up to you if—"

There's a problem.

Sabine isn't looking at me. She's looking behind and above me, at the outcropping.

A second too late, I smell the wildcat.

Gods be damned. I was distracted, and it was downwind. "Oh, fuck—"

Sabine's lips move in a silent request only the wildcat can hear, and even before I can raise my bow, it leaps off the boulder with hateful eyes reflecting back my own startled face.

CHAPTER 9
SABINE

In the dark, all I can make out is a jumble of movement. The wildcat yowls and hisses. I scramble to my feet, back pressed against the damp outcropping. My heart is beating so fast I'm afraid it's going to burst right out of my chest.

He found us.

My limbs are numb from sleeping on the bare ground, and my head is still sluggish. Dazed, I feel along the outcropping toward Myst. A small amount of light comes from the east. It must be almost morning. How long did I sleep? A few hours? I hadn't intended to sleep at all, only to shut my eyes.

The wildcat yowls again. Wolf grunts as he tussles with the beast. I force myself to look away. I hate this—hate that it came to this.

The wildcat started following us as soon as we left Wolf's campsite. It was after Myst initially, but once I spoke with it, it agreed to protect us as far as the forest's eastern border. Like most wild animals, huntsmen are its greatest enemy, and it was eager to thwart one of them.

There's a crack like a bone breaking. Man's or wildcat's?

A frightened cry bubbles up from my lips. My feet are aching, my legs beyond sore. My pulse hammers like a woodpecker between my ears. Panic clogs my airway like there's a fist around my throat, squeezing until I can't breathe.

I can't get to Myst—Wolf and the wildcat are between us.

She rears up, tossing her head.

Run away! she yells.

I feel frozen—I can't leave her—but Myst is my brave girl. She'll be okay on her own. She can sure as hell run faster than me.

There's another grunt as Wolf and the wildcat collide, and I flinch. Reaching the end of the outcropping, I climb until I'm on higher ground, and then run blindly.

Where can I go?

My mind doesn't want to think. It only wants to act. Rocks and roots stab at my soles. Months ago, my feet would have been tough enough to pass through the woods barefoot, but not since the Sisters ensured my calluses had softened in preparation for my marriage.

Shit. I won't get far like this.

Wincing as pain stabs my feet bottoms, I spot a fallen log in the early morning mist. It's hollowed out, big enough to hide me. Maybe the sweet rot of wood will mask my scent. Desperate, I dive for the log and scramble inside. It's damp and loamy and dark. I crawl in as far as I can, pulling in my feet. My bruised rib throbs. Between the two ends of the log, I just barely fit. Dirt and debris fill the humid air, straining my already limited breath.

Be quiet, I tell myself while clutching my aching rib.

But I can't stop my heart from beating.

I can't tell my lungs not to fill.

For a few seconds, nothing happens. I can only see a small portion of the forest from within the log. Muffled by the wood, it's impossible to hear what's happening out there. Are they still fighting? For all I know, the wildcat killed Wolf. Myst and I could be free. Assuming Myst got away . . .

I'm churning in my own fears when a branch snaps. I swallow a gasp—

The wildcat falls with a thud right next to my head.

It's dead. Its glassy eyes see nothing. Its neck is bent at an angle. Its fur is matted with blood.

I scream.

Before I can move, Wolf grabs my ankles at the other side of the log.

I kick and scream as he drags me out. All I can think about is the dead wildcat. If he killed it so easily, what will he do to me? Panic overtakes my reason, and I thrash as Wolf pulls me the rest of the way out onto the damp forest floor.

"Sabine. Stop!"

He tries to grab my wrists, but I smack at him with my remaining strength. From the corner of my eye, I spot Myst nearby, tied by a rope to a tree. She rears up, wanting to help, but there's nothing she can do.

"Let me go!" I scream, trying to scratch his face. I'm

dimly aware there are already deep, bleeding scratches on his neck made by claws far sharper than mine. But at this moment, I could care less if Wolf Bowborn is hurt.

He wrestles me until he manages to pin my wrists. I try to fight him, but it's useless. He holds me to the ground with his weight, breathing hard.

"You didn't have to kill it!" I yell, rage making my voice ring out like a bell. My heart aches for the wildcat. If I'd known it would die, I never would have asked it to keep watch while I rested. I keep wriggling under Wolf's weight to get free. Sweat pours down his face. He's breathing nearly as hard as I am.

"I did," he says with only slightly more composure than me. "You sent a wildcat to kill me, Sabine!"

It's only then that I fully take stock of Wolf's wounds. Besides the scratches on his neck, deep punctures in his bare chest near his ribcage ooze blood. His hair is never tamed, but now it's complete havoc.

The edge of panic fades in my chest, but my anger doesn't. I buck my hips as I writhe.

Wolf briefly closes his eyes as though pained. "Stop moving, Sabine. I like you squirming under me too damn much."

My body goes slack. A bird calls far in the distance. A rock digs into my back. The fight fades out of me as the sobering realization hits that it's over. Wolf found me. Was I a fool for ever thinking there was a chance he wouldn't?

Myst paws the dirt, frustrated. A strong breeze rattles the trees, dropping pine cones. It feels as though the whole forest is as charged as I am.

And then all my anger comes to a head, and I start sobbing.

I cry thick, ugly tears. Tears I don't care if Wolf judges me for. I'm crying for the wildcat. I'm crying for my own lost freedom. I'm crying because I never had any real damn freedom to lose in the first place.

Wolf's hands slacken around my wrists. He huffs an exhale up at the sky.

"Fuck," he murmurs.

He pushes off me but doesn't release my wrists. As I sob into my forearm, hiding my face so I don't have to show my defeat to the world, he tugs me into his lap and wraps a hand around my back. He doesn't offer comforting words. A monster like him knows nothing about how to comfort a person, and there's nothing anyone could say, anyway, to take away the pain.

'Sorry that I captured you, now let me take you to your villainous husband?'

But he holds me like he wants to help me, and despite everything, there is solace in his arms. It's simple biology. Wolf is huge, and with his arms folded around me, I feel shielded from danger.

But of course, that's a farce—*he's* the danger.

I'm too exhausted to do anything but slump against him and bury my face in his chest. Physical contact is not something I'm very familiar with, unless it involves pain. This is all new to me. Being held. Every part of my body flush against someone. Feeling his chest rise and fall beneath my cheek.

He strokes a hand down the remains of my braid, which is mostly undone by now. His touch is rough by nature, though I can tell he's trying to be gentle. He just doesn't know how.

That's when I have to admit that for as angry as I am, Wolf Bowborn is not my enemy. He might be my jailor, but he wasn't the one who commanded this twisted ride. It's his master who deserves my ire. Rian Valvere. The Lord of Liars. My future husband.

Once my sobs taper off, Wolf brushes my hair aside and says, close enough to my ear that his lips scuff my temple, "Don't try to escape again, Sabine. The Valveres will send more than just me to hunt you down. They'll punish you. You don't know what that family is capable of."

His face remains kiss-close to mine. He's breathing in deeply like he wants to drink me up, sweat and tears and all. Like he hungers to know how I taste.

I pull back, searching his dark eyes, trying to read him.

What game is he playing? Does he truly believe he's *protecting* me?

"I'm going to let you go now," he says measuredly. "Don't run. You know it won't end well."

He raises his hands, and I scoot out of his lap. Slowly, he stands. Myst has settled down. She exerted herself even more than I did.

Wolf looks at me expectantly, and I nod my head in obedience.

"Good girl," he murmurs.

He frowns at my bruised feet. One look at Myst tells him she's too exhausted to carry me. So, without warning, he scoops me up. I let out a surprised squeak as he carts me in his arms like I weigh nothing. I'm grateful for his borrowed shirt; otherwise, he'd have his hands all over my naked body. As it is, his rough palm cups my thighs as he carries me through the forest to a small clearing at the side of a stream.

"Stay," he commands, plunking me down on the mossy bank. "I'm going back for Myst. Bathe, if the water isn't too cold for you."

I can tell in the way he's carrying himself that he's exhausted, too. He's holding his hurt shoulder stiffly. There are lines etched around his mouth.

"I won't go anywhere," I say in a hoarse voice. There's no point in running again. I certainly don't intend to get another animal killed, like the wildcat.

He tromps away, leaving me by the stream. Wet grass slides against my legs. A mirthless laugh bursts out of me, turning into a sob. Wiping my face, I climb into the water. It's frigid, but my body is already numb, and it feels good to wash mud and muck off my skin. I shake out Wolf's shirt and hang it on a branch, unwilling to wash it and spend the rest of the morning naked while I wait for it to dry.

In a few minutes, I hear Wolf return with Myst.

"Sabine?" he calls from a distance, respecting my privacy.

"Let Myst off the rope. She won't run."

He seems hesitant, but does as I ask. Myst picks her way to the edge of the stream, blinking down at me.

Come in, I say. *You're even filthier than me.*

As she splashes into the water, I cup water with my hands to pour over her back. Using my fingers as a comb, I wash away the mud that I rubbed on her sides to disguise her. I feel so stupid now for thinking I could outsmart a huntsman with Wolf's skills. His godkiss is one of the more potent ones I've seen. It makes me wonder why, out of everyone, the gods chose to bless him.

He can keep you safe, Myst says, as though she knows who is in my mind.

My eyebrows raise as I scoop another handful of water. *Oh, so what, you're suddenly in favor of the man who just hunted us like beasts?*

No. But he is strong. He is loyal. He will be loyal to you, if you make him.

The water drains out of my cupped hands as I figure out what to make of this. It's so like a horse to think of safety and nothing else. Yes, Wolf is physically capable of being our protector, but the man is a *brute*. He's the last person I would trust with my fate.

Well, what does a horse know? I quip as I climb out of the stream. *You can finish washing yourself.*

Myst rolls in the shallow water as I wriggle back into Wolf's dry shirt, then tromp a dozen paces to where he has a fire going. The flames' warmth stirs some life back into me. Wordlessly, Wolf tosses me half a loaf of bread and some cheese. I tear into the meal ravenously.

He watches me steadily. Overhead, the sun is rising. He takes a bite of his own bread. "We'll spend the day here so you and Myst can sleep, then return to the forest road tomorrow."

"How considerate," I mumble around a mouthful. "I'm surprised you aren't chomping at the bit to get back to your precious master."

He doesn't take the bait. I wish he would—I'd rather have his quips than his pity.

The silence is painful as my meal settles heavy in my stomach, giving me cramps as the morning stretches on. Wolf busies himself with sharpening his knives as I stew in my feelings until, finally, I yawn into my palm. Exhaustion has a way of dulling anger.

Wolf glances at the yawn, then clears his throat. "I've been patient, Sabine, but the time for games is over. You're never running away—you get that now, don't you? I'll always catch you. Always. So, tell me your lover's plan."

His tone is a command I don't dare deny, after watching how easily he killed a wildcat. Still, it's hard to spill my secret. I wish I could keep Adan to myself for just one more day.

Swallowing a dry bite of bread, I vacillate on where to start.

"His—his name is Adan. He came to the convent to—to castrate the goats," I explain in fits and starts, feeling exposed under Wolf's scrutiny, like a butterfly splayed on a mounting board. "He was the most beautiful boy I'd ever seen."

Under duress, I tell Wolf the story of how Adan and I met. He didn't have old Mr. Porter's decades of experience, and the baby goats caused such a fuss that Sister Rose called me in to use my godkiss to convince the animals to submit to him. Together, Adan and I tended to each of the sixteen goats. I would hold them and whisper reassurances while he heated his knife. By the third goat, we knew each other's names. By the sixth, each other's greatest fears. By the sixteenth, I was ready to run away with him.

Adan told me about his huge, chaotic, but loving family. About his desire to study the healing arts. About his dream to see the ocean. He said there are port towns where no one cares where you're from or who you are. His eldest brother made a good living in the shipping business, and Adan promised we could stay with him and his wife until Adan found work.

"I'll come back for you, Sabine," he said, stashing his knife among the tall grass behind the kidding barn. *"One week from now, under the pretense of looking for my knife that I must have left behind. Be ready."*

His plan was for us to make our way to the port town of Salensa, borrow money from his brother, and then arrange for a third party to buy Myst. But the next day, my father's letter arrived ordering the Sisters to prepare me for marriage to Lord Rian.

Right before they locked me away, I managed to get a bird to take a message to Adan. The bird returned a note back, which a beetle smuggled into my room through a crack. It read: *At Middleford, escape your guard and ride east. Follow the signs to the Old Innis Mill. I'll wait for you there, my love.*

"So that's where I was going," I finish in a small voice. "To the Old Innis Mill. From there, Adan knew backroads to get us to Salensa."

When I finish the story, Wolf looks disgusted. Well, it isn't surprising that someone like him isn't into love stories. He probably likes tales of soldiers dying in bloody, gruesome battles.

My body shudders with exhaustion, and I can't suppress my yawn. Wolf's expression shifts, and he rolls out the blanket near the fire. He nudges it lightly with his toe.

"You should sleep."

"Aren't you going to tie my wrists?"

"No. I don't intend to close my eyes."

The truth is, I'm so tired that even my bones are singing for the blanket. I stretch out between Wolf and the fire, dragging one side of the blanket around my shoulders. Immediately, the weight of fatigue sinks over me.

"Good night, Basten," I mutter.

It's midmorning, and I don't know why I called him by his real name, but I'm too tired to hunt for the right words.

He pauses a beat as though caught off guard at the sound of his own name—as though it reminds him of something he lost long ago. A second passes before he says softly, "Good night, Sabine."

CHAPTER 10
WOLF

As Sabine dozes next to me, I keep rehashing how she swooned over that idiot goatherd. The most beautiful boy she's ever seen? I groan up toward the trees. *May the gods kill me right now.* She's been locked in a convent for twelve years—he's the *only* boy she's seen. If all it takes for Sabine Darrow to fall in love is a couple of hours with some idiot, then by that logic, after a few days together she must be fucking head over heels for me.

But she's not. She hates everything about me.

I don't blame her. All I've done is force her across half of Astagnon while men ogle her. And make her sleep on the ground. Oh, and break the neck of her latest four-legged friend. Though to be fair, it was either me or the wildcat.

At least it's clear nothing happened between her and the goatherd, not even an innocent peck. That boy really is a dolt. If I had Sabine Darrow ready and willing in some goat shed, I'd do a hell of a lot more than daydream about the goddamn ocean . . .

Shit. I really need to stop thinking like this.

Beside me, Sabine mumbles something incoherent in her sleep. She tosses, knocking the blanket off her feet. Her expression contorts like she's having a bad dream, and it's all I can do not to stroke the loose hair off her face and hope it helps her sleep.

I'm so damn proud of my little violet. I know she's disappointed that her escape failed, but she doesn't realize just how far she made it. She did better than anyone would have dreamed a sheltered noblewoman could: Covering Myst in mud, sticking to the stream, staying downwind to hide her scent, setting the wildcat as a trap. Not to mention fighting me tooth and nail. I wonder if Rian knows what a headstrong girl he bought himself. Will he like a feisty bride? If she were mine, I'd goad her just so she would writhe underneath me again, her cheeks flushed pink and that fire in her eyes . . .

Shit. *Shit. Knock that off, Wolf.*

Sabine curls into a ball, cold without a blanket on her feet. She tosses again in her sleep, this time rolling up against me. When her arm brushes my leg, she wiggles closer like she's a deathrattle snake in search of warmth.

My breath stills. I could replace the blanket around her feet, but then she might not stay curled against me. And I really, *really* like the weight of Sabine Darrow at my side. Far more than I should.

Watching her sleep is such a goddamn tender scene that my chest feels too tight to breathe.

Briefly, I close my eyes. Is this what it's like to have a

woman? I've only ever known whores and the occasional courtesan who will deign to sleep with the Valveres' huntsman. All those times, we sure as hell weren't sleeping soundly. But there is something so damn intoxicating about just being in Sabine's presence. I don't care that she'll never be mine to take to bed. Being near her is enough.

I'll talk to Rian in Duren, I tell myself. *I'll be her bodyguard. At least I can keep her safe.*

When she stirs, I saunter off into the woods to take a piss so that she doesn't realize that she slept against me. When I come back, she's stoked the fire and already has a pot of water boiling. A clutch of wild duck eggs rests on the blanket.

"Where did you get those?" I snap.

She ignores my tone as she drops the eggs one at a time into the pot. Her chin tips toward a grove of maidenhair ferns. "There's a nest over there. I left half of the eggs. It seemed cruel to take more than we needed."

The more I see Sabine use her godkiss, the more I realize how valuable it is. At first, talking to mice seemed like a cute trick. But I underestimated how her power could keep her alive in the woods, help her forage for food, even break free of binds.

She's fucking incredible.

Over the next few mornings, we fall into a routine. Sabine makes breakfast while I pack up camp. It's no longer me providing for us while I order her to sit and stay. We're more of a partnership now, though I don't have any illusions that it makes us friends. After all, I destroyed her dream of escape. And she sent a fucking wildcat to kill me.

Yeah, we have a few issues.

"Here. Your shirt. It stinks, by the way." Sabine gives me my shirt, and we continue the ride. The path passes a few gnarled apple trees that must have grown from an ancient traveler's tossed-off apple core. Myst strains her neck but can't reach the high fruits. I toss a rock to knock down some apples for her. As she munches them out of my palm, she doesn't flinch at my presence like she used to.

Has this cranky mare started to trust me?

We pass only a few homesteads until midday, when we enter the village of Charmont. It's the largest settlement within Mag Na Tir Forest, a sort of county seat. The spire of the Monastery of Immortal Meric rises like a knife blade over the rooftops. We pass washerwomen hanging clothes, children kicking a ball made of fabric scraps tied together. The children are too young to realize Sabine's public nakedness is unusual, but the washerwomen gape. One woman catches a boy and whispers to him. He takes off down a dirt path toward the center of town.

Great. Spreading the word. *Just what we fucking need.*

And as soon as we reach a blacksmith's forge, villagers are already lining up along the road. Men stare at Sabine with wolfish gazes. I bristle as protective instincts harden my muscles.

The longer this ride goes on, the more I question Rian's motives. Was this about establishing his power not just to Sabine, but to everyone whose path we cross? *If he is willing to force his own bride into such a display,* people must say, *imagine what he would do to enemies who crossed him*. I've known Rian to devise some vicious spectacles, but this one simply feels cruel.

When we were boys, he wasn't like this. I was eleven when he saw me in that fighting ring; he was thirteen. Jocki had tied a blindfold around my eyes to show off my godkiss power, and even without my vision, I'd knocked the other boy on his ass, off sound and smell alone. Halfway through the fight, I smelled aloeswood incense among the watching crowd. The only times I'd smelled it before were when the Valvere family paraded through the streets of Duren in full fae regalia as part of the Festival of Immortal Popelin.

So, I knew one of the Valveres was in the crowd, even before I won the fight and took off my blindfold. What no one anticipated was for young Rian Valvere to climb into the ring and take my fallen opponent's place.

"Don't go easy on me," he commanded. "And don't fetter yourself with the blindfold. I want to know the extent of what you can do."

Well, fuck, I thought. *This rich little lord has screwed me now.* Jocki would skin my hide if I shamed a Valvere through defeat, but the boy himself was ordering me not to throw the fight. So what the fuck was I supposed to do?

I got lucky that Rian was a skilled fighter. He put up a good enough defense that no humiliation was necessary. The third time I knocked him to the ground, certain that each time he'd get up and scream for the guards to execute me, he simply stood back up with a serious set to his jaw and said, "Go again."

Jocki's nerves finally got the better of him, and he shut

down the fight. That night, guards came to the old stables and dragged me out of the stall I shared with four other boys. I was certain this was the moment I'd be thrown in a dungeon for daring to win against the son of Duren's high lord, but instead, the guards took me to the Valveres' private soldier barracks. They shoved stew and bread in my hands. They gave me a cot and blanket. Clean clothes, too.

Basic necessities, and yet to me they were unthinkable luxuries.

I spent the next year with the Golden Sentinels, learning to soldier, and serving as Rian's personal sparring partner. Day after day, fight after fight, we came to know one another like brothers. Rian introduced me to the Sin Streets that his family oversaw, ribbing me good-naturedly when I drank my first ale and lost my first hand of Basel and fucked for the first time. He taught me how to stay out of his father's notice. Lord Berolt was—is—a devil in every sense of the word. Cruel, greedy, merciless, decadent. And eerily obsessed with godkissed. The Valvere vice houses are filled with godkissed fighters and whores. They employ godkissed servants in Sorsha Hall. Berolt likes to test them, display them, pull their strings to prove to the world that even though he isn't godkissed, his power is greater than magic itself.

To me, Rian will always be that thirteen-year-old boy who took me under his wing, despite the fact that I belted him daily in the ring. And, yeah, it's true that he's changed over the years. Like a tree pruned to climb along a garden wall, there was only one path Rian would ever be allowed to grow into: A Valvere.

I'd bet my last coin that Sabine's ride was Lord Berolt's idea.

High atop Myst, Sabine nudges me in the shoulder with her toe. She nods toward a gaggle of market women lining the road. Their eyes fix more on me than on Sabine as they giggle to one another.

"You're getting your fair share of attention," Sabine points out wryly.

I could care less if some village women like the way I look. I know the effect I have on women. What interests me more is the little pinch of jealousy that puckers Sabine's lips.

Despite my better judgment, I grin. It feels fucking incredible to see Sabine Darrow jealous.

"Imagine how they'd drool if *I* was naked," I say, needling her further. "Maybe we should take a break in this town. I'll disappear behind a shed with one or two of those girls for an hour."

She lets out a huff and rolls her eyes. "By the Immortals, the end of this ride can't come fast enough."

I'm still smirking when a small group of red-robed men steps into the street, blocking our path.

The smile melts off my face.

Sabine signals Myst to halt.

The men wear the gold-trimmed, crimson robes of the Order of Immortal Woudix, God of Death. Cutlasses hang from straps over their shoulders. Their faces are stiff. One of them clutches a gilded copy of the Book of the Immortals like a shield.

Fuck. Goddamn judgmental priests. This is the last thing we need.

"By the authority of the Immortal Woudix," the one in front intones. "The village of Charmont disaffirms the presence of this vulgar spectacle."

He wears a tall, peaked red hat with silken fringe, marking him as the Patron—the head priest. The gold-studded fringe brushes his dark eyebrows almost like a crown across his brow. Fitting, as the Red Church believes they're as mighty as kings.

I groan inwardly down to my bones. "If it offends you," I seethe, "then step aside and we'll be out of your way."

"I'm afraid it's too late for that."

The crowd begins to buzz. Tension gathers over the village center like morning mist. These priests worship Immortal Woudix, the God of Death, which means they know how to use those cutlasses at their sides. They're as militant as priests come, and we've walked right into their town.

Except this *isn't* their town.

Charmont worships Immortal Meric—not Woudix—which means these red-robed acolytes traveled here specifically to intercept us. That would explain how sweaty they are beneath their miter hats. We changed course, so they were probably waiting to confront us back on the road to Middleford, and rode here when word spread of the new route.

Immortal Woudix, as depraved as the rest of the fae court, wouldn't give a fuck about a naked girl. Hell, he'd love it.

So why have these militant assholes really come?

I have a strong suspicion that it has nothing to do

with Sabine's state of undress, and everything to do with how the Grand Cleric who oversees the Red Church resents the Valveres' influence in Astagnon.

"Arrest this whore at once!" the Patron commands, signaling to his brethren. "She will be made to answer for spreading such depravity! Pull her down from that horse."

The four heavyset priests behind him stalk toward Myst and Sabine.

My thoughts come slamming to a halt.

Did he just call Sabine a *whore*?

It isn't until Sabine nudges me again with her toe that I realize I'm growling at them like my animal namesake.

"Wolf," she says low, worried. "What do I do?"

My fists ball at my sides. Arrows are too good for these miscreant priests. I don't want to give them the gift of a clean shot to the heart. I want to bloody my knuckles on their jaws. I want to tread my boots through puddles of their blood. "Nothing, my lady. You're mine to protect, and I'm going to fucking protect you."

CHAPTER II
SABINE

Wolf drops his rucksack and lurches forward, but two of the priests draw their cutlasses. Cries ring out through the crowd. Doors slam as more onlookers come out to witness the incident. The other two priests stride intently toward Myst. One grips the base of her mane to keep her from bolting—not that we could, anyway, with the street so clogged with villagers. It all happens in the blink of an eye, coordinated to perfection.

The fourth priest grabs my thigh just above the knee, trying to pull me down off her.

Myst, go! I cry.

She rears partway up, shaking off the man's grip on her mane. He falls back on his ass, to my delight. Myst dances backward a few steps. Her muscles bunch, but there's nowhere to go. She stomps her hooves, frustrated.

Too many people!

"You'll answer to the Immortals!" another priest cries.

He snatches a fistful of my long hair, tugging me painfully forward to try to pull me off Myst.

I cry out, and Wolf pivots sharply toward me.

Wolf takes one look at the man with his hands all over my naked body, and any shred of mercy he might have spared for the priests evaporates. The cords on his neck strain. He limbers up his sore shoulder.

"Get your goddamn hands off her," he threatens, "Or I'll rip them off your arms."

Unintimidated, the priest doesn't stop trying to drag me from Myst's back. His hand moves from my thigh to the side of my ass, fingers digging in to get a better grip as he pulls me halfway down.

"Let me go!" I shout, kicking at his face while I cling to Myst's mane with a death grip. The crowd goes wild. I'm on full display to them, with my hair all askance, as I struggle against my attacker. No matter how I struggle, he's much stronger than me.

Before I know it, my feet hit the ground. The priest grabs me from behind, wrapping one hand roughly around my breasts in an attempt to hide my nudity, but really just looks like he's groping me.

Oh, this stupid man. He's just made a huge mistake.

Wolf lunges for him like a beast, moving faster than I thought possible. *Holy hell.* Is he godkissed for speed, too? But the two priests with drawn cutlasses were anticipating this. The closest one slashes in Wolf's direction. Wolf dodges the cutlass with ease, countering with an explosive uppercut that sends the man crashing to the ground. The second priest attacks, but Wolf sidesteps the cutlass's blow and delivers a swift punch to the man's jaw.

Besides the unarmed Patron, only the priest who captured me remains on his feet. Wolf stalks up behind my attacker and locks a heavy hand on his shoulder.

He leans in to hiss in the man's ear, "You don't deserve to touch her."

He lands a devastating jab to the man's kidney area. As the air rushes out of my attacker's lungs, his meaty hands slip off me, and I'm able to scramble back to Myst. Wolf lays into the man with another strike to the kidney, sending him stumbling to all fours.

Wolf picks the broken man up, only to slam his knee into the man's middle and send him back to hands and knees again.

Wolf pauses to toss his sweaty hair up. For a second, our eyes lock. He's breathing hard, but doesn't have a single new scratch on him. He touches my arm with tender concern.

"Lady Sabine. Are you—"

The two armed priests cut off his question with a simultaneous attack from both sides. I suck in a gasp as Wolf dodges the cutlass blades slicing through the air. One of them nicks his left arm as he's bending forward, but he doesn't so much as flinch as a line of red appears on his shirt.

He snatches his bow from his rucksack and uses it as a staff to block the cutlass swings. With a weapon in his hands, he instantly has the advantage. As he parries their strikes with astonishing speed, I realize that he's *listening* to their bodies shifting—that's how he can move so fast.

One of the priests darts into the crowd and comes back with a length of chain from the blacksmith shop, which he tries to circle around Myst's neck.

Hell no.

I might not know how to fight, and I don't have a sword, but that doesn't mean I'm weaponless.

Rear up, girl! I tell her.

Myst rises to her hind legs, clipping the man in the chin with her hoof, sending him crashing to the road, unconscious.

Good girl! I cheer her on.

But my moment of excitement vanishes as the Patron sidles up beside me in the chaos, locking his hand around my arm.

"Lady Sabine Darrow. You're wanted by the Grand Cleric of the Red Church."

I'm so distracted by the fight that his words barely register. The Grand Cleric? The head of all ten orders? What does he care about some indecency in a tiny village?

Wolf spies the Patron dragging me away from Myst, and hurls himself against the militant priests. Explosive crashes between cutlass and bow erupt from the melee. I've never witnessed anything as viciously beautiful as Wolf fighting. He's got a stark grace to him, a masculine intensity. It doesn't take him long to unarm one of the men and kick his cutlass into the crowd. He slams the end of his bow over the man's head to knock him on his ass. The other priest stumbles back, doubled over from a blow to his ribcage.

Wolf takes advantage of the break in the fight to wrap

one hand in Myst's mane and grab his rucksack with the other. He swings up on her back with astonishing grace. He extends his other hand down to me.

"Sabine, take my hand!"

I strain away from the Patron until I manage to clasp hands with Wolf. He digs his heels into Myst's sides, and the momentum as she bolts forward is strong enough to wrench me out of the Patron's hold. Wolf settles me onto Myst in front of him. He wraps a strong arm around my waist.

Now, Myst, I say. *As fast as you can!*

She doesn't need any more encouragement. The crowd finally parts, giving us an exit. As she charges down the village's main thoroughfare, Wolf clasps me tightly, my back flush against his heaving chest.

We leave the acolytes of Immortal Woudix in the dust —but I fear it won't be the last we see of them.

❧

Myst doesn't transition out of a gallop until we're miles from Charmont, back in the thick of Mag Na Tir Forest. As she slows to a walk, my thighs burn, my ribcage aches, and my anger crackles over my skin, but I'm able to stash the worst of it away as I focus on calming my racing heartbeat to match her unhurried pace.

Behind me, Wolf presses his open hand against my stomach, holding me steady as Myst stumbles. His voice ghosts in my ear, "There's a crossroads ahead. We'll make camp in the woods a ways before it."

I nod, all too aware of how firm his hold is—and how I don't have on a stitch of clothes. I should feel ashamed, and I *am* embarrassed—but not as deeply as I once would have been. I lost track of time since we left the village. His steady arms around me were my only focus, trusting that this man would protect me. Not only because it's his job, but because Myst was right about Wolf: He's loyal. I know I'll never be able to compete with his devotion to Lord Rian, but I believe Wolf cares about me to some degree.

Enough to keep me safe.

And it's a strange thing—trusting someone. Especially someone sent to jail you. But I do trust Wolf, which is a foreign concept. A daughter should always love her father, but I hate mine. There was no sense of safety under his roof, even before my mother died. And the convent? That was even worse.

Other than Suri, who I only had the joy of knowing for a few days, Wolf is the sole person in my life who's stood by their word. Even Adan, though he holds my heart, is an uncertainty. As much as I want to trust him, I only spent one day with him—I barely know him.

I feel as though our intense days and nights have shown me who Wolf is. I could go years knowing a person and still never understand them half as well as I do Wolf. He's every bit the hardened hunter he presents outwardly, but he's also a damaged boy who was handed a heart-breakingly bleak childhood, made to survive by his fists and his godkiss, who convinced himself in some twisted way that he's grateful to be a servant. He's a man who sees me shivering and fetches a blanket. Who tries to comfort me, though no one has ever comforted him.

He's more than Wolf—he's also Basten.

And we only have eleven more days together.

I'd be lying if I said I wasn't fearful of what lies ahead in Duren. Until now, I haven't allowed myself to ruminate on a future married to Lord Rian. I convinced myself the marriage would never happen, because I'd run away with Adan long before we arrived at Sorsha Hall. But my escape attempt was an unequivocal failure. As frustrated as I am that Wolf caught me, I accept the stark truth behind his warning: The Valveres would hunt me down by whatever means necessary.

Maybe, in a twisted way, Wolf did me a favor.

But I'm not ready to face marriage to a ruthless man. Or a castle notorious for debauchery. Or marrying into a family with the reputation of cutthroats dressed in silk and gold.

Plus, I won't have Wolf to protect me anymore.

We make camp in a clearing covered with springy green ground cover that smells like thyme. Wolf winces as he pulls his shirt over the bloody wound on his arm, then tosses it to me, before he starts to build a fire.

I drag his shirt over my head, flinching at the cold wetness of his blood staining the fabric. Rubbing my tired eyes, I say, "Aren't you afraid the priests will see our fire from the road?"

He rakes his curtain of dark hair back as he studies the coals. "They won't be looking for us. The Order of Immortal Woudix isn't based in Charmont. They were only there to cause a scene. Sent by the Grand Cleric to stoke the ire of the Valvere family. They've long been rivals."

As I smooth his shirt down my arms, my fingers come away sticky with blood. From a distance, I can't tell if his wound has stopped bleeding. Hefting my tired body to my feet, I shuffle over to the fire and plop down next to him.

With a poke, I gently inspect the blood-smeared skin around his cut.

"What are you doing?" he snaps, jerking his arm away.

I ignore his tone, knowing that with me, he's all bark and no bite. "It looks like the bleeding has stopped. The cut is deep but sliced cleanly. That's good. I'll need water to wash it . . . " I look around for any indication of a stream nearby.

Wary, he jerks his head toward his rucksack. "The water flask is there."

I root around until I find it, and grab a handkerchief as well. Taking my place by Wolf in front of the fire, I gently wash away the blood from his arm.

"The Sisters taught you how to heal?" he asks.

"No." I wring out the handkerchief and then pat the area dry. "I learned by tending to my own wounds."

His bicep flexes on instinct. I can see a vein throbbing in his neck. From somewhere high above us, an owl hoots. He growls, "I could kill every last one of them for what they did to you."

My hand pauses as our eyes meet. The firelight dances in his dark irises. For a second, I forget who we are. That he's my jailor and I'm his master's bride. Here in the hidden contours of the forest, we might as well have stepped back in time one thousand years to the fae realm.

An age of magic when the trees sang, and puffy white cloudfoxes skimmed the air.

I don't know if all the stories in the Book of the Immortals are true—the mythical animals and cursed lovers and vicious battles between the gods—but being with Wolf makes me want to believe in fantasies.

Slow, he presses his palm to where his shirt hangs over my ribcage, gently feeling the bone. For a crazy second, I wish the fabric barrier wasn't between us, and he was holding me again like when we rode Myst together.

Stop that, you idiot, I chide myself, but it feels hopeless.

"You reinjured your rib in the fight, didn't you?"

I give a soft shake of my head, still unable to tear my gaze away from the firelight reflecting in his eyes. I did hurt my rib, but if I said that aloud, he'd stalk straight to the Order of Immortal Woudix's church and burn it to the ground. "No. I'm okay."

His hand remains cemented against my side in a way that makes me think he found as much solace in our horseback ride together as I did. That having me close meant something to him.

Over the next days, I keep thinking of his gentle touch on my ribs. The first time I saw him, I thought he was a gorgeous monster. Now, I'm starting to realize that for all his brutish ways, he isn't at all like the men who catcall in the villages we pass.

There's a part of me that wants to trust him with more than just my safety. That wants to lower my walls and ask for something I've never had: help.

The next time he lowers me down from Myst, I place

my hand over his and, gathering my courage, look him square in the eye as I say, "Wolf, I want you to teach me to fight."

CHAPTER 12
WOLF

I stare at Sabine like she's speaking the incomprehensible Immortal Tongue. Teach her to fight? For a moment, with her soft hand pressed against mine, the moonlight painting her skin with a beautiful glow, and her leaning toward me with those rosebud lips, I had thought, *maybe* . . .

But that can never happen.

Sabine Darrow isn't mine to kiss.

"I never want to be in the position again that I was in at Charmont," she says in a voice that nearly breaks as her hand moves to her opposite wrist, where the Patron grabbed her. "My whole life, I've done nothing while others abused me. In the convent, there was nothing I *could* do. I was ten years old when I moved there, a child outnumbered by adults. When I got older and stronger, they threatened to hurt Myst as a means to keep me under their control." She swallows, her throat catching on a lump of fear, but then her eyes turn determined.

She continues in a steely voice, "I know what they say about Sorsha Hall. The depraved court that the Valveres keep is as lawless as any fae gods' realm. If I'm to thrive there, I need to be able to defend myself."

Her request is sensible but naive. She may think she knows what she faces at Sorsha Hall, but she has no idea what she's about to walk into. Rian has his flaws, but buried somewhere beneath his ruthlessness, a moral compass still tries to guide him, as it did when we were boys. It's the rest of his family she should fear. His older brothers, Kendan and Lore, though they've both been absent for years: Lore heading the Valveres' shipping fleet far across the Panopis Sea, and Kendan as a captain for King Joruun's army in Old Coros—or at least, that's the formal word. Their father, Lord Berolt, was born with a broken moral compass. He built his empire of legal—and illegal—vices through blood and blackmail. There's a persistent rumor that he killed his late wife, Madelyna— Rian's mother—in a fit of rage when she birthed a normal third son, after a fortuneteller foretold that Rian would be godkissed.

All that's not even to mention the Valvere cousins and aunts and uncles and one especially vile grandmother, as well as the questionable company the family keeps: revelers and pirates, mercenaries and whores. All dressed up in fae finery that does little to hide their barbarous desires.

"Lord Rian will do everything in his power to ensure your safety, my lady." I speak my words carefully, even formally, to try to atone for the unchaste thoughts I was having earlier.

That you're still having, Wolf.

I tell that voice to shut up.

Sabine levels a hard look at me. "Will Lord Rian always be around?"

I wish like hell I could assure her that without a shadow of a doubt, she'll be safe at Sorsha Hall. If everything goes according to plan, *I'll* be watching out for her, and you can bet I won't take my sight off her for a holy second.

But then again, not even I can be around all the time. I have to sleep. I have to piss. And if I don't investigate the strange happenings at the Volkish border wall, who will?

My little violet is right: she needs to know how to defend herself.

"After dinner, then," I say.

Once we've rested and filled our bellies, I explain methodically, "You're at a disadvantage because of your size. The only opponent you could realistically defeat is another woman. I don't mean to belittle the strength of your will—I'm only speaking practically. If you tried to take on someone my size, well . . . "

I don't have to finish my thought. I dwarf her as we sit beside the fire. Even my shadow vastly overstretches hers on the forest floor behind us. I could break her with just my little finger.

Not missing a beat, she says, "So, then tell me how to fight women."

My eyebrows rise until I remember that for twelve years, it's been women who have hurt her.

Sabine is nothing like what I expected. She's a study in contradictions: soft and hard at the same time. It feels impossible that she's real. This is a girl who will share her meager food with a mouse, who finds sympathy even for the slithering, venomous creatures of the night. She's just as tender a morsel on the outside, with her creamy soft skin and round curves that beg to be squeezed.

And yet there's another side to her entirely. An angry, determined girl who refuses to be a victim. Who wants to know how to fight against anyone who crosses her, even old women. I want to know how one person can hold so much complexity. How her soul can bear so much rage and yet not break from it. Maybe if I can figure out how she still sees the beauty in life after everything that's happened to her, I can, too.

"Right." I push to my feet. "Stand up, then. First lesson: basic stance."

She eagerly springs to her feet as my borrowed shirt hangs down to mid-thigh. She raises her fists like a child would, too high, too forward, and utterly wrong. But stance is easy to fix. You can't teach someone determination, and my little violet has that in spades.

"Before you think about your fists, get your feet right." I move behind her, easing her arms down by her sides, and kick her feet shoulder-width apart. She totters off balance momentarily, and I snare her around the waist to center her.

"Here. Your hips carry a lot of power. Sink into your stance. When you throw a punch, you need the whole force of your body behind it, not just your arm."

Her hips shift beneath my palms as she rocks back slightly to put the weight in her heels. "Like this?"

It's a near-perfect stance, and I'm a little gobsmacked

by how readily she picks up instruction. "That's it, my lady. Now, you can think about a strike. Keep your elbow tucked in close to your body, like this." I grasp her wrist lightly to show her how to hold her arm. "Good. Now make a fist. Keep it loose. To strike, you rotate your whole body into it." I wrap my arms around her shoulders, pivoting her body as she practices striking.

After a few practice punches in the air, I move to face her. "Now show me as if I were your attacker."

Her face is alight, determined. She aims a slow-motion punch at my chest, and the moment it makes contact, I trap her fist.

"Aim for vulnerable spots. I'm strongest here in my chest. Go for the chin instead, or here, where the ribcage meets. That's more likely to throw your opponent off balance, especially if it's a woman."

"Like this?"

She drives her little fist into my solar plexus with all the force of a wisp of cloud blowing in the breeze.

I smirk. "Now put some force behind it." Her eyebrows rise at the suggestion of violence, but she smashes her fist harder against me.

"Try again," I order.

She hits with more force.

"Again."

She pauses, looking up. "What if I hurt you for real?"

I chuckle "Oh, little violet. You can't hurt me."

Her jaw tenses like she doesn't appreciate my bravado. She throws a punch, but this time, she strikes my chest squarely in my lefthand side, atop the wildcat's puncture wounds. I jerk, not because the pain is bad—it isn't—but because this clever little minx tried to pull a fast one on me.

"So you want to fight dirty, is that it?" There's an edge in my voice.

Her fist is balled tightly. "I want you to take me seriously."

"Oh, I take your safety as seriously as a blade to my throat."

She straightens, lifting her chin as she evaluates her small fists. "Now show me how to defend myself against a man."

"A man? Lady Sabine—"

"There must be something I can do. You're saying I should just take a man's brutality?"

She's already suggested I don't take her safety seriously, so I want to give her what she wants. She's such a little thing that it spikes anger in my veins to even consider how easily a thuggish man might overpower her.

"Your strength isn't enough, so you'll have to use other tools at your disposal. You can speak to creatures that bite and sting. Use that."

"Use animals?" Her face pales. She shakes her head in a single, definitive bob. "No. I can't."

It takes me a minute to understand. "Ah. The dead wildcat. I see. You don't want to put more animals at risk, is that it?"

Pain ripples across her face as she swipes at her nose.

Nodding to myself, I say steadily, "There are ways to give *yourself* claws, then."

She meets my gaze, very much intrigued. "How?"

I draw my hunting knife from the holster at my hip. It's a wide, ten-inch blade with a heavy brass handle, given to me by Lord Rian as a prize when I slaughtered a wolf that attacked one of the Valvere's prize horses.

I press the hilt into her small palm. "This hilt was made for my hand, not yours. When we arrive in Duren, I'll have a properly sized blade made for you. Something small and sheathed that you can hide beneath your clothes."

"Oh," she says softly, wrapping her fingers around the brass hilt. "I can't pay you."

Pay me? For keeping her safe? I would pay *her* a thousand coins if she only promised to keep a blade on her at all times. Even after crossing half of Astagnon together, she still doesn't seem to understand that I exist to serve her, not the other way around.

I give a low laugh. "Consider it a wedding present."

She gives me a wry look. "Not many people would associate weddings with knives." She toys with the blade's sharp point, pressing it gently against my heart. "I do, too."

I swallow a dry breath. *Because we're the same,* I think. *Both abandoned. Both made to survive on our own.*

A girl like that doesn't want rubies and gold. She wants claws.

She applies slight pressure to the knife's tip, bowing but not breaking my skin. "And what if, when we reach Sorsha Hall, I don't have a blade at the ready? Should I scream?"

"Hmm," I stall, not wanting to dismiss her suggestion immediately. Yeah, right. The chance of someone responding to a scream in Sorsha Hall is as fanciful as cloudfoxes. Sorsha Hall is no silent convent filled with soft prayer and incense. Screams are the fucking *standard*. There are always sporting fights in the ballroom, not to mention moaning from the bedrooms.

"Distraction," I say instead. "That's your best option. Divert your attacker's attention and run."

She squares her stance just as I taught her. "Like this?"

She raises her fist, ready for more sparring, but I hesitate as my eyes trail down her curves beneath my oversized shirt.

"I don't mean to offend your decency, my lady, but there's often only one reason a man would attack a girl who looks like you do. He'll likely be able to overpower you physically, but such an attack also leaves him open to vulnerabilities."

Her cheeks turn a pretty shade of rose as she puts together my meaning, and she lowers her fists slowly, but maintains her fierce stance. In a dry, steady voice, she says, "Okay."

"Okay?"

"Show me."

Anticipation blooms in my chest. I've already touched my master's bride during this sparring lesson far more than is appropriate, and now she's asking for more?

I can tell myself it's for her safety as much as I want— it doesn't mean I don't also jump at every chance to feel her soft flesh. I am truly fucked by how much I like touching her. A better man would tell her that it's enough, and she can continue fighting lessons with her husband as her guide.

But I'm not a better man.

"Down," I command, tipping my chin up.

She readily complies, lowering to her knees while keeping her round eyes on me. She sinks onto her bottom, then leans back onto her elbows in a submissive, reclined position, looking up at me expectantly through her long lashes.

Fuck. I could be hung for the sick thoughts going through my head to see my master's bride splayed out like that on the ground before me.

With a dry throat, I drop to my own knees, straddling her waist as I brace myself over her with one arm. She's kiss-close beneath me, her lips parted as her breath rises and falls shallowly.

I say hoarsely, "A man, especially an aroused one, will be most vulnerable in his groin. That's where you're going to want to hurt him. He'll expect you to struggle, so he'll be on guard. The best thing you can do is put him at ease. Don't fight him—at least at first. Make him think you want it."

She scowls deeply at the suggestion. Disgust laces her voice as she says, "No man bent on rape would ever believe a woman wants it."

Oh, little violet, I think, recalling all the vile conversations I've overheard in army barracks. *You don't know men.*

"He will," I vow darkly, so serious that the scowl melts off her face. "Men have an astounding capacity to lie to themselves if it's something they want to hear. Make him think you want it, and then, once his guard is down, you raise your knee up like this, as hard and as fast as you can."

I reach through my straddling legs to grasp the back of her knee, then pull her leg up to meet the underside of my crotch. She complies, shifting her hips beneath me to get a better angle. With her body fondling all around my groin, it's all I can do to keep my breath from giving out. I get no perverse pleasure from pretending to force a woman, but I sure as hell am drowning in arousal to have Sabine Darrow between my legs.

"If you have a knife, now would be the time to draw it." I take her hand and place it over my bare abdomen, above my soft inner organs. "Stab him on his lower belly. Here."

Her fingers blaze a path against my bare lower stomach as she feels for the place I indicate. I silence a groan rising in my throat. I'm not the only one warring with myself over all our touches and strokes. Sabine tries to hide it, but her body betrays her. She shows all the signs of a woman in heat: shallow breath, dilated pupils, the sharp, sweet smell of lust between her thighs. Maybe she gets as confused between fighting and fucking as I do. She can't have ever been in this position with a man before, so her innocent body doesn't know what to do with itself.

"Now, try it," I bark hoarsely, and pin both her wrists to the dirt above her head. Her coiled braid drapes around her face like a garland, her eyes searing up at me.

She drives her knee up to my groin. Not hard enough to hurt, but hard enough to jostle things that shouldn't be jostled. I free one of her hands, and she grabs a stick to act as a knife and presses its point against my lower abdomen.

"Good," I bark. "Again."

We go through the motions time and time again. Once Sabine masters the initial moves, she quickly wants to advance. She starts trying to distract me in various little ways so she can roll away, but I easily thwart her every time. She grows frustrated the more I foil her, her pulse thumping in her veins, her breath coming in little huffs.

"A man won't go easy on you," I challenge, perversely enjoying her frustration. "Neither will I."

She temporarily stops struggling, letting her body sag against the dirt as she scowls up at me. We've been wrestling enough that her wiggles have awoken every part of my body, and it's a damn battle to keep my focus on teaching her to fight instead of training her to do what I really want: wrap those pretty little lips around the specific body part she keeps battering with her knee.

"Had enough, my lady?"

She narrows her eyes. I think she's about to concede defeat, but then her attention shifts to something behind my shoulder. A wrinkle of uncertainty forms in my brain. God, not a fucking wildcat again . . .

Before I can look, a chipmunk jumps on my head.

I'm so startled that I release Sabine's wrists so that I can swat at the little devil, but Sabine uses the opportunity to shove me over. I've fought men with ten times her strength, so realistically, her effort does nothing, but I let myself tumble backward. Even I have to admit her trick was clever, and she deserves a prize.

Triumphant, she climbs over my chest to straddle my hips, victoriously pinning my wrists to the dirt over my head as she grins down at me, her chest rising and falling rapidly.

"Congratulations," I murmur, unable to tear my thoughts away from all the dirty things I could do to her in this position. "I thought you didn't want to use animals."

"I knew you wouldn't hurt it this time." To hold my wrists down means she has to lean so far over me that her long hair drapes my scarred chest like silken chains. She raises a cocky eyebrow. "You let me win, didn't you?"

Without thinking, I say hoarsely, "Yeah, well, I would let you do anything to me, beyond what even the most depraved gods could conceive."

Her expression softens with surprise. Her big round eyes blink down at me, aghast. Our faces are only inches apart, both our lips parted. I know I said the wrong thing, but fuck it. It's true. To feel her sweet body on mine, I'd happily let her stab me. She could knee me in the groin until the sun rises. I'd take any and all of the pain she wants to dole out just to have her touch.

A soft whimper escapes her sweet lips.

And I'm lost.

I'm so fucking lost.

She has all the signs of arousal. She wants me, but not nearly as much as I want her. I knead my hands around her thighs as they hug my hips, groaning as my fingertips sink into her luscious curves.

Her hips twitch in an instinctive little buck that makes her breath hitch in her throat. Her breathy pants fill my mouth, and then with one tilt of my chin, my last resolve breaks, and my lips are all over hers.

My mind would remind me that kissing Sabine is wrong, but right now, my brain isn't the organ calling the shots. Knowing exactly what to do, my body takes over. My hands finally claim the touch they've been craving as I anchor one hand to her hip to pin her squarely in the straddle. I push up on my other hand to sit upright, with her now in my lap. Not breaking the kiss, I scrape my fingers through the hair at her nape to guide her head into a deeper kiss.

Our lips are searching, greedy, as they war together.

It's like some spell has broken. Like waiting for rain after months of drought, feeling the drenching liquid flood my skin in relief that excites as much as it soothes.

Finally, I have the taste of violets on my tongue again. But kissing Sabine isn't like eating candied flower buds. It's devouring the whole cake. The whole fucking meal.

Kissing Sabine is *everything*.

I've wanted her ever since she fed that hungry mouse, when I so jealously yearned for her to offer me a morsel of the same kindness. Since I first saw her standing in her father's courtyard in that skimpy silk robe with her scent splashing around, tormenting me.

Her legs wrap around my waist, and she matches the movement by sliding her hands around my neck. With one hand on the small of her back, I press her closer, wanting to feel every inch of her body against my own. My mouth is hot on hers as I kiss and suck and taste. I trail my lips down her jaw, and she lets out a moan that sends blood rushing straight to my groin.

Fuck.

I break the kiss to give myself a chance to breathe. I'm

so flooded with desire that I can barely form thoughts. Our eyes lock, and it takes my breath away how beautiful she is. Freshly kissed, ready for more.

And that's when my brain decides to turn back on.

More? I think. *Hell, I've already gone too far.*

The realization of what I've done douses me like a barrel of ice water over my head. Fuck, fuck, *fuck*. This is Lord Rian's intended, and I've got my mouth all over her. A gut punch of guilt hits me hard enough to stun. What's wrong with me? I'm sick. I'm broken. I huff out a curse, and Sabine's eyes go wide.

Her pink lips are swollen. Her sweet face mirrors my own shock at what we've done.

I lift her by her hips out of my lap, dropping her ass on the ground. Then I shove myself to my feet, dragging a hand down the sweat soaking my face.

"Lady Sabine." My voice comes between heaving breaths. "Forgive me." I pace, unsure of what to do with my hands. "That will never happen again, I swear it."

She touches a stunned hand to her lips like she can still feel the ghost of my mouth. The worst of everything is that I can still smell her desire, and I know that if I kissed her again, I don't think she'd fight it.

"Basten—"

I can't hear any more. I can't be around her scent. I'm not strong enough to listen to her thumping heart and soft little moans. I stalk off far enough into the woods so that I have some space from her, but am still within range to listen for danger. Adrenaline pumps unchecked throughout my body. Guilt marks me like blood that I'll never be able to wash off. Rian will instantly take one look at me and see my sin.

"Fuck." I slam my fist into the side of a tree, growling like an animal. But no amount of pain can fix the broken parts inside of me.

CHAPTER 13
SABINE

In the morning, neither Basten nor I say a word about the kiss. We go about our morning chores of boiling water for tea and cleaning up camp, as though he didn't have his mouth all over mine, and I didn't have my thighs straddling his.

Everything with him, since we woke, has been "yes, my lady" and "as you wish, my lady," as though an over-abundance of propriety can make up for breaking his master's trust. Anyone could see he's drowning in guilt, but I couldn't care less about betraying my future husband. I've sworn no vows yet. The engagement wasn't even my choice. Everything about this ride is forced by Lord Rian, and so he's earned no loyalty from me.

Still, it was foolish. Basten is no friend of mine. He would throw me to the wolves if his master ordered him to. He doesn't even want to be here, tending to a spoiled lord's daughter instead of stalking prey through the woods. I trust that he will keep me safe, but not because of any loyalty to me—only because I belong to his master.

I don't know what came over me last night. Locked up in the convent, I've been starved for human touch. So many nights I laid awake, wondering what a man's body felt like. I would sneak to the chapel to flip through the Book of the Immortals to look at the most wicked illustration, belonging to Immortal Alyssantha, the Goddess of Sex. Those portraits showed Alyssantha and her lovers in all kinds of compromising positions that stirred a heat between my legs.

So wasn't it inevitable that I'd buckle under the first man's touch?

Basten stews in his guilt, and I wallow in my anger. Here I've been fantasizing about my first kiss for years, and it had to be with a brute who dumped my ass in the dirt after pawing me.

"We should be getting on the road, Lady Sabine," Basten says without looking at me.

Hatred makes my steps stiff as I tug off his shirt, smash it into his chest, and start to comb my hair over my bare breasts. He keeps his gaze in the opposite direction, like his eyes will burn out of his head if he even side-eyes my naked body.

Myst, I call. **The brute says it's time to go.**

She walks over, swinging her head between Basten and me like there is a visible, taut line of tension between us.

She whinnies. **Mate?**

I gape, utterly horrified. At least only I can hear her

voice in my head. ***No, we didn't mate! Don't you dare suggest something like that again!***

She snorts again, skeptical.

I mumble curses as I climb onto a stump and swing a leg over her back. Grumpy, I rearrange my loose hair to try to cover every inch of exposed skin. It's been almost two weeks since Suri helped me wash my hair with scented soap, and now the full, soft waves that her braid made are clumpy and oily.

Basten swings his rucksack onto his back and, wordlessly, we return to the forest road. He walks a few paces ahead, and I bore holes in the back of his head with my glare, cursing him for existing. If it wasn't for him, I wouldn't be here right now, shamed and naked, thighs rubbed red from riding bareback, in dire need of a bath. I'd be in Adan's arms. It would be *Adan's* mouth on mine. *Adan's* hands in my hair. *Adan's* hard body atop my own.

Basten has made it crystal clear that escaping from him isn't an option. I refuse to try again and put Myst or any other animal at risk of what happened to the wildcat. And yet, I'll be damned if I let these men steer my future. I will never marry the man who forced me on this obscene ride. Somehow—either before we arrive in Duren or after—I'll evade every gilded bond they've shackled me with.

I have to send a message to Adan.

Since I can't meet him as planned, I need to let him know that I haven't given up on us. It's the least I can do after letting Basten kiss me.

The thing is, sending a message should be simple for a godkissed girl who can talk to animals, but it isn't. Birds are able to travel anywhere in Astagnon within a day, but they don't think as humans do. Even if one volunteered to help, it would be impossible to explain directions. They don't understand the concept of town names, road names, or even people's names. The best they can manage is navigating by natural landmarks, but that's a challenge, since Basten has taken us into a forest where every valley looks the same.

I raise my voice, daring to break the tense silence that's pervaded us all morning. "You said there was a crossroads ahead, right?"

"A few miles ahead, yeah. We'll take the fork east, sticking to the woods."

The Sisters of Immortal Iyre didn't bother to teach me geography, so my knowledge of Astagnon's topography is fuzzy. The best I can rely on are the few conversations I overheard in my father's manor house, between him and Suri discussing the path I'd take to Duren.

"If we go straight at the crossroads," I suggest, "That would take us north to Blackwater, right? On the Innis River?"

Basten grunts. "We aren't going north."

My thinking is that if I can get to a town on the Innis River, I can find a bird willing to carry a message to Adan. The Old Innis Mill is situated inland along that same waterway, and with its large waterwheel, it should be a clear enough landmark for a bird to recognize. All it would have to do is follow the river until it spots the waterwheel.

"But heading north would be a nearly direct path to Duren," I press. "Otherwise, we're wasting time skirting through the forest."

"Blackwater is no place for a lady."

Basten clearly isn't inclined to have this conversation, but I pull Myst to a halt and wait, hands on my hips.

He turns around with a scowl like I'm a thorn in his side.

I clear my throat. "I want to go through Blackwater."

"What you *want* doesn't concern me, Lady Sabine."

I trade him a scowl. My position on top of Myst gives me the advantage of height, and I draw myself up to take full advantage of that fact. Theatrically, I hold up a lock of my oily hair.

"If you can smell anything beyond your own stench, you would know that I'm in dire need of a bath. I doubt your master would be pleased to have his new bride parade through town looking like a cat who's been wallowing in the mud. I need to stop at an inn to bathe before arriving in Duren."

He folds his arms tightly. "I told you, we aren't going north."

I lift a pointed eyebrow. "Are there any inns along the forest road?"

"There are not."

"Then we *will* be going north." I bore a hot gaze into his skull as I lean forward threateningly. "Lord Rian commanded I perform this obscene ride naked," I hiss. "But it's up to you if I arrive filthy or not, Basten. Give me this one dignity. You *owe* it to me."

His hard expression eases. Guilt flashes in his eyes again at my referral to the kiss. His throat bobs in a dry swallow. "Blackwater is a rough town," he presses. "A river port that draws riffraff from all the bordering territories. A lot of men pass through that town, looking for trouble."

I don't back down. "I have every confidence that a guard of your ability can protect me from a few pick-pockets."

He pinches the bridge of his nose, cursing under his breath. I know I'm not asking for the impossible—if we had kept the original route through Middleford, we would have passed through Blackwater anyway. So it's unlikely to be as rough as he claims.

"Fine," he says tightly. "One inn. One night. One bath."

I smile in mocking sweetness at him. "You could stand a little soap yourself."

Blackwater is three days away, which gives me time to think through exactly how I'll manage to send a message to Adan. It warms my heart to think of him receiving my letter and knowing that I didn't give up on him. It isn't the same as us being together, of course, but it would destroy me to think he might believe I abandoned our plans in favor of marrying Lord Rian.

I rub my fingers together absently, recalling Adan's touch. What a shame my first kiss was with Basten, instead of Adan. The best Adan and I managed under the ever-present eyes of the Sisters was to hold hands in the kidding barn. Seated in the straw with a goat in my lap, Adan's hand brushed mine as he reached for a towel. We both blushed, and then he smoothed his strong hand over mine intentionally.

Holding hands with Adan was like warm spring sun on my heart. I can only imagine what kissing him would feel like: hot noonday heat, maybe. Nothing like kissing Basten. The last word I'd use to describe that interaction was "sunny." Kissing Basten was like embracing a storm. Like being consumed in dark clouds, and claps of thunder, and bolts of lightning and . . .

. . . and I need to stop thinking about kissing Basten.

Okay? Myst asks me. *Breathing hard.*

By the Immortals, she misses nothing, does she?

I'm, ah, thinking of Adan—the Boy Who Shines Like Sunlight.

She snorts, displeased. *Oh. Him.*

She doesn't like Adan, but then again, he *did* come to the Convent of Immortal Iyre to cut the balls off the livestock, so he might not be my favorite person, either, if I was four-legged.

I tell her about my plan to send him a message, and her response is swift and strong.

Forget him.

For a horse, she can be awfully judgmental. I dig my heels into her sides and say, *What, you'd rather see me married to the man my ass of a father chose?*

She tosses her head in Basten's direction, several paces ahead of us. *I like that one.*

I grumble at her insistence that Basten and I would make a good match. Is she crazy? Granted, she *is* a horse. Maybe my expectations are too high if I'm expecting sage dating advice from a creature whose greatest joy is grass. But Myst has also known me longer than anyone. She belonged to my mother, and is the only thing I still have of her. No one in the world knows me as well as Myst.

I thought you said he smelled like a predator, I remind her.

He gives me apples.

By the Immortals, this horse will be the death of me. For once, I wish I could shut off my godkiss and listen to nothing but the wind in the trees.

What are you afraid of? Myst asks, tilting her head to look back at me.

The question lodges deep in my chest, reaching past my proverbial armor straight to my heart. I know that she isn't asking about what gives me jump frights. She wants to know what it is about Basten that sets my nerves on edge and makes my heartbeat stumble. Of course, I could remind her that I've already committed myself to Adan. My heart simply isn't free to search out another man. It's true that Adan and I barely know each other, but in that brief time together, I felt a stirring of love for the first time in my life.

What kind of a person would I be if I threw that away for a man with a permanent scowl and bullheaded loyalty to a tyrant?

There's no world in which Basten and I could be together, anyway. I'm intended to marry his master. Basten would never break his oath to the Valvere family, and I'm guessing that my future husband wouldn't love the idea, either, if I suggested I make out with his huntsman on our wedding night instead of him.

I shift my position on Myst's back to ease the ache in my thighs.

Basten glances back. "Everything all right, Lady Sabine?"

"It's my thighs," I admit with a groan. "It's fine when I'm riding Myst at a walk, but that gallop to get away from the priests back in Charmont left me aching. It's only gotten worse since." I sigh, then lift a shoulder as my irritation fades, replaced by the fond memory of the wind in my hair. "It was worth it, though. I never get to gallop like that. So fast and free. It was incredible."

In the Convent of Immortal Iyre, the Sisters wouldn't let me ride Myst beyond the convent's grounds for fear I'd run away. But the convent was a self-sufficient place with ample fields and gardens, surrounded by a high stone wall. Sometimes, in the middle of the night, I would sneak into the barn and mount Myst. The two of us would ride circles around the grounds beneath the moonlight.

Basten tosses back another assessing look, then barks, "Go on, then. Ride free."

I laugh mirthlessly until I see that he isn't laughing. My face sobers. "Are you serious?"

A week ago, I tried to escape. I even had a wildcat attempt to end Basten's life. Why would he now offer me to gallop freely ahead of him? Unless that's the point—he wants to prove that I can't ever escape, even at a gallop.

But there's no cruelty in his eyes. "You and I both know there's nowhere you can run that the Valveres can't find you. So, yes, I trust you to return. I can't hear anyone else in the woods for at least half a mile—it's safe. Ride

Myst as you like, as much as you like, across that distance and back."

My lips part, still wondering if this is a trick, but Basten hasn't shown any inclination toward twisted games like his master. He might be a brute, but he is as open as a book.

Myst. I nudge her with my ankles. *He's letting us run. For pleasure.*

Her answer is an eager whinny. I tighten my legs around her and wind my fingers through her mane to hold on. Leaning forward, I say:

Go.

Her muscles bunch beneath my thighs as she surges forward. She's a proud, spirited horse, and she's craved this rush of movement as much as I have. She was as much a prisoner as me in the convent, and I can feel how her legs stretch out gratefully as she eats up the road.

I cling on, her speed startling but invigorating. The ache in my thighs vanishes as adrenaline floods me. Soon, the edge of panic ebbs, replaced by sheer joy. I feel laughter spilling out from my lips at the same time that tears sting my eyes. My hair whips behind me like a flag proclaiming that I am my own kingdom, and no man shall rule me. Myst's hooves pound over the dirt road like she's skipping on clouds. The trees blur on either side of us. We crest a small rise, and the forest opens up below. I can see for miles from here. The river valley stretches beyond with a vastness I've never experienced, and it steals my breath. Far in the distance, the mountains of the Blackened Forest rise, where the border wall between Volkany holds back the cursed kingdom. A sense of awe wraps around me like enchanted mist at this vast, beautiful world. So many little towns and hamlets dot the valleys. I imagine all the people down there, working and eating and falling in love, an entire world open for me.

Myst crests the hill and charges downward at an even greater speed into the valley.

I open my throat and let out a cry.

It's magical, riding like this. No stone walls or gates cage us. Just me and Myst and the wind and the road. It's a freedom I've never experienced, and it's so awe-inspiring that it's too much for me to take in, like a harvest bounty overflowing its basket. My heart doesn't know what to do with this surge of power. I've been confined by walls almost my entire life. Even if the walls didn't lock me in, societal expectations would have done the same job. A lord's daughter in this world is only good for her ability to fetch a powerful husband. Until I met Adan, there was never any hope for a different fate. But now here I am, free as a hawk. I could steer Myst into the forest if I wanted. I could climb that big elm tree to see the view. I could plunge into a stream, and no Sisters would be there to scold me.

I've come so far from that frightened, damaged girl I was when I stood in a muddy courtyard in a silk robe. I've experienced more in the last seventeen days than in the last seventeen years—most of all, what I've learned is just how much *left* there is to experience.

I draw Myst to a stop at the next rise. We both pant to catch our breaths as we take in the sweeping view of the Darmarnach Mountains in the distance. My hair falls around me in windswept waves.

As I gaze at those distant peaks, I think to myself that I can never go back to how I was before. Now that I've had a taste of freedom, I will never settle for anything less. Basten might drag me kicking and screaming to Duren, and Lord Rian might lock me inside Sorsha Hall, but I will never marry him.

I'm done letting men decide my fate.

Come on, Myst.

It's painful to turn back and trot down the road until we reach Basten again, who all the while has had me on an invisible tether, but the hot seed of determination has lodged in my heart, and it's already sprouted.

Somehow, I will sever that tie and win *true* freedom.

CHAPTER 14
WOLF

Blackwater.

It's a cesspool of a town; like most port cities where transient people intermingle to trade goods or change travel routes, it draws the dregs of society. Spies. Prostitutes. Thieves. And it's in Duren's jurisdiction, so the Valveres control nearly every gambling hall and brothel within the town. When I first started working for the Valveres, they had me doing more unsavory tasks than hunting boar—the kind of jobs that weren't exactly sanctioned under their license to operate the legal vices. The nature of that work brought me to Blackwater more times than I care to remember.

As we cross the bridge into town, my stomach clenches. I threw a man off this bridge once. He hadn't paid his debts.

Not the kind of place you want to take a beautiful, nubile, naked lord's daughter, for fuck's sake. And yet as we step off the bridge into the town proper, I'm cautiously optimistic. The number of glances we get on the street is shockingly sparse. Sure, there are leers, but nothing like we experienced in Charmont or Polybridge. And then it hits me: In a town like Blackwater, a naked woman simply isn't *that* unusual. Whores probably cavort bare-chested in the alleys every night. The people here are used to such sensationalism, unlike the prudish villagers of Charmont.

Sabine doesn't seem troubled by the riffraff, either: vagrants slumped in doorways, mangy dogs, fortune tellers who'll steal your coin and spit in your eye. Her attention is riveted to everything we pass, like we're wandering through a mystical cave filled with fascinating treasures, instead of the Sin Streets.

The sizzle of cooking meat reaches my nose and makes my stomach rumble. Mediocre fiddle music comes out of a second-story window. As we pass a brothel with a topless whore leaning out the upstairs window, Sabine leans down to whisper to me, "Is that a Valvere pleasure house?"

Pleasure house? Fuck me. The girl is so innocent she can't even say *brothel*.

I grunt in the affirmative. "This is the legal vice district of Blackwater. They call it the Sin Streets. The Valveres own most of the businesses here, including that brothel."

A drunkard reeking of herb stumbles out of the brothel, blinking into the daylight. His eyes fix on Sabine riding Myst like she's Immortal Solene herself, awoken from her thousand-year slumber. And in a dirty town like this, she might be the closest thing to a god.

He gapes at her, and as she passes, tugs off his cap and presses it to his chest. I roll my eyes, but a part of me appreciates that finally, someone is giving Sabine the respect she deserves. Even if it is just a drunk.

She strokes her hair distractedly as she takes in a brawl outside of a gambling den called Popelin's Hazard.

"Immortal Popelin? The pleasure house was named for him, too."

"He's the God of Pleasure. The patron fae of the Sin Streets. The Valveres worship at his altar."

Foot traffic interrupts our conversation as we cross a narrow wooden bridge that spans a secondary branch of the Innis River. A few blocks downstream, the shouts of workmen come from the docks' direction as sailors load and unload cargo. The reek of sewage and dead fish is overwhelming. This is why I've always avoided crowds: the tidal wave of sensations is too much for my godkissed senses.

Bristling against the onslaught of sights and sounds and smells, I jerk my head toward a ramshackle building ahead at the end of the bridge, where the two branches of the Innis River meet, along with a stream coming from the northern section of town. It's a three-story structure that's seen better days, but at least the pansies planted in the window baskets give it a modicum of cheer. A pictorial sign hangs over the door, showing the meeting of three waterways.

"The Manywaters Inn. You get your wish, my lady." I give a mocking bow.

Sabine ignores my attitude as she peers intently at the widest branch of the Innis River, then at a flock of sooty brown swifts perching on a lamppost, then back at the inn.

"If there's a bath, it will do."

We board Myst in a stable a few blocks away, then enter the inn to inquire about a room. This isn't my first time in the Manywaters Inn. I have memories I'd sooner forget here, but there are only a handful of inns in Blackwater, and this threadbare hovel is the finest.

Scantily clad prostitutes might be a common sight in Blackwater and even in the Manywaters Inn, but the common room still falls silent when Sabine enters, with her long hair kissing the floor and nothing underneath. My skin bristles with the protective instinct to shield her from everyone's gazes, but realistically, the fastest way to get her to privacy is to get her into a room.

"A room. Your finest," I bark at the innkeeper, and thunk a sack of coins on the counter.

The elderly innkeeper is thin to the point of being skeletal, her sandpaper skin sagging around her neck as she adjusts her glasses and peers shrewdly at me.

"You've stayed here before, haven't you?"

I bristle again as Sabine turns a curious eye on me. "Just give me the room."

The innkeeper's eyes drag over Sabine's state of undress as though trying to fit her into one of the three categories of women she could be: prostitute, wife, or sister, and coming up short on all. Her mannered bearing makes it clear she isn't a whore. There's no ring on her finger. And Sabine and I look nothing alike—we clearly didn't come from the same parents.

"Two rooms?" she attempts to correct me.

"One." My voice grinds dangerously against my teeth. It might not be proper for an unmarried man and woman to share a room, but I don't give a fuck about propriety. There's no way I'm leaving Sabine alone for an entire night in a town like Blackwater, even behind a locked door with me asleep at the threshold.

The innkeeper's thin lips press together as she slides my coins into a drawer and hands me a brass key. I seize Sabine by the upper arm and drag her toward the stairs.

"Basten—"

"Call me Wolf in public."

"Wolf, you're hurting me."

I stop short, dropping my gaze to my hand clenched tightly around her arm. I ease my grip, forcing myself to take a deep breath.

"I apologize, my lady. I don't like crowds. I'm eager to get you into a room."

She nods as we climb the creaky staircase to the third floor, a glorified attic space. The key takes us to the last room down the hall. The boards underfoot are uneven, and the mattress looks to have seen better days, but there is a copper tub and a pleasing view of the Innis River. Sabine passes right by the tub and takes a particular interest in the view, wrapping her fingers around the windowsill and gazing upstream.

I shed my rucksack, bumping my head on the sloping ceiling. These rooms weren't made for someone as tall as me.

My gaze circles back to the bed as I unpack my bow and set it behind the door. I didn't ask Sabine if she felt comfortable sharing a room. She doesn't have a choice, anyway—but maybe I was a jerk for not even asking.

"I'll sleep on the floor," I grunt.

She turns away from the window, chewing on her lip like she's distracted. "Hmm? Oh. Right." She starts going through the rickety dresser drawers.

"I'll go downstairs," I say. "Ask for them to bring up hot water so you can bathe."

"Could you ask for some paper, too?"

My hand pauses on the doorknob. "What do you need paper for?"

She gives an embarrassed little laugh that brings a rash of pink to her cheeks. "Oh, it's the view—it's so pretty. I promised Suri that I would write to her about the voyage, and so I thought I'd sketch her a picture. I've been trying to find *some* pleasantry about this damnable ride to share with her. I figure it's better than a description of your snoring, isn't it?"

I snort as I saunter out of the room, being sure to lock the door behind me, and head downstairs. I toss another handful of coins on the counter. "My lady would like a hot bath brought up to her. Paper and ink, too. And clothes. Something to sleep in, undergarments, and a daytime dress. *Clean.* The nicest you can find on short notice. I'll pay extra."

The innkeeper nods to a young girl sweeping the foyer, who scampers off to run my errands.

"*Wolf Bowborn.*"

The sudden, unexpected sound of my name has me immediately laying a hand on my knife hilt, preparing to return to those dark days of the early work I did for Rian, but as I face the common room, an astounded laugh barks out of me.

I gape. "Folke Bladeborn?"

Sitting alone at the corner table, a half-empty flagon of ale as his only companion, is perhaps the sole person on earth I would consider a friend.

Folke is a decade my senior, his tidily matted locks already graying at his temples, but the look suits him. His light, russet brown face is pockmarked from acne in his youth, but the scars don't stop women from admiring him. His straight teeth don't hurt, either—a rarity in a town like Blackwater.

He grins broadly. "Come here, you devil."

I saunter over to his table, shaking my head at the odds of having run into him here—although perhaps it's not such a slim chance after all, given the type of traveler Blackwater draws. Folke and I trained together in the Golden Sentinel army. Both bastards by birth, we were given the surname "Bladeborn" to mean soldiers, and he still carries it. After he was wounded in a skirmish, the Valveres released him from service due to his permanently incapacitated leg. Still, a man has to eat, so Folke became a spy for whoever would employ him.

"You'll forgive me for not standing," Folke jokes, patting his bum leg. His cane leans against the wall.

I drop into the empty seat across from him, clasping his hand in greeting. His grip is as firm as ever. "They gave the pathetic likes of you a room here?"

"That they did. And what brings you to this hellhole, eh? Last I heard, you'd left this life behind. Gone straight."

"Yeah. Well. If that's ever possible." I glance toward

the stairs—I need to catch the servants on their way up with Sabine's bathwater so that I can unlock the door.

"I'll raise a glass to that." He lifts his flagon, notices I have nothing to drink, and then starts to flag down the bartender's attention, but I shake my head.

"I can't catch up at the moment, old friend. Regrettably. I've pressing duties." I glance toward the stairs again.

His dark eyes twinkle with mischief. "It wouldn't have anything to do with some stark naked beauty everyone's been buzzing about, eh? Judging by the gossip, I came down from my room too late to steal an eyeful."

I rest my big fists on the table, hunching forward over its candle, grinding my teeth at the thought of every man in Blackwater's impure thoughts about Sabine.

Folke laughs. "Easy, big fellow. Ah. So it *is* about a girl. Who is she?"

"Rian's new bride."

"Fuck." He downs the rest of his ale in one go, then wipes his mouth with his sleeve and leans toward me across the table. "You're properly fucked, aren't you, Wolf?"

"Why would you say that? Because I'm here with your ugly ass?"

"Because a man doesn't bristle at the mere mention of a woman unless he's extremely interested in fucking her."

I stem the slight tremor in my hands, not wanting Folke to know how close he's struck to gold. Folke's keen eyes mark my subtle tells anyway. He's a spy, after all, trained to pick up on clues. He blows out a long, resigned puff of air that makes the candle flame ripple. His voice is soft with pity when he speaks. "It's like that, then, is it? More than lust."

My hands ball into tighter fists. I messed up when I kissed Sabine, it's true, but it was just the effect of going a few weeks without sex and having a pretty girl splayed across my lap. It wasn't anything more. It *can't* be anything more.

"You love her?" Folke asks in an uncharacteristically tender tone, like me loving Sabine would be the most terrible and most wonderful thing in the world.

"Of course not. Don't be fucking ridiculous. She belongs to Rian."

Folke holds his hands palms up with a shrug as if to suggest that the two things are not mutually exclusive. She can belong to Rian, and I can also be in love with her.

Which is utter horseshit.

I stand, sending the chair sliding back a few inches, and give Folke a smirk that I hope hides how hard my heart is pounding. I rib him, "It was good to see you, Folke, even if you are looking like an old man these days." But I pause before turning away. "What brings you to town, anyway?" Though my tone is light, we both know the true nature of his work—it would be a shock if someone doesn't end up dead while he's in town.

His brown eyes catch the candlelight. He drums his knuckles on the table. *Rat-a-tat. Rat-a-tat.* For a second, I feel sure he will speak of Volkish raiders. *I* can't be the one to bring it up. I'd sound like a raving madman if I started spouting off about woken goldenclaws and Volkish bandits who crossed the wall after five hundred years of being cut off. There are enough fanatical street preachers professing that the sleeping gods will soon wake; I don't need to add to their ranks. Besides, people have been prophesizing their awakening for centuries.

And what's happened? Fuck all, that's what.

Still, my pulse taps like torturous water drips as I wait for his answer.

He leans forward over the candle, eyes skimming the common room for any sign of eavesdroppers, but we're alone except for an old man in the corner. "Business that concerns Old Coros."

"Old Coros? You're working for King Joruun?"

He wavers in his answer. "I'm working for the royal advisors. The king's health is . . . failing." His eyes bore into me with an alarming urgency. "They're concerned about what could happen to the throne after his passing. If he doesn't name a successor, a power vacuum will open, and there are those who are eager to fill it."

King Joruun's health has been failing for twenty years, but something about Folke's tone makes me suspect the end is nearer than anyone thinks. I prompt, "Who?"

"I'm in Blackwater to meet with a former priest who claims the Grand Cleric is scheming to transform Astagnon into a theocracy."

I snort. "Fucking priests. We had a run-in with them on the ride. Five of them, armed, couldn't stop a naked girl from crossing the street—they can't overthrow a kingdom."

Folke scratches his thumbnail along his bottom lip. "Well, they aren't the only ones with an eye toward the throne, if rumors are to be believed."

"Who else?"

"Your employer."

I shake my head to clear out my ears, certain I didn't hear him right, even with my heightened senses. "Rian?" I scrape my nails back through my hair. "No. You're mistaken. He would have told me if he had any aspirations for the throne."

Folke's steady stare makes me second guess myself, but what he says is impossible. Rian trusts me more than anyone, which is why he sent me to guard Sabine. The Valveres already have the lion's share of wealth and power in Astagnon; do they need the crown, too?

"The Valveres have a legitimate claim," Folke says. "Lord Berolt is a distant cousin of the late king's."

Yeah, *very* distant. I'm aware of Lord Berolt's supposed claim to royal blood, but I'm also keenly aware that the royal genealogist is known to accept bribes over five thousand coins.

The stairs creak. Two young men carrying boiling pots ascend toward the third floor. I root in my pocket for the key to Sabine's room.

"I have to go. This news . . . You're wrong. Lord Rian wouldn't lie to me."

"He's called the *Lord of Liars*, you idiot." Folke's words have sternness but also fondness, like an older brother chiding his younger sibling.

My nails bite into my palms. A vein twitches in my arm. I've punched men for milder insinuations about Lord Rian. Somehow, Folke is mistaken. A plot to steal the Astagnonian throne is extreme, even by Valvere standards. If Rian was even slightly entertaining the idea, I would have been the first one he'd confide in. Hell, he'd conscript me to storm Hekkelveld Castle, the home of the king, and throw open the gates for him.

Then again, I've been in the woods more often than not the past few years. Could I have missed something? Am I out of Rian's circle of trust?

"Stay alert out there, Wolf," Folke says, not joking this time.

I knock my fist on the table, both an acknowledgment of his warning and to emphasize again that I trust my master and won't bend on that.

"You as well, old friend."

CHAPTER 15
SABINE

Someone knocks on the door.

I jerk back from the open window with a gasp. The little nut-brown swift flits from the windowsill to a nearby branch, my message fastened around its leg with a thread pulled from the curtains. To write the note, I had to make do with a scrap of torn wallpaper, and a stick from the cold fireplace with a burned charcoal end. The kindly swift agreed to deliver my message to Adan and focused intently on my directions. I think it understood. I hope it did.

Go, little friend. Hurry! I urge it with a wave of my fingers. I swing the window shut as the person in the hall knocks harder.

"Sabine, it's me," Basten barks. "The water for your bath is here." He pauses. "Are you decent?"

Decent? Have I ever been decent on this ride? *Um, no, Basten, I'm naked. Like always.*

I tug the bedsheet off and wrap it around me like a shroud. "Yes."

He unlocks the door to admit a pair of young men who strain under heavy cauldrons of hot water. Basten glares at them as they head toward the copper tub, making it clear he wants them to keep their eyes on the boiling water, not me. They empty their buckets and quickly shuffle out under Basten's close scrutiny.

Basten closes the door behind them. Steam rises from the copper tub. The scent of lavender soap permeates the air.

He drops a bundle of clothes on the bed.

"What's that?" I ask, curious.

"A dress. Undergarments. For you." At my confused look, he adds nonchalantly, "I thought you must be tired of wearing my shirt, given how often you tell me I smell."

He bought me clothes? It *is* appealing to dress in real clothes—clean clothes!—even though I'll only have the chance to wear them for a single day. Here, in this room. I can't go even as far as the common room in a dress, or Rian will know I broke his rules. Still, I'm touched that Basten thought to grant me this kindness.

I wind a curl of my hair around my finger and say quietly, "Thank you."

Basten shrugs it off.

Petting my hair, I eye the hot water enticingly.

He picks up on the hint. "Go ahead, while it's hot. I'll keep my back turned while you bathe."

He tromps to the window, thrusting open the pane I so recently shut, and pretends to take great interest in the goings on of Blackwater.

I sneak glances at his back as I shed the sheet and slip into the bathwater. If he'd returned only a minute sooner, he would have caught me sending the swift to deliver my message to Adan. If he'd found me out, would he have told Lord Rian? Would he have punished me?

Given my meager supplies, my message to Adan was necessarily brief:

Call off the plan. I'm sorry. I love you.

The last line was a stretch, but I panicked and added it out of guilt. Whether I'm in love with Adan or not, it's simply too risky to involve him in any escape plans. Basten has proven with terrifying certainty what he's capable of, and I can only guess what other tracking resources my future husband has at his disposal. If I were caught with Adan, they'd likely hang him for seducing a lord's betrothed.

I climb into the tub and recline back. As the hot water unwinds my aching thighs, and washes away days of grime from the road, my worries slowly unlock.

Basten was right about one thing: I really *don't* know Adan. What I thought was love at first . . . now I'm not certain. Maybe it was just a handsome face and a friendly smile. Maybe it was Adan's promise to take me away from everything. Maybe I was just desperate for a tender touch —any touch—after so much neglect.

I have to admit that a small part of me is, shamefully, glad to call off the escape with Adan. I crave freedom more than anything, but I'm not certain anymore that I want it with a boy who is essentially a stranger.

Besides . . . I can't stop thinking about the kiss with Basten. If I truly loved Adan, wouldn't I have thought of him when I let Basten put his lips all over me? Wouldn't I feel more guilty?

Because I don't feel guilty at all.

I scrub the scented soap bar over my skin, washing away layers of dirt, and study Basten's muscular shoulders straining his shirt.

That kiss. By the Immortals, that *kiss.*

It took my breath away, and I might be inexperienced in the ways of men's bodies, but even a rock would know that Basten was *fully* invested in our tryst, too. In the weeks we've spent together, he's only broken his absolute fealty to his master twice: the first time was to let me wear his shirt, and the second was when he kissed me.

Me.

I'm his weakness.

I'm the only thing that makes his resolve falter.

And maybe I can use this fact. It's painfully evident that, given Basten's powers, I'll never escape from him. But there's a chance that I could redirect his loyalty, just as Myst suggested.

I groan inwardly. *She'd gloat to no end to know she was right.*

Still, would it even work? Would Basten ever choose me over Rian? He's so damn stubborn in his devotion to a man who clearly cares nothing for him. I want to shake him, to save him. To show him he's better than someone's servant. He's smarter than even he realizes—he uses vulgar words like a brute, and he clearly had no formal education, but he has a naturally sharp mind, and he's picked up polished language from his time around Lord Rian. If he wanted to, he could speak like a nobleman. Between his intelligence, stature, and godkissed abilities, he could amass more wealth and power than the Valveres. He could *rule* that family.

I wish he saw what I see—the potential of an uncut gem.

"In Charmont," Basten asks, while keeping his attention out the window, "You said the Patron mentioned the Grand Cleric, didn't you?"

I wonder why he's suddenly thinking back on Charmont. "Yes, he said the Grand Cleric wanted to see me. I can't imagine why." I sink further into the tub, splashing the water gently so it makes a lovely rippling against my skin. Basten's jaw twitches at the sound. "Why do you ask?"

"No reason." But something must be on his mind, because not a minute later, he says, "What do they say in Bremcote about Volkany?"

"Volkany? The cursed kingdom?" What on earth has him asking about that forgotten place? It was walled off five hundred years ago after the war, and the only times I've heard it mentioned were in stories meant to frighten children. *Bloodthirsty godkissed soldiers from Volkany will come turn your blood to ice if you don't eat your cabbage.*

"I don't know—nothing, really. The Sisters at the convent believed Immortal Vale's resting place was somewhere in the Volkish forest. That he'd wake soon, and fae would rule the earth again. The usual refrain. They also believed the moon was a giant firefly . . . I wouldn't put too much stock in their words." I give him a slant-eyed look. "Why, are you trying to give me nightmares?"

"Nightmares?"

"You know. Volkany's beasts. Birds who spread disease like rain. Monstrous horses that summon fire. Or their vicious soldiers with a fondness for impaling their enemies, then making the corpses dance with magic?"

His forehead is so pinched that his eyebrows nearly touch.

I flick a small splash of water his way. "Come on, Basten. I'm only joking. All that happened centuries ago."

"Hmm." He scrubs his hand over his stubble, thinking.

I finish scrubbing my scalp and hair, and then dunk myself under the water to rinse off, coming up with a gasp for air. I climb out, dripping, and perch on the bathtub's edge while I towel off. "You should bathe, too, while the water is still warm."

I think he might press more about whatever has him concerned with Volkany, but he drops it. Without turning my way, he gestures toward the pile of clothes on the bed. "Dress yourself so that I can turn around."

I deadpan, "Yeah, gods forbid you see me naked."

He snorts, but still grants me privacy until I shimmy into the long white chemise that laces over my breasts, and then pull on a mauve wool outer gown that drapes over it. The fabric is new and clean, and as I smooth my hands over its folds, I marvel at how I feel like a different person wearing clothes.

It's like I've been an animal these past few days, sleeping in the dirt, eating roasted meat from a fire, wearing nothing but bad dreams. Suddenly I've rejoined the actual world, and I feel both incredibly relieved and, strangely, a little lost, like I don't know what to do with my hands anymore.

"Your turn in the tub," I say.

After he turns around, Basten takes his time studying me in the dress while I finish toweling off my hair. I can't quite read his expression. He looks like he's trying to solve some secret code in a language he doesn't know.

Finally, he says with a note of fascination, "I've never seen you in clothes."

It's true. Since he walked through my father's gate, the most I've worn is a silk robe or his own oversized shirt. Heat blooms on my cheeks as I straighten a twisted hem on my left sleeve cuff. It's ironic, but for some reason, I feel *more* embarrassed standing before him clothed than naked.

To ease the heavy silence, I blurt out, "If it's true what is said about men's lustfulness, then I'm sure my present state must disappoint you."

I meant it as a joke, but Basten doesn't laugh. He remains grave as he holds my gaze with an iron focus and says, "A wrapped present can be even more enticing than an unwrapped one, my lady."

A shiver dances up my spine as I think of Basten taking his slow, intentional time unwrapping me from my coverings to pounce on the gifts within.

Great. Now my cheeks are *blazing*.

I trade places with him at the window as he drags his shirt over his head and tosses it on the bed. Even though I keep my back turned, the sounds of him stripping out of his boots and pants and easing into the warm water with a masculine sigh stoke my curiosity until it's aflame. I've seen Basten's bare chest almost every night, but what lies below on a man's body is a mystery. All I have to go off are the illustrations in Immortal Alyssantha's sections of the Book of the Immortals: One, in particular, comes to mind, featuring Immortal Alyssantha and Immortal Samaur, naked together with their fey lines glowing. The God of Sun's member enters the goddess's sacred center while her ankles rest on his shoulders; her head is tipped back in ecstasy, his tanned hand squeezes her breast.

It's all I can do not to wonder if Basten has ever had a woman in that position.

The innkeeper brings us supper, and we sit at the table and eat with actual silverware like two civilized people. It feels foreign and strange to be with Basten like this, instead of crouched around a campfire, and it thrills me as much as throws me off balance.

I'm so busy savoring the wine and warm-baked, buttery bread that I don't even notice we've talked all evening, until Basten lights a candle. To my surprise, dusk slipped in at some point and darkened the room.

I stifle a yawn.

"You should sleep, Lady Sabine. Tomorrow, we'll press on north, and be in Duren within two days." He stands and arranges his rucksack on the rug, by the fireplace, as though he's planning on using it as a pillow.

It's now or never.

Slowly, I untie the wool overdress and tug it over my head, leaving me in the long chemise. I can't bring myself to meet his eyes as I draw back the bedcovers.

I clear my throat. "You don't have to sleep on the floor, you know. We shared a blanket in the forest. It's no different to share a bed."

He considers the soft, clean sheets as I slide into them, making an exaggerated show of leaving the other side open in invitation. But he doesn't make a move toward the bed—yet.

I pat the other pillow insistently, keeping my voice light. "I can see how your shoulder pains you—you need a night on a mattress. Otherwise, how will you be able to throw punches at all the men leering at me tomorrow?"

He gives a faint laugh, though his eyes remain serious. Wordlessly, he dims the lamp. Then, finally decided, he tugs off his shirt so that he's only in his pants.

"Very kind of you, Lady Sabine."

The mattress groans as his weight sinks onto it. It's all I can do not to roll into the dip his massive body creates.

I ease back against my pillow, my heart walloping. "Good night, Basten."

"Good night, my lady."

In the lantern's dim light, I stare up at the rafters. My body is exhausted, yet I've never felt more awake. Though we've slept next to each other before, something about sharing a bed *does* feel different, despite what I assured him. I'm aware of every crack of his joints and rustle of his pillow. The tension is so visceral that it feels like there's a third person in bed with us.

I briefly close my eyes and recall Myst's advice.

Make him loyal to you.

Gathering all my courage, I roll over to face him. Gods,

I hope he can't hear how fast my heartbeat flutters. But of course, he can.

"Basten?" I whisper. "I'm worried about what happens when we get to Duren. When I marry Rian and—and the wedding night."

He has one arm folded under his pillow, his raven-black hair loose and sinfully silky now that it's clean. I have to stop myself from reaching out to stroke it. He's close enough that I can see the dark stubble dusting his chin.

His eyes simmer like he's sensed danger and knows to proceed with caution. Gruffly, he says, "Trust me, Lady Sabine, no man would be disappointed to find you in his marital bed."

My throat bobs in a dry swallow as I try to calm the nerves that his gravely voice stirs in my belly. "It's just that . . . I don't know what to do. To please a man, I mean."

His jaw parts as he drags in a breath, like breathing through his nose alone isn't enough anymore. He says haltingly, "Some men like an inexperienced woman."

I slowly trace my finger along the lines of the bedspread's quilted pattern, watching the rise and fall of his breath beneath the covers. Demurely, I look up through my eyelashes. "Do you?"

Basten lets slip a stifled moan. A tremor shudders throughout his body like he's been brushed by feathered wingtips. He seems to be at a loss for words. Eventually, he says evasively, "I've never been with a virgin. I wouldn't know."

I can feel him trying to throw up walls of resistance

with every word. He wants me, I'm sure of it, but he wants to serve his master more. His stubborn loyalty is like a set of iron shackles around his wrists.

But I'm determined to win his devotion at any cost. So, I channel my inner Immortal Alyssantha. Digging for every ounce of courage I possess, I snake my bare foot beneath the covers in his direction until my big toe strokes his ankle.

His eyes sink closed. Another groan escapes his lips.

"But you've had women before, surely?" I ask, feigning innocence.

His throat bobs. "Yes."

"And you know what to do."

His voice is hoarse. "Yes."

When he opens his eyes, his gaze fixes on my lips like he doesn't dare look directly into my eyes. I bring my thumb up to my mouth, which has his attention, and bite down gently on my fingernail. "Maybe you could train me? Like how you taught me to fight, in the woods?"

My heart hammers like a blacksmith shop. Am I really doing this? I've never done anything so bold, and it's both terrifying and exhilarating at the same time. I feel like I'm playing with fire, and I don't know whether I want to get burned or not.

Basten rips his attention from my lips and sears me with a hard look. His eyelids are half-lowered, his eyes simmering. He knows exactly what I'm trying to do, and he doesn't appreciate how much he likes it. In a warning voice, he murmurs, "Sabine, what the devil are you—"

On impulse, I press my finger to his lips and whisper in a rush, "I'm not asking you to break your vow to your master. I know I belong to him—but, well, you could pretend to *be* him. Show me how to please him. You'd be helping him. And me. What's more loyal than that?"

His look is heavy with warning, even the threat of punishment, for suggesting something so indecent. *But he isn't saying no.* The mattress groans with the strain of his breathing. On impulse, he throws back the covers and rises from bed, pacing over the worn rug.

"*Fuck,*" he curses sharply.

Sensing his indecision, I let silence do my work for me. Sitting up in bed with the sheets pulled up over my chemise, I gently bite my lip as he prowls back and forth, while pinning me with a glare so licentious it's about to ignite the curtains.

Back and forth he paces, back and forth, never taking his eyes off me. Finally, he stops. His chest heaves hard as he repeats, "Pretend?"

My heart shoots into my throat. By the Immortals, is this really happening? I force myself to nod slowly as I whisper a quiet assurance. "No one ever has to know."

He paces once more in a final, last-ditch effort to resist. Then, decided, he slowly prowls back to the bed. His energy has shifted. The air crackles, but it stems from anticipation now, not resistance.

He leans over me with a predator's menace that makes me shrink back against the pillows. I stare up at him as he grips my chin, letting his thumb drag over my bottom lip.

"I swore a vow. I broke it once, and I won't again. But if you want to know how a man takes a woman, I'll tell you. I'll tell you exactly what I would do with you if you were my bride."

His thumb sinks between my lips, feeling along the hard edge of my teeth and grazing my tongue in a way that feels staggeringly depraved.

"First," he says in a low voice, "I would kiss you on the lips. Here." His thumb paints down along my jaw. "And then I would kiss you here." His hand glides down my throat to the dip at the base of my neck. "Then here."

A moan travels up my throat, emerging as a whimper. His touch is both rough and confident as he marks my sensitive skin. Anticipation snaps throughout my body as I wonder where he'll touch next. Beneath the sheets, my legs squeeze together to try to quell the heat building there. I sink further into the pillow until he's directly over me, caging me with one arm braced against the headboard.

I swallow. "Then what?"

His eyes flash with desire. "Then," he says, moving his hand to the laces across my chest, "I would do something about this chemise." His rough fingers skim over the laces without unfastening them, merely dragging back and forth in a way that's so tantalizing it might as well be torture. He's so close to unwrapping me, but he won't.

So determined not to break that vow.

"Once you were bare, I would kiss you here." He rubs his thumb against my godkiss birthmark. "And here." His hand falls to the chemise's neckline. "And here." The pad of his thumb presses over the chemise on the hard bud of my nipple.

The rub of fabric between my nipple and his finger

creates friction that infuses me with desire. I swallow a gasp as I arch my back. When I finally catch my breath, I give a raspy, "And then what?"

Basten drops his head to my ear in a way that makes his loose hair caress my cheek like a feather. His voice turns wickedly deep. "Next, I would peel you out of these clothes. I would put my mouth on every curve. I'd lick every freckle. I'd worship every inch of you I could get my lips on."

Dear gods. I'm speechless.

"Since it would be your first time," he goes on, "I'd go slow. I'd make your body as ready as a ripe peach, dripping with juices, begging to be plucked."

My thoughts go numb. It's like my mind is a candle that someone snuffed out and lit a bonfire in my body instead. The shudders of anticipation scrolling through me are pure torture. I agonize over how his lips are so achingly close to grazing my ear, but he won't actually kiss me.

More. I need more.

The bed frame squeaks as he shifts his weight to lean further over me. One of his hands draws the covers down to my waist while the other paints a slow caress over my belly, fingers kneading the chemise like he wants to rip it off.

This has already gone too far. I know it has. I meant to seduce Basten into helping me escape, but I didn't expect to elicit such exquisite need in myself, too. It's not too late to stop it, and yet every time I think about turning my back to him and losing his hot touch, my body forcefully objects. My skin's never felt a man's touch like this before.

My lungs are hungry, my breath shallow with the same fierce exhilaration as when I rode Myst at breakneck speed through the forest.

Suddenly, it isn't about seduction anymore. I'm not sure it ever was. It isn't about using Basten for some distant gain.

It's about *me*.

It's about that feeling I had while riding Myst. I feel that same yearning for freedom now. Whether it's riding free on a horse, or choosing the man I want to take my virginity, it's all the same—determining my own fate instead of letting others do it for me.

And I want to choose Basten.

So, *so* badly.

He gazes down at me with a challenge. We're both waiting for the other to stop this. But neither of us does. I can feel the moment tip on its side until it's out of control, and I know there's no going back now. I roll my hips beneath his open hand on my belly. With my free hand, I trail my fingers along my neckline.

Meeting his questioning look head-on, I murmur, "Don't stop now. Then what would you do?"

His eyes glaze over with raw desire. Not breaking eye contact, he begins to bunch up my chemise's fabric around my hips, inch by inch, in painfully tantalizing slowness. His voice takes on a wicked velvet rumble. "You've ridden horseback often, so you're probably already torn. That's good, because it will hurt less when a man fills you with his cock for the first time. Regardless, I would ensure it's the pleasure you'd remember, not the pain."

I can't breathe. I can't think. My skin begs for Basten to touch everywhere at once. To do each and every one of the filthy things he inventoried. I squeeze my thighs together, but it's impossible to tame the writhing heat at the base of my stomach. Like a flood, it spreads through every nerve until I feel as fragile as glass, begging to be shattered.

I moan his name. *"Basten."*

He ghosts my ear with his lips as he says huskily, breathing harder now, "And then I'd toy with your pretty cunt to get you ready to take me." His hand finds the chemise's hem bunched around my hips. "First with my fingers. Then with my tongue."

I moan louder.

His fingers fondle the inside of my thigh. Back and forth in slow, long, torturous strokes from my knee up to my groin and back. My hips writhe, hungry for more spoils, urging him to move his hand higher, to the tight little knot that so badly needs his attention.

I grip the back of his bicep so hard that it must leave bruises. His breath teases my neck, his lips so damn close to mine that I think I'll burst if he doesn't kiss me.

"If I were Lord Rian," he says, his breath coming hard and fast, "I would make damn sure you came your first time. Not once, but again, and again, until your body shuddered in my arms with its last ounce of strength, and I could smell the slickness sliding down your thigh."

Holy gods. My fingernails curl deeper into his arm. I might even be breaking the skin. I don't care. This game we've played has been fun, but I want my prize, now. No one has ever spiked my emotions as much as Basten, and I can't fathom any man but him taking me.

Not Adan.

Not Lord Rian.

Basten is the man my heart wants and my body craves. Basten is my freedom. Basten is how I will change my mantra after years of the same desperate plea: It's no longer "*They can have my body, but my mind is my own.*" It's now "*My body and my mind are mine.*" No one can use my body anymore unless it's my choice to give it to them.

And I want—I need—to give it to Basten.

I tilt my head so my lips skirt the stubble along his jaw's edge. Breathy against his skin, I say, "What if I don't want you to be gentle the first time you fuck me?"

I wait with bated breath to see what reaction this gets.

The last ounce of Basten's resolve vanishes as thoroughly as though it never existed in the first place. After one long, covetous look, he pounces on me with all the energy of a huntsman who doesn't intend to let his quarry get away. He curls one big hand around the back of my neck to tilt my chin toward him, as his other hand gropes down my hip to grab an entire handful of my ass cheek.

No more games, no more waiting. His lips are achingly close to mine. Heat prickles along each ridge of my spine, setting my nerves on fire. I need to hold onto something. My hands go around his neck, fingers weaving through his hair like clinging onto Myst's mane.

But he still doesn't kiss me.

He won't break the vow.

Damn him. *Damn him!*

I tug on the back of his neck, whimpering as I try to pull his lips to mine, rolling my hips under him.

His voice is hoarse. "You have no idea how much I want—"

His voice cuts off mid-thought as his head jerks to the side, like he heard something. His eyes are suddenly clear, alert. His body goes perfectly rigid overtop me.

Blinking hard, dizzy from desire, I push up to one elbow. "What is it?"

"Smoke." His eyes zero in on a spot on the wall while focusing on his sense of smell. He says tightly, "The common room is on fire."

This is such a stark turn of events that my brain can't switch back on fast enough. I shake my head. *I don't want this to end!*

Helplessly, I object, "I don't smell anything . . . "

But my words trail off. Of course Basten, with his godkissed senses, would smell smoke long before I would.

He sits upright, gazing down at me with dilated pupils, his breathing still fast. It's clear there is only one thing in this world he wants right now more than to fuck me—and that's to protect me. He drags a hand over his face. Instantly, he switches into guard mode. "I have to get you out of here."

He grabs my wrists.

My body is still slick with desire. My pebbled nipples haven't gotten the message about the danger. The dull throb between my legs demands attention, and frustration swells in my chest as he drags me out of bed.

"Basten, wait!"

I lick my lips, trying to find words. But my brain is

blank. I don't know how to tell him how much I wanted him, how much I still want him. That now that I have a taste of freedom, I don't intend ever to go back to the way things were before.

His expression softens in understanding. Briefly, he cups the curve of my jaw. "This . . . You . . . " He starts again. "We have to go, Sabine. Get dressed."

Finally, I snap out of my haze and realize how dangerous it is to stay in a burning building. Dragging a hand over my scalp, I take quick stock of where I left the overdress on the bottom bed rail. I tug it over my chemise, then crouch to look for my shoes under the table.

Without warning, my heel pushes down on a loose nail sticking up from one of the floorboards. Pain stabs through my foot. My knees buckle. Dropping to all fours, I let out a cry.

Basten is by my side in an instant. "Sabine?"

"My foot!" I gasp.

He makes quick work of inspecting the puncture wound that's oozing blood. Acting fast, he swings his rucksack over one shoulder, and then picks me up off the floor. Carrying me in his arms, he tromps across the room and kicks the door open.

Smoke billows up the stairs. A woman screams from a different floor. Doors slam, and feet gallop as the other guests hurry to flee.

I wrap my arms around Basten's neck, burying my face in his massive chest, as he carries me through the smoke, and out into the night's safety.

CHAPTER 16
WOLF

Smoke billows out of the windows and doors of the Manywaters Inn. The street is thick with coughing guests who have escaped the fire, and more people rush from nearby houses to help put out the flames. With the Innis River just a stone's throw away, people swarm the bridge, lowering buckets tied to ropes to fill with water.

As I carry Sabine, I scan the crowd for a familiar face, but Folke isn't among the survivors in the street. With his wounded leg, he can't climb down stairs easily. If he's not here, there's a chance he's still in the building.

"Have you seen a man with a cane?" I shout to a burly older man who is leading the efforts to put out the fire. "Light brown skin. Mid-thirties. Graying hair."

Unable to spare me much attention, he quickly shakes his head.

Fuck!

The flames throw heat on us as the inferno reaches the second floor. I tote Sabine through the crowd, to the recessed doorway of a fishmonger's shop across the street. I ease her onto the stoop, then set to investigating the wound on her foot. The nail cut deep but cleanly, which means as long as I can stop the bleeding, she should be fine. There's always the risk of infection, but we'll be in Duren the day after tomorrow, and Lord Rian has teams of healers at his disposal—even one with a godkiss that can mend torn skin. He'll ensure that she's showered with medical attention.

I rip the hem off her dress and use the fabric strip to bind her bleeding wound. She gives a hacking cough, her lungs clogged from having passed through the smoke. Her eyes are watering, ringed in red. She rubs them with the back of her hand like they ache.

I smooth a hand down her hair. "Sabine, can you walk?"

"I think so." Her voice is scratchy from smoke, but doesn't waver. My little violet is so damn brave. She rests her hands on my shoulders as I help her to her feet. Delicately, she exerts some pressure on the ball of her left foot, testing it out. She gives a shaky nod. "It's okay if I don't put much weight on it."

A dusting of soot streaks her cheek. I can't resist rubbing it away with my thumb, stroking her soft skin with my calloused finger, wanting to erase any imperfection on her flawless face. My heart thrashes inside my chest like a trapped animal. She's safe, but it terrifies me to think of what might have happened if I hadn't gotten her away from the fire.

One of the inn's upstairs windows shatters. Screams come from the street, where the men and women throwing buckets of water on the structure are struck by sharp glass shards. With a mighty boom, flames erupt out of the broken window.

I pull Sabine into my arms, holding her tight, even though we're safely out of harm's way. Then, I cup my hands around her face, guiding her to look me in the eyes so I can be sure she understands me. "I want you to go to the stables. Take the rucksack—it'll be stolen in a second if we leave it here. Get Myst. I'll be right behind you."

Her round, glistening eyes fill with worry as she latches onto my shirt with one hand. Breathless, she asks, "Why, where are you going?"

"The fire—I have a friend in there. I have to make sure he made it out."

I left things with Folke on a bad note. There are painfully few people in this world I'd consider a friend, and I'd pass through hell for any of them. I can't walk away before I know that he survived.

Another upstairs window explodes behind us, and Sabine flinches and leans into my chest. My hands automatically circle her back. Briefly, I let my head sink on top of hers, so I can breathe in the scent of her hair.

Not five minutes ago, I was willing to tear both our worlds apart to be with her. I was so tempted to stab Rian in the back, and let the sleeping gods damn me for eternity, just to act on what could happen between those sheets. My body is still hot and hard with yearning.

If the fire hadn't interrupted us . . .

It would have been a mistake to sleep with Sabine. But fuck, what a wonderful mistake.

"Go." I help her into the rucksack's straps, then urge

her toward the street. "Quickly. You'll be safe—Myst will protect you. I'll be right there."

She gives me one last wide-eyed look that's both fearful and trusting before darting down the street, struggling under the rucksack's weight, limp-running toward the stables.

I watch her go as long as I can, but I can't delay. The fire is spreading. Folke still hasn't emerged from the building. As I hurry through the crowd toward the burning inn, I promise myself that Sabine will be all right. She's dressed, so she doesn't stand out. Her long hair and looks would normally garner plenty of interest from the riffraff out at this hour in Blackwater, but everyone's attention is on the fire, not the girl limping away.

Sweating, soot-streaked men hurl bucket after bucket of water on the inn's facade, but the flames have already climbed too high to save the structure. Knowing this, the men divert their efforts toward wetting down the neighboring buildings to try to quell the flames' spread.

Shouldering my way through the crowd, I head straight for the burned-out front door.

The burly older man grabs me, coughing. "What are you doing? Are you crazy? You can't go in there!"

I throw off his arm and plunge into the burning inn. The common room is clogged with smoke, forcing me to press one sleeve over my nose and mouth. My eyes burn. Flames feast on the wooden tables and lick their way up the curtains. Broken earthenware dishes litter the floor.

Fighting through the smoke, I make my way to the stairs.

"Folke?" I yell up, though the fire's roar drowns out my voice.

There's a crash behind me. Sparks rain down as a ceiling joist cracks. Raising my arm against the shower of sparks, I see a figure stagger through the doorway between the common room and the kitchen.

It's Folke. *Thank the gods.* He leans on a broken stairway spindle as a makeshift cane. His face is streaked in soot, and a dark substance that might be blood. His rope-like locks are a mess. But my initial relief folds in on itself when, with his free hand, he raises a crossbow in my direction.

What the fuck?

My ingrained training kicks in with an order to dodge out of his range. I hurtle myself against the inn's reception desk just as Folke lets loose the arrow. The arrow's wake whips the air as it speeds by me, missing my neck by an inch, to lodge in the rear wall.

I'm hit with a burst of anger. I explode on him, "Folke, *what the hell—*"

"Behind you!" he shouts.

I pivot just in time to see a knife blade slash toward my shoulder. I evade on instinct, bending backward over the desk, so the blade slices through the air above me. A man in a dark cloak whirls back around with well-honed moves and raises the blade again.

I don't have the luxury of time to figure out what the hell is going on. My attacker strikes again. He slashes his blade with such startling speed that I can barely duck in time. If I didn't have my godkissed ability to detect the subtle tells in his movements, he would have slit my throat. I still wasn't quite fast enough, and the blade's tip grazed my scalp. A bolt of pain ricochets through my head.

I scramble behind the desk, keeping it between us as a buffer.

By the fucking Immortals.

His speed is inhuman—he's godkissed.

This makes the fight infinitely more challenging. In my youth, fighting in Jocki's rings, I was paired with other godkissed fighters whenever they could find one. A four-teen-year-old girl with godkissed strength slammed me to the ground so hard that my tailbone still aches when it rains. A godkissed boy from the distant deserts of Kravada could call the winds to toss me around like a leaf. Still, I managed to defeat both of them. There's only been one godkissed fighter who ever bested me, and his gift was goddamn *speed.*

Folke knocks another arrow and raises the crossbow. "Wolf, Pruitt's Creek!"

Pruitt's Creek. He's referring to a skirmish we were in against rebel agitators hiding out in a logging camp south of Old Coros. We lit their timber stores on fire to add the cover of smoke while we attacked. I instantly understand the maneuver he's suggesting.

The cloaked attacker circles the desk's edges so fast that he's almost a blur. Struggling to stay a step ahead of him, I scramble into the center of the common room. He's there in a flash, but I'm able to anticipate his trajectory with my keen hearing, and put the charred tables between us.

Folke keeps his crossbow at the ready, waiting, waiting.

Smoke now fills the entire upper half of the common room. My throat is raw, and my body wants to double over with a coughing fit, but I squelch the urge. Plunging myself into smoke may not be the smartest idea, but it's the best chance I have. My opponent, while fast, can't pursue what he can't see.

I, however, can hear his heartbeat as clearly as if it was a resounding gong.

He stalks through the smoke more cautiously now, unable to see where I'm hiding. I can only imagine his eyes are as blurry and stinging as my own, doubling how difficult it is to spot me. This is how it went down in Pruitt's Creek—I lured the agitators into the smoke, where I had the advantage.

Once I hear his heartbeat closing in, I bunch my leg muscles and, with a battle cry, hurl my full weight against him. He might be fast, but I outweigh him significantly.

We slam to the floor. The air pushes out of his lungs, and I use the opportunity to smash a fist into his nose. I won't have long—once he's recovered, he'll use his speed to strike me faster than I can block him.

"Folke!" I shout.

"On it! Move out of the damn way!"

Still dazed, the attacker struggles against me, but I'm able to pin him to the floor with my knee. I toss my hair back, straightening to give Folke a clean shot at his head.

I hear the rasp of Folke's finger on the trigger before the arrow is even free. At that exact moment, the cloaked man snaps back to attention. Blinking to clear his watery eyes, he uses his godkiss to slam a fist into my chest. He isn't the strongest man I've fought, but he immediately brings his fist back for another strike before I've had time to recover.

But then, it's too late for him.

Folke's arrow slams into his neck. The man's body wracks with pain as he claps a hand over the blood spurting from his neck. I keep my knee dug into his chest, not taking any chances, until a gurgle of blood spills out of his throat, and he finally goes still.

Letting out a deep exhale, I crawl off him, on hands and knees on the floor, where the air is clearer. Finally, I let out the hacking cough that's been torturing my lungs. Phlegm and soot scratch my throat as I hack onto the floor.

"Folke." Mustering my strength, I push to my feet and stagger to where my friend is slumped against the door frame between the kitchen and the common room. Blood flows steadily out of a cut on his temple, and more of it stains the front of his shirt—but at least he's upright. I clap a steadying hand on his shoulder. "Who the fuck is he?"

Folke drags his sleeve over the blood coating his face. "A spy. I don't know who for, but I'd hazard a guess it's the fucking Red Church. They must have gotten wind of my mission. Sent him to stop me."

My fingers tighten on Folke's shoulder, supporting him. His heart beats erratically from blood loss. The smoke is so thick, I can barely make out his features.

I ask urgently, "He knew you were here? He started the fire to flush you out?"

Folke sways, weak from his wounds, and slumps down the door frame. At the same time, a ceiling joist splinters. As flames roar, an oak beam cracks and crashes down to the charred furniture, bringing a good portion of the ceiling with it. Clouds of ash and debris rise around us. With all the new fodder, the flames spread faster, eager to eat up anything able to burn.

I grab Folke by the shoulders. We have to get the fuck out of here.

CHAPTER 17

SABINE

I'm numbed to the pain in my heel as I half-run, half-hobble down the Blackwater streets. Townspeople race past me in the opposite direction to help put out the fire at the Manywaters Inn. Or maybe they're hoping to loot what remains of it—I don't know. What matters is that no one cares about the barefoot girl with a limp, and that's exactly how I want it.

For once, I'm a nobody. Not a lord's daughter. Not a godkissed bride. Not a naked prisoner. Just a girl trying to get to her horse.

My shoulders ache from the rucksack's weight. Basten makes carrying it look effortless, but I don't have his strength. Groaning, I slide it to the ground, so I can catch my breath.

Behind me, smoke rises high into the night. My throat seizes up at the terrible image of Basten trapped in the burning building, unable to get out. Who is this friend he's risking his life for? That damn loyalty of his is going to get him killed.

Basten, please be okay. I need you.

Sweat rolls down the hills of my cheeks, dampening the corners of my mouth. The reek of smoke permeates everything from my dress to my hair to my skin. I keep willing Basten to appear on the street behind me, but there's no sign of him. My heart races so dangerously fast that I'm surprised he can't hear it, wherever he is.

I need him to get me out of this town, but the need doesn't end there. Somehow, his safety has become of paramount concern to me. He's become my companion, my shadow, my friend just as much as my bane. It's a struggle to think of waking to another sunrise without his grumpy ass by my side.

Wiping my brow, I glance ahead at the street. The lantern hanging outside Myst's stable swings in the breeze. Grimacing, I shoulder the rucksack again and hobble over cobblestones in its direction. My heel throbs. My lungs ache from the smoke, making it a challenge to take a full breath. By the time I finally stagger through the stable's entryway, I'm so exhausted I could collapse.

It's empty, the stable's staff long since gone to bed.

Myst is there, in the last stall on the right where we housed her, and I sigh deeply.

There you are, pretty girl.

Panting, I drop the rucksack on the straw-covered floor and limp toward her in exhausted relief. If there's a soul in the world that warms my heart as much as her, I've yet to meet them. And yet, as I reach her stall gate, her head jerks toward me in alarm. Her eyes flash so wide I can see the whites around her irises.

Not alone!

My stomach tightens at her words. I know my brave girl, and she doesn't look scared, exactly—more like she's wary and unsure how to communicate to me what is happening. I reach for the latch on her stall, shaking my head in confusion.

I don't understand—

Then, a boot scuffs behind me as someone steps out of the stall across the hallway. A male voice calls, "Sabine."

My lungs snag on a startled breath. Gripping the stall door, I whirl around, my muscles shaking as adrenaline pushes them past their limit in case there is danger—

A boy steps out of the stall, the stable's lantern light making his fair hair glow golden. He's a few inches taller than me, and moves with the lithe grace of a hound, slim but undeniably strong. His eyes are the green color of clover, flecked with bits of brown and gold. His nose is straight and proud. His cheeks are round, wickedly dimpled in a way that stole my attention the first time I saw him. Even though it's spring, his skin glows with a permanent sun-kissed tan.

He's so handsome that he belongs in one of the Book of the Immortals' illustrations. He's exactly as the animals call him—The Boy Who Shines Like Sunlight.

"*Adan?*" I gasp.

All feeling floats out of my body. My head spins, and I have to grab onto the stall gate to hold myself steady. For a moment, I wonder if I inhaled so much smoke that I'm hallucinating.

"Sabine. My love." His boot scuffs as he takes a shaky step toward me like he, too, doesn't believe it's real. "Thank the Immortals."

I'm still gaping in stunned silence as he closes the distance between us and sweeps me into an embrace. He hugs me tightly, burying his face in my hair. His breath is shallow as he utters soft prayers of gratitude to the sleeping fae.

My body remains rigid. After everything that's happened tonight, my mind can't process that Adan is here, in a stable in Blackwater, whispering his love in my ear.

I lean backward for some air, resting a shaky hand on his chest.

"What . . . " I lick my dry lips as I gaze into his startling green eyes. "What—what are you doing here?"

"All of Astagnon is talking about Lord Rian's bride's naked ride. It isn't hard to follow where you've been. I overheard talk that you changed course, so I rode day and night to intercept you."

"But—but you couldn't possibly have gotten my message. I only sent it today!"

His brow furrows. "Message? No, I didn't get any message. What did it say?"

I stare at him with no words on my tongue. He doesn't know that I called off the escape and planned to stay with Basten until I had a better plan for leaving. His eyes search mine, waiting for my answer, and I can't bring myself to tell him the truth. I haven't felt guilty until now, staring at those guileless green eyes.

Adan is just as handsome as the first time I saw him—and just as much a stranger.

The boy holding me in his arms, stroking my face, and looking at me with such tender love is an utter unknown. How many hours did we spend together? Five? Six? Maybe he is as heavenly as I imagined—or maybe he isn't. I really don't know.

What was I thinking to believe myself to be in love with him after such a short time?

You weren't thinking. You were desperate for someone to save you.

Struggling with the onslaught of confused emotions, I run a shaky hand along my temple. "The message . . . It doesn't matter. I—I just can't believe you're here. The inn catching on fire . . . " I swallow around a lump in my throat. "What are the chances?"

He barks a laugh, shaking his head. "I wasn't about to leave anything to chance when it came to you."

It dawns on me what he means. "*You* started the fire?"

"An associate. I needed a distraction to give you a chance to get away from your guard. I knew you'd run to Myst the moment you escaped him."

My thoughts still can't catch up to reality. Let me get this straight . . . He thinks I fled from Basten, not that Basten sent me here to escape the dangerous inferno. Holy gods, this is going to be a mess to sort out.

Basten.

Oh, no. Basten will be here at any moment. What will he do when he finds Adan and me together? He's spent the last eighteen days slamming his fists into men's jaws for merely catcalling Lord Rian's future bride. And Adan intends to *run away with me*.

Basten will kill him. Really, truly, kill him. I don't think he'll use a knife, either—he'll want to use his fists to get the job done in the most painful, punishing way possible.

"It isn't safe here," I say in a rasping voice, grabbing Adan's sleeves.

He nods in grave agreement. "I know. My brothers are waiting for us at the docks. They have a boat at the ready. We can take the river downstream, to a safe place I know."

I stare at him as my thoughts stumble and stumble. He expects me to leave with him. And why wouldn't he? He doesn't know about my first, catastrophic escape attempt, or my message calling off our future together.

Blinking, I stutter, "Adan—"

He continues urgently, "We'll have to leave Myst here, but I promise, it won't be for long. She's too recognizable, and we can't take a horse by boat, anyway. We'll come back for her. I swear."

"N—no," I stutter. "You don't understand."

He cups my face, gazing into my eyes. "What don't I understand, my love?"

Once more, words don't come. How can I tell him we were fools to think we loved each other after a single day? By the gods, maybe he *is* just as saintly as I first thought. After all, he upheld his end of our promise. He's here. He moved heaven and earth to rescue me. Even his brothers are risking their lives to get me to safety.

I'm the one who was going to break our pact.

What am I supposed to tell him, that I've developed some kind of twisted entanglement with the guard meant to deliver me to Lord Rian?

I'd sound crazy.

Maybe I *am* crazy.

I've barely spent more time with Basten than I have with Adan. There's still so much I don't know about him, even if his grumpy, endearing growls do make my heart stumble. Am I being as foolish now, thinking this thing with Basten means something?

No. It isn't the same. What I have with Basten—it's unmatched.

Regardless, the truth is that it doesn't matter. Whatever I feel for Basten, whatever we could become to each other in the future, it isn't Basten Bowborn's name on my engagement certificate. I'm to wed Lord Rian, not Basten. There was never a world in which Basten and I could be together. I'm betrothed to his master, and his asinine sense of loyalty isn't going to let him break that oath. I'd hoped to earn his devotion so that he'd help me escape, but the chances of that were always slim.

Just look at the present moment. Where is Basten? Risking his life to help an old friend, that's where. Not here.

"Sabine, come on."

Gripping my hand, Adan makes for the exit. Torn, I throw a desperate look back at Myst, who kicks her front hoof against the stall.

Don't go, she says. ***Don't go!***

I have just enough time to touch her velvety muzzle for all too brief a moment before Adan pulls me away.

I'm sorry, my brave girl, I say as I stumble along with him. *I'll come back for you. I promise. This is the only way I can escape my marriage.*

She puffs angrily and continues kicking the stall. I'm vaguely aware my cheeks are wet with tears. My heart aches to be torn away from her, though it was always the plan to separate and then buy her later under a false name. In the meantime, Basten will find her—he'll take care of her for me.

Adan stops at the stable's entrance, scanning the street before wrapping a hand around my back and leading me in the opposite direction from the still-smoldering inn. I hobble on my wounded foot, feeling as stunned as if I'd fallen through ice into a freezing lake, unable to trust that I'm making the right decision.

But, I saw a chance—and I had to take it.

Maybe Adan will turn out to be the love of my life, after all. It doesn't really matter. Right now, he's only a means to an end. He can get me out of Blackwater and hide me from the Valvere family's forces. This is the best shot I have for true freedom.

As to matters of the heart, well, right now, I need to save my damn ass.

Gritting my teeth, I banish all other thoughts out of my head—and my heart—and hurry with Adan toward the docks.

Adan's vessel is a single-mast sloop that's seen better days. Crabbing cages clutter the deck, along with barrels and some wooden buoys. It's a humble fishing vessel, or at least disguised to look like one.

Three men sitting on the crab cages bolt to their feet when they see us hurrying down one of the docks. Moonlight bathes them in a bluish glow. These must be Adan's brothers. They share his fair hair and sunkissed skin, though they seem older than him by at least a decade. Strange—Adan never mentioned he was the youngest of his family by far.

Of course, Adan hasn't told me much at all. He's a stranger.

My pulse scrambles as I worry, once again, if this is the right decision.

"Quickly," one of the men orders, holding out his hand over the gap between the dock and the boat. "Pass her to me."

Adan helps me step precariously onto the rocking sloop, where I clutch onto the deck railing to steady myself. He jumps onto the vessel behind me, and immediately starts untying the rope tethering us to the dock.

"Get her hidden," one of his brothers hisses sharply to Adan. "I'll handle the boat. Here."

He shoves a bundle in Adan's arms.

Clutching the bundle under one arm, Adan takes my hand, leading me toward the cabin. "Hurry, Sabine. We can't take the chance anyone sees you."

I follow him down a narrow set of stairs to the tiny cabin—if it can even be called that. It's barely large enough for a person to lie down in, and half of it is currently packed with fishing nets. I have to stoop to keep from hitting my forehead on the ceiling.

Adan motions for me to curl up on the fishing nets, and then he starts pulling clothes out of the bundle. A crofter's dress. Worn leather shoes. A white bonnet.

"We assumed you'd be naked," he explains with the ghost of a half-grin, motioning to my sage green dress.

"Oh. Right." I don't want to reveal that Basten gave me my dress, because that might raise too many questions. "I, um, grabbed a dress from a clothesline while I was running from my guard."

"He's one hell of a brute, isn't he? Maks and Bertine have been following you since Polybridge, looking for an opportunity to overpower him and take you, but we didn't anticipate he'd be both godkissed *and* as strong as an ox."

Apprehension prickles the hairs on the back of my neck.

Adan's brothers have been following me? Yes, Basten is strong as an ox, and now he's too far away to help me if I should need it. So is Myst. I'm on my own.

I swallow down a pebble of fear rising in my throat. "Where are we going? Those *are* your brothers, right?"

Adan nods, distracted. The sloop rocks sharply as we enter the river's current. I grip the edge of a crate to steady myself a second before my head would have knocked against the low ceiling.

Adan rests his hand on my knee, his gaze eating me up now that it's just the two of us in the shadowy cabin, with only a thin beam of moonlight slicing down from the stairs to light up his green eyes.

He smooths his hands down the hair on either side of my face, drawing me closer. "By the fae, Sabine, I've wanted to do this every second since I laid eyes on you."

He pulls me into a kiss. Startled, my breath stalls in my lungs. His kiss is more aggressive than I'd have expected, his lips demanding my response. My thoughts freeze. Operating on instinct, I go through the motions of kissing him back, because my brain can't function fast enough for any alternative.

But as our lips play against one another, I feel nothing. I'm too shaken from the fire and everything that came before it. My body feels only numb. Adan breaks the kiss with a satisfied moan, unaware of my arrested ability to process what just happened. He passes the bundle of clothes to me.

"You should change into these. We don't want anyone recognizing you or the clothes you were wearing." He stares at me, expectantly, and my pulse raps against my temples.

I blink. "You mean you want me to change here? Now?"

He gives a laugh that rings bitterly. "Every other man can see you naked, but not me? Is that it?"

My lips part, but only silence emerges. *That's* what he's thinking about right now?

His eyes soften as he runs his hand down the contour of my face. He gives a slight chuckle. "I'll go up and give you some privacy. But there's one other thing. How I said Myst was too recognizable to take with us? The same goes for your hair. It'll identify you immediately." He draws a long, thin knife from the bundle. "I'm sorry, I truly am, but we have to cut it off."

A tightness knots in my chest. "My hair?"

"I know you prize it, but there's no other way."

He doesn't understand. I don't prize my hair, not in the slightest. In fact, my hair is the symbol of the binds that kept me imprisoned in the convent and my father's house. I was forced to grow it out as long as possible to make me more appealing to a suitor.

Just one more way Adan is a stranger, and I am to him.

"Do it," I say, tilting my head to give him the right angle. He seems surprised by my readiness, and he looks regretful as he saws through the thick tresses at my nape. I close my eyes, feeling the gentle tugs on my scalp like a thousand tiny fingers. Separating me from those shackles. Transforming me into something new, no longer the pretty girl able to fetch a high price.

When it's done, and the rope of my severed hair is clasped in Adan's fist, I run a tentative hand along the rough-cut edges that hang an inch above my shoulders. A part of me feels missing. Without my hair's weight, my head feels too bobbly. And yet, at the same time, free.

Adan carefully stuffs my severed hair into the bundle. I suppose we can't just leave it out loose in the boat.

One of his brothers shouts something down, and Adan squeezes my knee. "Stay down here. Don't make a sound."

Before he leaves, I snare his wrist as a shard of fear cuts into my chest. "Adan, everything's going to be all right, isn't it?"

He gives me a smile that, in the dark shadows, doesn't

quite reach his eyes. "Everything is going to be exactly as it should, Sabine."

And then he leaves me in the dark hull, uncomfortable on a pile of damp fish nets, crammed between reeking barrels, and all I can think is: *This doesn't feel like freedom.*

CHAPTER 18

WOLF

"Folke?" I shake him. "*Folke?*"

He slumps further as his eyes roll back in his head. Cursing, I catch him before he falls and hoist him onto my shoulder, groaning from his weight. His lame leg hasn't stopped him from training to be one bulky motherfucker.

Struggling under his heft, while my eyes water from the smoke, I stagger toward the door. The flames reach a pocket of fuel somewhere in the rubble, and explode with a blast of heat that singes my face. Glowering, I fight past the heat and finally lurch through the door.

The moment I'm out of the building, I suck in a breath of fresh air like I've been underwater. My legs give out, and I drop to my knees, letting Folke's unconscious body crumple onto the street.

Maybe not the gentlest approach, but hey, he's lucky I saved his ass.

Townspeople rush forward to help us.

I jerk my head toward Folke. "My friend—help him."

The burly leader shouts for two men to pull Folke's body to safety.

I totter on weakened legs to a lamppost near the bridge, and lean my weight against it while I try to catch my breath. With Folke out of the worst danger, my thoughts double-back hard on Sabine.

She must have made it to the stable by now, so she's with Myst. That's good. That damn stubborn horse will keep her safe. Sabine knows better than to try to escape again, but still, every fragment of my body urges me to get to her. Rian might have sent me on this mission to protect her, but I'm no longer doing it for him. Every last shred of me is dedicated to nothing but her safety. I'd rush into ten burning buildings for her. I'd fight every godkissed warrior in Astagnon. I'd slaughter anyone, man or woman, who so much as laid a finger on her in malice.

But there's one more thing to do first—I have to find out who the hell the godkissed spy is.

Against the warning cries of the townspeople, I stride back into the burning inn. Raising my arm to protect my face from the wall of heat, I duck away from the worst of the smoke and pick my way over debris to the place where the spy fell.

I stop abruptly.

His body is gone. Only a streak of blood marks where he fell. Bloodstained bootprints form a line back toward the kitchen.

"*Fuck.*"

A cough claws its way up my throat, and I bend over and retch. Then, I stagger after the tracks, trying to scent him, but the smoke is too overpowering. I plunge through the kitchen, where flames have eaten half the ceiling, and escape through the open back door into an alleyway.

It slopes sharply uphill, where a staircase leads to a different sector of Blackwater.

Climbing the stairs with great effort is the spy.

With a growl, I race after him. He glances over his shoulder, eyes simmering with fury. His cloak hangs askew from his neck, the hood fallen back to reveal shoulder-length blond hair and rugged features. He's got a decade or two on me, and his advanced age, paired with the critical wound in his neck, means he's too weak to use his speed fully.

It doesn't stop him from trying, though. He lurches up the stairs, moving with odd, short bursts of brief speed, then having to slow.

Rushing up behind him, I grab him by the arm and throw him against the nearest brick wall. He winces, clapping a hand on his bleeding neck wound. Folke's crossbow arrow juts out from the tendon, squirting blood with every pump of his heart. Drawing my hunting knife, I hold it to his blood-soaked neck.

He can't last long. He'll bleed out in minutes, so I need answers fast.

"Who do you work for?" I demand.

Chest huffing with exertion, he bares his teeth. Then his lips purse and, to my surprise, he forms a sharp whistle.

A caw sounds from overhead. I pitch my head up as a massive bird swoops low over the alley, its wingspan greater than an eagle's. Its feathers shimmer like stars against the moonlight, rich with iridescent colors that belong to no goddamn bird I've ever seen.

It opens its beak, and a burst of virulent blue dust blasts in my direction.

"Fuck!" I release the spy, rolling to the ground to dodge the dust. It's comprised of midnight-blue particles like ash, and it reeks of sulfur and rot. An ashy flake lands on my cheek, and the skin swells and oozes. A few paces away, the spy slumps to the ground, more sprays of blood spurting from his neck wound. He tries to whistle again, but his lips are too slick with blood.

His body gives one final tremor before he stills.

Breathing hard, I watch the sky, but there's no more sign of the bird. What in the name of the Immortals just happened? There's no bird in Blackwater—hell, in all of Astagnon, with iridescent feathers like that. That can breathe fucking *disease*. I only know of one creature capable of such magic, and it hasn't flown in these skies for a thousand years.

My mind spins as I crawl over to the spy's body. He's dead. Moving fast, I hunt through his pockets. Some coins, a key, a hunk of cheese wrapped in wax paper; not much, until my fingers snag on a piece of paper in his inside jacket pocket. I unfold it quickly.

The writing isn't in the Common Tongue. It's in a language I don't speak, but I do recognize the alphabet.

It's fucking Volkish.

Cursing, I flip the paper around, then freeze. There, scrawled in the corner, is a short line written in the Common Tongue: *Godkissed girls, ages 18-25, white, with fair hair.*

A terrible dread coalesces in my mind.

What if this spy wasn't after Folke at all?

I shove back the spy's hood to get a clearer look at his face. He's tan, with blonde hair a shade lighter than his skin tone. That's not rare in Astagnon, especially in the north. But almost all of Volkany's population has his coloration. And given the starleon—a mythical bird that should be asleep but could have awoken in a kingdom that's been blocked off for five hundred years—my veins ice over.

"Sabine," I murmur as terror grips me like a hand around my throat, and shove to my feet to race toward the stables.

My vision blurs as I shove through the crowd, shouting for people to get out of my way, though whether the blurriness is from tears or the lingering sting of smoke, I'm not sure. Thank the gods my other senses tell me where to go. The smell of straw and manure leads me the few blocks to the stable, where I hurtle through the open door, hoarsely calling out her name.

"Sabine? *Sabine?*"

The only answer is my voice echoing back. Fear snaps in my chest. Every second hurts as I jog down the aisle, searching each stall. Horse, water trough, hay. It's the same in all of them. Nothing else.

Sabine isn't here.

My heartbeat locks up my bodily functions so that I can barely think. Myst is in the last stall, kicking angrily at her stall door like something is wrong. *Yeah, no shit.* Where the fuck is Sabine?

"Yeah, yeah!" I shout at Myst. "I know!"

A dark object slumped in the corner catches my eye. It's my rucksack.

Fuck, fuck, fuck.

I grab it, drawing in Sabine's scent. Smoke. Violets. There's even a hint of my own scent on her, which makes me groan with longing and frustration. She was here. She was right fucking here.

I grip one of the stall bars to quell the panic clawing up my throat. *Get it together, Wolf. You're a hunter. So fucking hunt.*

There are several sets of footprints on the stable's stone floor. Sabine was barefoot and had the ball of her foot bandaged. I quickly hone in on a drip of her blood near Myst's stall. *That better fucking be from her foot wound and not anything else.*

The other prints belong to a set of men's boots. It's just one man, and large, given the print size, but lighter weight than me.

I close my eyes and draw in a deep inhale, scanning for other scents besides Sabine's. *There.* I didn't catch the other scent at first because of the overpowering reek of smoke, and because a stable naturally smells like livestock.

But this smell isn't horses.

"Fucking *goats!*"

My eyes snap open. It's that motherfucking goatherd lover of hers. Adan. She said the animals called him the

Boy of Sunlight, or something, which means he's likely blonde. Just like the Volkish spy who started the fire.

Gods help me.

I slump against a stall door, feeling the blood drain out of my face. The dots begin to connect at dizzying speed, forming a picture I'm not ready to see. It looks like this: Sabine's lover has been planning this for months. Not alone, but with a team of Volkish raiders targeting godkissed people. Judging by the note I uncovered in the spy's pocket, they've been tasked with finding girls like Sabine. For what purpose? Holy gods, I don't want to know. There aren't many reasons a cursed kingdom, cut off because of its lawlessness, would want pretty, young, magical women.

Somehow, Adan found out that a girl fitting the desired description was at the convent. He wormed his way in and seduced her. The announcement of Rian's betrothal to Sabine must have thrown a kink in his plans, so his team staged the inn fire as a distraction to steal her away. It wasn't about Folke or the Red Church at all.

It was all to get Sabine.

"Fuck!" I yell again. My muscles twitch, making me pace to burn off the edge of adrenaline. My breath heaves like billows. It isn't good to breathe this fast and hard—if I pass out, what use will I be to Sabine?

This is my fault. I was supposed to guard her. She was mine to protect. An hour ago, I had her perfect body under mine, the moans on her lips for me, her hips writhing in need. She might hate me, but she can't deny that she also wants me. In some twisted way, she's come to trust me, at least enough to let me worship her body with my hot touch.

And I failed her.

Myst whinnies, kicking her stall door again, and it feels like she's kicking straight against my bruised heart. Rage claws down my back, leaving my skin feeling raw. I'm supposed to be better than this. I'm the best goddamn hunter in Astagnon. I know a trap when I see it—so how could I have missed this?

Growling, I plant a punch into a stall door, hard enough to splinter the wood. Blood weeps down my knuckles, releasing a metallic odor. But the pain isn't enough. I pull my arm back for another punch, but Myst whinnies sharply again.

"I know," I spit in the horse's direction with a clenched jaw. "I fucking know! It's my fault!"

Myst stamps her hooves angrily, turns in a tight circle, then rears up in the stall. Steam shoots out of her nostrils. Her black eyes stab me like twin blades, sinking deep into my already rotted soul. She slams back down to the ground.

This crazy mare is trying to tell me something.

I grip her stall's bars, licking moisture into my crack-led, dry lips. "Myst? Do you know where she went?"

Myst whinnies and kicks the door urgently.

"You saw them, didn't you? You saw the man who took her?"

You're talking to a horse, Wolf, a voice reminds me. I don't have Sabine's godkissed ability to talk to animals, and I can only imagine that Myst has no clue what the sounds coming out of my mouth mean. But Myst and I are perfectly clear on one thing: We both care about Sabine.

The three of us have been together on the road for weeks, silently adapting to each other's quirks and habits. She's a stubborn horse, I'm a stubborn man; but Sabine is the sun between us, keeping the both of us firmly in her orbit, circling her so steadily that we haven't knocked heads with each other too hard before now. And maybe we can call a truce.

I roll open Myst's stall door, holding out a staying hand. "Okay. Look, you haven't always liked me, and I haven't always liked you. But we have to put our differences aside for Sabine. Agreed?"

She snorts again, but it's mollified. Her hoof scrapes against the straw-covered floor. I ease into her stall another step, keeping my hand extended like I'm taming a wild animal.

"Easy, Myst. I'm a friend."

Her black eyes roll, but she doesn't bite my outstretched hand, which is a good sign. Slowly, I place a hand on her mane, and another on her back.

"Don't worry, crazy mare," I murmur, a trace of affection in my voice. "There aren't any two souls in this world who want to find her more than us. We'll get her back."

I heft myself onto her bare back, wrapping my legs around her sides, and grip a fistful of mane. Riding bareback isn't my strength, but Myst and I are a team now, and she readily heeds my direction.

I scoop up the rucksack on our way out of the stable, and then let all other stimuli fall away except for Sabine's scent. I hone in on it on the street, ignoring the distant crowds still putting out the fire, the reek of smoke, and the townpeople's shouts on the wind.

"This way." I nudge Myst, and we follow Sabine's scent for a few blocks, eventually ending up at the docks, where her scent abruptly ends.

Well, fuck. That means she boarded a ship, and scent is nearly impossible to track over such a large waterway. But I'm a hunter. This is what I do. Sabine said Adan's original plan was to rendezvous at an old mill, and a mill needs a river to turn its water wheel.

So, I click for Myst to head upstream, and the two of us set off at a gallop—Sabine's best friend and the man who will move heaven and earth to get her back.

CHAPTER 19

SABINE

When I wake up, my mouth is parched. I feel jolted out of sleep, with lingering nightmares flashing in my mind. I don't know how much time has passed. Hours, maybe? My muscles are cramped from sleeping on a knotty pile of fishing nets, my limbs balled up in the sloop's narrow cabin. The crofter's dress Adan gave me is itchy.

I comb my fingers through my hair instinctually, freezing when it doesn't have its usual heft. For years, in the Convent of Immortal Iyre, I fantasized about being free and light, with shoulder-length hair blowing in the wind as I rode Myst at breakneck speed through open fields. Now, I'm outside the walls, but I don't recognize this version of myself from any fantasy. Not this frightened girl in a hole that reeks of fish.

The sloop jolts again, and I realize we're docking somewhere. The repetitive rocking of floating on the river has been replaced with clomping footsteps on the deck overhead. Someone calls out, then throws a thunking rope.

My breath goes rickety. I grip the cabin's narrow walls to steady myself against the boat's jostling. I barely have time to chase away the remnants of nightmares and get my head on straight before the cabin's trapdoor is thrown open.

Bright sunlight stings my eyes. I turn away from it, holding up a shielding hand. Adan's silhouette eclipses the opening.

"We're here." His voice is laced with excitement like a kid on a summer morning. He extends his hand down to me. Outside, seagulls' lazy caws, mixed with a warm breeze, unwind the worst of the knots that formed in my muscles overnight. In the light of day, my fears look overblown. Adan saved me. He might be a stranger, but that doesn't make him a villain. He could truly be the kind-hearted boy from a big, boisterous family who wants to take me to Salensa and marry me.

Even though my rational mind tells me all this, however, my gut doesn't believe it. I saw something in Adan and his brothers last night that scared me.

Still, I'm here, now. And gods, I want off this stinking boat.

So, I let Adan help me up. It's mid-morning, judging by the sun's position. On deck, I get a clear view of an open river valley. An overgrown apple orchard hugs one side of the river, and the other is bare fields, plowed into tidy rows in preparation for planting. The dock belongs to a mill with a rusted-out waterwheel; it doesn't look like it's been operational in years.

On the riverbank, a blonde man in a cloak sits atop a horse with four more saddled horses at the ready.

I glance at Adan's two brothers, who are unloading duffle bags of supplies and affixing them to the saddles. Last night, they didn't bother to introduce themselves. They still don't.

"Where are we going?" I ask Adan, nodding toward the horses, trying to keep my voice from breaking and betraying my nerves.

"A cottage—it's a few hours' ride. It belongs to a friend. We'll be safe there until we can travel to Salensa."

We mount the horses and ride inland through the overgrown orchard, which gradually blends into woods. I can't be certain of where we are, but the Blackened Forest sits somewhere on the north side of the Innis River. From everything I've heard, the trees there tower like monoliths, and the leaf cover is so dense it gives the forest its name. Surely Adan wouldn't be taking me *there*—it's the opposite direction from the coast.

The further we ride, the shorter his answers get. His brothers say nothing, unless it has to do with the route. I try to memorize any landmark tree or noteworthy stream we pass, in case I need to return this way. Not that I expect things to go bad, but I'd be lying if the possibility of needing a sudden escape wasn't fixed in the back of my mind.

Finally, we descend into a hollar, where a cottage crouches in an overgrown clearing. Though sawdust on the ground indicates it's had some recent repair work, it looks largely abandoned. Tall grass grows higher than the front porch. The windows are boarded up.

My heart sinks all the way down to my tailbone. This cottage doesn't feel like freedom, either.

Inside, the cottage is in only slightly better condition than it looked from the outside. There are two rooms: a tiny bedroom with bunks, and a main room with a table and chairs, an ancient iron stove, and two rocking chairs by the fireplace. Even though it's spacious, it feels crowded with the five of us—but it doesn't matter, because Adan's brothers soon go outside to chop firewood.

Adan starts to leave, too, and I grab his hand in a rush of nerves, my gut telling me that I shouldn't be here. "Wait. Don't leave me."

"I need to talk to my brothers."

"About—about the route to Salensa?" I hate that the rise in my voice sounds so damn naive, but I have nothing left to cling to but this thread of hope.

"Yeah," he says dismissively. "Stay here."

Alone in the cottage, I don't know what to do with myself. Everything feels cold, foreign. I don't want to sit in the hard chairs. The beds' straw mattresses look moldy. When I check the kitchen cabinet, there are pewter plates and earthenware cups, but no knives. They've all been taken away.

I pace, gnawing on my bottom lip.

Another hour passes before the door opens, but it's not Adan. It's the elder brother with a scar on his upper lip. He sets a sloshing bucket of water next to the stove but doesn't leave again. There's something distasteful about him I can't put my finger on; he's handsome enough, though old—nearly old enough that he could be my father, now that I see him closer up. This is really Adan's brother? He's dressed slovenly. It's been a while since he shaved. I don't want to guess when he last bathed.

He takes a few slow, menacing strides into the cottage, eyeing me up and down like I'm a full banquet after a long fast. *Not* the look any man should give his brother's paramour.

I step back, fear cropping up in my chest, as I place the table between us. "Um, where's Adan?"

His laugh sounds a lot like a sneer. "Oh, he'll be busy for a while. Why, worried he'll interrupt us?"

Now, my heart blows up with fear. This man's casual delight in my fear sends desperation rising like a tide in me. There were no knives in the kitchen, but maybe there's a fire poker—

I try to skirt my way closer to the fireplace, but the man steps in, blocking me. His blue eyes travel down the length of my body like he's mapping out every step of a route he's about to take. A small, fearful sound escapes my throat.

He grins. "Fuck what Adan says. You're too sweet not to sample."

Terror thrums through me. My mind cedes way to my body, which knows what to do. I make a break for the door, but he catches me around the waist, chuckling gruffly as I struggle against him.

"Easy, girl. I'll make it fast."

His words drill into my bones until I think I'm going to crumble, but some deep well of strength inside me keeps fighting. I kick and squirm, but he's got wiry strength. He drags me, struggling, to the table and kicks a chair out of the way so he can set my ass on the tabletop. He grabs the back of my skull with one hand, while trying to pry my knees apart with the other.

"Too bad you don't have that long hair," he says huskily, his voice heavy with threat. "Something to hold onto. Like the reins of a horse. Bends a girl to your will, but no bother—I can make do."

His hand fists painfully in my short hair. Crying out, I try to pry his fingers off. His brothers outside must hear my cries, right? Where's Adan?

"Stop fucking moving," he growls, his terrible grin gone now.

"Let me go!" I shout, baring my teeth. "Adan will *kill* you!"

"Adan? Adan isn't in charge."

He shoves me back against the table. I try to lock my knees together, but he manages to wedge his body between my thighs, then shoves fistfuls of my skirt up around my waist. His hand probes roughly around my cleft. He gets a finger beneath the band of my panties, but before he can shove them aside, I buck my hips to push him away.

"Wait!" I gasp, my mind's gears whirling as fast as my lungs are pumping for breath. "Wait, not here. Not, um, like this. At least—at least do it in a bed."

"I told you," he says curtly, "shut up, and it'll be over soon."

"Please, it's—it's my first time. At least do it in a bed. I —I won't struggle. I'll make it easy for you, I promise, as long as you don't make it hurt."

A crack opens up in his dogged determination. He grunts, releasing his hold on my hair. He jerks his head toward the bedroom. Slowly, I sit up. I can't believe it, but Basten was right. Men will believe whatever they want to believe when their cock is involved.

He barks, "Go on, then, get in the bedroom—"

I knee him in the groin immediately, using the momentum from sliding off the table for extra oomph. His eyes go round as he clamps his hands over his cock and balls. With a cry, I hurl my weight at him to knock him down. He doesn't fall over, but he stumbles back a few steps. As soon as a path opens to the door, I lunge for it. *Go, go, go.*

I throw open the door—

And stare into Adan's startled face as he clutches firewood in one arm, with an axe in his other hand. For a breathless second, time stops, as we both struggle to make sense of the situation. He's blocking the door—I can't get past him.

His eyes shift to look at his brother behind me, and there's a moment when understanding snaps in them. He dumps the clattering firewood on the floor as he storms into the cottage. His shirt is sweatstained from chopping wood, buttons open halfway down his chest. His hair, normally tamed, hangs wild.

Before I can rush out the door, he slams it shut and fastens the latch.

"Maks, what the fuck are you doing?" he demands, the axe tight in his fist.

The elder brother is still hunched over from the pain in his groin. "She fucking kneed me!"

"Yeah—she should have rammed your balls all the way into your brain, you idiot!"

My body is still swimming in adrenaline, unable to float back to solid ground. Clinging to the back of a chair to keep myself upright, I fight to calm down. It was so close to . . . He was going to . . . But it's all right now. Adan is back. And even though I've known Adan only a few hours more than his brother, I pour all my trust into him.

I have to. He's all I have now.

Adan sets the axe down by the stove, then paces tightly, muttering curses under his breath. With each passing second, my heartbeat slows as my body attempts to register that the danger is over. My whole body shakes from the final purge of adrenaline, and I sink into the chair before my legs give out.

"No one would have known," Maks huffs defensively.

Adan thrusts a finger in my direction while he yells at his brother. "You know they would! What did you expect me to tell the king, eh? That she slipped and fell on your cock? She's supposed to be untouched!"

"His court doesn't give a shit about chastity."

"He's the *king*, you idiot. He said he wanted the girls unharmed and untouched. What part of that don't you understand? Don't you think, if it were allowed, I would have fucked her myself? If anyone deserves to, it's me. I found her in the first place!"

Fear finds a crack in my numb bones and works its way back in. It sifts through my body until my skin slithers with it, and something unlocks in my brain. *This. This. This.* My gut was right all along. I should never have taken Adan's hand in that Blackwater stables . . .

A small exclamation slips from my lips. I feel gutted from throat to bowels.

Then, as my panic crests, my eyes fall to the axe.

Adan must realize where he left it at the same time that I do, because as soon as I scramble out of the chair and dive for it, he does the same.

"Sabine, stop. Don't, goddammit!"

We wrestle on the floor as we both try to grab the axe. Maks snakes his hand behind the woodstove from the opposite direction to grab it, but his arm doesn't reach. I kick and claw blindly until my fingers slide over its smooth handle. The axe falls, clattering to the stone floor.

"No!" I cry. Gathering my strength, I lunge for the handle again—

But Maks stomps his boot down on my hand. I scream as I feel my bones crunch. Pain radiates in lightning bolts down my arm.

Maks snatches up the axe. Adan ensnares me around the waist and drags me away from the stove. My hand hurts so bad that I feel like I might black out. It's all I can do to flail and kick, but between the two of them, they make quick work of picking me up, shoving me into a kitchen chair, and binding my wrists with thick coils of rope.

Fighting against the rope, I squeeze my eyes shut against the pain in my hand. It's sprained, if not broken. But pain is nothing new. Pain I can deal with. It's the ropes that frighten me. The axe. The terrible things Adan said.

Think.

Think.

If an animal is close . . .

Adan rubs his cheek where I clocked him with my foot while we were wrestling. His green eyes lock onto me. "Goddammit, Sabine!"

I spit at him, "You lied to me! You always planned to abduct me! You said—you said the king . . . " My voice falls off, because I don't know how to finish my thought. None of it makes any sense. I can't fit together the pieces into any sort of coherent picture. According to Adan and Maks, King Joruun is behind this? He's a frail old man who hasn't left Old Coros in a decade. He has a reputation for monotonous speeches about taxation, not kidnapping girls.

"You can't get out of the cottage," Adan says evenly, rubbing the bruise forming on his cheek. There's ice in his eyes. He's dropped the act now, and there's no doubt that he was playing me the entire time. "The door and all the windows lock from the outside. The rest of our men are standing guard." He must notice that my attention shifts to the chimney, because he gives a mirthless laugh. "We blocked the chimney, too, so if you're thinking of calling to any creatures to swoop down and save you, you can forget that idea."

My mouth goes dry as my greatest fear comes true— I'm entirely alone. I have no one to help me. No birds. No rodents. No wildcats. *No Myst.* My heart squeezes to think of my brave girl, who tried to warn me in Blackwater not to go with Adan. There was a reason she didn't like him from the start. She could sense his nefarious intent, even if she couldn't put it into words that I'd understand.

But wait.

Adan and his brothers—who don't seem to be his brothers at all—plugged any entrances large enough for a mouse, but this is an old cottage made of rough-hewn logs and crumbling mortar. There have to be tiny cracks.

I tap into my godkiss to send a silent signal out into the nearby forest. It isn't long before I feel the buzz of many answering voices, who close in toward my call. I can feel each of their presences as though we're connected by an invisible tether, as they crawl and shimmy and slip between cracks in the cabin's logs barely big enough for a breath.

A honeybee alights from a crack in the wall to land on my cheek. Its tiny feet patter over my skin, its wings vibrating against my eyelashes as it crests the hill of my cheekbone. Another one zips across the cottage to land on my forehead. One by one, more honeybees join them until I have hundreds swarming my face and hair.

We help, the bees buzz in one collective voice.

Adan and Maks stumble backward like they're looking at Immortal Solene herself, the Goddess of Nature, cursed to suffer a thousand bee stings after betraying Immortal Vale by sleeping with his rival. It would be useless to use the bees against my captors—the honeybees could sting them a hundred times and still not kill them, but I have other ideas.

Adan shouts sharply, "Bertine! Iskander!"

The other two men storm in through the door. It isn't lost on me that if they heard Adan just now, then they must have been close enough to hear my screams when Maks tried to rape me. Anger drips down the back of my throat, setting my belly on fire, prodding my rage until it's buzzing like the bees.

My four abductors stare at me, covered in bees, in shocked bewilderment.

Moving my lips slowly so I don't unintentionally harm the bees crawling around my mouth, I say in measured words, "I have a reaction to bee venom—a single sting almost killed me once. Whatever King Joruun is paying you, if you lay one finger on me, I'll be dead in minutes, and you'll lose every last coin he promised."

CHAPTER 20
WOLF

Dusk chews up the forest as Myst and I stand on the edge of a clearing, facing a cottage that's seen better days. We've been pursuing Sabine and her captors since daylight. We followed the river from Blackwater for half a day to the Old Innis Mill, where a fishing sloop was docked. Buried under waves of briny stink was the delicate scent of violets. We tracked five sets of horse prints into the woods about twenty miles south of the Blackened Forest—and now we're here.

They're inside. Sabine and four men. I'm sure it's her —I'd recognize the swift patter of her heartbeat as surely as my own. For the last five minutes, Myst and I have been waiting as I listen for details of their conversation and movements, so I can track how best to attack.

But now they've been strangely quiet. They've used each other's names—Adan, Maks, Bertine, and Iskander —but only to pass around a bottle. I hear their glugs of booze, their boots scuffing, a rocking chair's creak, but barely more than a few spoken words, like all five of them are just sitting around staring at one another. I shift on Myst's back, fingers tightening in her mane.

"I don't like this. Something's wrong."

The buzz of a bees nest somewhere close dulls my ability to pick up on smaller sounds. I'm about ready to dismount, say fuck it, and simply kick the door down, but then one of the men speaks.

"*You can't stay like this forever, girl,*" he snaps in frustration. "*It's been hours.*"

Sabine's voice, gravely with exhaustion, replies firmly, "*Then do what I told you. Leave. Go back to the river. Once a bird confirms that you're on your boat, we go our separate ways.*"

She's negotiating with her captors? With what fucking leverage? What could possibly be the source of this stand-off?

Myst blows steam into the cool night air. She's getting impatient. So am I. Night darkens the forest, and the growing shadows ignite my desire to slit each one of their throats and listen to them choke on their own blood. It's a sound I'm going to fucking relish.

"*I'm not giving up the bounty!*" another man barks.

I still can't be certain of the scenario in that cottage, which is a major disadvantage. There's one of me and four of them. I'd confidently take those odds if I knew what kind of fighters they were, so I could play to their weaknesses. But I don't know if they're soldiers or farmers, fishermen or spies. They could be godkissed, like their speedy friend back in Blackwater.

But there's one thing I do know: Sabine is, at the

moment, alive. And I can't say how long that state will last.

I pat Myst's shoulder like we're old comrades. "Have we heard enough, my friend?"

Her muscles bunch under me, ready for action even after our long ride. It brings a grim smile to my lips. This crazy mare might just have won me over. Besides, she's not the only one antsy for a fight. The familiar prickle of anticipation shoots up my spine until I'm licking my lips, squeezing my calves around the horse, flexing my hands into fists and straightening them again. Fantasies play out in my head of kicking open the door, sinking my knife blade into every last one of them. The cottage is too tight to use my bow, or else I'd shoot them each through the eye first to prolong the pain.

The ache to fight them is visceral, arousing.

Is Sabine frightened? Does she believe I'll come for her? I can hear her body's clues, but that doesn't mean I can read her mind.

"Let's have some fun," I murmur in dark delight as I dig my heels into Myst's sides.

The horse surges forward like she's been anxiously awaiting my signal. Her hooves pound over the hard-packed ground as she stampedes toward the cottage with thrilling speed, not showing any signs of slowing. She thunders up the porch stairs. The whole cottage rattles.

Then she rears up, a bloodcurdling whinny on her lips, and brings down her front hooves to break down the door.

The door splinters around its meager bolt. I ride Myst

straight into the cottage, ducking to get through the door-frame, greedily drinking in the chaos our arrival causes.

The four men jump to their feet. They're blonde. Burly. Volkish raiders for sure. But they're unarmed and half-drunk; their guard was down. The sudden appearance of a mounted rider *inside* their kitchen has them scrambling for weapons. One of them snatches an axe. Another grabs a heavy cast iron pan. Another moves to block Sabine.

Sabine. She's in a chair, her hands bound. Garbed in a peasant's dress. Her long hair is gone—cut to her chin. Bees crawl all over her face. It's a horrific scene, straight out of the Book of the Immortals.

There's something else. Some people's bodies emit a spoiled-fruit scent when around bees if they're highly susceptible to bee venom, and Sabine reeks of it.

If she gets stung . . .

She starts to scream to me, but the man clamps a meaty hand over her mouth to muffle her cries, flinching as bees sting his palm. My heart shoots to my throat, afraid she's stung, too. But she controls the bees—so why is she putting herself at risk?

She's doing this on purpose. Her insurance policy. Clever fucking girl.

"Who the hell are you?" the man with the axe roars.

He's the youngest. Maybe twenty years old. The bland kind of good looks that would make him a prize in a village of a hundred people and utterly insignificant anywhere with a larger population. The perfect type of unintimidating boy to appeal to a skittish, naive girl who's been locked away for twelve years with old women.

"Adan, I take it?" I growl low. "Yeah. I always knew you'd turn out to be a motherfucking bastard."

With a cry, Adan draws his arm back to swing the axe at my thigh. Myst sidesteps to dodge before I even have to signal her. I swing my left leg over her back so I can dismount in a slide, which sends me slamming into Adan and knocks us both to the floor. His head glances off the kitchen table as he falls, which makes him drop the axe. I land in a crouch with one knee pinning his arm.

My nerves burn from the pleasure of his scream.

It's fucking on.

I love this—love the fight. It's fucked up, but that's what happens when you raise a boy on a diet of violence and starve him for anything else. My only reward in Jocki's fight ring came when I drew blood. So when it appears on Adan's temple, dripping onto the floor, I lick my lips.

Two of the raiders try to corral Myst into the bedroom, but she turns a tight circle, knocking over chairs, and snaps a kick at them with her hind legs.

The fourth man, with a scar on his upper lip, still has his hand on Sabine's mouth. He tries to drag her toward the bedroom, but she struggles against him. All at once, the bees leave her skin. There's a second when they're suspended in the air, ghost-like, and then they zero in on her captor.

"Fuck!" he yells.

Good fucking girl.

The scarred man—his voice gives him away as the one named Maks—trips backward over the rug as he flails to try to wave away the bee swarm. He crashes against a cabinet near the corner, writhing.

Sabine pushes to her feet, her heartbeat like a chugging engine, as she spins toward me. "Basten—"

While my attention is on her, Adan scrambles out from under my knee and crawls under the table to the other side. He snatches up the axe with a flush of triumph.

I chuckle darkly. I'm enjoying this way too much, and I haven't even taken my knife out.

I straighten to stalk after him, but then one of the other men grabs Sabine by the arm and drags her toward the busted-down door. My jaw clamps.

I whistle for Myst. The horse takes up most of the kitchen area, wreaking chaos by knocking over dishes and trampling their belongings. She clocks the man's trajectory toward the doorway and beats him to it. Her hooves clatter over the shattered wood, and she doubles back, blocking the open doorway. The man freezes, clutching Sabine, as he realizes there's no way he can get past the horse.

Hell yes, crazy mare.

I hear an intake of air a second before Adan runs at me with the axe. It gives me enough time to duck, then straighten, tug the axe out of his slackened fist, and kick him squarely in the chest, sending him crashing back against the fireplace.

My fingers tighten over the axe handle, relishing its heft. My tongue snakes out to wet my lips. As much as I'm itching to smash the handle into Adan's nose, I can't let that other bastard keep putting his hands all over Sabine.

I pivot sharply toward the man holding her, and raise the axe. His eyes go round, but he doesn't release her. He dances back and forth, trying to anticipate where I will strike. But all he's accomplishing is giving away his own future movements.

I see his nearly imperceptible glance toward the bedroom and swing the axe down just as he lurches toward it. The flat part of the blade clips his arm. He cries out and releases Sabine roughly, knocking her toward the stove.

"Iskander!" one of the other men cries.

I catch Sabine in my arms, half-dragging and half-carrying her negligible weight to the furthest corner, away from the action. There's a space about two feet wide and two feet deep between the corner and the kitchen cabinet—I shove her into the nook.

"Stay here." I spare a second to cup her cheek, verifying there are no sting marks on her. "Don't move. Don't watch."

Her giant round eyes swallow me whole, drenching me in her fear, but also a low blaze of righteous, sizzling, bloodthirsty thrill that's as wicked as my own.

She says evenly, "I want to watch."

Fucking gods. This woman. She gets my heartbeat pounding and my blood throbbing. She's going to be the death of me.

I have to tear myself away from her when one of the lugs —who must be Bertine—hurtles the cast iron pan across the room at me. I throw open the cabinet door to block it, and it clatters to the floor. Bertine runs at me, but I dive under the table to dodge him, crawl beneath it, and then snatch up a chair on my way up from the other side. Swinging it by the back, I smash it into Bertine's head. It clips him in the skull, sending him to the ground, unconscious.

My blood sizzles in delight to see him fall.

Iskander throws a punch, but I catch his arm and use his momentum to sling him toward the stove. His head smashes into it. Maks leaps over the fallen man to try to get to Sabine in the sheltered nook, but I grab a coil of leftover rope from when they bound her wrists, spin it into a quick lasso, and let it fly. It snags his raised right foot as he runs. I pull taught hard enough to yank him to the ground.

I whistle to get Myst's attention. She whinnies from the doorway, tossing her head. I throw the rope's end to her. She picks it up with her teeth, then stomps backward to drag the struggling Maks across the floor. His hands flail to find purchase. He screams for help.

Myst rears, then brings down her hooves on the wriggling man's chest. There's a bone-shattering crack. A sickening squelch. His breath goes silent.

Bees buzz relentlessly, leaving the remaining three raiders flinching under their stings, but the swarm leaves me alone.

I check on Sabine with a quick glance, my throat bobbing.

Adan, still with that damn axe, and Bertine, bleeding from a head wound, rush me simultaneously. Time for my knife. I wait until the last moment to draw it, then slide it out with one smooth movement and stab it straight into Bertine's chest. The man buckles, his eyes bulging. Blood pours down to coat my hand as I chuckle low—but when I try to pull the blade out to turn it on Adan, something's wrong.

The goddamn blade is stuck in his ribs.

Cursing, I tug it again, but it doesn't want to come free. Bertine gurgles as blood fills his mouth. I try twisting the blade. No use.

With Adan rushing me with the axe, I go to my backup plan. I spin Bertine around as a shield just as Adan slams down the axe. Its blade lodges in the cleft between Bertine's shoulder and neck, hacking a slice all the way down to the man's ribcage.

Horrified, Adan releases his hold on the axe, stumbling backward.

I also release my hold on Bertine, and he falls, dead.

Bees swarm on Adan's face, raising red welts, but he's numb to them as the horror of his accidental kill dawns on him.

It's the perfect opportunity to punch his pretty fucking face. I land a hook square on his jaw, then follow up with a cross punch to his stomach. Adan's attention snaps back to the fight, ducking and weaving to avoid my next hook punch. But I predict his intention with my heightened vision, and grab him by the arm so I can throw a jab to his nose that sends him crashing to the floor.

He recovers fast—and grasps the axe.

He swings it in a sweep toward my ankle, but I see it coming and jump over the blade. Then, I stomp on its flat side, pinning the weapon to the floor and Adan's hand with it. Groaning in pain, he has no choice but to release it.

Before I can land a downward kick on Adan's head, Iskander comes to by the stove. He heaves pieces of firewood at me with all his strength. I block each one, but it's a distraction, and Adan manages to crawl away.

Iskander heads for Sabine in the nook, and I see red. But before I can stop him from getting to her, Adan hooks my ankle with his own. He wraps his legs around my ankle, pinning me. A furious growl roars out of me.

He's going to fucking *bleed.*

Before Iskander can get to her, Sabine darts out of the nook and dives for Bertine's body. She wrenches my knife out of his ribs, the blade slickened and worked loose by his deflated chest, and stabs Iskander in the belly just as he reaches her.

Right in the soft organs—just where I taught her.

I'm so fucking proud.

I kick Adan off me with a yowl, and take the knife from Sabine. With one quick jerk, I slit Iskander's throat, finishing the job. His body slumps against the cabinet.

Blood coats Sabine's face and hair. Her hands shake— it's the first time she's stabbed a man. Little noises squeeze out of her throat. She looks up at me with an indescribable sea of disbelief in her eyes, and I'm drowning, I'm drowning, I'm drowning...

From the corner of my eye, I spot Adan lumber toward the door.

I peel away from Sabine with a growl. It's time to finish this fucker. Luckily, Myst is on the same page as me. We make a good team, that crazy mare and me. She snorts loudly, stamping her hooves, preventing him from leaving.

Driving him right back to where I want him. The rope attached to Maks's corpse spans the cottage floor. I slice off a length and come up behind Adan, wrapping it around his neck. His hands fly to the rope, trying to free it while he struggles for air. I drag him to the same chair he imprisoned Sabine in, shoving him down. Looping the rest of the rope around him, I secure him to the chair and finally release the hold on his neck.

He gasps for air with his damaged windpipe.

"I've killed many men," I murmur in his ear while both sets of our eyes are fixed on Sabine across the kitchen. "But none I'll relish as much as slitting your throat. That girl, there? The one you thought you could take from me? Whatever bounty you thought she was worth, I assure you, she's worth it one hundred times over. I would tear the living world down to the gods' underrealm for her—and I'll happily butcher you."

I place the blade against his throat and slide it through, slow and clean. His dying gurgles are a rapture. The blood pouring down his chest drenches me in ecstasy. His—

"Basten?"

I whirl toward her small voice in the corner, forgetting my bloodlust. Her. That's all that matters. That's all this bloodshed was for—just her.

"Sabine."

We come together. She slips on a blood slick, but I catch her as she stumbles. My hands circle her waist like a lock clicking into place. I hug her close to my chest, almost afraid to believe it's over, and that she's safe. My chin rests on the crown of her head. Her body folds so perfectly into mine. She and I fit together like we were made for one another. And fuck, if my groin doesn't harden in acknowledgment of that fact. I'm practically choking on the flood of adrenaline that swells from the fight. I want her. I want to bathe the blood off her. I want to tear her out of this foreign dress. I want to take her right here with four corpses still bleeding out on the floor.

But I tuck away that need; her care comes first. I smooth my hands over her blood-spattered face. Her cut hair is unexpected, but the length suits her. It frames her perfect face better than any gilded border ever could.

Tenderly, I comb my bloodstained fingers through her hair, tucking a short lock behind her ear.

"You're not stung?" I ask.

She shakes her head. "The bees were careful. They didn't sting me. Or you. Or Myst."

My little violet protected me just as I was safe-guarding her.

She delicately touches a scratch on the side of my neck. "You're bleeding." She uses a corner of her sleeve to wipe away the blood, and then on impulse, presses her lips to the wound like I'm a child in need of comfort.

I groan as I tip my head back. I'm barely able to breathe. Too affected by the perfection of this beautiful girl who keeps me guessing with her every move. It's a rush: To know that she's safe. To know that my brutality hasn't scared her away. To know that she's a force to be reckoned with in her own right. I want to hear her heart-beat every night when I fall asleep. I want to feel the vibration of her blood as she lies next to me. I want to drown in the scent of blood and violets until there's nothing in the world but her.

"Don't," I rasp out, and then lick my lips, and correct myself. "Don't stop."

She continues to move her soft lips over my neck in little kisses that makes my skin tingle and my body go still, afraid the slightest movement will make her stop. When she eventually breaks contact, she nestles her forehead on my shoulder. I'd bleed for her. I'd break bones for her. I'd cut my own heart out of my chest if she only asked it of me, and I'd willingly die at her feet with the still-pumping organ in my hands, an offering for this girl whose worth rivals the gods.

CHAPTER 21

SABINE

Basten's shirt smells of smoke from the inn, but it reminds me of our campfire nights in the woods. Those long, star-filled nights when the two of us burned so bright in our hurt, rage, and loneliness that we weren't able to see that the one thing we needed was just across the flames.

My hands twist in his shirt's fabric, the same shirt I wore for all those black nights. The shirt that hugged me, that sheltered me. Why didn't I see how Basten has always been watching out for me, even since that first night when he lent me his shirt?

And now he's killed four men for me. It leaves my mind reeling and my breath hot. I never knew how intoxicating it could be to see someone go to battle for me. He butchered these men. Dropped bodies to my feet. All this blood. This carnage. The air is charged like the aftermath of a lightning strike—so much energy with nowhere to go.

Clutching his collar, I tip my face up. We're whisper-close. A drop of blood rolls from his hairline. This time, I don't wipe it away. I watch it blaze a course down his perfect temple.

What would my life have been like if I'd had Basten in the convent? My whole life, all I've known from the people who were supposed to care for me is perverse abuse at their own hands. For so long, I've longed for safety. Someone to fight for me, or better yet, to show me I have the strength to defend myself.

Basten has done both.

And what about him? An orphaned boy, forced to fight anyone who might be a friend. He trembles under my gentle touch like he's never experienced a single tender thing before.

I didn't see before now how alike the two of us are. We both grew up painfully alone, relying only on our wits and godkisses. So it's no wonder that we tried to throw up walls when we found a like soul, instead of recognizing each other.

And now I'm about to lose him. When we reach Duren, he won't be there for me when I need him. I'll never again feel how entirely his arms surround me, like a coat tailored perfectly to my frame. I'll never know if his broken parts ever mend.

As I clutch his collar harder, I feel like I'm falling from a hundred feet, falling, falling, falling, and the only thing to hold onto is him.

"You came," I whisper.

"Little violet, of course I came. I'd cross the gods' ten realms on hands and knees for you."

He's filthy, covered in blood, just like me. We should clean ourselves up, but I can't bear to have this moment end. With the pad of my thumb, I smooth a drop of blood off his bottom lip. "What happened in Blackwater?"

"I shouldn't have left you, even for a second. It's my fault that they—"

I lay my finger flat across his lips, silencing him. "It isn't your fault."

He shakes his head. "Sabine, when I saw you were taken . . . When I smelled that bastard's taint on top of your own scent . . . " Rage contorts his face to the point where it feels like he'll explode. He drags a hand down his face, trying to bring his emotions into check.

Myst whinnies at the door.

All dead?

I start to answer her, but before I can, Basten says in a voice heavy with exhaustion, "Yeah, crazy mare. We got her. We did it."

I wrinkle my nose, confused. "Wait. Did you—did you *hear* her?"

"No. But that horse and I? We understand each other well enough without words."

He weighs as much as two of you, Myst snorts at me. *Tell him he walks on his own feet from now on.*

I can't help but smile, wondering how in the world the two of them got along well enough to team up to rescue me. Then, I look at Adan's body, and grow serious.

"Basten, there's something I have to tell you. King Joruun was the one who hired Adan and his men to bring me to Old Coros."

Basten pulls back to search my eyes for an answer to a

question he doesn't understand. His eyebrows furrow. "King Joruun? Are you certain?" He hesitates. "What exactly did they say?"

"That the king wouldn't want me, well, *touched*." My voice bottoms out on the final word, as I feel the ghost of Maks's hands between my legs. My throat goes bone-dry. My muscles seize up from the echo of past danger, and Basten must pick up on it with his heightened senses, because he lightly grips my chin with thumb and forefinger.

"*Did* they touch you?"

A whimper slips out before I can swallow it. My body shakes. Basten's eyes darken like storm clouds, and he shakes his head as I hunt for words to explain.

"No—you don't have to say it, Sabine. I can find out myself." As carefully as picking up a bird with a broken wing, he leans close to smell my neck, then over my shoulder, to the palm of my hand. Then he turns to the dead bodies.

"That one," he says, pointing to Maks. "He tried—but didn't get far."

I give the ghost of a nod.

His grip on my hand tightens possessively. "I'd ask Immortal Woudix to bring that bastard back from the dead, just so I could kill him all over again." He takes a shuddering breath. A moment passes, then he says quietly, "They weren't talking about King Joruun."

It takes me a second to realize we aren't talking about Maks anymore. "But who—"

"They meant King Rachillon."

I stare at him. I've never heard the name.

He explains, "They were Volkish raiders, Sabine. A king might have hired them, but not ours. It was King Rachillon of Volkany."

Bewildered, I stare blankly like he's telling me a fae story that happened long ago to people far more important than me.

"King Rachillon?" I pronounce it as he did, *Rah-shee-yan.*

I've been so sequestered for the last twelve years that any news that might have dribbled across the Volkish border didn't make it into the Convent of Immortal Iyre. The last I heard, Volkany didn't even have a king. "I—I don't understand. Why would the King of Volkany want me?"

It feels unreal to even say, like we're operating within a dream.

Basten mutters to himself, "That's a damn good question."

He brought up Volkany in the Manywaters Inn. I wonder if he knows more than he's saying—or at least suspects more—but his clenched jaw tells me his thoughts are locked inside his own head for the time being.

※

We leave the bodies in the cottage. Enough hungry creatures are in these woods to clean them up for us. Exhausted and dirty, we ride Myst through the woods, parallel to the river in case the raiding band has more members. The moon is high by the time Basten finally stops Myst so he can listen through the trees.

"There's a waterfall close by," he says. "Just over that rise. We'll be safe there. The water will drown out our scents and sounds. Maybe we can even bathe."

My muscles are wrung to the bone as we ride the final stretch. Soon, I hear the falls, and then glimpse the silver moonlight reflecting off its water. It's a tall and narrow waterfall that tumbles off the edge of a shallow cave, crashing below onto rocks before reforming into a meandering valley stream.

Basten leads Myst into the shelter of the shallow cave. We begin stripping off our blood-soaked clothes, so we can wash. The waterfall's roar fills the silence as our bared flesh catches the moonlight. Basten has seen me naked a thousand times, but suddenly I feel shy. When he extends a hand to help me over the rocks, I cross my arms over my chest.

"I can't hide behind my hair anymore," I say quietly, knowing he can hear me despite the waterfall.

Basten pauses, keeping his eyes pinned squarely on my face out of respect, pretending the night hides everything below shoulder level. "The raiders cut it off?"

I nod. "To disguise me. I don't miss it—only the cover it gave me."

He tucks another strand behind my ear. "I like you this way. You weren't meant to be weighed down."

Gingerly, I test out the falls by extending one foot, shrieking from the burst of cold—but it's a welcome shock to my system. I dip my hand in the falling water, then my head, then fully stand under the crashing water and tip my head back, letting it scour me clean.

Basten joins me beneath the falls, scrubbing his scalp in the frigid onslaught. He turns his face skyward, letting the water pound his face. It has to hurt, but he doesn't flinch.

The roaring water is too loud for us to talk much, but he sees me struggling to wash blood off my back and comes up behind me to help. His hands cup my shoulders as he guides me to stand beneath a water stream. His hands work to wash away the blood, kneading my tense muscles until they melt under his deft touch.

After bathing, we wash our clothes and lay them out to dry, then I bundle up in a blanket while he slings a towel around his waist and builds a fire in the lee of the cave. A light mist floats off the waterfall, making me shiver despite the crackling flames.

"Come here," he barks, patting his knee. "You need to be closer to the fire."

He gathers me in his lap, securing the blanket around me so I'm bundled up tight enough that a wolly worm couldn't slip through. I don't know which is more comforting, the blanket or Basten's arms. I let myself relax against his chest, watching the fire, as my mind dulls to match the waterfall's steady roar.

A long time passes in silence.

I don't think either of us wants to break this moment. We're safe. We're clean. We're *together*. One wrong word could topple this delicate house of cards, scatter us to the wind, when all I want is to be in his arms forever.

Somehow, his hand finds its way to mine, and it feels

good to do something as simple as holding hands. The firelight flickers over his busted knuckles. I run my thumb lightly over his damaged skin, recalling how charged he was during the fight. How charged I was *watching* him. He made the fight look effortless—like a game. He brought down four powerful raiders in minutes.

What would he do to the Sisters who beat me?

On impulse, I bring his knuckles to my lips and softly kiss the scrapes.

A moan rumbles in his chest. "I like it when you do that." His mouth is close enough to my ear to hear him over the waterfall's roar.

"Do what?"

"Treat me like one of your animals. So damn tender."

For a second, I wonder about kissing him on other places on his body. Bathing in the falls reawakened me, charged me again like during the fight. My breath feels shallow. My teeth keep hunting out my bottom lip, seeking the grounding bite of pain. The bath reinvigorated Basten, too—it's more than evident. I don't need heightened senses to perceive the attention of his stiff cock pressing against my ass through the blanket.

My hips shift in his lap like they have a mind of their own. His breath catches briefly. Then his hand moves from the chaste position holding my hand to my bare shoulder, exposed from the slipped-down blanket, his thumb rubbing in long strokes.

My vision blurs. I'm breathing too shallowly. My head fills with fantasies of what could happen in this cave behind the waterfall, where we might as well be the last two people on earth.

Quelling a rash of nerves, I whisper, "I realize now it was never about Adan, only what he offered me."

Basten is quiet before he asks, "Love?"

"Freedom." I swallow a bundle of nerves lodged in my throat. "That's what I want. Not jewels. Not a high lord. Not a castle. I want to feel like I do when I ride Myst at a gallop. Like the only path ahead of me is the one I make." I hesitate. "With whom I make it."

He doesn't reply with words, but his body answers for him. His thumb glides along my neck, working out the tight muscles there for a long time, like it's his own knotted thoughts he really needs to untangle.

"You're to marry Rian," he says.

There. It's spoken now. At least it's out in the open, this thing we've been circling. The topic of my impending marriage hasn't come up as often in the past few days as it did at the ride's beginning, and I can't help but feel that Basten has been fighting to put it out of his head as he and I grow closer.

I turn in his lap to face him, the blanket still wrapped around my chest, my legs dangling over his right thigh.

"I don't want to marry Lord Rian. I want to go with Myst to Salensa and see the ocean." I hold his gaze with every ounce of my courage. "I want you to take us there."

I nearly lose my voice as I ask the thing I'm terrified to ask. My heart knocks around in my chest in an attempt to escape the possible sting of rejection. I understand that he's devoted to Lord Rian. In fact, I'm so damn sick of hearing about his loyalty to that man that I could scream. But Basten has killed for me, he's sinned for me—is it so different to betray for me?

Yes. For him, it is.

And that terrifies me. Myst advised me to flip Basten's loyalty from Rian to me, but I'm not sure I can. I offered him a bribe in the woods—he wouldn't take it. I offered him my perfumed body on the inn's soft sheets—he still wouldn't kiss me.

His voice is grave when he answers, "Sabine, you don't know what you're asking."

"I know exactly what I'm asking." I hold my locked gaze steady. "I'm asking you to break your vow to your master."

His throat bobs. "I made a promise."

"So did your heart." My voice breaks. "It made a promise to me."

His jaw falls open, at a loss for words. I can see the torment traveling through his eyes. He rakes a hand through his damp, dark hair, tangling his fist in the long strands.

He finally moves me off his lap and unfolds himself, standing up to pace in front of the fire, securing the towel around his waist. At each turn, he throws me a guarded look like I might stab him in the heart. Is he wrong? Will I?

"Sabine—" he entreats.

"We'll pose as husband and wife on the road to Salensa so we can travel freely," I interrupt in a rush. "Once there, I can get work on a farm tending to livestock. You can hunt."

He gapes in disbelief that I'm serious enough about this to have thought it out. He repeats in a distant voice, "Pose as husband and wife?"

A portion of the question hangs there, unasked. I

glance down at my hands clasped in my lap. "If it's about sex . . . "

He barks a hard laugh. "It's about sex. Gods, yes, it's about sex. But it's about so much more than that, Sabine. You know it is."

A catching sensation snags in my throat. My body alone isn't enough to tempt him, but can I dare offer him more? My heart is all I have left to give, and if I surrendered it, I'd have nothing. I made the mistake of falling for Adan, and I'm terrified of thinking I might be in love again, only to be wrong.

I start, "I know you feel loyalty to Rian—"

"Yeah, yeah. I know what you think. That my loyalty is blind and unmerited, but it isn't. Rian is like a brother to me. More than that. I'd be in the gutter if it weren't for him. Hell, I'd be dead."

"He's not a brother, he's your *master*! He *pays* you!"

He continues to pace as our voices rise to a shout above the waterfall's roar. Myst just steadily munches on grass while she watches us trade barbs. Basten readjusts his towel. His chest heaves. Every one of his muscles is on edge. He looks more frightening now than he did facing off against Volkish raiders.

Finally, he stops. The firelight casts shadows over the smooth dips and rises of his muscles, making him look inhuman, like one of the fae gods themselves. "I need more than sex. I need more than a few days with you, or however long it takes us to get to Salensa and for you to grow bored of me. No. I need *everything*. Not now, not yet. But I have to know there's a chance this could be more."

My lips part. He's turned the ultimatum back on me,

and I'm even more nervous now than when I first proposed we run away together. What exactly is he asking? If I could fall in love with him? If one day, pretending to be husband and wife will become real? How am I supposed to answer that? I'm not even sure I know what love is. The last person who showed me unconditional love died twelve years ago.

"I can't read the future," I whisper helplessly. "I can't make any promises."

A muscle in his jaw jumps. "Well, I can't betray Rian, if you can't give us a fucking shot."

By the Immortals. What does this man want from me? Weeks ago, I wouldn't have hesitated to lie to him, but we're far beyond that. The least I owe him is honesty.

Can I see a future with him?

He stares me down with more heat than comes from the fire.

My heart opens like a cracked door, letting in the faintest rays of light. "I—I want this, Basten. I want you. Now—maybe forever. That's the best I can give you." *Maybe. Maybe. Maybe.* So many maybes I'm drowning in them. So many maybes I'm terrified.

He stills. A strange calm comes over his face, like he's given into a battle he didn't know he was fighting. "Okay."

"O—okay."

And it's done. It's sealed. My mind can hardly process the fact that after so many days of wanting to escape my fate of marrying Rian Valvere, I'm getting my wish. Not only that, but so much more. I'm getting freedom. I'm getting the *sea.* And gods—*gods*—I'm getting Basten, and that's the best part of all. I can't predict what the future holds for us, but as terrified as I am of letting that door in my heart open wider, the light is pushing through.

The waterfall pounds steadily behind him, so I can't hear his heartbeat, but I imagine it's thudding as hard as mine. He takes a jolting step toward me like this isn't real. Like it's a dream. He sinks to his knees next to me. His eyes drink in the sight of me in the blanket and nothing else.

My body turns on like a star, blazing for him. I grab him by the shoulders. My voice catches as I whisper huskily, "All those things you said you'd do to me at the inn? I want you to do them to me. *Now.*"

How many times have I fantasized about that game of pretend? How many times has he?

His hot palm rests at the base of my neck, heavy like an iron necklace. "We both know that if this happens, everything will change. If we start, I don't think I'll be able to stop."

I whisper, "I don't want you to stop."

He has a single moment of hesitation, then his eyes spark as he stands up and gives the order, "Lay back."

I'm shaking as I lay on the cave floor, still wrapped tightly in the blanket. Basten looks me over from my head to my toes like a present he can barely keep from tearing into. He stands on either side of my hips, then lowers to his knees to straddle me.

My pulse scrambles like buzzing bees in my veins. His body weight on my hips feels good, but my stomach is roiling, my thighs trembling.

He places his hand flat on the base of my neck again,

slowing my breath. "Let your body relax. I'll go slow. I'll take care of you."

Of course he can hear how wildly my heart is beating. How I'm both excited and afraid of what's to come. Once I'm fighting for steadier breaths, he moves his thumb to my mouth, dragging it over my bottom lip and letting the fingertip graze the hard edge of my teeth.

"I've thought a million times about how I'd fuck you."

In the inn, he never kissed me, only touched the burning places he would want to. Now, my breath stalls in anticipation as he lowers to close his lips around mine. True to his word, the kiss starts slowly. He's taking his time, savoring this. His lips guide mine toward deepening the connection, and then his tongue pushes against my lips' seam. They part for him, and he slides his tongue over mine in long strokes that I instinctively match.

He groans into my mouth as he pulls back. His index finger moves down my neck to settle in the hollow at the base of my throat.

My skin is already snapping, craving his touch, before he plants his lips on my neck. He breathes hotly onto my skin, then licks the hollow at the base of my throat with the tip of his tongue, like lapping up honey.

I moan.

His lips blaze a trail lower on my chest, to where my godkiss birthmark rides on my breastbone. His hands find the blanket's edges, coaxing me to release my tight hold on it.

My arms lock, a last attempt to hold the blanket around me. My final wall. But he gently eases my arms away from my chest, guiding them to lay flat at my sides.

He unfolds the blanket one side at a time, slowly exposing my bare, full breasts.

He takes a moment to appreciate the sight. His hand cups the heft of my left breast, squeezing and fondling softly. His fingers deftly roll the nipple until it hardens like a pebble. My head tips back on the blanket. His touch feels like magic. I want it everywhere.

Without warning, he takes my nipple into his mouth. A gasp springs to my lips as I arch my back, thrusting the nipple further between his lips. He claims it, sucks it, then gently bites down.

I cry out. "Basten!"

"That's it, little violet. Tell me what you like."

It's getting hard to think. I'm trying to remember what came next at the inn. What hot, filthy promise did he moan against my skin? All I can concentrate on is the growing spark catching fire in my lower half.

He releases my nipple to plant hot kisses along the contours of my stomach. A freckle on my ribs. One near my navel. Another on the curve of my right hip. As his lips move lower, he peels back the blanket, opening me up to the waterfall's cool mist, the fire's hot blaze, and his own covetous look, until I'm entirely nude.

This is as far as our game of pretend went at the inn, but now, it feels like only the beginning. I gaze up at him, gently biting my bottom lip. "And now what?"

"This."

His hand cups the wet heat between my legs. I swallow a moan, my hips bucking against the weight of his palm. He presses the rough base of his hand against the tight knot at the top of my groin, then slowly sinks one finger into my core. He stops at the first knuckle, stroking me shallowly and slowly.

I moan, bucking my hips to try to force his finger deeper. "More."

He chuckles as he presses his finger further into my heat, stroking faster. Then he adds a second finger. The hard base of his palm continues to rub me from the outside.

I whimper, hardly knowing what I'm experiencing. I didn't know it was possible to feel like this. That with just one hand, Basten could make me feel like I'm soaring. His fingers stroke in a steady move that has me rolling my hips up to meet their rhythm.

"That's it. Ride my hand. You're doing so good. I can smell your slickness. Can you hear it? I can. It sounds like snowmelt dripping from rocks."

I should be embarrassed, but it only lights me up more to think of how his godkiss perceives my response to him. I can't hide anything from him—we have no secrets.

A pressure I can't put a name to builds between my legs. I can't focus on anything but riding out the sensation, seeing where it will take me. But all too soon, Basten pulls his fingers out.

I moan an objection, pushing myself up to my elbows.

He chuckles again as he licks my glistening juices off his fingers. "Gods, your taste," he moans, lapping at his fingers.

The move steals whatever I was going to say right out of my mouth, and I gape. "What are you doing?" This is all new. It's terrifying. It's exhilarating. The waterfall roars steadily, dulling my thoughts.

"That's only the start," he says. "I warned you what would happen."

"What—what else are you going to do?"

"Lay down. Like this." He presses my back to the blanket, then bends my knees to point toward the cave's roof. My thighs squeeze together instinctively, but he grabs each knee and gently pushes them apart.

My pussy is spread for him like a banquet. Heat reddens my cheeks, but he doesn't look embarrassed. Far from it. He looks primed to gorge. He brushes his thumb over the sensitive outer edges of my core like pressing into a ripe peach.

"I've lied awake so many nights thinking about having your cunt quiver beneath my mouth."

My eyes stretch wide. "Wait, your *mouth*?"

He's already got his face between my legs, his arms prying my legs apart against their instinct to clench together. He licks the outer edges of my cunt, sending lightning bolts shooting into my belly. His tongue slides around my slick heat, stroking like he did with his fingers, but this is another level. His mouth is so warm, the things he does with his tongue so confident. So *ravenous*. In seconds, the building pressure feels like it's about to explode.

"That's it," he whispers against my body. "You're doing so well. Moan for me. Moan where it feels good. There? You like that?"

He seals his lips over the tight bud at the top of my cunt and gently sucks.

And some deep, dark part of me goes wild. My entire body seizes up like a fist, trembling and pulsing, and then all at once, the hold shatters. Lightning crashes between my legs, and a tingling rumble of thunder rolls through my muscles. It's ecstasy. It's pain. It's heaven. It's sinful. It's frightening and new, and I already know that I'm going to need to feel this again and again.

While my body is still shaking from the aftershocks, Basten sits up, wiping his mouth with the back of his hand. I try not to think about his godkiss. How intensely he must perceive my scent, my taste. His eyes are heavy as he gazes down at my quivering body, and there's an edge of darkness there. The hint of violence I know he craves because it's all he's known. But he promised he'd go slowly for my first time, and his hands are tender as he wrenches my legs back apart, staring down at my cunt.

"You're slick as melting ice. Are you ready for me? Do you want me? Say it." His fingers tease the poor, oversensitive bud that's still throbbing from what he's already done to it.

"I want you," I breathe.

He removes the towel around his waist. His cock is thick, heavy. Enormous. It juts out with a readiness that makes my inhale stall in my throat. *That* is supposed to fit inside me? Fuck the gods. He's going to split me apart with that massive tool.

"Go ahead," he commands. "Touch it. Take me in your hand."

I hesitate. My trembling fingers graze the smooth tip, where a pearlescent drop glistens. His cock is smoother than I expected. It strains into my palm with throbbing urgency.

He briefly closes his eyes, and I realize how much my

touch pleases him. It gives me a strange feeling of power to know I can put that look on his face.

"Kiss it," he barks.

Is he serious? These are the things described in Immortal Alyssantha's chapters, things I wasn't sure anyone but the debauched fae gods did. But one look at Basten's hooded eyelids confirms it: Oh, yes. He's deadly serious.

With shaking lips, I gently kiss his cock's tip. It tastes salty, not as bad as I'd feared.

He groans as he pushes me down to the blanket again, leans over me, then wraps his hand around his cock to line it up with my entrance.

"I'll go slow. Don't be afraid."

He holds me like a fragile doll as he presses the tip of his cock against my center. It enters an inch, pushing me apart with its stiff insistence. I can't describe what it feels like. Like . . . like pleasure and pain, a thorn and a rose, fire and ice. Basten pushes inside another inch, pausing there, giving my body time to adjust to his enormous size.

"Gods, you feel good," he mutters. "So fucking tight."

His muscles are twitching. Sweat drips down his chest. He's straining not to thrust all the way into me like I know he wants. He pushes in another inch as my body gushes desire, stretching to make room for him. Once he's halfway in, he starts moving in slow, shallow thrusts. Each thrust lets him enter a little further, and my hips begin to roll in a matching rhythm.

"Keep moving your hips like that . . . that's it. That's fucking it. You're so tight."

With a groan, he sinks all the way into me. It's so deep

that I gag, my eyes bulging, unable to believe how far he can reach inside me. His balls slap gently against my ass as he pulls out, then slides back in.

"Does that feel good?" he asks wickedly. "Do you like it?"

I give a shaky nod, not trusting myself to think. Words? What are those? All I am is a ball of dry tinder, ready to combust. He grabs my ass cheek to get a better hold, and thrusts faster, riding me harder.

"You take it so well, little violet. You're so wet for me."

His words drip over me like honey. It feels good to hear the praise. I've fought so long. To survive, to defy my surroundings. I'm tired of fighting. I want to be possessed, used, taken care of, stuffed with pleasure.

The pressure builds until I'm keening, and I choke, "I don't think I can take any more."

"Oh, you can take it." His strokes are long and deep, spearing me.

I feel the lightning and thunder coming again. I tip my head back, trying not to fight the rising storm. My body twitches in a thousand different places, and then all at once, comes together in one shattering clap. I cry out. Pleasure drenches me like I'm under the waterfall, being pounded by the full force of nature. This time, the wave is stronger, claiming my body in tight little pulses that go on and on until I'm flying.

With a masculine groan, Basten thrusts into me one final time. The deepest yet, so deep I feel his cock inside near my navel. It throbs and pulses in my swollen core. He stays buried in me for a few breaths, wringing the last morsels out of our pleasure.

When he finally pulls out, his hot seed seeps down my inner thighs. Dear gods—it's pure wickedness. He drags me into his lap, and wraps the blanket around my quivering body, holding me in the thick walls of his arms, I wrap my arms around his chest, my face pressed to his godkissed birthmark.

We're spent. Both of us.

I don't know who falls asleep first, but neither of us lets the other go.

CHAPTER 22

WOLF

She's so fucking pretty I can't rip my eyes off her. The dying firelight paints fingers of light on her. Why sleep, when she's in the waking world? I never want to fall asleep again.

My cock is hard, aching to take her again as I remember how it felt to push inside her tight pussy to claim her virginity. It's never been something that matters to me, unlike some other men. I don't get off on the idea of an untouched pussy, but the idea that my cock will be the first and last one Sabine takes is so satisfying that my balls tighten.

I could fist my own cock right here while I watch her sleep. She's mine now—no one else's. I can touch her however I want, in whatever way feels good to her. I'd crawl through any battlefield to hear her whimper again like she did when she came.

She has her back to me, her perfect little ass pressed to

my groin. The scent of my seed on her thighs makes me drunk with pride. I move aside the blanket to look at her. Her cunt is hot. Glistening. Even in her sleep, she's wet and needy.

I can't help but reach around to take one of her tight nipples between my fingers and roll it softly. Just as I hoped, the action elicits a little moan deep in her throat. In another second, her pussy is throbbing, coated in slickness, begging to be filled again.

"That feels so good," she mutters, still half-asleep. "Do it again, Basten."

I pinch her nipple harder. "Look at me when you ask that."

There's a sharpness to my command that makes her jump. She rolls over, more awake now, blinking those innocent, sleepy eyes up at me. I didn't talk to her like this the first time I fucked her. I wanted her first time to be tender, for her to feel powerful and adored. But now it's getting hard to hold myself back from the bottomless well of lust that has me imagining so many filthy things I want to do to her.

Quietly, but with a boldness in her eyes, she whispers, "Do it again, Basten."

Her obedience makes me groan—that this beautiful girl will let me do such debased things to her. She's so willing. So bold. All the terrible, violent things I've done . . . and she still lets me put my hands on her.

Have I found someone who gets me? *I* don't even understand the fucked-up things I do. But this girl lets venomous snakes coil up next to her for warmth. If any woman could ever love me, it's Sabine Darrow.

"Please," she whispers groggily, snaking a hand under the blanket toward my groin.

"You're insatiable," I mutter, barely able to restrain my own desire. "You just had my cock. You already want it again? Greedy thing. Very well, then tell me. Tell me how you need it."

Her hips are already fidgeting. "I need you inside me."

With a cruel smile, I stroke the outside of her cunt with one finger, teasing her without giving her the fullness she wants. "What would you do for it? Would you beg?"

"You bastard," she groans, pushing her cunt harder against my palm, trying to ride my fingers.

I chuckle darkly. "Now you're starting to understand what you signed up for. Lay back. Keep your eyes on me this time when I fuck you."

This time, I don't hold back when I thrust into her. It's easy to tell what she likes. Her body gives it away as clearly as if she were whispering instructions against my ear. I know when to hold back, when she can take more. And she takes it so fucking well, everything I have to give her. Having sex with Sabine feels like worship. I've never entered a church in my life, never bowed to one of the Immortal's shrines, but now I understand reverence for the divine.

Fuck the gods—I'll pray to her.

"In Salensa," I say between heaving breaths as I pump into her, "I'm going to call you my wife. What are you going to call me?"

"Husband," she breathes.

"That's right. I don't care if it's fucking pretend. I'll

still fuck you every night. Our neighbors will hear your screams from the window."

She makes the most delicious little noises. Her nails dig into my shoulders hard enough to leave half-moon bruises. Gods, I want to fuck her into oblivion. I want to fuck her like an animal. I want to fuck her until she forgets every god's name and only remembers me.

My balls draw tight. I hold back, wanting her to come first. And she's so goddamn close. Her pussy is quaking, ready. She just needs to be sent over the edge. I move my hand between her legs and flick my fingernail against her clit while I thrust long and deep into her pussy, and that's all it takes.

As soon as she cries out, I bury myself deep inside her one final time. I want to mark her. Even if I'm the only one who can smell my seed leaking out between her thighs. I come hard, shoving all the way to the hilt, wanting every drop of my cum planted deep inside her. It's feral, this instinct to fill her up to the brim.

After I pull out, she lazily drapes herself over my chest, yawning as she mutters, "Immortal Iyre didn't know what she was missing with her whole chastity thing."

She falls back asleep, sated, using my chest as a pillow. The poor, exhausted thing. She's been through so much. She needs her sleep, because I have so much more planned for her. Ever since I laid eyes on her, I've had to pretend I didn't fantasize about her—about my master's bride.

I stroke her short hair, misted with droplets from the waterfall's spray.

We've fucked twice now with no precaution. I normally wouldn't be so stupid, but I didn't predict this would happen. And after the million times I've been kneed in the groin in the fight ring, I've been told it's highly unlikely I'm capable of siring children. Still, I'll try to be more mindful next time, but what if she falls pregnant from the two times I've already planted my seed in her? Staring at the cave ceiling, the answer comes to me like a rush of falling water.

Fuck me, I'd be the luckiest man to walk the earth. First to have Sabine's sweet cunt wrapped around my cock, then to have her belly swollen with my child.

Thinking of her like that is going to get you hard again, Wolf . . .

But in seriousness, what if she *does* fall pregnant? What kind of a father would I be? The gods know I don't have a role model for the job. Jocki, who forced me into the ring? Lord Berolt, who killed his own wife? Certainly not my real father, whoever the bastard was.

I bite the end of one thumb, scraping my teeth against the nail. Trying to figure out if I've just totally fucked over any future children, cursing them with *me* for a father. And a husband? How am I going to fuck that role up? We said we'd only pose as a married couple, but I made her promise it could happen one day. Was that cruel of me? To want her love, when I know I can never return it? Because as much as she consumes every last corner of my mind, I'm incapable of love. I'm too broken. Whatever I might have once called a heart is a burned-out shell. I can want her. I can crave her. I can protect her with my dying breath, but love is impossible for someone as damaged as me.

Fuck. Why did I think a bastard like me could give her the life she deserved? I have no money. No title. No talents except with my fists or a bow. She's a goddess. Men have probably been vying for her since she was twelve years old. As awful as her life was in that convent—and as much as I want to wring those Sisters' withered necks—maybe it was better for her. She could have been sold off as a young bride to some wrinkled old lord who'd stuff his shriveled cock down her throat each night. Her ass of a father might have done her a favor by waiting for Rian's proposal.

Rian—he's the type of husband she deserves. Yeah, he isn't virtuous by any stretch of the definition. There's blood on his hands, too. But he'd be able to give her the life she merits. Beautiful dresses, days of leisure, servants to wait on her. What do I have to offer? I can protect her, but beyond that? Rabbit stew and deer pelts?

My jaw clenches as I watch her chest rise and fall in her slumber. *No—don't think like this.* She chose me; it's not like I'm forcing her to accept life with me. She has every right to decide what she wants, and if that's rabbit stew instead of Balaysian caviar, so be it. I'll give her the best life I can. I'll fight like hell to make her happy.

The crunch of grass reaches my ears. Myst is munching through the armfuls of grass I gathered for her from the valley. I tear my eyes off Sabine and go to the horse, leaning against the cave's rocky wall.

"You didn't want to go to Duren anyway, did you, crazy mare?"

She stops eating to nuzzle my pockets, until I pull out the hunk of cheese I'd been saving for breakfast. I hold it out in my palm. "Yeah, yeah. Here."

I stroke her silky white hair as she enjoys the cheese. Before I left, Rian ordered the stableboys to clear out his prize stallion's spacious stall to make room for Myst, and even bought the finest Spezian tack as a welcome gift for Sabine. He paid a fleet of seamstresses to make dresses in her measurements. He ordered the metalsmith to make a wedding ring out of Cratian gold, inset with an ancient diamond, the Titan's Tear, so famed that it's even mentioned in the Book of the Immortals. He even commissioned a painting of Immortal Iyre in tribute to Sabine's patron goddess of virtue—of course, *that* might have been premature.

He's wanted her for a long time. He spent a year planning for this. He entrapped her idiot father into a rigged card game to get him so deeply in debt that he'd do anything to clear the books.

I scratch my nails hard against my scalp, but the pain isn't enough. Myst watches me steadily with her velvety black eyes as I fidget—resting a foot on the rocks behind me, pacing toward the falling water, then doubling back.

When I agreed to run away with Sabine, I knew the price. Backstabbing the only person who's shown me an ounce of concern. It comes down to a simple toss-up, like Rian's favorite game, the coin flip with his Golath dime. Sabine or Rian. Rian or Sabine. One of them was always going to feel my knife in their back.

And it sure as hell wasn't going to be her.

I close my eyes, pinching the uneven bridge of my

nose, broken so many times in the ring that I've lost most feeling in it.

"Wolf. Come on, you lug. Get up." I can hear Rian's voice now from many years ago. *"The whorehouse on Second Street has two new girls. Twins. We can fuck them together, eh?"*

I'd been finishing up a drill in the Golden Sentinels' training grounds. The army camp was just north of Duren's walls, pushing up against the edge of the Blackened Forest. It was strange for Rian to interrupt me while in a drill, and I was about to tell him to fuck off, when I spotted Lord Berolt's carriage pull up near the archery range.

A blade of fear sliced into my belly.

Lord Berolt always had a fascination for godkissed people, but now, according to dark rumors, he'd started experimenting on aging godkissed whores who'd outlived their beauty, or nonessential godkissed soldiers.

I had to quickly wonder if my skills counted as essential.

"Come on, Wolf," Rian insisted, his voice light, though there was fear in his eyes as he glanced at his father's carriage. *"Tell your commander I ordered you to wrap up early so you can wet your cock on a twin."*

He got me out of there before Lord Berolt started perusing the training grounds for viable candidates for his experiment table. It wasn't the first time Rian saved me, either. He always sheltered me from his father's attention. Downplaying my godkiss, insisting I was just a brute who was useful to train against. Always masking his real intentions with a smirk and a quip.

Now, Myst's stomach grumbles. She sniffs my pockets for more cheese. I shake my head fondly at her, glad to be distracted from the past.

"Whoever heard of a horse who liked cheese? I don't think it's good for you, crazy mare." I crouch by my rucksack to dig for a different treat for her, and my fingers brush over crumpled paper. I pull out Lord Charlin Darrow's letter.

I haven't given the letter much thought since we left Bremcote. The Darrow wax seal glistens in the firelight with the emblem of a sheep's head. It occurs to me that Lord Rian will never receive this letter, now that I'm not returning to Duren. I could throw it in the fire. I could let it turn to dust, forgotten in the bottom of my rucksack.

Or I could read it—why the hell not? What secret was so meaningful for Lord Charlin to think it could possibly sway Rian?

Still, I pause before breaking the wax seal, still bound by years of fealty. But then I take in Sabine's sweet, slumbering form beneath the blanket, shivering without my warmth beside her, and my heart knows I'd damn myself to the underrealm for her.

With a finger jerk, I break the seal and open the letter. I don't know what I expected to find. A minor scandal that Lord Charlin discovered; a bribe of some ilk. Maybe a pitiful wager on a horse race in an attempt to regain his fortune.

But as soon as I read the first line, the condescension melts off my face.

A tremor starts in my left hand. No—no, this can't be right. *This can't be fucking right.* I have to read the first few lines twice. My vision blurs, making me hold the letter to the firelight to keep reading. And by the Immortals, it goes on and on. Each line more bone-chilling than the last, filling my stomach like a poisoned meal.

The things Lord Charlin claims in the letter are impossible. He's a liar or, at best, a confused old man. But he swears to have proof of his unimaginable claim—a claim that is so consequential to Sabine, to me, and to Rian that it will change everything.

The old drunk really did have one hell of a secret.

I don't know how many times I re-read the letter before crumpling it in my fist. My heart beats erratically. I'm at war with myself. Who else knows this secret? In the letter, Lord Charlin claims he told no one. So I could throw the letter in the fire. Pretend it never existed. If Charlin himself ever tries to bring it up, I'll arrange for him to have an unfortunate accident.

No one has to know.

But Lord Charlin, and now me, *aren't* the only ones who know. And that's the whole fucking problem. Because this letter makes it very clear why the Volkish raiders targeted Sabine. I'd thought they were just after pretty godkissed girls that fit her description, probably to use as whores.

But I was wrong.

They weren't after girls *like* Sabine—they were after *her*.

And if what Lord Charlin claims is true, then they'll be back for her. King Rachillon will send his best spies and raiders. He might send a whole fucking army.

What am I going to do against an army? Oh, I'll fight like hell for her. A band of raiders? That's easy. Even a battalion? I'd give it a fair shot. But not even I can go up against an army. There's only one person who can— someone who *also* has a big fucking army.

My pulse scrambles in my veins. The waterfall's rush is too loud, driving me to distraction, and the campfire smell is too strong. I'm overloaded by senses. My godkiss is going haywire.

I slump against the back of the cave, raking my nails down my face.

"*Fuck!*"

I'm at war with myself. I don't know what to do with this information, this threat. A soft horse muzzle knocks into me gently. Myst blinks steadily at me, concerned.

I take the horse's face in my hands, staring into her bottomless eyes.

"I'm fucked, Myst."

The last remnants of that burned-out shell of my heart crumble into ash. Because I know what I have to do now. Salensa? A fantasy. Why did I ever think I could keep Sabine safe, anyway? That I could make her happy? Hell, even before I'd learned the contents of that letter, I knew I wasn't good enough for her. I'm a bastard from the streets. I have nothing. I don't even own my bow—that's Rian's. Everything is Rian's.

And now, she is, too. She has to be. Because I don't have a choice.

"She's going to hate me." I squeeze my eyes shut, pressing my forehead against Myst's. Sabine can't ever know what's in that letter. No one can. Which means I'm going to have to lie to the only woman on this earth who I've wanted to share absolute honesty with. "I have to *make* her hate me."

CHAPTER 23
SABINE

I wake languidly, stretching my limbs over the blanket laid out on the cave floor. The waterfall's steady rush was a balm that had me sleeping better than I can remember. My thighs are sore from so much riding, and the puncture on my foot aches, yet I feel restored. The dream I was having still traipses through my mind. I'm on the beach, gathering seashells as festive music drifts on the air from Salensa's nearby town center. Big shells, small ones, whole ones, broken ones. They're all beautiful in their own way. Each time I find one, I run back to add it to the collection Basten grudgingly carries for me in his hands. He acts as grumpy as ever as he tromps through the surf, but the doting amusement in his eyes betrays his joy.

Laying back, I close my eyes and listen to the waterfall, imagining it's the rush of the Panopis Sea. I wish I had Basten's senses, if only for a day. When we get to the sea, I want to hear every bubble pop in the ocean surf.

Feel every grain of sand scouring my feet. Taste the layers of salt in the water. What will I say to the sea creatures? What will they say to me? Dolphins and fish and octopuses—if octopuses are even real. I know only what I've gleaned from overheard snatches of conversations.

"Basten?" I call.

He's not in the cave; he must have woken early to hunt breakfast. I smooth my hand over the rumpled half of the blanket that still holds a trace of his warmth. A secretive smile breaks across my face as I roll over and feel a soreness between my legs. Pressing a hand to my mouth, I giggle up at the cave's ceiling.

By the gods, the things we did last night . . .

What I said to Basten was true—I don't understand how anyone could consider such pleasure sinful. For twelve years, I've had the virtues of chastity drilled into me. In Immortal Iyre's chapters, she's constantly accosted by male fae who crave her body—Vale and Woudix and Popelin—and even Alyssantha, who wants to train her as a concubine. Iyre dutifully rejects their advances, preferring her needlepoint. I was taught that Iyre was the model for all young noblewomen. What a farce. Who would choose embroidery over sex?

It isn't until I tug on my chemise, mostly dry and clean of bloodstains, that I notice Myst is gone, too. A hitch catches in my lungs. That's odd. Basten *and* Myst gone? He must have ridden her into the forest, but I can't guess why. Maybe the waterfall drowned out the sound of game, and he had to travel deeper to hunt.

No matter. My stomach growls, but I can wait. Last

night's coals are still warm, so I blow on them until the fire roars again cheerfully. I trail a hand along my neckline, toying with the lace collar. Now that I know that every sinful act in Immortal Alyssantha's chapters is fair game for humans, I can't stop fantasizing about Basten and I recreating every contorted position in those illustrations.

If I can bend backward that far . . .

My cheeks start to blaze. I clear my throat, smoothing out the chemise's wrinkles to give my hands something to do. The chemise may be stiff and secondhand, but at least it covers what it needs to. It occurs to me that I never have to ride naked again. Lord Rian's cruel game is over. We've won, Basten and I, by deciding not to play.

Another hour passes before I finally hear Myst's hoofbeats. They ride into the cave, a skinned squirrel carcass dangling from Basten's belt. So much for making Basten walk on his own two feet, I guess. I smile to myself at how the two of them—the two souls I love most—have become friends.

Basten dismounts and crouches in front of the fire to add a few pieces of wood, his dark hair curtaining his face, his body hulking and hunched. His face has fallen into its familiar scowl like the settling of an old house. I roll my eyes fondly. *My wolf is so grouchy before he has his breakfast.*

I feel giddy as I teasingly throw my arms around his neck and plant a kiss on his stubbly cheek. He stiffens, which only makes me hug him harder. Last night, he touched my body in places I didn't even know existed.

There's no room this morning for crankiness. We're about to voyage to the ocean. Every night, we'll mimic another sinful pleasure from the pages of the Book of the Immortals. For the first time in my life, I feel like I've captured true happiness in the palm of my hand.

"Good morning," I breathe sweetly against his ear.

He gently shrugs out of my embrace so he can attend to the roasting squirrel. For a few minutes, preparing breakfast has all his attention. Finally, he drags in an unsteady breath. "Is your dress dry?"

His voice is hard. He's determined to be irritable, which pokes a small hole in my good spirits, but I check my dress's outer layer where I laid it out to dry.

"Yes, mostly. Oh wait, the hem is damp."

"That will have to do. We need to get moving."

I can't put my finger on why Basten would be acting so distant unless it concerns last night. He doesn't regret it, does he? That's impossible. No one could regret the way we came together. He certainly seemed to enjoy it last night . . . and again early this morning.

Turning to Myst, I ask in my mind, **Where did you two go?**

Village, she answers as she chomps grass. **Four hills away. He sent a message.**

I turn to Basten, frowning. "You sent a message this morning? Where?"

He briefly shoots a damning look toward Myst, but he has to know that she and I tell each other everything. As he tears into a freshly roasted hunk of squirrel meat, he mutters, "North. To tell them we'll arrive tomorrow afternoon."

I give him a crooked smile, confused. "North? Salensa is west."

Did our lovemaking knock something loose in his head last night? He's a hunter. He knows directions as well as he knows that the sky is up. My heart starts squeezing strangely, thrashing like a snared rabbit.

"We're going north," he grunts curtly.

My crooked smile stretches wider, increasingly uncertain, as I shake my head back and forth. What is he talking about? The only town of consequence in the north is Duren. Other than that, it's just the Blackened Forest, and eventually, the border wall with Volkany. I may be no master of geography, but there's no plausible way that heading north could take us to the coast. In fact, going anywhere near Duren would only put us squarely in the Valveres' territory—straight into the enemy's den.

An invisible fist tightens around my throat as a dawning fear sinks into me like fingernails down my back. My heart starts thrashing harder, a trapped animal who now sees the hunter closing in.

He's betraying me.

The certainty of it pierces me like a blade. *Dear gods.* It can't be true, can it? I'm overreacting. And yet I know in my core that I'm not. Basten is taking me to Duren just like he always planned. He's going to deliver me into Lord Rian's arms despite everything that happened last night, all our whispered plans and promises. Despite the fact that he had me moaning his name. Despite his own passion!

I gape at him in disbelief. Is it true? Basten is just

another man who will tell a girl anything to stick his cock in her?

I stare at him as I slowly drown in disbelief. My lungs struggle for breath. Panic sinks into my bones. My voice is barely audible as I whisper, "It—it was a lie? Salensa? You're still taking me to Rian?"

His jaw locks as he stands and brushes ashes roughly from his palms, not meeting my eyes. "Oh, come on, Sabine. Not even you can be that naive. You know I work for the Lord of Liars. I've learned a thing or two about lying."

I flinch like I've been slapped.

I still feel numb, but the trapped rabbit in my chest refuses to go down without a fight. As anger coils in my chest, I snarl, "So you just wanted to fuck me? You played me?"

He scoffs as he starts rolling up the blanket to pack in his rucksack. "I guess you have me figured out, little violet."

There's a meanness in his voice that is utterly foreign. Basten is many things—grumpy and cold and quick-tempered and violent—but not mean. We've spent every hour of every day together for weeks, and I've never heard that tone. He doesn't play games, either. Everything about Basten is as unpretending as the animals that make their home in this forest, who couldn't deceive even if they wanted to. It's one of the things that draws me to him. He isn't about games. He's the opposite of the man who bought me as a bride and forced this twisted ride.

I *know* that about Basten. I know *him*, maybe even

better than he knows himself. And everything he said to me last night wasn't a lie.

My lips purse tightly. "No. I don't believe you."

He stiffens again, but only briefly before cramming the blanket into his rucksack like it's insulted him. "Believe it, little violet. You've been locked away too long. You're pretty but not smart. Men lie—accept it."

There it is again—that cutting blade that isn't him.

With my heart thrashing in my throat, I rest a shaking hand on Myst's arched neck. My brave girl. Thank the gods I have her. She's always brought me back from the brink of panic.

I ask her, *Tell me more about where you went this morning. I want to know exactly what happened from the moment he woke.*

She leans her weight into my palm. *He never woke.*

It takes me a second to catch her meaning. *You mean he never slept?*

You slept, he did not. There was a leaf in his bag. Its markings scared him. He smelled like fear.

It can be difficult to understand an animal's meaning, even if their words are intelligible, I can't make sense of what Myst is trying to tell me. She sometimes calls paper a leaf, but that's my only clue.

I stomp over to Basten's rucksack and start wrestling to pull out the blanket he's stuffing in, searching for this mysterious piece of paper.

"What the hell are you doing?" Basten snaps.

"Where is it? *What* is it? Myst says you read something that upset you." I tear into the contents of his rucksack with feverish intensity, past hard rocks of stale bread and leather pouches of coins. As soon as my fingers graze on a folded paper, he seizes my wrist and wrenches my hand violently away from the bag.

"Sabine, stop!"

"You're lying!" I snap, feeling the sting of desperate tears in my eyes. "Something else happened—last night, you meant what you said! I know you did! You were ready to run away together and damn the rest of the world, so what in the gods' names did you read?"

His eyes crackle dangerously as his fist closes over my wrist. With his knee, he shoves the rucksack away with an angry grunt. "Fine. You're right. I did mean it last night, when you were offering me your pretty little cunt. But what Myst saw me reading? It was the list of Lord Rian's rules for this ride. No great mystery, I assure you. It reminded me of my duty, that's all. That as much as I want to bury my cock in you in every village from here to the coast, you're a silly girl I've known for a few weeks. Rian will always matter more." For the first time all morning, he looks directly into the depths of my eyes as he readies the final blow. "I'd be an idiot to throw away his patronage for some cunt I could get anywhere."

There is such crass cruelty in reducing me to the parts between my legs that I'm rendered speechless. I stare at him like I'm looking at a stranger. Who the hell is this man in front of me? It isn't Basten. It isn't the man who slaughtered an entire raiding party to save me, then kissed me tenderly after.

Fury seizes me. Before I know what I'm doing, I deliver a sharp slap to the same place on his cheek where I kissed him only moments ago.

As my chest heaves, I spit at him viciously, "How could you do this?"

He stretches his sore jaw. In a deathly quiet voice, he says calmly, "There's no use in running. I alerted Lord Rian by messenger that we'll arrive tomorrow, which means he'll send Golden Sentinels to meet us on the outskirts of town. Either I'll catch you, or they will."

My eyes sting. This can't be happening. It can't be real. My mouth is dust-dry as I gape at him with so much unspoken devastation on my lips that I don't even know where to start.

As soon as Basten sees the tears in my eyes, he looks away. Sunlight filters from the trees beyond the cave, glimmering over the falling water. His tone is softer as he murmurs, "Rian has always been the right match for you, Sabine. He has an army that can protect you if there is ever danger."

I wrinkle my nose in bewilderment. "Danger? What danger? Basten, I don't need an army. I need a friend. I thought—I thought I needed you."

As my voice breaks, he hisses a curse under his breath. He shoves to his feet like he can't escape me fast enough, and paces near the waterfall's stream.

My mind fogs up like it's filling with the falling mist. That snared animal in my chest is bleeding out, afraid this is the end. The cave's walls make me feel caged in. Suddenly, I'm back in the convent's walls. *Trapped. I'm always so fucking trapped.* And there's no way out this time; it's too late. Every person who was supposed to care for me has hurt me. My father. The Sisters. And now Basten, too.

275

Tears blaze a trail down my cheeks, dripping onto my lap. The creep of hatred runs down my skin as I shove myself to my feet. If Basten is going to shatter my world, then I'll break his, too.

Steeling my voice, I threaten, "I'll tell Rian that you fucked me."

"Go ahead," Basten says steadily, as though he's been expecting this. "He won't believe you. *I'm* the one he relies on to determine who is a virgin. Besides, who will he trust, the vengeful bride he bought against her will, or his oldest confidant?"

Pure hatred chokes me as I realize he's trapped me once more. Because he's absolutely right. I could swear on Immortal Iyre that Basten had his cock inside me, but Rian will believe Basten. Men always believe other men.

I hate him.

I hate him so much that the thorns of it snag in my gullet until I taste blood.

I close the distance between us and, with a growl, scratch my nails down his face. A blood line appears on his cheek before he captures my wrists, preventing me from scratching him again as I struggle.

He murmurs softly, "There's the wildcat. Still alive after all."

"I wish I had true claws to rip open your throat!"

He's ruined every bedtime story I told myself those long nights in the convent. That one day, I'd get out and fall in love with some beautifully flawed man. I had to harden my body to survive the Sisters' abuse, but it only went muscle-deep. It was armor over a tender heart. Because every night, I fell asleep whispering stories to the mice about love. I kept an ember of hope burning that one day I'd find someone who would make all the suffering worth it.

I can forgive myself for falling for Adan. A dangerous lapse of judgment. But Basten? I gave Basten my heart. I cut open my tough exterior and allowed him inside. Like a delicate spark, all it took was one huff to put it out.

And now? I'm extinguished.

I'm numb.

I'm wreckage and ash.

The only thing left in the wastelands of my heart is rage. Rage that he destroyed a girl's dreams. Rage that he toyed with me. Rage that he put loyalty to a high lord who doesn't give a shit about him over me.

I angrily wipe away my tears. Then, with a voice edged in steel, I vow, "You will never touch me again, Basten Bowborn. You will not speak to me. You will not so much as look at me, or I'll send every bird in the sky to tear you apart with their beaks and feast on your flesh. You ruined me."

He keeps his eyes on the waterfall. "I'll tell Rian you're a virgin—"

"I'm not talking about my body!" I snarl. "You ruined *me!*"

My voice is breathless and broken. He ruined the hopeful girl I was, the girl I could have been. Because it's impossible to see a future now. For a brief, shining moment, it was so clear, like in my dream on the beach. Basten and I together. Now, the future is like staring into a deep pool with no end. I never got to see the ocean. Never put my feet in the sand. Instead, I feel tossed in murky waves, plunged into stormy waters where I can't tell which way is up.

I tear at my chemise's laces as fresh tears blur my vision. Because he's won—not Basten, but Rian. Because ultimately, it all comes down to Rian. He wants my naked obedience, and I have no choice but to surrender it. I tug angrily at the fabric until it pools at my feet. The waterfall's cool mist fans over my bare skin, making me shiver. I don't even have my long hair to shield me anymore.

Basten tugs his shirt over his head and tries to press it into my hands. In a strange tone, he says, "Here. Wear this. Damn the rules. Rian will take out his anger on me, not you."

A cruel laugh bubbles from my throat, sounding more like a sob. It's a hell of a time for him to break the rules.

"I don't need your help." I ignore his offered shirt. Instead, I rest my hand on Myst's withers. She lowers to her knees so I can swing one leg over her back. Without my hair, I feel fully exposed, as though the entire forest can see through my skin to the shredded heart beneath. But the forest? I can trust that. Nature will never betray me like a man.

Myst stands, and I tower over Basten.

"You will regret this, Basten Bowborn. I'll *make* you regret it."

A white moth flutters out of the cave's shadows and lands on my left breast, just above my heart.

The little moth extends its silken wings over my skin. A woefully insufficient shield for an entire broken body. The tiny thing can't shelter me from what's coming. But it's trying. It isn't giving up. So neither will I. And for half a breath, the murky waters I've been drowning in clear. For a glimmer, I see hope. I don't know what exactly awaits in Duren. I can't read the future. But I *can* steer the reins that I'm given.

And every bullheaded man in my life—my father, Lord Rian, and especially Basten—will see how a woman's defiance can burn brighter than the stars.

CHAPTER 24
WOLF

We travel in silence for hours. Sabine said not to speak to her, and that suits me fine. Because I wouldn't know the first fucking place to start. I broke her heart in the waterfall cave; I had to. I had to make her believe that I was as much a bastard as they used to call me—Basten the Bastard—and build up her hatred until she gave up hope of a future together. Given the contents of her father's letter, there's only one way to keep her safe, and it's sure as hell not the two of us cozied up in seaside inns. It's with Rian's private army of five thousand Golden Sentinels.

An owl swoops down from a pine tree to land on Sabine's right thigh, and I flinch. It started happening as soon as we left the waterfall cave: This unnerving parade of winged creatures flocking to her. First, a tiny white moth landed on her left breastbone. It was joined by a half dozen more moths, brown as bark, settling on her belly. By the time the waterfall was out of earshot, a raven came to roost on her shoulder. Then a fucking goose, white as snow, nestled on Myst's withers between Sabine's legs and extended its wings like a loincloth.

Every few minutes, a new winged animal joins the flock.

A nuthatch on her knee. Delicate lace moths on her breastbone, like a neckline. Colorful butterflies on the curve of her hips.

Is she doing this? Calling the animals? If she is, then her message is pretty fucking clear: If everyone in her life will deny her even the dignity of clothing, then she'll clothe herself with the creatures of the forest.

But something tells me she *isn't* calling them, at least not with words. That the insects and birds are coming on their own, drawn to her pain like moths to flame.

It's unnerving, this ever-expanding mantel of winged beasts she is surrounding herself with. Another raven perches on her opposite shoulder, wings stretched toward the sunlight filtering through the forest canopy to give her the uncanny look of an angel. But not a gentle maiden of the clouds—oh no. Dressed in birds and moths that match the forest colors, Sabine looks like she's stepped out of the pages of the Book of the Immortals. There's a tale in Immortal Thracia's section where the stars are dimmed by magical lanterns erected by the other fae, so their revelries could continue into the dark night. As Goddess of Night, this offended her. In her anger, she transformed herself into a giant egret whose powerful flapping wings put out the lanterns.

I don't know if the ancient fae actually had the ability to transform themselves into beasts—it seems beyond even their magic. But watching Sabine shield her broken heart with an armor of wings, I believe in the divine.

My own armor, the leather breastplate with the Valvere crest, does fuck-all to shield the remains of *my* tramped heart. I have only myself to blame. I destroyed the one good thing in my pathetic life. The only chance I had for happiness. Guilt weighs me down like my rucksack is filled with boulders. She hates me, but it's nothing compared to how much I hate myself for what I did to her.

Still, I don't regret my choice. Sabine's only chance is through Rian's protection. But I sure as hell regret taking her to bed, and promising her I'd run away with her. In that moment, I was ready to swim across the fucking Panopis Sea for her. If I'd only read her father's letter earlier, I never would have let it go as far as it did.

And now I've lost her forever. I was a fool to think I ever had a shot with her in the first place—it never would have worked out. I don't get nice things after the sins I've committed.

The first time I killed a man, it was to spare Rian from having to do it. Rian was eighteen, I was sixteen. We were sparring in Sorsha Hall's courtyard, when Lord Berolt dragged in some scum who had beaten a prostitute to death in one of their brothels. He ordered Rian to carry out the man's death sentence. Rian hesitated at the idea of taking a life, even a villain's, so I stepped in to do the task with my fists. Halfway through, Rian joined in. That first murder bonded us; we both had blood on our hands.

The murders got a lot easier after that first one. I didn't mind when it was killing bad men, and at first, that's all it was—rapists and abusers who had crossed the

Valveres' business empire in one way or another. I could easily justify their deaths. In my way, I was making Duren safer, not just for the Valveres but for riffraff like I'd been as a boy and whoever my whore of a mother had been. And I was good at it. So good that when Rian stepped into his father's shoes as high lord, I was the first one he'd summon if he had a job. Slitting throats became as second nature as scratching an itch.

My abdomen clenches like something I ate isn't sitting right, like the past is trying to claw its way back. Not all the jobs Rian gave me were as justified as those first ones.

So many sins.

So many innocent people I killed. Women I've hurt. Families I destroyed with extortion and threats.

But I got out. It was hard as hell, but I got out. I told myself I'd never return to that work. My kills are now served on the dinner table—not dumped in the paupers' mass grave. But to guard Sabine's secrets, even from herself, I'm afraid of what I'll have to do.

That night—the final night of the ride before we reach Duren—I tie Sabine's wrists and ankles again. As much as I want to stay awake to watch for danger, I need sleep. I don't think she's foolish enough to escape, but desperate people do desperate things. Hell, there's not a small chance she'd try to throttle me in my sleep.

It would be a kinder death than I deserve.

With the blanket wrapped around her, the birds and

insects roost in the tree branches overhead, waiting until they're needed again in the morning. It's like a goddamn jury of black-eyed demons up there peering down at me, ready to cast down my own death sentence.

Once Sabine is asleep, I pull out her father's crumpled letter but don't open it. For all I know, that damn goose overhead can read and will tell her what it says. I don't need to read the letter, anyway. Every word is burned into my head like a branded nightmare.

What I'm trying to decide is, should I give it to Rian? Of course, with the broken seal, he'll immediately know that I opened and read his private correspondence—a sin punishable by the dungeon. But I'm less concerned with the dungeon than what Rian would do with the letter's information.

There's a chance he'd see it for the threat it is, and surround Sorsha Hall with his sentinels, even if it means calling back entire battalions from Old Coros and the southern border, where he rents them out to the crown. That's what I'd do. That's what any caring husband would do.

But the Valveres are a different breed. There's a chance that Rian will see it as an opportunity instead. With King Joruun's failing health, and the crown's future in Astagnon on shaky ground, this could be the fuel he needs to make a run for the throne, if what Folke said about his ambitions is true.

It would be foolhardy, stupid even. Practically a death sentence. But the Valveres drink down risk like wine.

I stuff the letter back in the rucksack, deciding it's too risky to show to Rian. Instead, I'll only tell him about the note in the spy's pocket that indicated Volkish raiders are targeting girls like Sabine. I'll tell him about the starleon, too, and how there must be a breach in the border wall. I can convince him that Sabine needs extra protection without revealing the true reason.

I'll be there, too. As her bodyguard. Shadowing her. Ghosting her. Guarding her door while she sleeps. She'll hate it, but she'll have no choice but to accept it.

As I drift off to sleep, thinking about ancient dangers seeping across the Volkish border, I recall an incident about a year ago, when a hermit from the Astagnonian side of the Blackened Forest stumbled into one of Sorsha Hall's masquerade balls. He was delirious and dehydrated, raving about how he narrowly escaped death from a monoceros, a vicious black-scaled horse with a sharpened horn capable of doling out fiery ruin on anything in its path. Monoceros all went to sleep a thousand years ago, along with the rest of the fae's mythical beasts. Even back in the Immortal Age, there were only ever one or two known to exist.

The hermit was laughed out of the castle. His tale was lifted straight from the Book of the Immortals, a scene when Immortal Artain found a monoceros with a broken leg trapped in a thick mud pit. Naturally, everyone assumed the hermit was crazy. And maybe, now that I think about it, he *was* confused, melding Immortal Artain's story and his own, but that doesn't mean he didn't *actually* see a monoceros.

If it's true that goldenclaws, starleons, and monoceros have awoken, then what's next? The fae themselves?

Fuck.

All night, dreams plague me. The border wall crumbles in a giant earthquake, the boulders that form it tumbling down our mountains to smash the Blackened Forest flat, blazing a path for all the ancient, dark magic buried in Volkany's soil to rise again, spreading into our kingdom like poison ivy, until everything is choked out from the sun.

In the morning, the first thing I see is a goddamn owl peering down at me with yellow eyes. It had better the hell not shit on me.

I rouse Sabine, who for a sleepy second smiles up at me, forgetting her hatred, until it comes crashing back like a bucket of ice water.

And she turns away sharply, refusing to look at me.

My chest sags.

I can take her hatred. But that flash of love I saw briefly before it was dashed—*that's* going to kill me.

CHAPTER 25

SABINE

As soon as I settle on Myst's back, a motley collection of owls and dragonflies and crows land on me. This isn't the first time animals have come to my aid unbidden. They sense a need in me, just as I do in them. If they're hungry or cold, I offer them what I can. But I've never experienced anything quite like this. The creatures covering my nakedness have a mind of their own, as though something greater than all of us summoned them. For maybe the first time, it makes me believe in the old stories. That magic threads through everything, not just the few godkissed, whether the fae are sleeping or not. That magic connects us all.

Golden Sentinels are waiting for us two miles outside of Duren. They're so well trained that they say nothing of my state of undress, though they keep a wary distance from the birds, throwing my animal companions alarmed looks. *Good.* I want them to be afraid.

Rian's soldiers escort us past villages and farmsteads,

where children run out to wave banners made from scrap fabric and cheer for us. For *me*. There are no leers here, no catcalls, not even titillated curiosity.

"Lady!" the children call as they wave. "It's the new Lady of Sorsha Hall! Look at the birds! Hullo, my lady!"

Their warm reception throws me off. Shame? That I expected. I was prepared for it. To keep my head high and my chin tipped against the people's slander, as I've borne for the last three weeks. But this is different. What were these people told? To welcome me? Show me respect? Maybe it's just another twist that my future husband has thrown into his game.

"Just ahead, my lady," a mounted sentinel says, motioning to a bend in the road ahead. "The gates of Duren."

Duren might be known as "Sinner's Haven," where one can bet on dog fights in the arena, or have women of any skin color ride one's cock, but from the outside, the town looks unexpectedly solemn. The city's high stone walls are plain except for slitted windows and guard towers. The only decoration is two white banners, emblazoned with an image of a red key, rippling in the breeze on either side of the gate.

Oh, great.

My stomach sinks. Red on white is the color and emblem of Immortal Iyre, who Lord Rian must think is my patron goddess because of my time in the convent. Why, in the name of the Immortals, would I worship anything related to my abuse?

Basten, walking a pace ahead of me, glances back at

me. It's only then I realize I'm growling so quietly in my throat that no one but him can hear it.

Once we pass through the gates, however, everything changes. The city's dour exterior walls give way to a veritable symphony of color and activity. Paper lanterns hang from house gables and street lamps, painted to depict colorful scenes from Immortal Iyre's life. The air is heavy with the scent of brewing ale, roasted meats, salted smoked fish, fritters and puddings. People line the narrow streets three rows thick. Children run and shriek, energized by the festivities. I'm immediately struck by the residents' fashion, much finer here than in a provincial town like Bremcote. The women wear asymmetrical hems to mimic the fae gowns in the Book of the Immortals, and their hair is twisted into immortal braids. More than a few wear pointed golden caps on the tops of their ears, secured by a delicate chain, to further mimic the ancient fae. Some have painted light blue fey lines on their arms and necks. Almost everyone—men and women alike—line their upper eyelids in bold colors to make their eyes appear winged.

The streets fill with cheers. Small children scamper up to me, bearing baskets of cut flowers that they toss at Myst's feet so she treads on a carpet of petals. It's all so overwhelming—and frankly unexpected—that my brow pinches tightly.

Am I supposed to be honored by this?

Too much noise, Myst says as her muscles tense beneath my thighs.

I smooth a hand down her long, arched neck. *I know, girl. I know. We both must be brave.*

As the Golden Sentinels lead our procession, I catch exclamations of surprise from the crowd. People are entranced by the winged creatures clothing my body like a gown of feathers. Murmurs travel through the crowd ahead of us, but since I don't have Basten's keen hearing, I can only overhear broken pieces.

". . . *wings like an angel . . .* "

"*Supposed to have long hair covering her, isn't she?*"

"*. . . the lord's planning?*"

"*. . . no, not the lord's doing. It's her. An act of defiance!*"

I straighten my spine and roll my shoulders back, the twin ravens perched there extending their wings. Lord Rian draped his city in white to welcome me, his chaste bride, and I've arrived in dark woodland colors. It gives me a grim sense of satisfaction to think of how this transgression will stoke his ire.

My body is my own, my gown of living wings announces to the crowd. *No man will command me.*

A pace ahead of me, Basten keeps his head down, ignoring the festivities. It hurts to even look at him. I feel like one of the stained glass windows that hung in the convent's chapel. Such a window starts as broken glass, but when soldered together with iron, comes out stronger than before. Basten might have smashed my heart, but I will pick up the pieces. I will weld myself back together into something mighty.

The main street veers, and ahead, the brick walls of Duren's famous arena rise, with vast canvas sheets strung up high to shade the seating. It's quiet now, the games halted for my welcome procession. We pass through a market with smiling vendors selling bolts of clothing, giant cheese wheels, and roasted nuts out of barrels. To my surprise, Duren is an astonishingly beautiful town. It's vast and chaotic, a buffet of intriguing sights and sounds. There's no sign of rubbish or emptied chamber pots in the gutter. I might not have much experience in large towns, but something feels off. Too scrubbed and purged. I don't just mean that Rian had the streets cleaned for my arrival, but that this whole procession was carefully planned to show me only a portion of Duren. After all, this town is called Sinner's Haven. There must be whores, beggars, cockfights. Where are all the scrappy orphaned boys pummeling each other for coin in the streets, like Basten?

As we pass an alley, I crane my neck to peer down its length. Shadows mask its contents, but the smell of opium and lurid perfume tells me enough.

Yep. I'm not seeing the *real* Duren.

It's all just another trick.

My winged friends stay with me faithfully as the soldiers lead us up a hill to the towering structure on the city's pinnacle: Sorsha Hall.

The high lord's castle is an impressive homage to ancient fae architecture. Its gray stone walls rise in turrets topped with polished copper spires that blaze in the sunlight. To the left, a portion of a hedge maze is visible within a walled garden, along with marble statues of all ten Immortals. Upper balconies are draped in luxurious velvet curtains that billow in the breeze. Elaborate bay windows are framed with gilded arches and inlaid with stained glass windows depicting scenes from Immortal Popelin's life—the patron god of gamblers and revelers. Lanterns from within give the windows an ethereal glow, making the castle look magical. The main doors are adorned with metal accents in the shape of a gold coin, a symbol of both wealth *and* games, in case anyone were to mistake which family's house this is.

A fragrant canopy of flowers, woven of intertwined strands of vibrant blossoms, shades a small welcome party waiting for us on the front steps. The men and women are Valvere family members—they must be, given their similar features. They wear sumptuous, revealing fae clothing, with off-center buttons and closures on the men, and immortal braids and pointed gold earpieces on the women. Their makeup is so extravagant that they look almost freakish; harshly winged eyelids in blues and blacks, powdered white faces, bold fey lines traced along their limbs. They whisper among themselves with furrowed eyebrows, glancing pointedly at my rebellious collection of winged creatures.

And then there's him—Lord Rian.

He looks different than he did a year ago. More lines in his otherwise youthful face, a dark shadow of a beard that wasn't there before. He stands on the center stair, arms folded in casual patience. The tailored cut of his clothes suggests lithe and well-honed muscles. His beard is tamed into a precise band around his jawline, and his hair is shorter than the current fashion, as though he values the control a tight cut gives him. He's undeniably hand-some, though his features aren't as elegant as the rest of the Valveres. His features are coarser, heavier. Maybe, in part, he stands out from his family because of his simple attire. A black doublet over a shirt of the same color, with the only nod to fae style a decorative armored plate harnessed to one shoulder. His eyelids are subtly winged with a single line of blue.

Ask anyone, and they'd tell you I've stumbled into unbelievable luck to be chosen by him. Handsome, powerful, wealthy. I can only imagine how many women have tried to snag his attention at the infamous Sorsha Hall balls, dreaming of becoming a Valvere bride.

They can have him. *Please*, I want to scream. They can have it all.

Myst draws to a stop in the front courtyard. Basten hangs off to the side, keeping his distance. This is his home, and yet he looks uncomfortable here. With his bow and hunting boots, he's a denizen of the forest, not the city streets. Yet he murmurs greetings to a few sentinels standing guard—friends of his, or at least associates.

Rian waits for an extra beat before descending the stairs. It feels calculated. Always calculated. When he steps into the sunlight, I draw myself up to my full height atop Myst, prepared to defy any attempt to intimidate me.

His eyes run from the raven on my shoulder to the moth perched on my toe, and I hold in a breath, ready for this confrontation—

But he turns to Basten instead, ignoring me. "Wolf. Am I fucking glad to see you." He slings one arm around Basten's shoulder, pounding on his back in greeting, and then mutters, "*Tamarac.*"

"*Tamarac,*" Basten repeats, bowing his head.

I have no idea what the Ancient Tongue word means, but it clearly holds some deep significance between them. I lick my lips, suddenly nervous that I've gotten everything wrong. I assumed Basten's loyalty was a fool's errand. I didn't think any master respected a mere servant.

Huh.

The bond I see between the two of them—it's deeper than I thought. And with their dark hair and hungry eyes, Rian and Basten don't look altogether dissimilar. Their features don't match—Rian is far too lithe, and Basten is much too heavyset to share blood—but they have something alike I can't quite put a name to. Then it hits me: they're like gemstones cut from the same quarry, only with his wild mane of hair and dirt-streaked face, Basten is a rough-cut stone, raw and flawed and unrefined. Rian is as cut and polished as the gems glistening on his family's jewelry.

When Rian finally addresses me, I'm so disoriented that my head is spinning.

"Lady Sabine. Welcome to Duren. To you and your . . . friends." He acknowledges the birds and insects in a playful tone that I'm not sure is derisory. "I see the rumors of your godkiss were not exaggerated."

Scrambling to regain my composure, I keep my head high, though my pulse is pounding. "They were not, Lord Rian. And I suppose I'll discover the rumors of your *lack* of a godkiss were also not exaggerated?"

Though I mean it as an insult, he barks a laugh and claps his hands as though I've delighted him.

"May I help you down?"

I hesitate at his outstretched hand. It doesn't feel right. Basten has always been the one to help me dismount. My body is used to surrendering to his rough and steady grip as he lifts me effortlessly to the ground.

For a second, my heart splits all over again, gushing and gushing from the fresh wound.

I briefly squeeze my eyes closed. I will *not* let them see me cry. They don't deserve my tears.

I force a smile and say loudly, "It would be my pleasure to be handled by a gentleman after the past few weeks."

A smile quirks Lord Rian's lips as he glances over his shoulder at Basten. "Hear that, you beast? Of course, you did. Didn't win any fans on the ride, did you?"

Basten merely scowls up at the sky, pretending he didn't hear.

I take a breath before placing my hand in Lord Rian's. His palm isn't lined with dirt like Basten's, but it is calloused. The goose nestled on Myst's withers takes flight, as do the moths along my thigh that would be crushed when I dismount, but the rest of the animals remain. Rian's strong fingers close over mine, and with controlled grace, he guides me—still bedecked in feathers and mothwings—down from the horse.

He motions to a servant at the bottom of the stairs holding a folded velvet drape. With a wry smile, he says, "I had intended to sweep in like a dashing hero and offer you a cloak to cover your body, but I see you've handled that yourself." His dark eyes flash as he assesses each one of my winged friends. "You'll soon learn that nothing travels faster than gossip in Duren. The people are already calling you the Winged Lady, and talking about how you used your godkiss to mock my rules of the ride."

His candor is unnerving and, frankly, suspicious.

I stare him down as I challenge, "Such rules were made to be mocked."

A secretive smile pulls at his lips. "You hate me, naturally. I expected no less. But you should know that the ride wasn't about humiliating you, my lady. Immortal Solene professed the virtue of our natural states. Her own famous ride was meant to demonstrate the sacredness of coming into a marriage as we are, not hidden behind costuming. My wish was that you and I meet at our most basic level. Simply a man and a woman."

Gods, this man is eloquent. He almost has me falling for his own bullshit.

"Hmm," I purr evenly. "So then why aren't *you* naked?"

His smile stretches wider, and I realize I've fallen into one of his traps. "So eager? Soon enough, my lady. And here I thought you were chaste."

His eyes spark tauntingly.

"No . . . I didn't mean . . . " I garble.

He only grins wider.

Despite myself—despite the hell this man has just put me through—I almost appreciate his humor. Because the one goddamn thing I could use right now is someone else to laugh at the futility of my situation.

"I'll take that cloak now," I say stiffly, turning to the servant, who comes forward at Rian's beckoning.

I first take a moment to gently touch each of the dozens of birds and insects who left the forest to help me on my journey.

Fly away, my friends. You have my gratitude. Thank you. Thank you.

Almost as one, the animals take wing. The cloud of flapping wings rises into the sky like a puff of chimney smoke over the spires of Sorsha Hall. Rian takes a subtle step to the right, which blocks my brief flash of nudity from the crowd's view.

How fucking thoughtful.

The servant drapes the cloak over my shoulders, and even before I've fully secured it, Rian presses one hand to my back and motions to the stairs.

"Now, my lady, you have the dubious honor of meeting my family. My father couldn't be here to receive you, but you'll meet him later."

He introduces me to a woman about my age, with intricately painted fey lines on her exposed skin, and her raven black hair coiled in a thick immortal crown. "This is Lady Runa Valvere, my cousin." The painted woman gives me a smile that looks warm but feels cruel. Next, we move to a middle-aged couple drenched in exotic perfume. "This is Lord Gideon, my uncle, and his wife, Lady Solvig. And this sublime woman is my grandmother, Lady Eleonora Valvere."

The elderly woman is dressed in a gossamer-thin toile gown with an exaggerated asymmetrical hem. His grandmother snakes out a hand and seizes mine. Is this death grip supposed to be a handshake? Her eyes are foggy with cataracts. Her ears, I'm shocked to see, have been mutilated through years of binding to come to a fae point, though the effort left them scarred, and I feel sick to my stomach that a person would suffer like that in the name of fashion.

"She can control animals? All types?" Lady Eleonora snaps. "Eh, girl, is that true?"

Something unpleasant ripples over Rian's face as he explains in tight patience, "Yes, grandmother, I believe you missed the impressive display of her power just now, when she humiliated me by arriving with an animal entourage."

The elderly woman grunts, nodding to herself. I wait, but there's nothing more. I suppose that's all I'll get by way of welcome.

Rian then introduces me to Sorsha Hall's head servants, their names coming at me so fast it's a whirl. My thighs feel slack. My throat is parched. It's all I can do to stay upright instead of slumping into an exhausted, over-whelmed puddle.

"We'd intended to hold an engagement ball tonight, to continue the welcome festivities," Rian says, sweeping a hand toward the town's decorations. "But when I received word of your attack, I thought it best to post-pone. Wolf indicated you'd need some days to recover."

He motions to Basten, who's halfway up the stairs, speaking with a Golden Sentinel on duty. Basten stops at the mention of his nickname and glances at us. For a brief second, our eyes meet. My heart tightens against my will. Even breathing hurts.

Basten eventually drags his eyes off me, returning to his conversation, though his hands are now tightly fisted at his sides.

"Serenith will show you to your room," Lord Rian says, motioning to the head maid, a woman of fifty with a thick and precise immortal braid woven with gray ribbons. "You'll forgive me for not taking you myself, but urgent business requires my attention. If you need anything, or if you want anything changed to your liking, tell Serenith."

I blink. Annoyance snaps in my chest. Rian arranged all this extravagant fanfare only to speak to me for five minutes?

Well, what do you want, you dolt? The less time the better.

"Of course," I say tightly. My thighs are trembling with exhaustion. All I can think of is getting to a chair to sit. I just have to maintain my composure for another few minutes . . .

But as soon as I climb a step toward the main set of doors, my muscles give out. My toe catches on the stair's edge, and I stumble. The marble stairs rush up to meet me before I can catch myself—

Until two strong hands close over me.

It's Basten. Of course it is. He's there for me, keeping watch, even now when the distance between us couldn't be greater. My throat bobs with a painful swallow.

He lifts me to my feet like I weigh nothing and doesn't let go, like his heightened senses perceive that my muscles are shaking, and I need support. One of my hands clamps onto his shoulder from instinct.

Our eyes meet.

Something stirs back to life in my broken heart. For weeks, I've entrusted this man with my safety. I've gone from loathing the sight of him to realizing that I actually very, very much adore the sight of him. The last thing I wanted was to fall for my jailor, so naturally, in a twist of fate, that's exactly what happened. Yesterday morning, I was dreaming of a future with him. And even though my brain now screams at me that he's a lying bastard, the furthest corner of my heart hasn't yet gotten the message.

Part of me still wants him—wants to move back in time to the waterfall cave.

I may not be able to speak telepathically to Basten as I do with animals, but on that same deep level, I'm certain he feels it too. We're bonded through the scars of the road. The wildcat. The Red Church's confrontation in Charmont. Adan and the Volkish raiders—the bloodbath. How can I separate myself from him after all of that? Our fates have woven together time and time again until I'm not sure where mine ends and his begins.

A breeze kicks up. Fragrant petals flutter down from the woven flower canopy to dance around us like a rainfall of sunflower yellows and rose reds. Basten briefly closes his eyes. His fingertips dig in around my waist.

Low enough for only my ears, he murmurs, "Little violet..."

And that's all it takes to wake me up: his nickname for me on his lips. At once, I remember how he moaned those words while thrusting his cock into me, his hands worshipping my curves, his lips marking me as his.

Anger curdles the blood in my veins.

No. He doesn't get to pretend like there's anything left between us but hatred.

I tear away from him, hugging Rian's cloak like a suit of armor. I forge my words into iron as I lock my gaze to Basten's, and say in disdain, "I'll be grateful never to see you again, Wolf Bowborn."

CHAPTER 26
WOLF

The moment Sabine disappears into Sorsha Hall under the guidance of Serenith, with a pair of sentinels marching behind her, Rian turns on me sharply. His well-rehearsed smile vanishes. I like him better like this—when he's just himself, not pretending. It's getting rarer to see these days.

Keeping his voice low, he hisses, "What the fuck really happened on the road?"

The message I sent yesterday only briefly mentioned Sabine's kidnapping and the fact that I killed everyone involved.

"It's a lot to tell you," I say, gaze shifting toward the Valveres. Those vipers. Especially old Eleonora, who only pretends to be senile. I know they have their ears pricked. As do the servants, half of which are spies. "Where's Lord Berolt?"

It's strange that Lord Berolt isn't here to greet Sabine. Though it would be less of a greeting and more of an assessment. The moment Rian returned from Bremcote, a year ago, saying he wanted to marry a godkissed girl, Berolt got a fucking hard-on. He's always craved godkissed offspring—I guess a godkissed grandchild is the best he can hope for now. I don't know if he still performs his creepy experiments on godkissed, but at least Sabine's child-bearing ability will spare her from his attention.

"A squabble at the Titan Taverna," Rian says. "Just a hiccup, but he was required."

He jerks his head for me to follow him into the castle. We pass through the arched foyer with its stained-glass window depicting Immortal Popelin's dark brown grinning face, up a spiral flight of stairs, and down a long hallway to his bedroom. It's an enormous room, the bed occupying only a small portion. He has a formal office elsewhere on the second floor, but this is where he conducts most of his business—the giant table with its map of Astagnon carved into the top, a desk stacked with books, a pair of leather seats where we've shared many a drink, and a rug that has seen so much blood I can't fathom how the servants keep getting the stains out.

"Tell me what happened," he says, going immediately to the sideboard where he stores his liquor. "No—first, tell me about her. Does she hate me as much as it seemed?"

"She does," I grunt.

"Good. That means she has some sense in that pretty head. I'll change her sentiment soon enough—mark my words." He sloshes amber liquid into two crystal glasses and then passes me one. "What is she like?"

"Angry. Headstrong. Oh, and she fucking hates Immortal Iyre. You should take any shit down that has her emblem. Do you still keep tigers in the cells beneath the arenas? If so, don't let her near them."

Rian chuckles, not at all intimidated by the fact that his new bride could send every one of the exotic beasts he uses for fights to rip out his throat. "Is that how you got that scratch on your cheek? She sent a wild animal after you?"

Sabine gave me the particular scratch he's referring to, but it's close enough to the truth that I just nod.

"What else?"

I hesitate. Where do I start with Sabine? She's a riddle of contradictions. Her kindness knows no end, yet she won't hesitate to claw a villain like me. She watched me murder the Volkish raiders with dark delight. Then she daydreamed about us frolicking on the beach.

She's more multifaceted than that hefty diamond waiting for her in her wedding ring.

"She was beaten and neglected in the Convent of Immortal Iyre. All twelve fucking years she was there. They kept her locked up. Tried to keep animals away from her so she couldn't use her godkiss. If I were you, I'd give her every semblance of freedom you can. Trying to pin her down will only push her away. Encourage her godkiss, too. Let her talk to every four-legged thing in the castle. Give her perches for her room, dog beds for the floor."

Rian listens closely, then goes to the door, waves over the chamberlain, and commands him to do what I've suggested. When he returns, he takes a long, thoughtful sip of his drink.

"She's a beauty, isn't she?"

I know that testing tone in his voice. I've heard it a million times, and I know how to handle it. With a shrug, I say wryly, "Only if you like a perfect face and perfect body and perfect hair." I throw back the rest of my drink as casually as I can.

Rian laughs, clapping me on the back. "You see, Wolf? This is why I sent you to accompany her. Everyone else lies to me. But you see a beautiful fucking girl and call her a beautiful fucking girl. What happened to her hair, by the way?"

I stare into my empty glass. "Her kidnappers cut it off."

His face darkens. "Hmm. Well, it doesn't matter. Ferra can restore it when she returns. Go on. Tell me everything."

Leaning on the map table, I recount the journey's highlights—leaving out some key points, like how I promised Sabine I'd betray my duty and then fucked her until she was moaning my name. Red creeps over my neck as I try to stick to the Red Church's interference in Clare-mont and how we changed course as a result, then the fire in Blackwater, Sabine's kidnapping, and the rescue. I'm not the best liar. Sure, I've learned tricks from the Valveres, but it never comes naturally to me. Fortunately, Rian's had a few drinks already today, judging by his breath, and he isn't at his sharpest.

As I finish the story, my eyes fall to his four-poster bed at the other end of the room. My throat tightens. Before I can stop them, images flood my head. Is Rian going to fuck Sabine in that bed? When? *Tonight?*

I manage to tear my thoughts away from the mental picture of my master and the girl I crave fucking each other, and focus on the most important part of my report.

"The spy who set the fire at the Manywaters Inn was one of the raiders." I hesitate before delivering the rest, knowing how significant it is. "They were sent by King Rachillon."

One of his eyes twitches; otherwise, his face betrays no emotion. After so many years running a gambling empire, he knows how to mask his true thoughts. Does he already know about Volkish incursions into Astagnon? About King Rachillon's rise to power?

I can't fucking tell.

His hand dips into his pocket for his Golath dime, which he absently toys with between his fingers. "You're certain?"

"They told Sabine as much. And they had the Volkish look. Not to mention the starleon—where else would it have come from if not across the border?" I fold my arms tightly. "Did you know about the wall breach?"

He lifts his shoulder with the decorative harness in an ambiguous shrug.

I add, "On the road, we heard of several more godkissed kidnappings. And there's that business up near the border I told you about. The possible goldenclaw who killed a godkissed girl, though now I'm thinking she wasn't killed, but abducted. And not by the goldenclaw, but raiders who came across with it. With your leave, I'd like to investigate the area more thoroughly."

At the time, Rian dismissed my suggestion about a goldenclaw's appearance as readily as he had the hermit last year who claimed to see a monoceros. Now, I wonder if my report wasn't the first he'd heard of a goldenclaw in the Blackened Forest. If maybe he's known about ancient magic crossing the border for years.

"Don't worry about it, Wolf," he says, waving his fingers. "I'm sure if such things were happening, I'd know."

There's an edge to his voice like he *does* know about it —probably far more than I do.

"Rian—"

"Enough." He claps a hard hand on my shoulder, silencing my objection. His eyes start hard, but it isn't long before they soften, and he says with sincerity, "You brought Sabine to me. I'm grateful. I knew there was no one else who could." His smile turns devilish. "I think you've earned yourself a night in Alyssantha's Boudoir. Work out some of that aggression from the raiders, eh? Tell the madame I said you could have as many whores as can wear out your cock."

He winks.

Guilt ties my throat in fucking knots. I want to scratch off my own skin to get rid of the memory of thrusting into Sabine, being ready to betray everything in the world I held dear for her. And now what the fuck am I supposed to do? Fuck a whore and wish it was her, while Rian seduces the girl I want? Help him win Sabine over by telling him all her secret hopes and fears? Attend their fucking wedding?

My nerves jangle like carriage bells.

Keeping my voice gruff, I sidestep the offer to whore the night away in Duren's finest brothel, and say, "On the point of Lady Sabine's safety, given that Volkish raiders already targeted her once, I think it best I keep watch over her. You said yourself that you don't trust anyone else to do it. Post me as her bodyguard."

Rian takes his hand off my shoulder, then returns to toying with his Golath dime as he leans against one of the leather seats. There's an odd gleam in his eye. "I'm surprised, Wolf. I thought you'd be thrilled to return to the solitude of the woods instead of babysitting a spoiled noblewoman." He cocks his head. "Did you fall under her spell?"

I ball my fist behind the table, where he can't see. Scoffing, I bark, "Of course not."

He assesses me closely, searching for the truth. It's a while before the tension breaks and, with a tight smile, he says, "I was merely teasing. Wolf Bowborn's heart is made of stone, isn't it?"

I laugh lightly, nodding.

Rian paces by the map table, arms folded, deep in thought. Finally, he shakes his head. "I'm not granting the post, however. You can go back to your grouse."

Surprise cuts through me, forcing my spine straight. Harder than I should, I demand, "Why not?"

Rian's eyes gleam dangerously. "Because you had the choice between my personal service or the woods, and you chose the woods. You wanted out, Wolf. Of this family's business. Of this life. I *let* you out. It's too late to decide you want back in."

The air in my lungs is all sharp edges. My pulse raps hard in my veins. I didn't know that asking to get out of the business of murder, extortion, and arson had borne such a weight on Rian. He's wounded. Stung. Ever since I changed my surname to Bowborn and took up a quiver, he's been more distant, but I chalked it up to the fact that I was gone hunting for weeks at a time, whereas once we'd been together daily. But now it's clear—he distanced himself on purpose the last few years. I left that rough life, but he never can.

Taking a deep breath, I say, "My lord, I truly believe that Lady Sabine—"

He claps another hand on my shoulder. It isn't angry this time, but it is conclusive. His voice holds a trace of regret as he orders, "Go shoot grouse, Wolf."

CHAPTER 27

SABINE

I've never stepped foot in any structure as grand as Sorsha Hall. It dwarfs my father's manor house like a kitten before a lion. Even the chapel at the Convent of Immortal Iyre, with its altar of prized treasures—a golden chalice, a crystal decanter—is laughably plain compared to the riches in the castle's entryway alone.

My head spins at the dizzying opulence that drips off every surface. The stained glass windows bathe the decor in muted rainbow colors: the crystal chandeliers, the ornate candelabras, benches upholstered in velvet, the high arched ceilings. The delicate, spicy smoke of aloeswood side-winds out of ormolu incense holders placed at every window's base. I'm overwhelmed by the assault of so much grandeur. The colored light stings my scratchy eyes. The smells of incense and roasting meat and musty drapes are too rich, too cloying. Maybe I'd feel differently if I was at my prime; but I've come off a hellacious twenty-one-day ride. My thighs are chaffed raw. My bones ache from sleeping on tree roots every night. I've been kidnapped, nearly raped.

I couldn't care less about a gods damned tapestry, even if it was woven by Tarrian priests.

"You'll note that the architectural molding here varies from what we saw downstairs," Serenith tells me, pointing a graceful finger toward chiseled stone accents along the window frames. "These are fae axe patterns, in honor of Immortal Vale. Though the Valvere family worships Popelin, they still wanted an ode to the King of Fae."

I limp after her, wincing with every step on my heel's puncture wound. We've traversed so many staircases and hallways that I feel trapped in one of Immortal Meric's endless mazes. I'm shivering beneath the cloak, though the castle feels warm. It's all I can do to keep putting one foot in front of the next.

"Lord Rian thought you'd enjoy staying in the east tower bedroom. It gets excellent morning light, with a view of the Darmarnach Mountains. The room formerly belonged to Lady Madelyna, Rian's late mother. It has remained empty since then, used only for occasional guests. Unfortunately, that does mean you will be removed from the rest of the family's residences. Lord Rian resides in the keep on the third floor, and Lord Berolt and Lady Eleonora have suites in the north tower."

This is the one good piece of news I've heard all day— that I'll be far from my husband and that viperish grand-mother of his.

When we reach the east tower stairs, my vision blurs into fizzing dots, and I have to steady myself against the stone wall. Serenith looks back at me in concern, though I don't lie to myself for a minute that she cares about me. Only as much as Rian will hold her responsible for my well-being.

"My lady? Do you require assistance?" She holds up a hand to the two Golden Sentinels behind me, ready to give them a signal.

My shoulder slumps against the wall as, slowly, my vision clears. I don't want those soldiers' hands anywhere near me. Breathing hard, I grit my teeth and mutter, "I can make it."

Slowly, painstakingly, I climb the spiral stairs to my bedroom. When Serenith opens the door, I temporarily forget my exhaustion. I stop at the threshold, afraid to step inside, like crossing a portal into the dreamworld.

Serenith called it a bedroom, but I call it a palace. There's a canopied bed draped in velvet, piled high with quilts and fur coverlets. A marble wash basin and matching marble bathtub are already filled with steaming, fragrant water steeped in flower petals. A monstrously huge walnut wardrobe hulks opposite the bed, carved with allegorical forest scenes from Immortal Solene's life. And the ceiling! It's *painted*. A work of art on a ceiling? I've never heard of such a thing. It's a portrait of the full fae court, all ten Immortals, seated on a fae hill surrounded by playful cloudfoxes and twisting, enchanted vines.

My head is tipped back so far to marvel at the artistic feat that I lose track of how spent my body is, until a wave of dizziness hits me. I stumble.

One of the guards moves forward, but I catch myself on a bedpost and wave him away.

As I'm regaining my breath, a line of servants appears at the door, laden with more decorations and furnishings. Serenith immediately begins directing them.

"Yes, you two. Remove that painting of Immortal Iyre. And you. Place that perch next to the window on the left. And you—set the cages there."

I watch in dazed confusion as the servants remove an impressive portrait of Iyre, her skin fair as snow and marked with soft fey lines, and replace it with one of two playful cloudfoxes chasing each other. The rest of the decorations are even more confounding. Empty wicker baskets lined with blankets, wooden perches, cages made of woven rattan.

"What is all this?" I ask, befuddled.

"Lord Rian ordered us to bring places to house animals," Serenith informs me. "Naturally, with your godkiss, he assumed it would be important to you."

"But that rattan cage—a mouse will chew through it in two minutes."

"Perhaps there was a misunderstanding," she says, lips pursed. "He indicated that you'd prefer not to have animals caged, only given places to sleep."

My mind reels as I stare at her in boldface disbelief. How could Rian possibly know how sensitive I am to anything being caged? "Lord Rian said that?"

"He was very specific. Was that wrong?"

"No, no, it isn't wrong."

She doesn't seem to understand the significance of his orders. Ever since my mother died, people have tried to keep me from animals. In the convent, it was a way to control me. The only strength I had was my godkiss, so they gave me a room far from the barnyard and stable. I had to sneak visits to Myst at night. My only friends were the few mice and nuthatches who could squeeze through my room's cracked walls, and I'd be beaten if found with them. Likewise, the first thing Adan did when he kidnapped me was to seal off the cottage to keep me from calling to animals for help. It's been how the world keeps me powerless.

And now Rian, who knows nothing about me, who has every reason to keep me powerless too, *encourages* my godkiss?

Did I misjudge him?

This thought knocks the last remaining strength out of my legs, and I sink onto the edge of the bed.

Serenith looks at me with genuine concern. She snaps at a young maid, waving her over. "Lady Sabine, this is Brigit. She'll be your lady's maid, if you find that acceptable."

"Huh?" I stare blankly, then try to wet my lips. "Oh. Yes, sure."

Serenith murmurs the low orders to Brigit, "Help her bathe. A maid is bringing food up. Then she needs rest."

"Shall I summon a healer?" Brigit whispers, eyes pinned to my swollen foot.

Serenith responds quietly, "Bronwyn can work on her while she's sleeping."

Their words slip and slide around my ears, like something isn't quite working in my brain. All at once, exhaustion hits me. I didn't realize until now how hard I've fought to make it this far still standing. My mind is still charged, ready for the next challenge. But my body can't take anymore.

I fall back on the covers, weariness cutting all the way to the bone, and before I know it, my thoughts fade into oblivion. Nebulous shadows dull my memories until I'm falling, falling, falling into the unconscious abyss.

My dreams aren't quite dreams. They're flashes of memories mixed with fantasy. A painfully beautiful god beneath a waterfall. Feathers sprouting from my limbs. From somewhere deep, I hear a rattling voice, though it turns more into a nightmare as it echoes in my head.

Out, the voice says. ***Get out. Now.***

I wake to the sound of giggles.

It's such an improbable sound to hear in my new prison that I assume I'm still asleep. I blink my eyes open, and then I'm *positive* I'm dreaming, because I'm staring at Immortal Thracia with her bronzed hand resting on a goldenclaw's shaggy back.

The bedroom ceiling painting.

Everything rushes back to me like an opened dam. Wincing, I push myself to a seated position. Every one of my sore muscles protests. My empty stomach complains.

"Oh! You're awake!" Brigit, seated on a stool at my bedside, blinks at me in surprise. Her hands are cupped around a small gray mouse. She quickly transfers it to a woven basket on the floor, then rushes to her feet and helps me sit up.

"Here, my lady. Lean back." She fluffs the pillows before easing me into a reclining position. The pillows are buttery soft, supporting me like clouds.

With a rasping voice, I say, "How long did I sleep?"

She glances at a porcelain clock on the desk. "Almost three days, my lady."

Three days? I'm not surprised. I feel like I could sleep for a dozen more. My groaning stomach certainly verifies the timeline.

"Why—why do you have a mouse?" I ask her.

"Oh, it's for you, actually. That huntsman brought it while you were sleeping. He had, um, unrepeatable things to say about the damage it did to his rucksack."

I peer down at the mouse on the floor, delighted to discover that it's the same one from the forest that's been stowing away in Basten's bag. Was it the strange voice in my head last night? Or was that a dream?

Hello, friend. I say. **How good to see you!**

Hello! It says cheerily.

A tightness pulls at my chest that Basten brought me the little mouse, even though it gave him so much trouble on our journey. I almost wish I'd been awake when he came so that I could have seen him . . .

Stop it.

Brigit leans forward with twinkling lights in her eyes. "I think your godkiss is *incredible*, my lady. You should hear what the people are saying about how you defied Lord Rian's command by arriving covered in all those birds. It was a sight to behold!"

Do the people of Duren not like their high lord? Or are they just happy for any gossip?

"I hope you don't mind that I washed and dressed you," she continues, and for the first time, I realize I'm wearing a soft cotton chemise with satin ribbons at the collar. "And the healer attended to the wound on your foot and scratches on your arms. She's godkissed."

I free my foot from the silken sheets to examine the puncture wound. It's entirely healed, not even a scar. "She couldn't do anything about my sore muscles?"

Brigit's face falls slightly. "She's at the army barracks presently, but now that you're awake, I'll call for a fresh bath with herbs for your soreness."

She gives a thick cord near the door a tug, signaling to the servants downstairs. Then she scampers over to the wardrobe, proudly throwing open its doors. "After your bath, you can select any gown you wish. They've been made just for you."

One glance tells me the clothes are just as opulent and costly as everything else in Sorsha Hall. Clarana silk, delicate patterned lace, metallic-threaded damask, brocaded satin. The colors range from sky blue to midnight black and everything in between. Brigit opens smaller drawers, tilting them to show me the glistening jewelry inside.

She's so proud to show off these riches that I'd be a monster not to smile. "Lovely—it's all lovely. I'd really like some food, though."

"Oh! Of course. What would you like?"

My lips part, unsure. What would I *like*? Not even in my father's manor house was I ever asked that question. My mind scrambles; in my grogginess, all I can think about is the gruel I've eaten for twelve years.

At my strange silence, Brigit says, "I'll just have them

bring an assortment." She returns to the pull cord and tugs it twice this time, then pops over to the door, cracks it, and whispers something to the guards on duty.

Soon, servants bring steaming boiling water to fill the marble tub, and Brigit helps me ease into it. A sprinkling of ground eucalyptus and lavender scents the air, and Brigit rubs coarse salts against my skin, which hurts in a delicious way. She scrubs my hair with rosemary oil until my scalp tingles. I stare blankly at the dresses, so Brigit selects a sage-colored silk gown for me, embroidered with a leaf pattern. The hem pulls up high on one side, showing off a good portion of my leg, but it isn't nearly as revealing as much of what I saw on Duren's streets.

While she's brushing my damp hair, someone knocks at the door, and Brigit rushes to answer it. I hear a brief exchange, and then smell the most deliciously mouth-watering scents of roasted meat and fresh bread.

"Oh, thank the gods. I'm *starving*." I push up from the dressing table and spin, ready to pounce on anything I can get in my mouth—

And freeze.

Lord Rian is at the door, tray in hand. I glimpse a flash of Brigit's backside as she disappears into the hallway.

Swallowing a knot in my throat, I sink back down to the stool. As intimidated as I am by his presence, my mouth still waters at the smells coming from that tray. I glimpse fresh berries, haunches of roasted game bird, hunks of cheese that have me licking my chops.

"Lord Rian. You—you brought my food yourself?"

"You'd have preferred a servant?"

"Well, yes." I'm too damn hungry to think up a clever

retort.

A genuine laugh erupts from his chest. He sets down the tray and drags over two stools. He doesn't have to beckon me to the table—my feet are already taking me there, eyes pinned greedily to the food. As I sink onto the stool, I can hardly decide what to tear into first. The bowl of spiced nuts? Some kind of meat dumpling? A creamy burdock soup? When Brigit said she'd request an assortment, I didn't think she meant a *banquet*.

There's something that looks like stuffed gamebird drizzled in a golden sauce, and I tear into it with bare hands, not caring if Rian thinks I have no manners. So what? He made me eat over a campfire for the last twenty-one days. He can stand to see his bride act like a savage.

With luck, I'll disgust him.

But he doesn't seem disgusted as he watches me gobble down sliced herring on bread, and pear tarts, and cheese topped with plum sauce. He smiles broadly, captivated, as he pours us both brandy.

"Are you determined to fatten yourself so I won't want to marry you? If so, I'm afraid you're out of luck. I like women of all sizes."

I pause briefly in chewing to roll my eyes. I'd give him sharper words, but my patience is better when I have food to focus on. "Let me guess, you planned this. You know I'm starving, so you deliver a king's feast with your own two hands. You mean to control me with food."

His head pitches to the ceiling as he laughs. "My lady, you've quite a vivid imagination. It's only *quail*. If I wanted to manipulate you, I'd have served swan."

To him, this feast is beggar's food. But for me, wealth doesn't mean money. It means a full belly. And knowing I'll have a full belly again tomorrow and the day after that. The contents of this tray are more valuable to me than the priceless artwork hanging on Sorsha Hall's walls.

Out.

I pause, a plump raspberry posed in front of my lips. There it is again—that voice. Definitely not in a dream this time. It tickles the same part of my mind as animals' communication, but there's a foreign feeling to it, unlike any animal I've ever known. The voice rings with anger, too. The chill of it leaves me feeling like wind just swept through the room.

"Lady Sabine? Are you well? Is it indigestion?" He's teasing.

I shoot him a hard look as I set down the raspberry. "Basten didn't say you were funny."

His eyes gleam oddly as his head cocks. A long beat passes before he says, "He told you his real name? What else did *Basten* say?"

There's an odd note in his voice. I realize I might have said the wrong thing. I don't want Rian to suspect anything happened between the two of us. As much as I want to hurt Basten, I realize now that I'd be stabbing myself in the foot, too. For better or worse, I need Rian to like me. Until I can figure out a plan, I need to play his games, and keep my food and safety secure.

Fortunately, I'm spared by a demanding rap at the door. The wine jostles in our glasses. I jump.

Rian's brows lower, displeased. He barks loudly, "What is it?"

But his demeanor changes when an older man enters.

He's around my father's age, with the same graying hair and lines on his face, but the comparison ends there. The years have diminished my father. This man seems to have only strengthened with age like petrified wood. His height is imposing, as is his doublet made of leather and ultrafine chainmail. On most people, decorative armor is merely a shiny accent—on him, it's a threat.

"Lady Sabine," Rian says like he's tasted something bitter. "This is my father, Lord Berolt."

Fear weighs me down like an armful of boulders as the man looks me over purposefully like a filly at auction. He might not be High Lord of Duren in name anymore, after having turned over that title to Rian, but it's painfully clear that this man still wields massive power.

His first words to me are an order. "Show me your godkiss, girl."

My first instinct is to look to Rian for help; Rian, who's the last person I'd consider an ally. But the sheer menace of his father has me scrambling for any straws.

"My—my godkiss?"

"Yes. A demonstration. I want to see your power with my own eyes."

"Father," Rian says in a low, tight voice. "Lady Sabine just survived a vicious abduction; perhaps we don't immediately thrust her up on stage?"

"Nonsense. Show me, girl."

My chest fills with lead as I slowly pick up a crumbly piece of tart crust with shaky fingers.

Come here, little mouse. I'll share my food with you.

The mouse scampers across the floor in cautious

bursts, pausing to sniff the air. He makes a wide arc around Berolt's feet to where the treat rests in my palm.

"There," Rian says curtly. "See what you need?"

Berolt grunts, dissatisfied. "I want to see her command something bigger. One of the army's hounds. Or better yet, one of the tigers. And no offering it food—*I* could lure a mouse with a pear tart."

My nerves don't go away, but they're rapidly being eclipsed by anger. Who does this man think he is, to command me like a puppet? I'm to be his daughter-in-law, not his servant.

I'm about to risk the dungeon and tell the mouse to piss on this man's shoe, when Rian rests a hand on my knee and squeezes. I pause. The touch is a signal: *Don't.*

"I'll arrange something," Rian says with purposeful vagueness. "Now, there's the engagement party to plan, so if you're done extending a warm welcome to my bride—"

"I'm not." Lord Berolt snaps his fingers. "Stand up, girl. I want to see exactly what my son's coin has bought him."

Before I can object—if I even dared—Lord Berolt seizes my arm and drags me to my feet. His wrinkled hand feels the contours of my hips and stomach, manhandling me like livestock. My thoughts lurch to a halt. Bile rises on my tongue, the bad taste enduring no matter how many times I try to swallow it down.

"She's ripe," Berolt says. "She might give me a godkissed grandchild. You should start on that soon, Rian."

My mouth forms into a stunned "o," so aghast at this man's crassness that I'm entirely speechless.

Rian, clearly used to such behavior, pops a spiced nut into his mouth and murmurs, "I should like to get to know my bride first."

Berolt gives a derisory snort. "Hurry, or with a pretty thing like her, I have half a mind to do the job myself."

I actually gag, but at the last minute, am able to mask the sound as a cough. *Fucking gods!* And I thought Rian was the one to worry about. Now I see that disease is most rampant at the base of the family tree. I'm reminded of something Basten said. A terrible rumor that Lord Berolt killed Rian's mother when Rian was born without a godkiss, contradicting what the fortune tellers predicted.

Is *that* the great mystery of why Rian chose me as his bride, despite essentially ignoring me at the Preview? They think because I'm godkissed, I can give them godkissed Valvere children? There are ample godkissed women, but not many among Astagnon's nobility. If Rian wanted a godkissed bride of noble birth, there were only a handful of options.

Rian's jaw tightens as his father's hand wanders further up my belly toward my chest. Rian shoots to his feet, knocking a silver fork off the table. He's of formidable height as well.

"Oh—about the incident at Titan's Taverna," Rian says, his tone seamlessly switching to business as his body herds his father away from me and toward the door. "I overheard that Theo Laganon is back in the bottle. I thought we might post a few undercover sentinels at the pub next time . . . "

Berolt mutters a response, and after a low conversation at the door, Rian manages to eject him from the room. He spins back to me, wipes a slow hand down his face, and then gives a humorless smirk. "Now you understand how he built such an empire. He takes whatever he wants."

His tone may be darkly joking, but he looks shaken by the incident, too. My lips are trembling now that the assault is over, the danger gone—at least for now. Rian takes one look at my face and shakes his head.

"No—no, don't fear him, Sabine. I can handle my father. He won't touch you."

"He just did!"

Rian concedes the point with a head tilt. "Well, I promise you that he won't make good on his threat, how about that? And neither will I, for that matter. You and I haven't discussed it yet, but I have no intention of forcing you into my bed before we're properly wed. I could frankly care less if you worship Immortal Iyre. But I know you're a virgin, and I'll honor that."

A cruel laugh rests at the base of my throat. A virgin? Oh, how I could raze this castle to the ground with the truth. If he was only smart enough to believe me.

"You want me to trust you?" I ask bitterly. "To believe you'll keep me safe? You forced me naked across half of Astagnon! You're a *villain!* If Wolf hadn't been there—"

I snap my jaw shut, biting off my words. It won't do any good. Angrily, I glare at Rian until he finally gives a tight sigh and leaves me alone.

As if I needed one more reminder that creatures on two feet can never be trusted.

CHAPTER 28
WOLF

As soon as I'm back in my shithole of a house, I throw myself head first into investigating what's happening at the border wall. Okay, so it's not entirely a shithole. Until a few weeks ago, the game warden's residence, just outside the city walls between the Golden Sentinel barracks and the start of the Blackened Forest, suited me fine. It's as simple as cottages come; a single room with a large fireplace and a sleeping loft, and a porch where I store my bows and arrows. It's quiet. Peaceful.

Now, the quiet is fucking killing me.

I always thought I wanted solitude. The few times I've had soldiers in my house to share a bottle of ale was tolerably pleasant, but I was always anxious for them to leave. Now, I can't stop glancing at the empty second chair, at the bed that's only ever used on the left hand side.

Hunting isn't any better. I'd thought it would take my mind off a certain girl with flowing locks, but all I can see in the woods are animals that remind me of her: owls, geese, mice. I have to force myself to fire the killing arrow, reluctant now that I know they could be friends of hers.

So as the days pass, I fill every second I'm not hunting with my quiet investigations. Rian forbade me from formally examining the breached border wall, but what he doesn't know won't hurt him. He made it abundantly clear that he's been withholding things from me, so I'm only returning the favor.

Pouring over maps, I mark the route I'll take to hike up the Darmarnach Mountains to reach the wall's westernmost checkpoint. None of the checkpoints are manned now; they only were for the first hundred years or so after the great war, when people began to forget that the terrible crimes Volkish godkissed soldiers committed didn't just happen in ghost stories. But there are still ruins where guards once stood, and that's a likely place for a breach. With the difficult terrain, it would take a month to traverse the entire border wall, so I plan on sticking to the section closest to Duren. From the first checkpoint, I'll follow the wall east around the Tulle tributary, skirting through the Blackened Forest until I reach Havre Peak. Even that short section will require four or five days. It'll be tricky to find an opportunity to be absent that long without raising suspicion.

In the meantime, I've been quietly asking around among old contacts. Deep in the Sin Streets, there are information brokers who can find out anything for the right price. I get a lot of raised eyebrows when I mention King Rachillon and Volkany, but eventually, a spy informs me that there's a Volkish whore at the Velvet Vixen, a mid-level brothel, who came to Astagnon under myste-rious circumstances as a child. It's the best lead I have.

On the evening I head into town to speak to her, however, I find myself running smack-dab into the last thing I need: A giant fucking mural of Sabine painted on the side of a grain warehouse. It portrays her draped in birds and dragonflies and moths, her arms extended in defiance. The artwork is amateurish, so I can't imagine Rian commissioned this. Which means the people of Duren have already taken to her enough to immortalize her. Well, of course they fucking have. Who wouldn't? She's a goddess.

Somehow, after seeing that mural, I find myself in the Cloudfox Tavern instead of the Velvet Vixen. After more drinks than I care to count, I stumble back outside, stare too long at the mural, and then head to the Valvere stables.

Other than a few grooms shoveling shit at the oppo-site end, it's empty. I find Myst in the first stall, which is so luxurious that it's nicer than my cottage. Her mane and tail are perfectly groomed. Her white hair gleams, freshly washed. She's happily munching on honey-rolled oats.

"Hey. Crazy mare. I've fucking missed your long face." I lean on her stall door, pressing my forehead to the iron bars that top the wooden lower portion.

She comes over and nuzzles my forehead, getting horse slobber all over me. I scoff and wipe it away.

She gives a soft neigh.

"How am I, you ask? Oh, just fucking great. I'm always great. A lone wolf, don't you know?"

She snorts.

I reach between the bars to scratch her behind the ears. "Okay, you got me. I miss her, too. I guess I got used to the two of you slowing me down. To her scent. It's like violets—that's the first thing I noticed about her."

On some level, I'm aware that I'm drunk and talking to a horse. Utterly ridiculous. But being around Myst calms the black pit that's been growing in my chest. I close my eyes, pressing my forehead to Myst's, letting the scent of horsehair take me back to the ride from Bremcote. Those black nights with Sabine.

Gods—it fucking hurts.

I can smell a trace of violets in the air; Sabine must have been here recently, visiting Myst. My heart starts hammering, and my groin twitches as I breathe in that delicate scent. It's almost overpowering. I could swear it's getting strong enough to drown me.

Fuck, I downed too much ale . . .

Someone clears their throat behind me. "What the hell do you think you're doing?"

My eyes snap open. Sabine stands behind me, her hands perched on her hips and a scowl on her pretty face. She's wearing a lavender gown the same goddamn color as violets. *Fucking perfect.* It's an off-the-shoulder neckline, exposing her bare shoulders and the top of her godkiss birthmark. The air stalls in my lungs.

I didn't think it was possible, but I'd forgotten how beautiful she is.

"Lady Sabine." I sober up fast, wiping the back of my hand over my mouth. "What are you— Where's Rian?"

Her hate-filled eyes burn into me hot enough to banish me to the underrealm. She lifts a hand toward the stable entrance. "Just outside. He saw someone he wanted to speak to. He'll be in shortly."

I can't read her tone. Alcohol dulls my heightened senses, makes me just as obtuse as everyone else. I clear my throat. "Have you set a wedding date?"

Her eyes flash hotter. "No."

I can't stop my eyes from sliding down her short hair, softened with a braid along the front, to her fine leather riding boots. I swallow hard. "You look well. Has Rian been keeping his hands to himself?"

I wince as soon as the words come out. *Stupid, Wolf. Stupid.* I bent over backward to make this girl hate me, the last thing I need is for her to know how fucking jealous I am.

Her eyebrows rise at the bold question. "Can't you tell?" Her voice is edged like a blade. "Can't you *scent* him on me? Do I smell like fresh sex?"

My groin tightens at the same time that my jealousy combusts my skin into fire. She's needling me. I know she is. My sense of smell isn't so dulled that I would miss the telltale scent if they *had* fucked. But even knowing this, I suck my teeth, fighting to calm the wave of covetousness that rolls through me.

"I wouldn't be surprised if he had taken you," I answer evenly. "He's certainly wanted you long enough."

Her mask of anger slips long enough to show confusion. "What do you mean? He ignored me the first time we met. The only reason he wants to marry me is because it's more likely I'll give him a godkissed child."

A bitter laugh tears out of me. "Are you serious? You believe that? He came back from Bremcote last year with fire in his eyes. He knew he wanted to marry you the second he saw you. It didn't have a thing to do with your godkiss. Fuck, he plotted for months to entrap your father in debts so he'd have no choice but to give you to him."

Her eyes widen—she didn't know that her father didn't fall into debt by his stupidity alone. But then her pretty brows furrow. "But Rian never showed any—"

"He runs a gambling empire, Sabine. He knows how to hold his cards closely."

She goes quiet. The silence stretches between us, only broken by the sound of shovels at the far end of the stable, and the stomp of horses in their stalls. All the fight goes out of me as I bask in her gorgeous presence. What I would give for one more day with her love instead of her hate. I'd find a way to snare the stars and put them on her dinner plate.

Something shoves me from behind, and I stumble forward with a curse. Before I know it, I collide with Sabine, our bodies pushed together. My hands secure her waist on instinct to keep us both on our feet. Her soft curves graze against my harder edges. Her scent bathes me like exotic oils. I feel the beat of her pulse, once so familiar to me that I fell asleep to its soft patters.

I look around to find Myst's head between the bars. That crazy mare pushed me!

I swear that goddamn horse is smiling.

"Sabine . . . My lady . . . . Forgive me." With apologies on my lips, I extricate myself from Sabine. It's so damn hard to let her go. I'd forgotten how perfectly she fit into my arms, like she's my world and I'm her gravity.

"No, no, it's alright." She's too flustered to berate me as she brushes the wrinkles out of her gown.

It's at that awkward moment when Rian walks into the stable.

The breath dissipates from my lungs. I'm instantly a paragon of control—not a lovesick drunk at all, oh no—as I give him a tight nod.

"Wolf." His voice lifts in surprise. "I thought you'd be in the forest."

"I brought down a stag this afternoon. I was delivering it to the kitchen."

"Hmm." He touches Sabine's back briefly, and I flinch. It's barely a touch, but it shoots me through with white-hot jealousy. What happened to her hatred of Rian? Her defiance? Does she really let him touch her like that?

She subtly shifts away from his touch, to my dark satisfaction.

Rian says smoothly, "I promised Lady Sabine that as soon as she was well, I'd take her for a tour of Duren on Myst. I believe there's a horse race in the arena tonight."

Yeah, that's not by chance. He wouldn't show Sabine the dog fights or warriors wrestling until one of them loses an eye. He picked the least offensive of the arena's entertainment.

I give a stiff nod. "Enjoy the tour, Lady Sabine."

I can't get out of there fast enough, but even before I reach the entrance, Rian calls, "Wolf. Wait."

He jogs over to me while Sabine strokes Myst's long neck through the stall bars. Once we're out of earshot, he lowers his voice.

"The job you mentioned. Being her guard. I changed

my mind—I want you to do it. You can start tomorrow night."

My heartbeats kicks up again in its steady hammer, unsure what to make of this. "What changed?"

A muscle jumps in his jaw. "My father. He's taken an . . . interest in her."

Revulsion turns my stomach, but I can't say I'm surprised. Lord Berolt has committed far greater sins than coveting his future daughter-in-law. This suits me, however; I can protect her from the old bastard and Volkish raiders at the same time.

I try to keep the magnitude of my relief hidden as I give a gruff nod. "Whatever you need, my lord."

§₀

I head straight to the Velvet Vixen after leaving the stables. If I'm going to be guarding Sabine, I'll have even less time to slip away and investigate the border, so tonight has to be the night I get answers, even if I am still sloshed and prickling with adrenaline after seeing her again.

I pound my fist on an oak door carved with a none-too-discreet outline of a copulating couple. A second later, Madame Anfrei throws open the door.

I cough at the wave of perfume that slams me in the face. It might mask other scents from her other customers, but I can easily pick up on the reek of body odor and opium.

"Wolf Bowborn," she says, folding her arms as she

leans in the doorway. "Haven't seen your handsome face in a while."

Madame Anfrei is a distant Valvere family member, by marriage. She divorced one of Lord Berolt's second cousins twenty years ago, and rather than being sent back to the hogwash village she came from, she took up management of the Vixen.

I lean in the doorway, keeping my face stony. "I'm here for business, Anfrei. I need to ask you some questions about . . . politics."

Her painted-on eyebrows arch dramatically. "Is that so? Hmm."

She beckons me to follow her with a hooked finger. My jaw clenches as I duck through the doorway into a darkened den of silk settees and lanterns draped in cheap colored cloths. It's the receiving room—private rooms in the back room are where the action happens. Girls lounge on the settees and floor cushions, perking up at my entrance. I'm a lot younger and less paunchy than most of their clients.

"If there's a private place we can speak—" I start.

My thoughts fall off a cliff as a girl walks in from the back, pushing aside a curtain. She's pretty and petite. Her honey-colored hair is pinned to make it look shoulder-length. Her face is scrubbed of fae makeup. And there are fucking wings strapped to her back, and paper moths pinned to her flimsy dress.

What in the name of the gods?

Madame Anfrei notices my attention and smirks. "Every man in Duren wants to fuck Rian's Winged Lady. A few women, too. Mathilde here fulfills their fantasy." Her cold eyes turn dangerously perceptive. "Why, Wolf Bowborn? Did you want a turn on your master's pretty new bride all that time you were with her, able to look but not touch?"

Her aim is too close to a bullseye, and I scowl and turn away from the girl dressed as Sabine.

Patience thin, I grab Madame Anfrei and drag her into the small closet of a bedroom that doubles as her office. I say, "Tell me everything you've heard about King Rachillon. I'll pay you."

"King Rachillon! That isn't politics, Wolf, it's madness." Before I can say more, she lifts a hand to silence me. "No. You aren't in that line of work anymore. I once took your coin for secrets, but Rian made it clear that you're out."

I groan. I'm getting really fucking tired of being stonewalled. "This isn't about Valvere business. It's—"

"It's always about Valvere business. Everything is Valvere business. Now, pick a whore or leave. Rian said you're to have anyone you want. How about that pretty thing dressed up as Lady Sabine, eh? Don't tell me you didn't have a hard-on every night watching her sleep naked."

My jaw clenches so hard I think the bone might shatter. It's getting harder to swallow my fury when I need answers as badly as I do.

"Fine." I force my shoulders to relax. "Fine. I'll take a whore, then. You're right. It's been too long since I've visited your fine establishment."

Her smile is both triumphant and nasty.

I return to the reception room and search out the

Volkish girl. The lights are intentionally low, but my heightened eyesight easily picks up on the one with warm skin and light blond hair.

"Her."

Madame Anfrei snaps. "Carlotte. You have a gentleman. Just don't expect him actually to have manners—we've all heard Wolf Bowborn fuck, and there's nothing gentle about it."

The other girls titter. One voluptuous brunette pouts that I didn't pick her.

The Volkish girl, Carlotte, takes my hand with a tempting smile and leads me to one of the back rooms. Walking down the long hallway, we're assaulted by grunts and moans from behind closed doors. She takes me to the last room, then starts to peel her gown's strap off one shoulder.

I lay my hand over hers. "I'm not here for that."

She laughs like I made a joke. "It's okay. I don't mind taking a tumble with you. Every girl in there was hoping you'd pick her. I mean . . . *look* at you."

I hold up my hands and start again. "I want to talk to you. That's all. I'll pay you the same price, but for your discretion, not your cunt."

She slowly realizes I'm serious. One hand nervously runs up her other arm. Eyebrows furrowing, she says uncertainly, "Why do you want to talk to me?"

In a low voice, I ask, "Were you born in Volkany?"

Her eyes widen, ringed with fear. "Where did you hear that? Not even Madame Anfrei knows about that!"

"Look, I don't hold it against you. I don't care where you're from, and you can rely on my silence. I'm just looking for information on Volkany from someone who's been there."

"But I haven't been there," she insists in a whisper, her eyes big and round. "At least not that I remember. I was brought to Astagnon when I was three. A market vendor found me wandering the streets. I only spoke Volkish. When I finally learned the Common Tongue, apparently I told her I was from over the border wall, from a Volkish town named Kittengen. I don't remember anything from that time, though."

"How did you get over the wall?"

"I don't remember. I swear. I'd tell you if I did." Her honesty rings true, and my chest rises and falls with a tired breath. *Another dead end.* But then she perks up. "There is, well, not a detail, really. Just a song I remember. I think my mother might have sung it to me."

I cock my head. "Sing it."

Her voice trembles as she sings haltingly, *"From slumber deep in realms unknown . . . dormant powers start to breed . . . first the king, and then the beasts . . . What do you do with sleeping gods? . . . Pray they don't awaken."*

She looks at me shyly. "It doesn't rhyme, I know. It was probably originally in Volkish, but I only remember the song's general meaning in the Common Tongue."

Sleeping gods awakening?

Dormant powers breeding?

It's a riddle—and I don't like the answer it's pointing to.

I pay the girl, and we play a game of Hazard for the duration of my paid time, so our lovemaking seems convincing. It could get her in trouble if anyone suspected I was here for information.

As I'm leaving, troubled by the possible meaning of the girl's remembered song, Madame Anfrei stops me. She holds up a folded letter addressed to her, bearing the Valvere seal.

"Look what was just delivered by courier. An invitation to Lord Rian and Lady Sabine's engagement party. It's to be held this Friday. A masquerade with a winged theme. How perfectly diabolical of Rian to embrace his bride's show of rebellion. They might just be well matched after all." She gives me a knowing smirk like she knows this is the last thing I want to hear. "I'll see you there, handsome."

CHAPTER 29
SABINE

Out.

GET OUT.

I wake with a start, sweat slick on my temples. There it is again. That voice. I've heard it more times than I'd like to count, and its source remains a mystery. My animal friends in the castle say they can't hear it. I never believed in ghosts, even though Immortal Woudix's story in the Book of the Immortals chronicles his ferrying ghostly souls to the underrealm. Are they real after all? Whatever the voice's source is, it feels angry.

Angry at *me*? Is it ordering me to get out?

It wouldn't be the first sign I've come across that I'm not safe here. Sorsha Hall is a warren of shadows. Rian only lets me see what he wants me to, just like his carefully cultivated tour of Duren. I've barely even seen *him* in the week I've been here. He's frequently absent on "business," and I don't think it's just overseeing the town's legal vices. Two nights ago, I heard the guards at my door discussing a team of Golden Sentinels who Rian sent to the border wall; they never returned.

OUT NOW.

I clap my hands over my ears, though it's useless since the voice rings from within my head. It's driving me mad. What time is it? After midnight, judging by the moonlight. Donning a silk robe, I throw open my door, ready to confront the guards outside about what's really going on in the castle. They *must* know something.

But I go still as stone when I find Basten on the other side.

He's traded his huntsman garb for the light sentinel armor that castle guards wear: brass shoulder plates and forearm guards, leather breastplate with the Valvere crest, a collar-like piece around his neck, and a baldric belt to hold his sword. Though the brass armor is polished to perfection, he still looks like he belongs in the woods. His hair is long and loose. His cheeks tanned from the sun.

"What the hell are you doing here?" I snap.

"Lady Sabine." His rumbling-stone voice rolls across the threshold between us. "From today on, I shall have the pleasure of serving as your bodyguard."

The formal tone doesn't suit him any more than the armor does. Though I must admit, it does something to me to see him in metal and leather. The armored plates make his already enormous frame even more affecting. I once thought he looked like a god—now, he looks as imposing as the king of gods himself, Immortal Vale.

And damn if my belly doesn't tighten at the sight of him. Naturally, that's the moment when I realize I'm in nothing more than a revealing chemise and robe. Cheeks blazing, I wrap the robe tighter over my chest.

Scoffing, I blurt out. "Are you *trying* to torment me?"

His brows lift innocently. "I'm merely obeying Lord Rian's orders."

"Oh, of course, you'd never do *anything* to transgress against your master." Fire sparks from my eyes as I lean in, sniffing. "You smell like cheap perfume."

His lips part for a quick retort, but then he stops, and a cold smile crosses his face instead. "Yeah. Well. Probably from the whorehouse I visited last night before taking up this post."

My jaw slackens as my cheeks blaze in outrage. I must be throwing off more heat than the fireplace. A whore? We've been in Duren barely a week, and he's already fucked someone else? I scramble for words, then shut my mouth. No. Basten Bowborn doesn't deserve my anger. He doesn't deserve a second of my thoughts at all.

"Did you require something?" he asks with infuriating calmness, pretending he's simply my bodyguard. "You seemed anxious to leave your room."

I recall the voice with an uneasy pull in my stomach. I'm not about to tell Basten that I'm hearing ghosts—he'd tell Rian, and they'd lock me up in a madhouse. So I lift a blase shoulder. "I wanted some fresh air."

He leans one hand on the doorframe, towering over me in his armor, trying to intimidate me. "I'd be happy to accompany you to the gardens, my lady, though I would suggest you change your attire first. As I understand it, Lord Rian doesn't want you to roam freely. Out of safety concerns, of course." His voice falls an octave. "Oh, and if you've got any ideas about using the servants' entrance in your room to sneak out, you should know that it's kept locked at all times. Besides, I'd hear if you tried to leave that way."

My fiery stare radiates white-hot hatred. So much hatred that it stalls the breath in my lungs. It's my own suit of armor, protecting my still-wounded heart.

"So," he says in a light tone. "A walk in the garden, then?"

I grip the door hard as my hand shakes with rage. "You know what? I've changed my mind. My engagement party is in a few days, and I want to look beautiful for my future husband, so I'd better get my rest. The night of the party might even be when I invite him back to my bedroom. I hope you won't mind standing guard while listening to our *moans* through the door."

I don't mean it, of course. I'd never let Rian touch me. Still, Basten's eyes go blade-sharp with jealousy, and before he can say a word, I slam the door in his face.

※

Sorsha Hall's parties are legendary throughout Astagnon. Even as a child, I'd heard rumors of them, whispered about by nobles visiting my parents in Bremcote. People's obsession with fae culture is stronger nowhere than the Valvere balls, which attempt to recreate the decadent fae courts of old. Feasts of exotic game, fanciful eye masks, feats of strength, wormwood-laced wine to bring out visions. Oh, and of course, unmentionable debauchery between couples—even throuples—in not-so-private hallways.

Still, after an entire day of being bathed and groomed, trimmed and coiffed, and sewn into a scandalously low-cut blue gown with slits on either side all the way to my upper thighs, I'm unprepared for the awe-inspiring sight when I step into the castle's ballroom.

Hundreds of paper lanterns containing votive candles hang from the ceiling. Their light reflects off the tall glass windows, twinkling as though the stars have lowered to the earth. A quartet of string musicians plays beautiful and strange fae melodies. The discordant combinations of notes shouldn't work together but do. The air is rich with the attendees' fragrant cologne and sumptuous scents from the overflowing tables of decadent foods.

The partygoers are dressed in fanciful clothes copied straight from the Book of the Immortals's illustrations, with the off-set closures and unbalanced hemlines that, like the off-kilter music, make me feel like I've stepped into a slanting world. The majority wear satin masks over their eyes or carry masks on sticks. Nearly every person's attire incorporates feathers or wings as part of their clothing, mask, or woven into their hair.

Standing in the hallway just outside the ballroom, Brigit comes up behind me, tweaking the positioning of the silvery goose-down wings harnessed to my back. After all, I'm the Winged Lady of Duren, the reason for all the celebratory feathers: No one would expect anything less than for me to have the grandest costume of all.

As soon as he spots me, Lord Rian drops his conversation with a man in a feathered cloak, and cuts a line to me. He doesn't wear a mask. His only adornment is a leather harness studded with iron rivets, and a subtle swipe of blue eyeliner, as always. The message of his plain attire is clear: He's above fashion. And it's true—somehow, he looks the most striking out of everyone here.

"Lady Sabine." He bows to kiss my hand, his eyes locked to mine beneath my white feathered eye mask. "Duren's beautiful songbird, who sings the language of nature as only the rest of us can dream about."

I would roll my eyes if I weren't still so stunned by the party's grandeur.

A few paces behind me, wearing his sentinel armor and not a single fluff of a feather, Basten gives a snort disguised as clearing his throat.

Rian straightens with a smile. "Come, songbird. Everyone is waiting to honor the future Lady of Sorsha Hall."

I force a smile, very aware of Basten's eyes on us. It's all I can do not to shoot him a glare over my shoulder. At least my anger dulls my nervousness. I find myself saying loudly, with my head tipped slightly in Basten's direction, "It would be my pleasure."

Rian leads me into the whimsical fray. Basten lurks at the edges of the ballroom, speaking with no one, drinking no wine, his eyes fixed on me as his charge, entirely focused on his task. It's hardly surprising that he fails miserably at enjoying himself. At least with him shadowing me from afar, I can almost forget about him.

"Lady Sabine." Lord Berolt, in a simple black eyemask, stands from the high lord's table to greet me with a heavy kiss on my cheek and a hot hand on my waist. I swallow back my revulsion. "The infamous Winged Lady. Do you enjoy that we've set tonight's theme around your famous act of rebellion? You see, it's worth wringing the rebelliousness out of your system now, before the wedding. Once you're a Valvere, we'll expect the same obedience as all Valvere wives."

An unpleasant taste coats my tongue. I'd love to spit it out, along with a vow that I'll never be a Valvere wife, but I force myself to swallow.

"Oh, I think rebellion is the *perfect* theme," I say through bared teeth.

Lady Eleonora, in a feathered peacock mask that sits askew on her face, barely glances at me, far more interested in the wormwood-laced wine that stains her withered lips. The other Valveres and nobles at the high lord's table raise their glass in a curt toast.

As high lord, Rian takes the heavy oak chair at the table's head, then motions to one draped in golden ribbons at his side.

"Sit, my lady," he commands. I sink into my chair as tightly coiled as a bundle of nerves, struggling to get comfortable with the costume set of wings against the chair back. I feel like an imposter. My chair and Rian's are practically thrones. Such finery should be treasonous for anyone to flaunt other than King Joruun. But the king is elderly and in poor health, so who's going to stop the Valveres?

The instant my backside hits the seat, a fleet of masked servants place silver trays before me and fill my crystal goblet.

"Take care with the wine," Rian warns wryly. "A few

glasses, and you'll be spouting off prophecies by the night's end like Immortal Meric."

I glance again at tipsy Lady Eleonora in her ridiculous mask—she looks ready to drunkenly prophesize the awakening of the gods right now, and the ball's just begun.

Though the food is delicious, my nerves make everything taste like ash. As the night stretches on, my heart knocks insistently in a reminder that this isn't where I'm supposed to be.

Rian stands and clinks his glass with a silver spoon.

"Lords and ladies of Astagnon, please raise a glass to my beautiful bride. Lady Sabine proved her perseverance on the ride to honor Immortal Solene, and charmed us with a striking demonstration of her godkiss upon her arrival. We are all fortunate to have the famed beauty in our city, but none as much as I." He gives an exaggerated, playful wink toward the crowd. "Hands off, you rogues. The lady is mine."

Polite laughter rings throughout the crowd. I stare at my plate, gripping the armrests so hard my knuckles are white, feeling like nothing is real.

"And now," Rian says, raising his glass. "It is my pleasure to announce that I will wed my bride here in Sorsha Hall, the ancient seat of my family, on the eve of Midtane. And you're all invited, you roisterers!"

"Here, here!" The attendees raise their glasses to us amid more cheers. The blood drains from my face. He set our wedding date? Midtane is scarcely more than a month away. Naturally, no one involved me in the decision any more than they did betrothing me to Rian in the first place. It was frightful enough when I was merely engaged to him; having this date set feels like an executioner's blade hanging over my head.

Rian turns to me with an outstretched hand. "Will you honor me with a dance, my lady?"

Sweating under hundreds of sets of staring eyes behind winged masks, I can't say no. My heart hammers as my trembling feet follow Rian onto the dance floor, where the crowd makes room for us. I don't know how to dance. When was I supposed to learn, while scrubbing floors? But Rian saves me. His confident hands steer me so that all I have to do is follow his guidance.

As I twirl and spin, my mind reels. Maybe it's the wine, or my numbing trauma, or the shock of Rian's wedding date announcement. Attendees' masked faces whirl around me like a nightmare.

What am I going to do? Rian might not be quite the devil I thought he was, but I'm no fool. I know that I haven't met the *real* him yet. He's an expert at hiding his true nature, and thus far, he's only presented a carefully cultivated facade. Still, I'll take that over a baldfaced villain like his father any day.

At least Rian has been respectful. He's gifted me anything I could want; but I feel nothing for him. He's handsome, but it isn't his face I dream about. He's rich, but I don't care about his money.

My heart doesn't surge for him in that dizzying, terrifying, bone-melting way that it has before. Halfway through the dance, my eyes seek out Basten at the crowd's edge. His face is stoic, betraying no emotion, the perfect unfeeling soldier. But I know he must feel something. In the waterfall cave, he pledged himself to me. He made love to me like I was the only woman in the world. I don't know why his sentiments turned, but he's masking his real feelings now, too. I know it. I want to tear down that mask, stare straight into his soul, and demand to know why he broke me.

After the dance, we return to the high lord's table, but the music doesn't restart for another song. With a devilish grin, Rian announces, "I've prepared special entertainment for tonight's celebration. A battle of strength between two of Duren's most famed fighters, Magnus Lancaster and Roland the Shade!"

He claps his hand together in a signal, and the crowd shuffles backward to clear a wide circle in the center of the ballroom. For the first time, I notice the inlaid wood on the polished floor isn't just a decorative pattern; it cleverly forms a game boundary. Among other markings, there's a circle delineating where a pair would fight.

Two hulking men stride in from the back entrance. They're clad only in leather breeches to show off their stacked muscles. Their faces are hardened as sea-beaten rocks, one with a short beard, the other with a deep scar across his jaw. One has a red "M" painted on his chest, and the other bears a painted blue "R."

"For an extra treat," Rian says, resting his hand on my shoulder. "I'd like to propose a wager to my future wife. Select a fighter, Lady Sabine. Should yours win, you may name your prize. However, if mine is the victor, you'll forfeit a kiss."

The crowd hoots scandalously, delighted by the

bawdy wager, though it has to be relatively harmless, as far as Valvere bets go.

My stomach flips, and my eyes skim over the two fighters trying to win my favor by flexing their muscles. The promise of violence at my engagement party, even as a game, seems a tasteless choice. My eyes happen to land squarely on Basten, standing a few paces behind the fighters, and my heart falters.

But then I think about how he smelled of a whore's perfume this morning, and my hands tighten in anger on the armrests.

"Wager accepted," I announce tightly, to the crowd's delight. "I'll take the one in red."

The two fighters step into the marked ring, dancing around one another with intimidating huffs. They're clearly well-practiced at turning violence into a form of entertainment. I let my eyes drift up to the hanging lanterns. Grown men pummeling each other for sport feels barbaric; then again, what better ode to the ancient fae, the original barbarians?

After some performative banter between the fighters, which energizes the crowd, the bearded fighter, Roland, throws a powerful straight punch, which my red fighter evades by sidestepping. Magnus counters with a lightning-fast jab, followed by a kick to Roland's midsection. Roland responds with a flurry of hooks and uppercuts, adding a theatrical touch of acrobatics, which has the crowd squealing in delight.

My attention flickers between the fight and Basten. He watches in mild interest like he's seen these productions a thousand times. And he *has*. For years, he was one of the fighters. Does it trigger him to see it again? Call back to his rough past?

If it does, he doesn't show it.

Roland surprises Magnus with a well-timed inside leg kick that sends him off-balance. But my fighter lunges forward with a flying knee, striking Roland in the chest. The crowd shrieks—I don't think Rian and I are the only ones with a wager riding on the outcome. Magnus is clearly the superior fighter, and I smile as I think of what prize I'll ask Rian for—one that he might actually grant.

A long ride on Myst beyond the city walls?

One of the new puppies that was recently born to a sentinel hound, which I could raise into an ally?

Or maybe a tour of the real Duren, including the Sin Streets, and everything he's been hiding from me?

But then Roland, worn down and near defeat, surprises Magnus with an explosive punch to the jaw. Magnus's head is thrown back, and he does a backward swan-dive to the floor. As soon as his back touches the polished wood, Roland lifts his fist in victory.

Excitement erupts as bets in the crowd are settled— and my eyes go wide as I realize what this means. Improbably, Rian's fighter won. Did he catch a lucky break? Yeah, unlikely. Chances are far better that Rian ordered whichever fighter I chose to throw the fight.

My dress feels too restricted as I shift uncomfortably in my seat, realizing I've been played. My cheeks burn crimson. The costume wings at my back dig into my spine.

I shoot Rian a glare. He smiles back wolfishly.

Damn the Valveres.

After Rian congratulates the winner and invites Roland to sit at the high lord's table—the far end next to the less favorable nobles—the energy in the crowd shifts. The masked attendees, sated by wine, no longer crave bloodlust. Now they only desire *lust*.

"A kiss!" Someone shouts. "May the Winged Lady give our lord a kiss!"

"Yes, keep your promise, good lady!"

My fists ball in my lap. Behind my mask, my eyes scan the crowd with rising panic. How can I get out of this? On instinct, I fall back into the old habit of unconsciously seeking out Basten for help.

He's standing by the ballroom's rear entrance. His arms fold tightly over his breastplate. Lantern light gleams off his brass shoulder plates. His eyes bore into Rian as Rian settles back into his chair. Yeah, I'm not the only one who figured out that Rian rigged the game.

"What do you say, my lady?" Rian asks loud enough for the crowd to overhear. "Of course, far be it for me to think a rogue like myself has earned a carnal kiss from such a goddess; I'll settle for one blown from your sweet lips."

It's surprisingly generous of Rian to offer me this way out of a real kiss, and while I'm certain he has ulterior motives, it does relax my tightly set muscles.

Glaring across the tops of the costumed attendees, I snag Basten's eyes.

He laid with a whore? Well, two can play that game.

"Fair is fair, my lord," I announce loudly, pushing to my feet and flouncing my harnessed wings theatrically before dropping my ass into Rian's lap, glad my feathered mask hides my nerves.

The crowd oohs and titters at my cheeky move. Rian's hands grip my hips, adjusting me in his lap with a touch of both suspicion and intrigue on his face.

Reaching behind my head, I unfasten the satin ribbon holding my mask on. Now, barefaced, I address the crowd —address Basten—in measured words. "I honor my wagers, my lord. You'll have your kiss."

OUT. OUT NOW.

The voice. It's back. It's *here*. My attention whips around the room, seeking its source. Picking up on my sudden distraction, Rian places a hand on my thigh to draw the crowd's attention back to us.

It works.

His calloused hand runs along my bare thigh, exposed by the dress's high slit, until more immediate matters eclipse my concern over the voice.

He shifts his hips in a way that makes me bob precariously in his lap. My heart *rat-a-tats*. His hand strokes my thigh languidly, in no rush. Leaning back in the throne-like chair, he gazes at me with half-lowered eyelids.

He's manipulating me. Making *me* kiss *him*, not the other way around. Forcing me into the initiator role so it will seem to the crowd that I'm desperate for it.

A perfectly willing bride.

I channel the fighters' theatricality and tell myself this is only an act. *Basten is watching*. His eyes are the only ones I care about. I want *him* to think I'm willing. That he isn't the only person putting Rian above all others.

I want to hurt him as badly as he wounded me.

An actress—just an actress. With a burst of courage, I lock my arms around Rian's neck and meld my lips to his. The clapping and hooting from the crowd make the paper lanterns quake. I thrust my nearly-exposed breasts against Rian's chest, squeezed tighter by the harness holding my wings, and throw all I have into the kiss.

Rian's palm glides along my bare thigh up to my ass. He's giving the attendees a show, just as I am. His lips take over, setting the tone for the kiss, deftly taking control now. His tongue flicks against mine, silently asking how far I'm willing to go. My dress feels tighter than ever. How far *am* I willing to go? Is Basten watching? Are his hands fisting at his side?

The kiss isn't as bad as I feared—in fact, I'm a touch breathless. Rian's unwavering confidence makes him an exceptional kisser, and now I get why so many women hunger for him. His teeth snag my bottom lip to bite gently. I'd be lying if I didn't say I felt a thrill, though it could just be the energy from the crowd focused on me as the center of attention.

GET OUT.

I break the kiss with a sharp intake of breath. The voice again, louder this time. It provides the jolt of reason that I need to remember that the kiss is only an act. But my breathlessness is very real. So are the goosebumps on my thigh as Rian's thumb strokes it in lazy circles.

From the corner of my eye, I see Basten swipe a tray of crystal glasses off the buffet table to the floor, smashing them in a burst of anger. A few people close by laugh like he's drunk, and no one else cares. I'm the only one who sees him flex his hand—there's a flash of blood on his knuckles—and then storm out of the ballroom.

I smile in grim satisfaction. I did it—I got to him. He would only react like that if he *did* care about me.

"That was . . . unexpected," Rian purrs in my ear, and beneath his seductive tone, there's a heavy note of suspicion.

He's not an idiot. He knows a bride he bought against her will and humiliated in front of half of the kingdom must loathe him. Then again, Basten told me once that men have an astounding capacity to lie to themselves when it's about something they want.

I give Rian a nervous smile, more shaken by the kiss than I expected, as I slide off his lap. Briefly, my eyes flicker to the rear entrance.

Basten is gone.

I hadn't planned for this, but if there was any good time to slip away and investigate the mysterious voice, it's now. For once, I'm not being watched.

"If you'll excuse me, my lord," I stammer, resting a hand on my heaving chest. "I—I'm short of breath. I'm just going to take a moment on the balcony."

Rian nods, his half-masted eyes grilling into me like he can read my lies but isn't going to call me out on them.

He murmurs, "Of course, songbird."

Placing a hand on the base of my throat, I slip through the raucous attendees, who've returned to dancing and drinking and fucking each other with their eyes. Struggling under the unwieldy weight of the wings, I head toward the balcony—and then double back to the rear entrance, and slip out when no one is looking.

CHAPTER 30
WOLF

Blood drips from the gash in my hand as I storm into the hallway. I can't get away from that fucking party fast enough. So many stinking bodies. That jarring fae music. The deafening cheers when Rian had his hand all over Sabine's ass.

Fuck.

Here I go again, fisting my hand so hard it's bleeding more. Where's a damn cloth...

The southern hallway is dark, its candelabras intentionally half-lit to foster a secretive air. Couples have already taken advantage of the darkness's cover. In nearly every alcove I stride past, shadowed forms rut together in winged masks, playacting like they're fae. The idiots. I hate Sorsha Hall's parties. I've never understood people's adoration of the fae—what have they ever done for us?

A woman's high-pitched moan of pleasure stops me in my tracks, and makes me briefly shut my eyes. For a second, it sounded like Sabine. Behind my eyelids, all I see is her perched in his lap with his hand on her bare thigh. When she kissed him, it took all my strength not to drag her off his lap, wrestle her to the floor, and fuck her in front of the whole damn court until there wasn't a shred of doubt who she belonged to.

Damn Rian. Damn this whole fucking castle.

I grab a crumpled napkin from where it's fallen off someone's plate and wrap it around the bleeding gash on my knuckles. Knotting it tightly, I slump back against a wall, tucked away in a seldom-used hallway lined with storage closets, where no one will see me rest my head against the cool stone.

What the hell am I doing?

I have to get my shit together. I have to get Sabine out of my head. Something bad is happening in Astagnon, and there's fucking blood in the water. There are so many trails to follow, so many possible leads. Where do they all come together? What does King Rachillon know that we don't? Are the gods truly awakening? Are all his preparations—breaching the border wall, kidnapping godkissed people—to prepare for their return?

All these questions screech to a halt the second I smell violets on the air.

Like a predator, my eyes snap open.

Twenty paces away, Sabine slips quietly out of the ballroom and tiptoes down the hallway opposite me. My spine straightens in disbelief at her boldness. Sneaking out of her own engagement party? What does that little winged wildcat think she's doing?

Hugging the shadows, she moves with purpose down the hallway. The same woman as before moans from the

WHITE HORSE BLACK NIGHTS

alcove, and Sabine freezes, presses a hand to her chest, then continues. I stalk her from behind, curious about what she's up to. She knows there's no escape from Sorsha Hall, so what's her aim?

At the end of the hall, she pauses. She stands still for a few seconds like she's listening. Nearly inaudibly, she whispers under her breath as though voicing a thought. "Who are you? What do you want?" It's so quiet that only someone with my hearing could pick up on it.

A second later, she turns toward the lower level stairs with purpose again.

Yeah—I don't like this.

The only things on the lower level are some potato storage and the dungeon, neither of which Sabine has any business rooting around. It's time to cut her little adventure short.

With swift, silent steps, I move up behind her and wrap my hand around her mouth from behind. My other hand locks around her waist. Her damn costume wings are between us, the feathers clogging my mouth, my heavy shoulder plates getting in the way, too.

She screams into my hand and bucks as I spin her around to press her back against the wall. It's too dark for her to recognize me right away. Wild-eyed, she struggles to slam her knee against my groin—hey, at least she remembered what I taught her—but I easily anticipate the strike and block her.

"Quiet," I hiss. "It's just me."

Her screams dry up, but her pulse is still shouting. Her breasts rise and fall like creamy pillows, shoved up and on display from her dress, the wings' harness squeezing them together. She stops struggling, but her eyes are still primed to fight.

Her wings crumple against the wall as I push her backward again. "I'm going to take away my hand now, and you're going to tell me where you're going."

Slowly, I remove my palm from her damp mouth, sliding it down to snare her neck instead.

Baring her teeth, she snarls, "What are you doing here?"

"It's my job to protect you. Did you think I'd let you out of my sight?" Her perfect breasts continue to heave, straining against the harness. "Now tell me where you're headed."

"I just needed a second of quiet!"

"You're lying," I say lazily, pressing my thumb to her jugular, where her pulse reveals her deception.

Squirming under my grip, she spits out, "Rian has secrets—you'll forgive me for wanting to know the truth about who I'm supposed to marry."

"Secrets hidden in the potato cellar?"

"What? I don't know. I'm just following a—a hunch. Secrets are always kept somewhere dark and deep, aren't they?"

She isn't telling the whole truth, but most of what she says isn't a lie. It earns her a lighter grip around her throat. The muscles there bob as she swallows, and I can't help myself. It's fucked up, but all I can think about is ramming my cock down that throat until she moans.

"You didn't seem so troubled by your husband's secrets when you had your ass in his hand," I say.

"What was I supposed to do? I lost the bet."

I growl, "You did it on purpose. You wanted to hurt me."

She's immediately ready with a jab. "Oh, like you hurt me? I'm not yours, Wolf Bowborn. You could have been fucking me right now in a beach cottage, but you chose not to. You chose *this*."

I see red at the accusation. My body hardens, adrenaline preparing it for a coming fight or fuck. But it isn't her I'm furious with. It's me. Her words strike too hard to the punishing truth.

"I never chose *this*," I hiss. Who in their right mind would choose this exquisite torment? To watch the girl I want with her lips all over another man?

She skewers me with a scathing look that tells me how wrong I am.

"Admit it," I say between my clamped teeth. "You were thinking about me when you stuck your tongue down his throat."

"What do you care?" she shoots back. "You had a whore ride your cock what, three days ago? You used me and threw me away!"

It takes every ounce of my strength to maintain the lie and swallow down the hate she's throwing my way. "I would never throw you away, Sabine. Not in the thousand years the gods have slumbered."

"Then why be so cruel?" Angry tears glisten in her eyes, and it breaks me a little.

My voice hitches in my throat. "There's much you don't know."

"Then tell me! What could possibly have changed your mind? Are you really so loyal to Rian?"

I hesitate. "It is about loyalty—but that's only one part."

"What else, then? Are you that broken? Did you just toy with me? Was it fun?"

My molars clench at the idea that I would ever hurt her for pleasure.

"You're sadistic," she hisses, cheeks burning crimson. "You're no better than Berolt and his wandering hands—"

My body moves against the accusation on instinct, hips pushing her harder against the wall. Her silly wings quake. My eyes flash like a wild animal's. "I'm *nothing* like Berolt."

She retaliates by shoving me with her full strength, and I grant her some space, taking a step back, pacing like a caged animal. She shoves me again in the chest with both hands, and then again, until my back smacks into the hallway's opposite wall.

I let her pin me, needing to see this thing through. And damn if it doesn't feel good to have her hands on me, even in hatred. "Tell me why you've been so cruel, Basten. I want the truth."

It's intoxicating, the beautiful flush of her anger. I could bathe in her hatred all night.

"I told you—"

She slaps me across the face. The sting of pain does something to me. The violence at her hand shoots straight to my groin. I close my eyes, fighting the urge to act on the adrenaline slamming through my veins.

I murmur, "Do it again."

She pauses, but only for a second. She slaps me again, even harder this time. I groan in demented pleasure and lick some moisture into my lips. "That's good. Again."

But she doesn't. I can feel anger sparking in her hand, wanting to lash out again, but not if I like it. Then, something shifts in her energy. Or maybe in mine. Her arm pulls back to slap me again, but I catch it this time, trapping her by the wrist and dragging her into the cage of my arms.

Our lips come together like warring armies, our passions crashing violently, hatred and love all mixed up, and it feels like stars colliding, like beautiful devastation. This is wreckage, but I'll die happily here. As my hands lock to her narrow waist, my lips can't drink her in fast enough. I want to consume her, to take everything from her. Her hands rest on my brass shoulder plates, trying to pull me closer. My little violet is so small compared to me. Even on tiptoe, I have to stoop to kiss her.

And it's not enough.

It will never be fucking enough.

I grab her ass and hoist her into my arms. Her beautiful legs wrap around my hips, her dress's saucy slits easily allowing the movement. My fingers squeeze handfuls of her soft flesh like sinking into a feather mattress after months on the road. My groin pulses. Now that my body has made up its mind between fighting and fucking, every drop of blood rushes to my cock.

"Basten." My name sounds so good on her breathy voice. "I *hate* you."

Her hips roll against mine, telling a different story. Whatever she has to tell herself is fine with me, as long as it keeps her lips on mine.

"I know, little violet. I know."

Supporting her with one hand, I use the other to tilt back her head to slip my tongue between her parted jaw. I taste her, lapping her up. When her tongue lashes back at mine, I think I'm going to die. The urge to touch her everywhere drills into me.

Her damn wings . . .

My damn armor . . .

I have to get it off. I tug roughly on my metal collar to loosen the leather straps, but then freeze as I pick up on footsteps and wine-slurred voices around the corner.

"*Did you hear that?*" someone says.

"*Hear what? You've had too much wormwood,*" the other responds.

"Shh," I hiss into Sabine's ear. "People are coming."

I smash my hand against her mouth, silencing her moans. Her hot breath dampens my palm. Her tight little body is like an unruly cat in my arms, refusing to stay still and silent. Fuck—she's going to get us caught.

I shift her in my arms, wanting to tear my armor off so I can feel her closer.

I rest my forehead on hers, my hand still pressed to her lips.

The blacksmith's hammer of her heart reverberates. Time stretches painfully as we remain unmoving, coupled against the wall, trying to be silent. It's dark here, but anyone would recognize the Winged Lady's costume and a sentinel's armor.

Whoever the approaching people are, they turn off in the opposite direction down the northern hallway, and a sigh rolls out of me.

Sabine mumbles something against my hand, but I shake my head slowly.

"Shh, little violet. We can't be caught."

She wiggles her hips insistently, and I swear the damn wildcat is as aroused by the possibility of being caught as she is afraid of it.

My groin tightens again, demanding I find a private place to fuck her senseless or risk combusting.

"Don't make a sound," I warn. "You're coming with me."

CHAPTER 31
SABINE

With one hand still clamped over my mouth, Wolf slips a small key into an unassuming door I hadn't noticed in the shadows. It's a servants' door like the one in my bedroom, though this one is plain oak since it can't blend in with the stone walls. He pulls me into a faintly lit passageway and eases the door shut, just as we hear more voices pass mere paces from where we'd been.

Once the voices fade, and silence surrounds us, he finally removes his hand.

"Rian will notice I'm gone," I say whisper-soft, my heart knocking. "He'll be looking for me at the party. If he catches us together . . ."

"Leave it to me, little violet. I'll hear if anyone comes." His broad palm cups my cheek like a golden chalice as he leans close enough to ghost a kiss against my lips. "Just try not to scream my name too loudly when I fuck you."

His lips claim mine greedily in a kiss before he takes

my hand, interlocking our fingers, and leads me down the passageway.

Dear gods. My heart flutters like a bird lured into a trap, sensing danger but moving in anyway. What am I doing? Have I lost my mind? Basten betrayed me. He slept with a whore. I shouldn't be here with him! But when I look at him, my resolve flits away into nothingness. Longing and need rush up to fill the void.

I hate him . . . I hate him . . . I hate him.

I also want him so painfully I'm about to shatter into pieces.

The servants' passageway is narrow, lit by brass lamps every twenty paces, which means we're continually plunging in and out of shadows. The walls are simple wood paneling with a muted green rug underfoot, meant to silence servants' footsteps.

"What if a servant comes?" I say breathlessly.

"We're alone. I'd smell someone if they were close. Everyone is in the ballroom to help with your party."

I'm missing my own engagement party. My fiance waits by my empty chair at the high lord's table. Well, so what? I never asked for any of it. Rian's been pulling my strings across half of Astagnon, and it's only fair I sever them.

Basten knows these passages by heart, which makes me wonder how often he uses them. *Is* he a servant? Expected to keep out of sight with muffled footsteps, so as not to disturb the Valveres? Or does he walk the primary halls freely as Rian's friend? I can't figure out where he falls between the servants and the family themselves—and I'm not sure he knows, either.

He leads me down a narrow passage. Then up two flights of steep stairs. There are so many turns my head spins. I've completely lost my sense of direction by the time he stops to unlock another door. When he eases it open, the smell of botanical perfume greets me.

We're in my bedroom.

"That key," I say as he slides it back into his pocket. "Does it unlock all the doors?"

"The ones servants have access to. But don't get any ideas." His eyes flash a warning. He knows me well enough to realize escape is always at the forefront of my mind. I can't help it. I've been imprisoned so long that my mind has carved a deep river of thought that only knows how to flow in one direction.

Moonlight streams through the tall windows. The lantern on my dressing table flickers; otherwise, it's dark. Basten strides to the main door and locks it with the latch. Then he turns on me with a huntsman's stalking menace. One hand goes to unbuckle the brass collar around his neck. He tugs the leather laces free, and it falls to the carpet with a muffled thud.

There's no misinterpreting the lustful look in his eyes.

I snag my bottom lip between my teeth to quelch the rush of blood to my lower half. I feel lightheaded. In the faint light, Basten looks more like a dark god than ever before. And gods, do I want him to take me like one.

This is wrong, I know. I'm engaged to another man. Years of studying Immortal Iyre's teachings on chastity tell me that I shouldn't be doing this. But how much loyalty do I owe Rian?

Not a damn drop.

Basten unbuckles his shoulder plates and slides them off one at a time, moving slowly so the metal doesn't clatter loudly. He unfastens his forearm cuffs. His eyes never leave mine. I feel snared, like a rabbit enchanted by a serpent's gaze. He stalks toward me slowly, next unbuckling the leather chest plate with the Valvere crest. He sets it on the foot of the bed.

With his shed armor, he stands in only his pants, his sword slung low on his hips, and a different shirt from the one I borrowed so many times that it felt like a second skin. My palms dampen with desire to twist the fabric in my fists. He steps close enough that warmth spills off his body. He places a heavy hand at the base of my throat.

"Say that you felt nothing in that kiss."

I know what kiss he means. Sitting in Rian's lap, arms looped around his neck, our tongues sliding together. But I don't want to give him the satisfaction of the truth.

"What about the whore?" I challenge. "Did you feel nothing with her?"

His palm slides up to encircle my throat's column as he leans in with barely contained impatience. "I didn't fuck any whore. I haven't had my cock in any woman since you, and I don't intend to. Little violet, don't you know I could never want any woman but you?"

My lips fall open to release a soft exclamation. This man is torturing me. He's going to destroy me. And I'm falling so willingly into the quicksand, begging for him to bury me whole.

"Basten," I moan softly.

His eyelids fall to half mast. "Say that again. Say my real name."

I swallow around a knot in my throat, caused by his hand still gently clutching it. "Basten."

Before I know it, he scoops me off the ground like I weigh nothing. My legs, able to move freely with my gown's side slits, clutch around his hips instinctively. As soon as our bodies are aligned, a deep, husky exhalation shudders out of him.

He spins me around and presses my back to the wall. The rough stone scratches down my back like fingernails. The beautiful goose down wings snag and break apart. Feathers rain to the floor. He doesn't seem to care that we're shredding a costume that must cost more than he makes in a year.

Our lips crash together in a kiss that's a battle of wills. His mouth is hot. His tongue licks and strokes over my own like it wants to sample every drop of me. The hard edge of his teeth drags against my bottom lip. He sucks the lip into his mouth, biting down just hard enough to send lightning shooting all the way to my toes. I fist my hand in the back of his hair, wrenching his head down to mine. This feels like a game, and both of us are determined to win.

His hands on my ass explore freely like I'm his prize to plunder. The dress's slits let him touch my most intimate places, guarded only by my satin panties.

"I need these off," he orders sharply.

I wiggle my hips, and he sets me down. He attacks the broken wings first, unfastening the leather harness around my chest and sliding it down over my shoulders. I fill my lungs to capacity, finally freed. But before I can step out of my panties, he kneels before me like he's about to worship the gods. Roughly shoving aside the dress's slitted fabric, he runs his hands along my panties' front seam. His hot breath cools the already damp fabric. He's so close to my cleft—he must be drowning in my scent. My cheeks burn to know that he can tell how wet I already am, my body craving him enough to flood my channel in preparation.

He hooks his fingers in the sides of my panties and slowly drags them down my legs, painting his palms along the smooth skin of my thighs and calves until he reaches my feet. Then he leans his forehead against my lower half and groans.

"Your scent. I've been thirsting for it. Nothing else will do."

He stands and undoes his pants, then grabs me by the ass again, shoving the dress's skirt aside to coax my legs around his hips.

My head falls back against the wall. What is wrong with me? I hate this man . . . but my body doesn't care. In fact, the hatred only makes me wetter. It's fucked up, but hatred is a powerful form of connection. For a long time, it was the only language I knew. And Basten is the same way. We were raised on violence, so no wonder we crave it.

We're both so damn twisted. So broken.

At least we're broken together.

His eyelids sink lower as he frees himself from his pants and presses his cock to my entrance. He slides the tip up and down my glistening slit as his chest heaves.

"Gods, you're so fucking wet."

My hips buck, unable to hold steady. My tongue darts

out to dampen my lips, which are dry from panting. But as much as I wiggle, he doesn't plunge any deeper than a shallow tease.

He demands, "Tell me how you were thinking of me when you were kissing him."

I bare my teeth as a white-hot flare of anger engulfs me. "I wasn't. I hate you—I don't think of you at all."

"You're so fucking pretty when you lie," he murmurs, and then finally takes me with one hard stroke.

A gasp tears from my throat as his cock fills me completely. *By the gods.* There is no feeling in the world like having Basten inside me. My juices make our union slick, but he's so big that it still stretches me in a way that brings both pleasure and pain. He takes a moment to bury his face in the crook of my neck, his cock sheathed to the hilt. Then he pulls out and thrusts in again.

I cry out, overcome by the pressure, and he clamps one hand over my mouth while supporting me with the other.

"Quiet," he breathes. "You don't want to alert the whole castle to the fact that I'm fucking Rian's bride."

But as he takes me against the wall with powerful thrusts, I can't swallow my moans fast enough. He keeps his hand against my mouth to muffle my whimpers.

"That's it," he says, low. "Show me how much you like it. How you can't fucking help but like it."

I wrap my trembling thighs around him tighter, our slickness making it hard to hold on. The dress's slits tear. The gown was already ruined—shredded by the rough stone wall, soaked in my desire.

His fingers dig into my ass as he thrusts hard and hot.

Our skin slaps together even louder than my muffled moans. I can feel every inch of him sliding in and out of me. It triggers some madness in me that shuts off my brain and turns me into an animal. Gripping his shoulders, I lift my hips to match his thrusts.

"Nod your head," he orders. "Show me you like it."

My head bobs against his palm. In reward, he adjusts his stance and thrusts into me even deeper. I feel swollen, needy. A storm is growing in my lower half that I can't stop. My thighs tighten as I rock my hips faster, calling to the storm. Wanting it. The heat is building so much that I can feel it coming to a head, and my pussy tightens around his cock.

"No," he growls. "Not yet."

He slides all the way out of me. He removes his hand from my mouth just in time for me to give an angry protest.

"Basten, please!" I pant, angry with him for making me beg.

"I said not yet." He carries me to the bed, where he drops my ass down on the fur coverings. He stands over me, gazing at my splayed body in the torn, ruined dress, and then shoves my knees apart, putting my core on full display.

He drops to his knees at the foot of the bed, his lips parted, and as it dawns on me what he has in mind, my eyes go wide.

"Oh no," I say. "Not *that*. It's too much. I can't take it!"

The last time he licked my pussy, I shattered into a million pieces. I'm afraid this time, I won't be able to put myself back together again.

He gives me a pitiless look as he lowers his mouth to my core. "Talk less when I fuck you."

He's merciless as he licks and sucks my swollen core. His tongue laps at my outer folds, caressing the curves. He lays his tongue flat to lick me from bottom to top, then captures my clit between his lips and sucks.

I cry out, then clamp my hand over my mouth to keep myself quiet. My heart is scrambling wildly. Any minute, Rian could come to the door looking for me. Or Brigit could enter through the servant's door to prepare the room for the night. We can't be caught. There's no telling what sick game Rian would punish us with.

But the pressure is building too fast. The storm is coalescing, aching to burst. Basten pushes a finger inside me, stroking my insides deeply while simultaneously sucking on my sensitive bud.

That's all it takes. The storm bursts. A wave of dousing pleasure drenches me like I've been swept underwater. My brain goes numb as I'm caught in the storm's thrall. I'm weightless, like campfire embers coasting toward the stars.

My head falls back against the quilt, throat opening to let ragged breaths tear out of me. As my knees fall to the side, my body utterly spent, Basten wipes his mouth with the back of his hand and then unbuckles the baldric belt around his waist that holds up his sword, the last of his armor. He lets the sword clatter to the floor.

I realize why when he crawls on top of me with a look that tells me he isn't even remotely finished with me, and that he needs full range of movement to accomplish what he has in mind. My breath catches in my throat.

"I can't come again," I pant. "Not yet."

"You can, sweetheart. You will."

He starts kissing the hell out of me. Arching my back, I lean like a cat into the hard planes of his muscles. He wraps a hand around my bowed back, then without warning, flips me over until I'm on my stomach.

"Basten! What are you—" My words die as he shoves the torn skirt out of the way, exposing my bare ass to the room's cool air. He grabs my hips and lifts them high so that I'm on my knees with my elbows on the bed.

His hands knead my ass cheeks, holding my hips prisoner with an iron grip. I realize he wants to fuck me like this, rutting from behind like an animal.

"This pussy belongs to me," he growls. "Do you understand? No other man touches it. Not Rian. No one."

A flare of anger makes a part of me struggle against his grip while, at the same time, another part of me wants to move closer to claim his cock. "My body is my own, you bastard. I'll do whatever I like with it."

"Not this. It's mine."

He rubs my entrance with the tip of his cock, and by the gods, this angle elicits a whole new wave of sensations. My traitorous body is gushing again for him.

He teases me with the tip of his cock pressed a little deeper into my swollen heat. "Tell me you want me, Sabine."

"I want you to fuck me," I bite off angrily, twisting my head so I can glare at him. "That's all it will ever be."

He pushes in another inch, so shallow it's torture. He knows exactly what he's doing. There's a dark, hungry depth to his voice as he says, "Tell me that you love me."

My heart thrashes like angry hooves against a stall door. How dare he, with his cock in me, say such a cruel thing?

I gag on my shock, spitting out, "I never said that!"

He rests a hand on my lower back, holding himself back from thrusting into me as he clearly wants. "You don't think I know what love looks like? Come on, little violet. I can read you like a book. You love me. You have for a while. Admit it, and I'll have you seeing stars."

His gruff voice is softer, coaxing. That same damn tone he used when he promised he'd run away with me. And I hate Basten for this more than anything else. For these fleeting glimpses of vulnerability that he offers so stingily. Moments when I can see the real him, the one he hides from everyone but me.

"Say it, Sabine. Say you love me. That's all you have to do."

His voice is so tender yet so commanding. His tone makes me want to trust that I can believe him, but I've fallen for this before. He'll show me snatches of this side of him, tempting me with the authentic person I know is buried there, but then the moment I lower my walls, he'll throw his own back up.

"I hate you," I breathe, eyes squeezed as tightly closed as my jaw is clamped. "I hate you so much it hurts. What I hate most is . . . I'm in love with you."

A ragged exhalation shakes out of him. His body shifts behind me, his hands firming over my curves. His cock strains at my entrance.

"Good girl," he breathes.

He gives me his whole cock, thrusting all the way in. I

gasp, leaning forward on my elbows as my vision blurs. He drags my hips back and sinks into me again. And again. His strokes are fast and worshipping now—a reward for giving him what he wanted. As much as I'm choking on anger, the feeling between my legs wins out. I push my hips back against his thrusts so that his cock hits the tingling place inside my channel. He reaches around to caress my breasts, fondling the nipples.

"That's it," he urges. "Take what you want. Take your need."

He knows how to work my body as expertly as he does a bow and arrow. Touching the right places, feeling for the sensitive areas, when to go easy and when to go hard. It isn't long before my pussy is quaking again, close to another release. With each of his thrusts, the buzzing intensifies. I rub against his cock wildly, not caring about anything but getting the release I crave.

He rolls my nipple between his fingers, and that breaks the pressure. It shatters over me like cracking ice, decimating me. Drowning me. Reducing me to nothing more than a quivering mass of liquid pleasure.

My thighs threaten to give out, so Basten grips my hips to hold me up as he pumps faster.

"Yes. *Fuck*. You're mine, little violet. Mine."

He comes in me with a final deep thrust, fully buried in my scabbard. I can feel his cock pulsing against my slick inner walls, pumping hot sprays of semen that fill me up. It feels so good. His hot come. His throbbing cock. And it's so wrong, absolutely filthy, a sin I'll never forgive myself for—but as necessary as breathing.

I slump onto the bed, still in the tattered masquerade

gown, while Basten goes to my wash basin and fetches a cloth. He comes back and cleans me up with a tenderness that makes my heartstrings tighten. I feel the terrible sting of coming tears.

Of all the cruel things he's done, making me admit I loved him was the worst. I didn't want to say it even to myself. I thought I loved Adan, when all I really loved was the idea of getting out of the convent and starting a new life. With Basten, I told myself that it was the same. My feelings for him were confused. It couldn't be love, because I didn't know what love was.

I should have known he could read the secret buried in my heart. The shame I never wanted anyone to know about. I gave him my heart, fully and without reservation, and even after his betrayal, I'm still so damn in love with him that I can't think straight.

I brush away a tear, not wanting him to see. I meant what I said: I love him, but I hate him, too. We just can't stay away from each other. Maybe it's this place. Duren. Sorsha Hall. With its sinful nature, this place is more dangerous than anywhere I've ever been. Even with Basten's loyalty to his master, and my fury over his betrayal, we keep getting pulled back to each other like circling planets. It's a collision course for destruction, I know, but I'm just as helpless to stop it.

Basten's weight sinks onto the bed beside me. He wipes away the tear that rolls down my cheek, chased by two more.

"I'll take care of you," he whispers in a tone that twists me up inside.

He tries to kiss me, but I shove him away, bitterly wiping away my tears. "You can't take care of me."

"Sabine. I can. I will."

"You can't!" I shove him harder, almost knocking him off the edge of the bed. Pushing to my feet in the tattered gown, I kick his armor toward his feet. "Get out!"

"Please." His jaw tightens. His throat bobs in a swallow as his walls slip a little further. "I couldn't stand it if you—"

"Get out, Basten," I hiss. "Take your gods damned armor and go!"

CHAPTER 32

WOLF

I fasten the armor that marks me as a Valvere soldier and leave Sabine's room, resting my head against her door as I mull over how completely fucked up I am.

Yeah, I lied to Sabine to protect her. It was justified. I didn't have a choice. But a good man would have stayed away from her after breaking her heart. He wouldn't have fucked her against a wall in her engagement party gown until she cried.

I can't help but keep moving toward her. I've never wanted anything as much as I want her. Not just the sex —though fuck, the sex is mind-boggling—but to have her love. To know that she thinks about me first thing when she wakes up and last thing when she falls asleep. To possess her smiles, her kind touches. To have *my* ring on her finger.

Stop it, Wolf.

What I want is impossible. She's engaged to Rian,

who can keep her safe. So I'm just going to have to swallow my feral possessiveness and watch them be together, knowing I'll never have what I want.

"Wolf?" a masculine voice says, tearing me out of my thoughts. "Were you just coming out of Lady Sabine's room?"

I jolt upright. Rian and two Golden Sentinels stand at the end of the hall, looking at me strangely. I was wallowing in my feelings so fucking hard that I didn't hear footsteps approach. That isn't like me. Not good. I'm losing my edge.

I straighten, one hand going to my baldric belt to ensure it's properly fastened. "The lady wasn't feeling well. I was checking on her."

Rian comes closer with slow footsteps. "She said she was going to get some air on the balcony, but then no one could find her."

I clear my throat, trying to hide my jumping pulse. "As her guard, I had eyes on her the whole time. I—I think she drank too much wine. I was about to call for Brigit to come attend to her, to help her out of her costume."

Rian smoothly turns to one of the soldiers. "Send for Brigit. And you." He points to the other. "Stand guard at Lady Sabine's door for the remainder of the night."

My heart starts slamming in my chest. Casually, I say, "I assure you, my lord, I am capable of—"

"I need to speak with you," Rian cuts me off, rubbing his hands distractedly. "Maximan can fill your post for the time being."

My lip curls at Maximan. I know him from my

training days. He's a mean old bugger, but a highly capable guard. If I had to pick anyone else to watch over Sabine, he'd be my choice—and not just because he's ugly as a coyote. Still, I hesitate.

A few minutes earlier, Rian would have caught me fucking his bride. Is there a chance he suspects something?

"As you wish, my lord," I say gruffly, though I have to force my feet away from Sabine's door. I hope like hell she cleans up the evidence of our tryst before her lady servant arrives.

Rian says nothing as I follow him down the long hall. I keep my face stony, trying not to reveal my scrambling nerves. If he knows about me and Sabine, I'd deserve the dungeon, but that doesn't mean I *want* to go there. Fuck me. People have a habit of disappearing into Sorsha Hall's dungeon and never coming out—I know, because I put half of them there.

My fears only increase as Rian leads me to the stairs to the lower level. Our feet clunk heavily as we descend. Oh, fuck, he really *is* going to lock me in a cell. Like I told Sabine, there's nothing of note in the lower levels except cold storage for foodstuffs and the dungeon. It's always made my skin crawl down here. So dark, lit only by a few cobweb-covered lanterns. And damp enough to grow mold in my lungs.

Then again, there are also old tunnels down here connecting Sorsha Hall to other parts of Duren. They haven't been used in years, but maybe Rian plans to take me somewhere in the city in secret. Other than the primary tunnel that goes beyond the city walls, I've never explored the rest of them. Most are collapsed. The castle's original stable was housed here, underground, but it's been in ruins for decades.

At the bottom of the stairs, Rian takes a sharp left, and I curse inwardly.

The fucking dungeon, I knew it!

My nerves jangling, I start, "My lord—"

He holds up a hand to silence me. "I don't appreciate having my engagement party interrupted, Wolf. But if there's any good reason for it, it's this one. Now, I must return to my guests before they sense anything is amiss, so I'll leave you to deal with . . . this."

Confusion snaps in my chest until we turn the corner, where Folke Bladeborn and another man slumped to the floor appear in the light of a flickering wall sconce.

Everything I feared about Rian's suspicion and my future in the dungeon vanishes.

"Folke?" I ask, surprised.

The last I saw him, he was unconscious outside the Manywaters Inn while the townspeople of Blackwater attempted to put out the fire. Now, he leans heavily on a new cane. He doesn't look good—his face ashen and deeply lined—but it would take a lot more than a fire to bring his bones down.

"He arrived an hour ago," Rian says evenly. "Through the old tunnels."

As a former Golden Sentinel, Folke is familiar with Sorsha Hall's secrets. He jabs his cane in the slumped man's direction. "I brought you a present, Wolf. For saving my hide." His grim tone is anything but festive, and it curdles something in my stomach.

I glance at Rian, but his face betrays nothing. So, crouching, I pull the hood off the man's face. It reveals blood-matted fair hair and a face that, while hard to make out with all the bruises, is so familiar it stabs me with rage.

The man wheezes, his eyes fluttering as he mumbles something in pain.

I shoot to my feet. "One of the fucking raiders?"

This broken and bloodied man is familiar to me because *I* was the one who broke and bled him. It's the raider who tried to rape Sabine. Maks—that's what the others called him. Myst trampled him, and I can't fathom that anyone could survive the bone-shattering beneath her hoofs, but apparently, I should have checked the bodies better. I was in such a damn rush to get Sabine out of there to safety.

Folke digs the end of his cane into an oozing wound in the man's side, eliciting a pained moan. Folke smiles in dark delight. "When I woke up in Blackwater, I followed your trail. Enough people saw you riding a white horse to point me in the direction of the river. And the Old Innis Mill is a known haven for raiders. Eventually, I found the cottage. Your mark was all over the carnage. This one was still barely alive."

My muscles quake with fury that this scum still lives.

"Folke thought we might be interested in questioning him," Rian explains, though I'm sure Folke is collecting a handsome bounty for bringing him here, too. "There's a chance the raider can tell us why they targeted Sabine. What business King Rachillon has with her and the other godkissed he's abducting."

A vein ticks in my neck. It's a challenge to tame my temper, when all I want to do is borrow Folke's cane to stab it deeper into every one of Maks's oozing wounds until he's screaming, but I need to be smart. I don't need Maks to reveal why King Rachillon wants Sabine. I *know* why he does. And if Maks *does* know Sabine's secret, then it isn't his answers I need, but his silence.

Still, I have to play along for now.

I give a hard nod. "Good."

Rian pulls me a few feet aside. His eyes have the dark gleam they get when he's plotting something. "You wanted back in the business, Wolf? Here's your chance. Use those fists like you used to."

Torture him, Rian means. Interrogate him. Beat the answers out of him.

I flinch, then try to mask the reaction by smoothing a hand down my jaw. "You made it pretty clear that *out* meant *out*."

"Things change," Rian murmurs, glancing distracted in the direction of the abandoned tunnels that stretch beyond the dungeon. In a low voice, he confides, "I sent a dozen of our best sentinels to the border wall to look for breaches. It's been four days. None of them have returned."

Dark omens drift on the cold air coming from the direction of the abandoned tunnels. The Golden Sentinels are among the most skilled mercenary army of all the neighboring kingdoms. If a dozen of the best didn't return, it means we're all in big fucking trouble.

"So, we need answers," Rian presses, his eyes jerking toward Maks. "Before King Rachillon makes his next move."

My hands tighten into fists. I know what I have to do, but I don't want to do it. I had to move fucking mountains to get out of this line of the Valvere business, and into something respectable. I swore to myself I wouldn't kill again in the name of Valvere greed.

But someone has to keep Maks quiet.

Folke watches me with a knowing, piteous gaze as he eavesdrops on our conversation. He, more than anyone, knows how badly I fought to get out of exactly what Rian wants me to do now.

I feel like I'm damning myself to hell as I quietly whisper, "I'll get you answers, but I want some of my own. Be straight with me. What do I need to know about King Rachillon? I know you know more than you've told me."

A muscle pulses in Rian's jaw as he leads me further down the hall, out of Folke's earshot. In a quick whisper, he informs me, "All of Volkany is shut off, even from their neighbors to the north and east. Only portions of the western coast are open. My brother Lore encountered a Volkish sailing vessel in neutral waters. He took captives. They told the story of how King Rachillon rose to power out of nowhere thirty years ago. Some claimed he was a monk living on an isolated island in a giant lake. He gained followers when he claimed to be godkissed with the power to wake the sleeping gods. No one believed it at first, but then he awoke the fae's mythical creatures—"

"So the goldenclaw I told you about," I interrupt sharply. "You fucking *knew* it was real?"

He snorts dismissively. "You were out of the business, Wolf. You only wanted to hunt. That information was for the inner circle."

My fists squeeze even tighter. My heart thunders. Peeking back down the hall, I see Folke kick Maks a few times until he coughs to show he's still alive. As much as I want to throw a punch in Rian's smug face for not telling me this, I have only myself to blame.

I asked to leave—he granted it.

"So Rachillon plans to wake the gods? Fucking hell." All those stupid street preachers prophesizing the gods' return will shit their pants when they realize they were right. They're going to lose a lot more than their bowels, though, once they learn what's truly coming for them under the gods' capricious reign.

We all are. Everyone in Astagnon.

"Rachillon needs to find the ten resting places, starting with Immortal Vale's," Rian warns. "That's all that's stopping him. So, he's sent raiders into Astagnon and neighboring kingdoms to abduct godkissed with talents that suit his cause. But that doesn't tell us why he targeted Sabine. Her godkiss doesn't have anything to do with tracking."

Rian is right in one thing: It isn't about her godkiss at all.

I take a deep, shuddering breath to try to let this information take seed in my brain. The fae gods have been asleep for a thousand years. There are no records that state *why* the gods went to sleep, despite the Red Church's preaching that it must be a test for humanity. A thousand-year test? Yeah, fuck that. The gods never gave a shit about humanity except as slaves. People focus on the beauty and dramatics of the gods, glossing over all their bloodshed. Now, centuries later, we've forgotten our former struggles and, like idiots, pray for our subjugators' return.

If Rachillon wakes the gods, an entirely new chapter will begin. And we here in Astagnon won't only have to deal with *their* tyrannical aims; the gods' awakening will throw the human world into chaos, too, and Volkany's first order of business once they're in league with the Immortals again will be to attack us. With feeble King Joruun on the throne, we'll fall like a house of cards.

The Volkish prostitute's childhood song returns to me. What was it? *What do you do with sleeping gods? . . . Pray they don't awaken.*

I realize that the song was about Rachillon's grand plan—which means he's been working on this for decades.

I move my head side to side to crack my neck, working out the stiff kinks in my body. I'm in good shape, but it's been a while since I've used my strength on any prey other than animals. Human bones are notoriously hard—it takes some muscle to shatter them.

"The prisoner needs to recover," I say matter-of-factly, gesturing to Maks. The last thing I want to do is help that rapist bastard, but it's a means to an end. "Lock him in a cell. Have someone clean him up and wrap the worst of his wounds. Give him food and water for a few days. We need him strong enough to last through questioning."

Rian strokes his short beard as he nods. The gleam in his eyes is sharp, almost twinkling. Damn, but I think he's *delighted* to have me back in the business of blood. And I get it. He and I were thick as thieves since we were boys, complicit in our sins, until I turned respectable and left him behind.

He rests a hand on my shoulder. "I must return to the party. Take some time off, Wolf, to prepare. Maximan can guard Sabine for a few days. Once you have answers—" He jerks his head toward the prisoner, "—we'll talk again."

I don't like the idea of Maximan on Sabine's guard duty, but right now, this is a lot more important to her safety than standing outside her door.

"Right."

He hesitates before saying, "*Tamarac.*"

It means "clear as water" in the Immortal Tongue. In our younger years, it was our signal that we'd always be transparent with one another, as close as if we were brothers. A feeling of guilt stalks out of the shadows to dig a knife into my side. I've lied to him. Betrayed him. Coveted his bride. And now, he gives me our old word for unshakable trust.

Guilt burns my throat as I murmur, "*Tamarac.*"

Once Rian leaves, I return to where Folke stands, folding my arms as I stare daggers down at Maks. I'll kill him eventually, and I'll make it slow and painful, so he suffers for what he did.

In a quiet voice, Folke asks, "Does Rian know?"

"Does he know what?"

"What the fuck do you think? That you're in love with the girl he's throwing an engagement party for upstairs."

I flinch again. My instinct is to throw a punch to shut up such a treasonous accusation, but Folke means well, so I tame my temper. Chewing the inside of my cheek, I eventually spit out, "I told you, I'm not capable of love."

He huffs a derisive laugh. "Yeah, yeah. And I'm a prancing cloudfox."

His words sting because they hit too close to the truth. I do care about Sabine, more than I thought possible. But I know in my bones that someone as broken as me can't love anything. I was never taught how. I never saw what it looked like. And even if I could love Sabine, I'd only find a way to ruin that love just like everything else. So, no, I don't love Sabine Darrow. I *can't*. But I can dream about her. I can fantasize about her smiles and her sweet little chats with her sweet little animals. I can yearn for her affection. I can obsess over her, possess her, do everything in my power to shelter her.

"You'll stay in town a few days?" I ask Folke, tearing my thoughts off Sabine with difficulty.

"What, to help with *this*?" He kicks Maks. "No, my friend. That's all you—I've been paid and want nothing more to do with Volkany. But I'll stick around for a drink."

The corner of my mouth hitches in what passes for a smile, under the circumstances.

ई

My body aches with exhaustion by the time I return to the game warden's cottage. The sun is just coming up over the Darmarnach Mountains on the eastern horizon. I think about the wall and the sentinels who disappeared there. About goldenclaws and starleons.

About gods who should stay asleep.

Though all I want to do is crawl into bed and sleep myself for days, I stoke yesterday's dying embers to get a small fire roaring again. Then, I wiggle out the loose brick in the hearth floor and set it aside.

Lord Charlin's crumpled letter rests hidden beneath it. After a long breath filled with foreboding, I open and re-read the letter one final time before banishing it into the underrealm forever.

It begins clearly enough.

Sabine Darrow is not my daughter; I've known since before her birth. My wife, Isabeau, arrived in Bremcote already pregnant, the victim of an unknown rape. Her secrets only came to life upon her death. Isabeau, it turned out, was godkissed and hid it for ten years . . .

The letter goes on to describe how Isabeau, in her desperation to flee her mysterious abuser, agreed to marry Lord Charlin. She was a great beauty, far too good for the likes of him, but he agreed to acknowledge the bastard child as his own, and shelter Isabeau and the child with the power of his title. She refused to speak of her past other than to claim she was from a small village in the north. Her only possessions were a tattered copy of the Book of the Immortals, a simple pewter charm Charlin assumed had belonged to her mother, and Myst.

She'd remained faithful to Charlin, but only begrudgingly served her wifely duties. Instead, all her love and energy went to Sabine. Sabine was the apple of her eye until Isabeau unexpectedly fell on a horseback ride, hit her head on a rock, and died tragically.

Then, something no one could have expected happened: The book and the charm, which Isabeau kept in an unassuming chest, transformed. *So did her body.* Her honey-colored hair turned almost white blond, her nose straightened, her eyes changed their shape.

It turns out that Isabeau was godkissed with the ability to cloak objects' appearances, including her own. The book wasn't a copy of the Book of the Immortals, but her personal journal written in Volkish. The pewter charm was actually a solid-gold coin inlaid with priceless glittering gemstones—a rare calling coin of the Volkish throne.

Lord Charlin paid a godkissed seer to translate the Volkish journal, then had the man killed to keep its secrets contained. The entries revealed that Isabeau's abuser was, in fact, none other than King Rachillon, who had just risen to power. He'd enslaved Isabeau as a concubine, but when they discovered she was pregnant with his first child—whom a godkissed seer foretold would be female and godkissed—she escaped by making her way to the coast and bribing her way on a ship to an Astagnonian port, then disguised herself.

Lord Charlin ends the letter with a clumsy blackmail attempt:

This game has just begun, Lord Rian. The public will turn on you if it emerges that you wed a Volkish princess. I possess the evidence—Isabeau's journal and the calling coin of King Rachillon. If you want to keep Sabine's secret, you'll pay dearly.

Lord Charlin Darrow

King Rachillon might be abducting Astagnonian godkissed who can help him locate the fae's ten resting sites, but that isn't why he's searching for Sabine.

It's because she's his daughter.

Has he been looking for her since Isabeau fled twenty-two years ago? What changed now; what new information did he discover? Since the raider in Blackwater only had the rough description of a godkissed girl around Sabine's age and basic appearance, I don't think the raiders—or even King Rachillon—know her actual name or location. They're just searching for any godkissed girls with those parameters to take back to Volkany, to see if she's the right one.

I'll make damn sure it stays that way.

I ball up Lord Charlin's letter and toss it into the fire, steadily watching the flames destroy the claim of Sabine's parentage.

Next, I'll have to find out how much Maks knows, then kill him before he can reveal anything, though I can't make his death too fast, or it might seem suspicious.

Then, I'll have to silence Lord Charlin himself. He might suffer a fatal accident. Or, at the least, I'll cut out his tongue. One thing is certain—no one, least of all Sabine—can find out that her bloodline curses her as a daughter to Astagnon's greatest enemy.

CHAPTER 33

SABINE

As Midtane—my wedding date—tiptoes closer, I find myself thinking often about my mother and father. They were such an unlikely match; all of Bremcote gossiped about the strange pairing. What did my mother see in Charlin Darrow? Was it about his money and title? She never struck me as the social-climbing sort. Though she was born a peasant, she possessed a natural aristocratic bearing, whereas my father, despite being an actual member of the nobility, had lowly manners and even baser appetites.

They never talked to me about their wedding. In fact, my mother refused to discuss anything about her past. I don't know if my mother selected the wedding feast menu, or smiled as her wedding gown was fitted, or chose the flowers to decorate the church nave. Maybe, like me, she was a forced bride.

I'll probably never know the truth behind their marriage, but one thing is for sure: I don't intend to be shackled to a villain for the rest of my life by a golden ring, as she was.

Get out. Out now.

The mysterious, angry voice continues to haunt me. I hear it at the least expected times, like getting out of the bath, or cutting roses in the garden, or visiting Myst. Sometimes, I hear it as I'm falling asleep, and I feel like it's my own voice urging me to escape from Sorsha Hall before I end up another broken wife. With Wolf as my bodyguard, I never had a chance to investigate the voice, but for the past few days, a different guard's been posted at my door.

OUT NOW.

The voice is relentless.

Once night falls, I press my eye to the keyhole and spy on my new jailor. He must be in his late fifties, but age hasn't dulled his sharp eyes. He's an unpleasant, old brute who likes to bark commands at me like I'm a dog instead of the future Lady of Sorsha Hall. But as keen as he is, he isn't godkissed with heightened senses like Basten. And I can use that.

Little friend? I call in my mind.

The forest mouse scampers out from under the bed. Rising to his hind legs, his little whiskers twitch.

Here!

Are you ready to do what we talked about? I ask.

He eagerly darts across the room to the servant's door, where he's small enough to slip under the crack. I pull my bottom lip between my teeth, biting anxiously as the minutes pass.

Ten minutes later, the mouse returns, tugging a brass

key between his jaw. I drop to hands and knees, scooping him up in triumph. His little heart beats fast from the exertion.

You did it! You're a hero!

He proudly grooms his tail. I set him on my shoulder and reward him with a stroke on his head, then pick up the key that he stole from Brigit.

Something feels off as I unlock the servants' door. A part of me still expects Basten to smell the mouse or hear the key turning, and storm in with his glaring midnight eyes. Dammit, a part of me even *wants* that. I haven't dared to ask where he's been the past few days, because I don't want anyone thinking I care about him. Rian is so shrewd that I'm worried he already suspects something.

Where *is* Basten? The last time I spoke to him was with tears in my eyes, when I yelled at him to get out of my room after we made love. I've thought about that night a million times since then. Hating that I still love him. Knowing the sex was a mistake but not regretting it. Wanting to see him—to know he's okay.

It doesn't matter. Basten is nothing if not a survivor. Wherever he is, he's doubtlessly fine, probably not pining away for me at all. This is my chance to investigate the voice's source, and I'll be damned if I'm going to miss it because I'm too wrapped up in thoughts about an asshole huntsman.

With the mouse on my shoulder, I make my way down the narrow passage, praying no servants are working this late.

GET OUT.

There it is again. I drift to a stop, concentrating. I try

to extend my thoughts throughout the myriad castle levels as I ask: *Who are you?*

The only answer I get is a wall of anger crashing over me. It's strong enough to steal my breath, and I grip the wood paneling to steady myself. Sweat breaks out on my brow.

It's rare to feel animals' emotions. Usually, I can only communicate with them through words, though when Myst feels strongly about something, some of her emotions spill over into my head.

It gives me the shaky fear that I'm not dealing with an animal at all—but something *else*. Something that really doesn't want me here.

OUT. OUT NOW.

The voice is so steeped in mad rage that it drowns out my own inner voice. Whoever the ghost is, it's so deafened by its anger that I don't think it can hear me.

Little friend, I ask the mouse, *Do you hear the angry voice?*

Its nose twitches. *No.*

All that really tells me is that it isn't another mouse, since animals can only communicate with their own kind. I'm at a loss for what to do until the mouse scales down my body onto the floor.

Wait, follow me! I know angry!

The mouse leads me through twisting passages and down two flights of stairs. I follow after with my heart thrumming in my chest, afraid of being caught sneaking around but too excited to care. This might not be the ultimate freedom that I crave, but it feels thrilling to explore just the same. The mouse leads me through more unassuming doors that I wouldn't have noticed otherwise. Luckily, Brigit's key works on the locked ones.

We descend until I'm sure we must be far below ground. The air grows colder. The mouse leads me to a descending staircase, this one comprised of rough-hewn stone walls plunging into darkness. A barred iron gate blocks the way. The mouse scampers through the bars, but I stop.

The key doesn't work, I say, frustrated as I rattle the gate.

The mouse climbs up the opposite side of the gate, and I hear a latch falling open under his small paws. The gate swings open.

The mouse continues eagerly into the darkness, but I don't have its superior eyesight. Without a lantern, every step plunges me further into pure blackness. There's no muffling carpet underfoot here, and my shoes clatter loudly on the stone, so I take them off and carry them. I keep my other hand pressed against the stones to help find my way without stumbling.

The air smells musty and dank, with a metallic note that shrinks my stomach. Growing apprehension tiptoes up my spine as I move lower and lower, unsure of where the mouse is taking me.

GET OUT!

A cry escapes my lips, startled by the voice's ferocity. It's so loud in my head that it feels like it's coming from an inch away. Somewhere ahead, there's a sharp thumping sound. The air has an odd taste—like iron.

My heart kicks into a faster clip.

Where are we going? I ask the mouse. I can't see it in the darkness.

Come, come, almost there!

My bare feet finally touch a dirt floor. I'm glad to leave the stairs behind, but I have no idea where I am. The darkness is as complete as a blindfold. Dragging my hand along the wall like Immortal Meric in the Prison of Night and Day, I follow the mouse's urging.

Eventually, a light shines ahead. It's flickering—a torch, not a lantern. Both fear and excitement grip my throat as I approach with tentative footsteps.

OUT. OUT. OUT.

We turn the corner, and the light grows bright enough to see that I'm in an underground tunnel. The rock walls are ancient, with crumbling mortar between the chinking where the original straw binding has disintegrated over the years. There's one other recent set of footprints on the dirt floor—a man's heavy boots.

Basten said the only things down here were a dungeon and potato storage. But I don't hear any prisoners' screams, and there sure as hell aren't any vegetables.

Maybe Basten doesn't know about this place.

The mouse pauses to make sure I'm still following him. Then he plunges around the corner.

Something crashes, and I freeze. There's a strange stomping noise, followed by a hiss that sounds almost like something huge breathing. For a moment, my courage wavers. There's something alive down here. Something big. Something angry—that wants me gone.

I swallow around my fear and force my feet forward.

More stomps come, then something that almost sounds like a horse's angry snort.

As soon as I round the corner, curiosity wins over my fear. I'm in an old, subterranean stable. There are dozens of abandoned stone stalls, most of which are caved in. Though almost everything is in ruins, a barrel of fresh oats rests in the corner. The smell of iron is stronger here.

More stomps come. Something kicks hard at a stall door.

Another snort.

With wide eyes, I move further into the ancient stable to discover that one stall has been newly repaired. Its door is reinforced with iron panels, though they're dented. The door's hinges are chained to the wall for extra support.

Holy gods.

The upper half of the stall door is barred, and behind it is a horse—only it isn't a horse.

The illustrations in the Book of the Immortals don't do this creature justice. It must stand twenty hands high, towering over even the tallest of Rian's prize stallions in his racing stables. Its build is powerful, like a draft horse, with a long arching neck and broad, balanced proportions that grant it both strength and speed. Its mane and tail are black enough to swallow the light, and black hair also feathers over its hooves. Its body is covered in glistening black scales. At its nose and around its eyes, the scales are as delicate as my smallest fingernail, but they give way to armor-like scales on its shoulders and flanks that are the size of my splayed hand.

A monoceros.

A fae beast that's supposed to be asleep, like the gods.

A horn as long and thick as my forearm juts proudly from its forehead. According to legend, it's made of solarium, a material a thousand times more prized than gold. When the horn catches the light, an infinity of colors shines in its depths like a prism. As beautiful as the creature is, it's deadly. A monoceros is only safe to be around indoors or under moonlight. If a monoceros's horn reflects sunlight, the solarium concentrates the rays and projects it into a powerful fey fire burst that incinerates everything in its path. Only a highly trained rider bonded to the creature can direct the fire burst.

The monoceros slams a hoof against its door, rattling the metal enough to send me scrambling backward with a hand to my chest. I can't believe what I'm looking at. The creature's beauty is great and terrible, only matched by its rage. Its eyes roll wildly. White foam clots at the corners of its mouth.

It slams its horn into the door, denting the iron again.

GET. OUT.

My hand goes to the base of my throat as the realization hits me that this was never any ghost trying to scare me away from Sorsha Hall. The voice wasn't even speaking to *me*. This poor monster has been a prisoner down here for who knows how long. Wanting to get out so desperately that it's driven itself mad.

Gaping, I take in the manure piles in its stall that have stacked up for days. Its water bucket is overturned. Its hair is matted and filthy. No one has groomed this horse in months—I don't think anyone has been brave enough to try.

It wasn't threatening me; it was *begging for help.*

My breath falters as the burden of this monster's pain sinks onto my shoulders. My heart squeezes in sympathy for it, followed by a sweep of anger through my veins. I know what it feels like to be trapped. To want more than anything to get free.

OUT, the monoceros drones in its familiar, hypnotic refrain as it stamps its massive hoof against the stall door. Its hoof is chipped from months of repeatedly kicking the iron.

Easy, easy, I say, holding out a gentle hand as I carefully approach the stall. *You're hurting yourself.*

For the first time, the monoceros seems to notice me. Its wild eyes sharpen with a glint of intelligence. I can practically see the gears working in its head, trying to figure out why it can understand my voice in its head. It snorts a sharp warning, not trusting me.

Fae? It asks.

I shake my head. *I'm not fae. You've been asleep a long time, my friend. The world has changed. I can tell you. I can tell you everything—*

My message dies as someone clears their throat behind me.

Oh, *fuck.*

I pivot sharply, adrenaline making sweat pour down my temples. My lips fall open.

"Rian?" I say breathlessly.

Rian stands on the threshold of the same tunnel the mouse led me through, with a lantern in hand. He's reclined against the wall like he's been watching me for some time. He must have followed me. A clap of annoyance snaps in my chest, even though I know I should be worried that I've been caught.

"You, ah, weren't supposed to see this yet," he says in a mockingly casual manner, like I stumbled upon an unwrapped present.

"How long have you been following me?"

"Well, I knew you were trying to find something when you disappeared from our engagement party. I was going to task Wolf with letting you escape your room, so he could follow you and discover your aims, but he's been otherwise occupied of late. And I had time."

Otherwise occupied? What does that mean?

Heart pounding, I jab a finger at the caged monoceros. "What the hell is this?"

"A monoceros," he answers plainly.

"I know what it is! Why is it here? How—how can it even *be* here?" My chest heaves as my voice echoes in the ancient stables.

Rian takes a few slow, unhurried steps into the stable. The monoceros snorts curtly, and Rian shoots it back a sneer. These two are used to one another, I realize. And there's no love shared between them.

"A hermit encountered it in the forest last year," Rian explains. "I had a team of sentinels trap it and bring it here, though it killed all but one of them, as it's killed most of the grooms who have tried to care for it. It hates everyone. It *loathes* me. It won't allow my father or grandmother down here anymore without thrashing so hard it threatens to bring the whole castle down. We haven't found any way to tame it—or even communicate with it." He gives the monstrous horse a look that's both hateful and a small bit impressed. "At least, not until now."

A muscle twitches near my eye. "This is why you wanted me, isn't it?" I can't believe it; this whole thing hasn't been about marriage at all, but my godkiss. "To tame your monster."

I stare at him with a twisted scowl as I realize how deeply his scheming reaches. For weeks, I've been under the false impression that Lord Rian Valvere bought me because of my prized hair and pretty face. I got it all wrong. He never wanted me for my body—he wanted me for my magic.

My voice is hoarse as I press, "The naked ride, the spectacle, the entire engagement . . . it was just for show?"

His cunning eyes gleam in the lantern light like dark stars. "A distraction so our enemies wouldn't suspect why we actually wanted you. So they'd focus on your beauty and not your power. Dark times are ahead, songbird. The awakening of the fae gods is nigh. Astagnon needs a strong dynasty, including every weapon we can wield. Monoceros have the power to raze entire villages to the ground." His voice catches. "I didn't go to Bremcote last year to evaluate a fighter; I went to evaluate you. Our spies reported on your ability, and my father wanted me to see if it was true. So, yes, my family wanted you for your ability. But I just wanted *you*. That's no sham, at least not on my end. I've wanted you at my side since I saw you looking so defiant, standing on a chair in a village church nave."

I stare at him like he's grown horse ears. Shaking my head, I blurt out, "But—but you barely looked at me."

A dark chuckle rumbles in his throat. He takes out his Golath dime, making it dance over his knuckles. "Do you want to know what the other men at the Preview said about you? No, I don't suppose you do, but I'll tell you anyway. They spoke of your sweet face and sweeter body, built for obedience to a husband. They cited your godkiss as proof of your docility—talking to animals, what could be more pure? I couldn't believe what I was hearing. Idiots, all of them. They were blind to what I saw."

"What did you see?"

"A beautiful girl who wanted to claw their eyes out. Oh, you have a sweet look to you, all right. I have no doubt there's a part of you that's as pure of heart as those men think, but there's another part of you that blazes like . . . like sunlight. Your anger. Your grit. Your ambition."

At the time, a year ago, I never dreamed Lord Rian had taken any notice of me at all, let alone peered into my soul. I'm shaken to my core. I force my chin high, not letting Rian see how deep his read on me is.

I sneer, "You saw all that in a half-second glance?"

He smirks. "Songbird, I make my living running card tables. If I couldn't read a person in a half-second glance, I wouldn't own this city."

The monoceros snorts, thrashing his horn against the door. The pounding echoes in my chest.

I shake my head, scowling. "You expect me to believe you fell in love after only seeing me once?"

"Love? Oh, songbird. Whoever said anything about love? I *wanted* you after one look. Your pretty lips. Your curves. I wanted that defiant girl, the same one who rode up dressed in a gown of wings to shame me. I see so much in you, Sabine. I want to encourage your power. Help you grow it." The Golath dime dances faster over his knuckles.

My jaw hardens. "So I'll turn this beast into a weapon."

"Well." He flips his coin, then catches it. "That, too."

My head drags back and forth at the depths of this man's scheming. "Fuck you."

My harsh words roll off him like water on river rocks. With a shrug, he says, "The fae realm is already awakening. You can see for yourself right here with the monoceros. It's only a matter of time before the gods themselves rise. Volkany is putting all its resources into preparing for the new era. And who will shepherd Astagnon in the coming storm? Old King Joruun, a sack of rattling bones on his deathbed, with no heirs? No—Astagnon needs new leadership. A deadly game is about to begin, and the players are already taking their places on the board."

"You wish to be king." The words tumble from my mouth in shock. I knew Rian was ambitious—but I had no idea he'd set his lofty sights on the *crown*.

His voice softens. "Songbird, you were meant to be a queen. The whole town saw it when you rode up in defiance. You're so much more than a backwoods lord's daughter. Our marriage can be as real or fake as you like behind doors, but we must appear united in public." He pauses as something glazes over his expression. "Unless .. . your heart belongs elsewhere?"

There's an edge in his voice that frosts my marrow. My fingers stretch and ball as I try to read the subtext in his pointed words. Does he suspect the affair with Basten? Did someone see us?

I run my fingers through my shorter hair, still unused to it, and turn to the monoceros's stall to buy time. Rian's question isn't as straightforward as it seems. I told Basten that I loved him, and despite the thousand damn times I've wished for it to be the opposite, it's still true. There's a corner of my heart that only beats for him. He worked his way into me like tree roots under a building's foundation, so intertwined that removing them would mean tearing down the whole structure.

But Basten had his chance.

I *have* to cut him out of my heart, even if it means breaking walls.

Still, that hardly means there will be freshly tilled ground for Rian to dig his roots into. Far from it. Because I know my enemy when I look him in the eye.

Rian is no friend to me.

The most he can ever be is a means to an end.

I spin back toward him, and my hand darts out to snatch the Golath dime as he flips it between his fingers. Squeezing the stolen coin tightly in the cage of my fist, I level Rian with a brazen stare.

He wants my hand in marriage and my magic at his beck and call. But I have my own desires. I've tasted the bitterness of captivity. The weight of oppression. I am no longer the imprisoned girl unaware of her own power. I am a force, fueled by my past, guided by the scars etched upon my heart.

I want my freedom—and freedom for the poor monster caged behind me.

I hold up my fist with the coin.

"The stakes are high for both of us," I say evenly, with

an unyielding gaze that challenges him as much as it entices. "So I'd like to propose a new game. Winner takes all."

A plotting smile slowly stretches across his face as dark curiosity dances in his eyes, and for a second, I worry about what I might have gotten myself into. But then my resolve hardens. *He* should be the worried one. The player with the best hand is the one with the littlest to lose.

And I have *nothing* to lose.

"Okay, songbird," he says. "I'll play."

The games are just beginning! Discover how the cards fall for Sabine and Wolf in *Silver Wings Golden Games*.

For a steamy bonus scene of the "one bed at the inn" chapter from Wolf's POV, join my author mailing list!

A NOTE FROM EVIE

Dear Reader,

PREPARE YOURSELF. I have much more in store for Sabine and Wolf as the gods awaken, kingdoms fall, secrets are uncovered, and hearts are at war. The cards are dealt and the games are just beginning . . .

Thank you from the bottom of my own black heart for picking up this book. It started as two separate ideas: A Snow White retelling, and a Lady Godiva-inspired horseback ride. As I tinkered with each idea, I realized they might meld beautifully.

I would absolutely love to hear from you in my Facebook reader group (search "Evie Marceau's Reader Group"). Also, the book community wants to know your opinion, so please leave a review!

xo,

Evie

www.eviemarceau.com/newsletter
(PS: get free bonus scenes when you join!)

Printed in the USA
CPSIA information can be obtained
at www.ICGtesting.com
LVHW041116180124
768903LV00064BA/630/J